ANNA OF ARIMATHEA

ANNA OF ARIMATHEA
THE ARIMATHEA CHRONICLES

SUSANNE BLUMER

Copyright © 2025 by Susanne Blumer

All rights reserved. No part of this publication may be reproduced, stored in a retrieval system, or transmitted in any form or by any means—electronic, mechanical, photocopying, recording, or otherwise—without prior written permission of the publisher, except for brief quotations used in reviews or scholarly works.

Published by Sutton Avenue Press

Black Mountain, North Carolina

ISBN: 978-1-945065-22-4

Cover design by Hannah Linder Designs

This is a work of historical fiction. While it draws on known events and historical figures of the first century, all characters' thoughts, motivations, conversations, and specific actions are imaginative interpretations. Any resemblance to persons living or dead, apart from documented historical individuals, is coincidental.

Scripture quotations, whether spoken or paraphrased in dialogue, are taken from the Holy Bible, New International Version®, NIV®. Copyright © 1973, 1978, 1984, 2011 by Biblica, Inc.™ Used by permission, or are taken from the King James Version of the Bible. Public domain. All rights reserved worldwide.

Printed in the United States of America 10 9 8 7 6 5 4 3 2 1

*For the ones who carry quiet wounds,
and the brave souls who learn to rise again.*

And for my husband, who never watched from the shore, but jumped into every adventure with me. Even the ones that made little sense to anyone else. You have been my companion in all of life's chapters, long before this story took shape, and the steady hand when the waters ran rough.

Thank you for being my Huckleberry.

INTRODUCTION

This story began with a question that stayed in my heart: who was Joseph of Arimathea, and what kind of life might have shaped the courage he showed? That wondering pulled me deeper into the world of first-century Judea. I began to picture the dust and noise of the markets, the weight of Roman rule, and the quiet faith of the people who lived in those days. And as I spent time studying and praying, a girl lingered in my heart as well. Her world took shape slowly, drawn from the sounds, textures, and hopes of the time, and I found myself seeing the Messiah through her eyes.

I have tried to portray those days as faithfully as possible through the lens of history, study, and reverence for God's Word. Though the story is fiction, the truth of Scripture remains unchanged and stands at the center of everything here. Come and step into first-century Judea for a bit. Walk its roads, breathe its air, and see what your heart finds there. I hope you love Anna as much as I do.

Susanne

PROLOGUE

JERUSALEM, 17 AD

Anna pressed her small hands against the rough stone wall of their courtyard, watching her mother clean the gash along the young lamb's flank with steady hands. The animal had caught itself on a splintered fence post, and the wound gaped open like an angry mouth.

"See how I hold her steady?" Sarah murmured, her voice calm despite the lamb's struggles. "Frightened creatures fight the very help they need."

Anna nodded solemnly, her five-year-old mind absorbing every detail. The way Ima's fingers never trembled, how she cleaned from the center outward, the mixture of herbs she pressed into the wound before binding it with clean linen.

"Will she be whole again?" Anna asked.

"With time and care, yes. The Holy One gave us hands to heal, little dove, just as He gave us hearts to see suffering."

Her mother smiled at her. "You have the gift, Anna. I see it in how you touch her."

Three days later, the lamb was running with the others, with only a thin pink line marking where the wound had been. Anna felt a warm glow of satisfaction as if she had helped in some small way.

Now, standing in Jerusalem's great marketplace, Anna walked next to her mother among the maze of stalls and shoppers. The air buzzed with voices speaking Hebrew, Aramaic, and languages she could not identify. Vendors hawked their wares from beneath dyed awnings. "Fresh figs from Jericho!" "Spices from distant lands!" "Pottery fired this morning!"

The smell of roasting almonds mixed with the sharper scents of leather and metal. Heat closed in on all sides, carrying the gritty taste of dust and the faint scent of animal sweat. Roman soldiers moved through the crowd in measured patrols, their bronze armor catching the afternoon sun. Anna had learned to keep her eyes down when they passed, the way all the Jewish families did.

The lamb's cry cut through the noise of the marketplace. Anna's head snapped toward the sound as if it had called her name.

"Ima, look." She tugged at the rough wool of her mother's cloak, small fingers clinging to the weave. "A lamb. He is hurt."

Sarah bent down, dark eyes following Anna's pointing finger to where a white lamb lay in a pen, apart from those destined for sacrifice.

"I see it, but stay close, Anna," Sarah told her. "The marketplace is no place for wandering. You may go to Miriam, but no farther."

Just a few paces away, Hannah, her mother's closest friend, was bent over a spice stall, gesturing as she bargained, her voice rising and falling in the familiar cadence of haggling. Her daughter sat perched on a sun-warmed stone ledge, weaving grass into crooked crowns. Miriam caught Anna's eye and waved, curls bouncing as she held up her handiwork.

"We should play in your garden when we get home," Anna said, slipping over to her friend. "I will sing the new song Ima taught me."

"Yes! And I will show you how to make these better. Yours always come apart." Miriam held up her grass crown, grinning.

But the lamb's cry came again, thin and desperate, tugging at her heart. Anna watched it struggle to stand on three legs, its broken limb dragging uselessly. People walked past without even glancing at it. A merchant sat in the shade next to the pen, counting his coins.

The Holy One gave us hands to heal, Ima had said. *Hearts to see suffering.*

"I will only look, Ima," she called over her shoulder, already weaving between carts and baskets. She scrambled up the wooden fence, small hands scraping against rough boards. The lamb huddled in the straw, eyes wide with pain.

"Shhh, little one," she whispered, crouching beside it and stroking its head. The smell of hay wrapped around her like home. "I know it hurts."

The lamb lay in straw soaked with its own blood, and Anna could see the bone protruding white through the torn skin, just like her lamb's wound, but worse. She stroked its head, and the wool was softer than anything she had ever touched, white as fresh snow. She hummed one of her mother's soothing songs, and the lamb's wild eyes seemed to calm slightly.

"Get away from there, girl!" the merchant barked. "That beast is worthless. No one wants a crippled sacrifice."

"He is not worthless," Anna said.

The man snorted, ready to argue, but his words drowned in the rising shouts from the grain stalls nearby.

Voices carried across the marketplace. "This barley is spoiled!" one shouted in Hebrew. "I will not pay full price for grain that will make my customers sick!"

"The grain is perfect!" the other replied hotly. "You seek to cheat me because I am from Galilee!"

Other traders took notice, murmuring among themselves. Anna looked up from the lamb, suddenly aware that the usual hum of marketplace activity had changed to something sharper, more tense.

"The barley smells sour," called out another voice. "I would not feed it to my animals!"

"You Judeans think you are better than everyone!" the Galilean merchant shot back. "Your money is no cleaner than ours!"

What had begun as a simple disagreement over grain quality grew into something larger and uglier. Anna saw people gather, the air thick with tension and the sharp sound of raised voices.

She looked back toward the spice stall where she had left Ima, but the crowd had thickened, and she no longer saw her mother's familiar blue head covering through the mass of bodies.

Hannah turned from the spice seller, worry creasing her features. She started, "Sarah, where is—" but the growing uproar swallowed her words.

A woman screamed. Another voice joined, then another, until the marketplace churned with noise. Pottery crashed as a stall overturned, shards skittering across the ground like broken teeth. Chickens fluttered from their cages, wings beating the air, feathers drifting in the sunlight.

The crowd swelled and heaved. Strangers rushed past each other, fear rising like a shout above the sudden quarrel. Merchants abandoned their scales, mothers clutched children to their robes, men reached instinctively for knives they dared not draw.

Sarah spun from Hannah's side at the spice stall. Her eyes found Anna in the pen, crouched in the straw with the wounded lamb.

"Anna!" Her cry carried above the noise as she pushed into the crowd.

Bodies pushed against her, jostling, stumbling. Someone shoved, knocking her sideways. She gathered her robes high and forced herself forward, but the fabric tangled about her legs as she tried to run. Breath tore from her throat as she fought toward the fence, panic pounding in her chest.

A centurion pushed through the chaos. His face was dark with fury, and his whip coiled in his fist like a deadly serpent. Behind him, soldiers poured out on horseback, their hooves ringing on the stone.

"Back, dogs!" he bellowed, his Latin harsh against the Hebrew shouts. "You think Rome will let you riot in her streets?"

He snapped the whip overhead, the crack splitting the air.

The horses moved forward slowly, carving a path through the crowd, nostrils flaring. Sweat, iron, and dust's stench permeated the air. The soldiers forced their way through like a flood, the crowd breaking, stumbling, and trampling over one another to escape. People scattered before them, but not fast enough.

Anna stood, clutching the lamb to her chest, her legs trembling under the weight. All around, fear burned through the marketplace.

"Ima!" she cried, frozen in place. "Help!"

Sarah reached the fence at last. With desperate strength, she hauled Anna up and over, pulling her out of the pen. The lamb slipped from Anna's grasp, crying out as it fell.

Sarah held Anna tight against her chest, her daughter's small face pressed above her shoulder. Sarah turned frantically, searching for a way out. Faces blurred around her.

Then a man charged past, shoving through with wild eyes. "Halt!" The centurion's whip cracked toward him, meant to drive him back. But Sarah and Anna were in its path.

The lash struck across Sarah's back. Anna shrieked as the metal end slashed her face, slicing the skin from temple to mouth. Heat ran down her cheek. Sarah gasped and stumbled, but did not release her hold on her daughter.

Anna, seeing the whip in motion again, raised her hands to cover her face, and they caught the full brunt of the second lash, pain searing her skin.

The horses nearest them snorted, ears flattening. One caught the sharp scent of blood and reared high, eyes rolling white, hooves thrashing.

Sarah tried to twist away, but her tangled robes caused her to stumble, and she let go of Anna as she fell to the ground. The horse came down hard, its hoof striking Sarah's head with a sickening crack. Its other landed on Anna's hip, agony exploding through her small body as her cry broke into a ragged wail. The rider reined in his horse and turned back toward the crowd.

Anna lay stunned, the world spinning around her. Pain shot through her, but she forced herself to move, crawling across the stones. "Ima!" Her torn hands groped for her mother, but Sarah's eyes had already gone empty.

Anna glimpsed Miriam, frozen, mouth open in a scream. The grass crown lay trampled in the dust. Hannah seized her daughter, dragging her back before the soldiers swept closer.

Sarah lay still. Anna heard the lamb close by, its cry sharp with terror.

"Sarah! Anna!"

She heard her father's voice, ragged, somewhere far and near at once. Strong hands lifted his daughter, held her against his chest, damp with tears. He bent over Sarah's body, then crumpled to his knees and pressed his forehead against her lifeless form as her name broke from him in choking sobs.

At last, he raised his head. "Help me! Please, someone, help me carry them home."

Hannah stood frozen, Miriam pressed to her side, both staring in horror. Several men stepped forward at once, faces grim. Together they lifted the lifeless and the living, bearing them through Jerusalem's streets toward the upper city.

Anna's world narrowed to the jolt of footsteps, the muffled sobs above her, the pain burning everywhere at once. Then, mercifully, the dark took her.

Darkness came and went. Sometimes Anna heard Abba's broken prayers, a physician's quiet voice, servants weeping. Pain lived within her like a creature that never slept.

"I want Ima," she whispered once, the words rough against her throat.

On the third day, the world came clear again. Her first thought was not of her wounds, but of her mother. Memory struck like a blow, Sarah's body folding, blood pooling bright as spilled wine.

"Ima?" she said. "Where is Ima?"

Abba kneeled beside her bed, still wearing his council robes from days before. They hung wrinkled and stained, his hair wild. At her voice, his head lifted sharply.

"Abba, where is Ima? Is she here?" She tried to sit up. Fire ripped through her hip, and she cried out.

Joseph stopped her, easing her gently back. "Little dove, you are hurt. You must rest."

"Little dove" was Ima's name for her. Abba never used it. Something felt terribly wrong.

"Abba," she said, lips trembling, "why will you not tell me? Is Ima here?"

He took a deep breath and a long pause before he answered. "Ima is with God now, little dove."

"No!" The cry tore from her, raw and jagged. Tears spilled hot down her damaged cheek, stinging the wound that had just begun to heal.

Joseph gathered her carefully against him, mindful of her injuries. His hand stroked her tangled hair as her sobs shook her fragile frame. "I am so sorry, Anna. I am so sorry." His voice cracked with his grief. "If I could have stood in her place, I would have. She loved you more than life itself. Rest now, child. You have much healing to do. Ima would want you to be well."

He stayed with her until exhaustion claimed her, whispering broken prayers between his murmurs of comfort.

The next morning, he returned and sat beside her bed, his face lined with sleeplessness and sorrow. "How are you this morning, little dove? Did you sleep?"

"Some. It hurts," she mumbled. "It hurts everywhere."

Joseph's throat worked as if he could not bear to answer. He turned his head toward the window, blinking hard at the sunlight pressing through. He flexed his hands uselessly, wanting to take the pain from her but knowing he could not.

Anna watched him in silence for a moment, then her memory stirred. "Abba..." Her voice trembled. "I remember the lamb. I dropped it. Do you think it—" Her voice broke, the words trailing away.

Despite everything, Joseph managed a faint smile. "She lives. Look over there. The merchant brought her here. He said you belonged together."

In the corner, the lamb lay on a folded blanket, its splinted leg bound neatly. At the sound of Anna's voice, it bleated softly.

"You saved her," Joseph said.

The door creaked. Hannah stood there, with Miriam pressed close to her side. Joseph waved them into the room, grateful for a distraction.

"We have prayed every hour for you," Hannah said.

Miriam slipped from her mother's grasp and crept to the bedside. In her hand, she clutched a grass crown. "Anna," she whispered, "I was so scared."

Anna looked at her friend. "I was scared, too."

Miriam placed the crown beside Anna. "I made this for you."

"Thank you," Anna said. "I will wear it when I am feeling better."

Miriam looked at the lamb. "I will make one for her, too," she promised.

Sarah's absence filled the room, but for a moment, Anna felt the comfort of familiar voices and the closeness of the friend she loved like a sister.

Anna caught fragments of the physician's words to her father over the next few days—"Did what I could," "The scar will fade but never disappear," "The hip... She will need help walking." A servant had already carved her a slender staff, though it lay unused beside her bed.

Weeks later, when Anna could travel, Joseph lifted her carefully into a cart bound for their country estate in Arimathea. The lamb rode beside her, wrapped in blankets like a fragile treasure.

Joseph settled next to her, his hands restless on his knees. "It will be good for you there," he said, forcing brightness into his voice. "The air is clean, and the hills are peaceful. The vines grow strong, and the servants ... The servants knew your mother as a girl. They will tell you her stories."

Anna nodded, holding the lamb close. Every bump in the road sent fresh pain through her hip, but she bit her lip and stayed silent. "Will you be there, Abba?"

He hesitated, then smiled too quickly. "As often as I can. My seat on the council keeps me in Jerusalem more than I would like. Remember that I am a member of the Sanhedrin. I must be here for important meetings. I would be with you every day if I could, Anna, but... You will love Arimathea so much, you will not even notice I am gone."

"I will notice," Anna said. Her eyes blurred with tears. "I never said goodbye to Ima."

Joseph looked away toward the city walls, jaw tight. "She loved you with all her heart," he managed. "And we loved her, did we not?"

"Yes," Anna said, burying her face against the lamb's wool. "Abba, will I ever see Miriam again?"

The question pierced him. He thought of the distance, of the silence that would fall between the girls, of the life Anna would now live apart. He forced another smile. "Of course you will."

It was a small lie, the only kindness he had left.

They rolled forward, and Anna pressed her face against the lamb's soft fleece as she watched Jerusalem's walls grow smaller behind them.

Somewhere above, she heard her father's voice: "Help me. I do not know how to do this."

The sky stretched blue and still overhead. The road unwound toward Arimathea. Anna clutched the lamb tighter, and the cart rolled on.

CHAPTER 1

Arimathea, 30 AD

The fever broke just before dawn.

At first, I did not trust my hand. I held my palm above Aaron's brow, then pressed gently to be certain. Cool. Not the cruel heat that had burned beneath my fingers through the long night, but the soft, blessed coolness of a child returning to himself. Relief struck so strongly that I swayed, and I had to set my weight more firmly upon my staff to keep from sitting where I stood.

Thank You, Adonai. Thank You for sparing him.

Aaron sighed in proper sleep, lashes dark against cheeks still flushed but no longer blazing. The faint whistle of air through his nose came steady now, instead of the harsh, ragged panting that had haunted the small hours. Beside him, Ruth had finally folded into the chair, her head leaning at a painful angle, her fingers still twitching as though they wrung cloths, the dark crescents under her eyes telling of a night spent holding her son's hand and whispering prayers and promises to a God who sometimes was deaf to the pleas of bakers' wives. Her lips still moved faintly even in her dreams, prayers still trying to reach heaven after her voice had given out. I let her sleep. She would learn soon enough that her prayers had been answered.

The room carried the breath of sickness, the rank, metallic tang of sweat and fever, the bitterness of willow bark softened with honey, the clean, green bite of elderflower, the damp wool of blankets that had been changed and changed again. My skin smelled of smoke and heat and the herbs I had crushed with a pestle worn smooth by my mother's hands.

Deborah filled the doorway with quiet presence, fresh linens folded over her arm, her eyes asking what her lips did not.

"The fever broke an hour ago," I said, my voice hoarse. "He will live."

Her breath left her in a soft rush. The furrows on her face eased. "Blessed be the Name," she whispered. "I feared we would lose him."

So had I, though I had never said it aloud. In the stillness of the night, I had feared it too many times to count. When his little limbs jerked and stiffened and his back arched like a bow, when his lips blued and when he lay too still, the silence pressed heavy on my chest. I had spent the darkest hours alternating between cool cloths and feverfew tea, my hands moving with the desperation of someone who knows that minutes often matter. *Not again*, I had begged, pacing prayers into the floor, *Lord, let this child live. Hide us beneath Your wings.*

"The willow bark mixture served us well." I checked my stores of the bitter tea that finally turned the tide, noting how little remained in the earthenware cup. "Though I had to sweeten it considerably with honey before he would take it."

"The elderflower was inspired, Anna," Deborah told me, and warmth stirred in my chest, despite my weariness.

Aaron stirred like a small bird waking, lashes fluttering open. "Thirsty," came a thin thread of sound, but wonderfully, impossibly clear.

"Of course you are." I reached for the cup as Deborah slid her arm beneath his shoulders, her touch unfailingly sure even after a night without sleep. Pain lanced through my hip as I leaned, the old wound reminding me of its presence, but I would not let it steal anything of this moment. I steadied the cup to his lips. "Drink slowly now. Tiny sips."

Ruth jerked awake. In a heartbeat, she had him pressed against her, tears falling into his hair. "My son. My precious boy."

"The danger has passed," I said, and it felt like speaking a blessing. "Rest and water now. He will need days to regain his strength, but the fever is gone."

"Thank you, my lady." Ruth lifted her face to mine, eyes bright and wet. "I do not know how to repay such a gift."

"There is no need," I answered, gathering vials and packets then rolling strips of linen into neat bundles before tucking everything into my satchel, the bittersweet breath of herbs rising from its seams. "Only care for him well."

My staff stood where I had set it, within easy reach, as familiar as a friend. I took it up and tested my weight. The ache sang along the old path from hip to knee as it always did after long standing. Yet here in a room that smelled of fever and hope, I had a place. Here, my hands were of use. Here I mattered.

We stepped into the morning light.

Cool air slid over my face, a thin veil of dew and damp earth. The first light lifted over the hills and spilled onto the path, turning the dust to pale gold. Fig blossoms breathed sweetness from the orchard below. My staff tapped its steady rhythm, sending well-known sparks of pain up my spine. Deborah walked beside me, linens balanced against her hip, and though she tried to make her steps even, I saw the small catch, the hand that drifted, too often, too deliberately, to the place beneath her ribs. My healer's instincts stirred as I watched.

"Abba sent word he will arrive by evening," I said as we reached my workroom. "Perhaps earlier if the roads are clear and the donkey willing."

"You have been counting the days," she said, lowering herself onto a bench with a small, controlled exhale that she hoped I would not notice.

"Too obvious?" I tried to make light of it, but my eyes clung to the new lines along her mouth, the fatigue that no washing would rinse away. "Deborah, are you well? It was a hard night."

"I am well enough. Only tired." Her smile came, faithful and thin, but stopped before it reached her eyes.

Deborah, who had held me through the fever-dreams and night terrors when my mother could not, who had stitched my wounds and taught me that mint grew sweeter if you pinched it back, that willow bark must steep exactly so many minutes to draw out its power. She had stood between me and the emptiness that wanted to swallow everything after my mother died. She could not be ill. I would not allow it. If I could name it, I could treat it. I would find a name and a way.

"It will be good to have your father here," she said, smoothing the air between us as if she pressed creases from the cloth.

"Yes," I said. "It will."

I hoped it would. Three, perhaps four times a year, if Sanhedrin matters and trade allowed, Abba came to us like a storm passing through, never staying long, rarely with time for an honest conversation with me. Duty clung to him like an outer cloak he did not think to remove, and something always pulled him away—grief or guilt or the endless demands of a world that saw him as Joseph of Arimathea first and my father second. Between us lay a desert of unsaid things, one I longed to cross.

I moved toward the window where the sun reached through the high arches and lay itself across the limestone in broad bands of gold. Below, the estate spilled down the slope, olive trees whose trunks twisted like the arms of old men lifting prayers, vineyards standing in soldierly rows upon the terraces, fig branches heavy with buds in the warm breath of spring. There, my garden spread in careful order, neat beds of coriander, mint and lavender, while jasmine climbed the courtyard in cascades of star-white blossoms. Even from here, I could taste pomegranate blossoms in the air and the clean cut of crushed thyme.

Abba would approve of the flourishing vines. He always did. Known as one of the best winemakers in Judea, he meant for that to continue.

I slipped into my best robe, the blue linen, the color of

deep water, dyed rich enough to catch and hold the light. The gold ring Abba had given me at twelve still turned easily on my finger, while Ima's silver bracelets circled my wrists. She had worn them on the day she died, and I wore them constantly, as if their weight could anchor her memory to this world. My bronze mirror gave back what it always did. The right side, I had been told, reflected her features—dark eyes, the graceful line of jaw, high cheekbones, and the full mouth that Deborah said loved to laugh — while the left told the story of my accident. Raised ridges that pulled at the corner of my mouth had not faded, even after thirteen years, and a deep groove ran from temple to jaw, carving my face in two—the side I could bear to look at and the side I could not. After turning away, I gathered my hair into a simple braid and drew it over my shoulder, smoothing the loose strands with my palm.

"I asked the servants to prepare lamb stew with mint fresh from the garden. Abba's favorite," I said as I returned to the workroom, the bracelets sounding a small, bright music. "And figs stewed in honey."

"And flatbread warm from the stones, no doubt," Deborah said. Her needle flashed and paused. "Do you believe food will keep him from going over his ledgers with Ezra?"

"Perhaps," I said, and could not help the small smile that came with it. "Likely not."

My fingertips drifted along the row of jars, straightening one that did not need straightening, feeling the roughness of my mother's old table beneath my palm. Bundles of drying herbs hung above us, their shadows making a canopy of small leaves upon the wall. In the center rested my mother's beloved mortar and pestle, mine now, its wooden surface marked by years of grinding remedies, of coaxing healing from root and leaf and bark, of knowledge passed down like a sacred trust. Everything in this room bore the marks of use and time. I was not the only scarred thing here.

"Do you think he will ever ... " The words knotted, then loosened.

Deborah's hands stilled. "What, child? Speak what you will."

"Arrange a marriage for me," I confessed. The question broke free before I could catch it. "I am nearly eighteen," I said. The truth of it pressed on my chest. "Other girls are wives and mothers by now. I long for what they have. A husband, children, and my own home. Instead, I stand in my father's house and wait. I want more."

My hand closed around my staff until the wood pressed grooves into my palm. "But who would choose a wife who limps, who bears scars upon her face? Even with Abba's wealth and whatever dowry he might arrange, who would say yes to what I am? Either no one has come forward to ask about me, or Abba has said no. I fear it is the first."

"Enough! You are not damaged," she declared, and the firmness in her voice startled me, as if she had struck the table with her palm. "Not in the way you speak of it."

"Sometimes I wonder ... " I could barely say the words out loud. "If this is punishment. For disobeying that day in Jerusalem, for wandering away, for causing her death." My breath faltered. "Sometimes I fear Adonai has hidden His face from me. Forgotten me."

She set the needle aside, stood and gathered me close as she had when I was a child, the familiar scent of wool and rosemary and the smell that was unmistakably hers surrounding me like a cloak. "You were five years old, Anna. A little child reaching out to comfort a wounded animal. The Romans chose violence that day, not you. Your mother shielded you because she loved you. Your father does not blame you. I do not blame you. Nor does Adonai."

Her words sank into the wounded places of my heart, and they stayed, warm as bread. Deborah laid her hand on my scarred cheek. "You are kind and intelligent, a healer with a steady hand and a tender heart. Any man would be blessed to have you. Adonai's timing is not ours, child. He sends mercies at hours we do not expect."

Hope flared too quickly, too bright, too dangerous. I stepped back before it could burn me.

"Enough of this," I said, breathing deeply to calm my emotions. "We have much to look forward to today."

The hours trailed into one another. Deborah's needle began its soft rhythm again. I opened my mother's journal upon the table, and the leather creaked in the way it always had, as if it sighed to be used. I had discovered the journal hidden like buried treasure in her healing room, preserved with such care that I knew she had meant someone to find it when the time was right. The ink of her letters held the shape of her hand, and I could almost see the moments where she had paused and lifted the pen to think. Today, I was drawn to her careful notes about grain poisoning and the terrible winter when death had come to the village uninvited.

"Look here." I beckoned Deborah to my shoulder. "Do you remember this? Seventeen cases occurred that winter because of darnel contamination when the separation was poorly done. She recorded them one by one — how to recognize the sway and stagger, how to purge the poison, and what teas to brew. Seventeen people who would have died without her knowledge."

Deborah leaned close, and the light caught the silver strands at her temple. "I remember. They came from the hills and from the road by the river, even through rain that cut like reeds. And she sent them away on their own feet."

"She drew these herself," I whispered. I traced the careful lines of seed and stalk. "Every mark was meant to guide the next pair of hands."

Deborah nodded, her voice low with memory. "Your mother was blessed with learning that few women possessed. Her father saw the skill in her hands and the hunger in her mind, and he sent for a scribe from Jerusalem to teach her. She could read and write as well as any scholar, and she used those gifts to preserve that which might otherwise have been lost when the last person who held it died. Instead of knowledge being scattered, she gathered it and bound it with ink." She glanced at me, a small pride warming her tired face. "And your father honored that same learning in you. He placed the reed pen in your hand, paid the teacher when some called it foolishness, and kept you to your lessons so that wisdom would not die with her."

Could she have made them for me, even when I was too small to spell my name? The possibility brought tears to my eyes, hot and unexpected.

That afternoon, I carried the journal to the courtyard and set myself where I could see the road to the estate. The sun warmed the stone bench through my robe as I waited. The shadows grew longer, painting the stones in rosy hues, but still no sign of Abba on the path that led to our gate. I smoothed the braid against my shoulder, stretched my back, and adjusted my robe, all the while keeping an eye and ear out for my father.

Just as I wondered if Abba would arrive at all today, footsteps sounded upon the path — firm, even, unhurried, the measured step of someone arriving on foot. Not Abba, then. He would come by donkey. I rose, set my weight upon my staff, and watched the bend in the road.

A solitary figure approached through the shimmer of the late-day light, travel-worn but moving with the easy stride of someone accustomed to long roads, sun-browned and straight-backed. His tunic and cloak were simple but well-made, his shoulders broad, and his stride sure. A stranger. He moved into the courtyard, and I saw he was perhaps a few years older than I, with brown hair curling at his shoulders and eyes full of light.

"Peace be with you," I called, keeping to the safer distance of the gate. "How may we help you?"

He looked at me, and the weariness of travel eased from his features. His mouth curved, brief and unguarded, dimples marking his cheeks. My chest went tight, breath catching somewhere below my ribs. I tucked a loose strand of hair behind my ear, willing myself to calm down.

"Peace be with you," he answered, and I heard a northern cadence in it. "I seek the house of Joseph of Arimathea. I was told this is the place."

A stranger asking for my father by name could mean trouble. "I am Anna," I said, careful to keep my voice even, though it sounded breathless to my ears. I cleared my throat. "His daughter. He is not here at present. What business do you have with him?"

His gaze sharpened, then widened by the slightest degree as if my answer surprised him. He stepped closer, and I saw the work of the sun along his cheekbones, the faint salt-whitened lines where sweat had dried, a faded scar across his cheek. A man young and strong, good to look upon.

"Anna of Arimathea," he repeated with a slight bow, and the way my name rested on his tongue made my pulse stutter. He straightened as though remembering himself. "Shalom. I am Andrew," he said. "I have come with a message."

CHAPTER 2

"Of course," I said, stepping back from the gate. "Please come in and rest. You must be weary from your journey."

Andrew followed me, and I became acutely aware of his nearness. The soft leather of his sandals whispered against stone, a steady hush. The scent of the road clung to him, dust and sun-warmed skin, and, beneath it, a faint salt note still lived in his cloak.

As I turned toward the main entrance and led him down the paving where the sun fell clean upon the stone, shame swept over me. My head covering lay forgotten inside, and every scar stood exposed to this stranger. New eyes made old marks feel fresh and raw. I longed to reach up and cover that side of my face, but that would only draw attention to it, and he seemed not to notice. Yet.

Better to be done with it. I faced him there and let the light have my scars. He was closer than I had thought, the afternoon brightness laying his features bare. We stood nearly face to face, close enough to see the sun lines at the corners of his eyes, the intelligence and kindness in his eyes, and his strong jaw. *He is handsome,* I thought, and laid my hand against my stomach to stop it churning.

"Your home is beautiful," he said, smiling at me, then looked around the courtyard with genuine appreciation. "It is quite peaceful." I waited for his eyes to catch on the scars, for the slight pause, the careful averting of gaze. Would he say nothing about my face?

"Yes, it is," I replied, the words coming out stilted. When had simple conversations become so difficult? I spent my days speaking with the sick and injured, the servants, and Deborah, yet this man's presence left me fumbling for ordinary words. I tried again. "Thank you. My father values the quiet of our estate."

I led him toward the main room, acutely aware of the way my staff tapped the paving stones. The rhythm sounded louder than it should, a small hammer striking the truth of my limp with each step, and each one sent a jolt through my body. He slowed to keep pace with me, making no comment.

"Please sit," I said, directing him to the cushions near the tall windows. Light slanted through the lattice, casting netted shadows across the woven rugs. "I will have refreshments brought."

Shira materialized in the doorway. One of the younger servants who always drifted nearer whenever the world promised a story. Interesting happenings were rare at our estate, though, so I could not fault her for that. I met her glance and tipped my head toward the kitchen. She vanished, fabric whispering in her place.

Deborah appeared as well, settling nearby with her sewing, as steady as the next breath. Her presence soothed me, and I wondered what she read in our guest that I had not yet learned to see. Deborah always saw things I missed.

"The vineyards look well-tended," Andrew observed as he lowered himself onto the cushions. "They are quite extensive."

"My father takes great pride in them," I said, easing down opposite him, taking care to hide the worst of my awkwardness and discomfort. "His wine is known throughout Judea."

"Yes, I have heard." His expression sharpened with interest, and warmth lit his features. Lines that spoke of much laughter creased at the corners of his eyes. I looked away quickly before he caught me staring. "I have also heard of your father by his reputation on the Sanhedrin as well."

"You seem to know much about my father," I said.

A small smile tugged at the corner of his mouth, and a dimple marked his right cheek. Unexpectedly charming, that small hollow.

"People in many places hold your father's name in high regard."

"What places?" I leaned forward, keeping my voice even. "Who speaks of him?"

"Those who value justice and discretion." He paused, choosing words as carefully as a man decides stones for a sling. "Men who seek to serve God faithfully, even in difficult times. My teacher speaks of him often."

Before I could ask more, Shira returned with a tray laden with bread warm from the ovens, soft white cheese, dried figs gleaming with honey, and wine cooled and tempered with water. She served Andrew first, as was proper, her youthful face bright with curiosity she tried and failed to hide, then turned to pour for me, though her eyes kept drifting back to our guest with obvious fascination. I found myself irritated by her lingering attention to him.

"Your hospitality is generous," Andrew said.

When he drank, I watched the way the light caught in his hair, the strength of his hands, the way his lashes threw shadows upon his cheek. I forced my gaze away and busied myself arranging the food on the small table between us.

"This wine is exceptional. I can see why your father's reputation extends beyond the council chambers."

"Thank you." I adjusted my mother's silver bracelets, seeking their familiar comfort. His eyes followed the motion. In the shafts of sun, he could see every scar on my hands.

An unasked question filled the quiet, and the answer rose of its own accord. "An accident in Jerusalem when I was five," I said.

"I am sorry," he replied, his voice carrying genuine sorrow and not the smothering pity that usually followed. "Such early suffering is a heavy burden to carry, yet it often shapes us in unexpected ways."

His tone opened a door. "I suppose it did. I tend to those who are ill when there is need, perhaps because I know what it is to be in pain."

"Being a healer is a rare gift. A holy calling," he said, his smile gentle and unforced. His eyes met mine directly, and I could not look away. "To ease another's suffering is to do the work of angels."

Holy. I studied my damaged hands, these faithful witnesses to loss and labor. Could such marked things do holy work?

"I do not believe what I do could be called holy," I insisted.

"Surely that is for Adonai to decide. Have you studied formally with physicians?"

"No, Deborah has been my teacher." I glanced toward the woman seated nearby with her needlework. "She has been like a mother to me since I was small, and she began instructing me in healing when I was still a child. Though I continue learning, she remains my guide in all things. She is the true healer here."

Andrew's mouth lifted. "She sounds like a remarkable woman."

"That remarkable woman is sitting right here," Deborah countered, warmth and amusement in her voice, looking up from her sewing. "Do not let Anna's modesty mislead you. She has surpassed what I know and has gifts that go beyond training. Arimathea is fortunate to have her."

"I am the fortunate one." I looked at her and found the same smile that had steadied so many of my days, though her face was drawn and shadows pooled beneath her eyes. "Besides my father, she and her husband, Ezra, have been the only kin I have ever known. Ezra takes care of the estate in my father's absence."

Andrew's expression grew thoughtful. "Yes, your father would need someone trustworthy if he spends so much time away. Having an absent father is difficult."

"You understand such things?"

"My father was a fisherman on the Sea of Galilee and often away. The sea called more strongly to him than home ever did." A shadow crossed his features, and he set down his cup carefully. "I understood that, even as a boy."

There was old hurt in his voice, carefully controlled but unmistakable. I leaned forward slightly, drawn by the pain I recognized.

"Did you follow him to the sea?"

"For many years, yes. My brother Simon and I worked his boats, mended his nets, brought in the catch." He gazed toward the window, though I sensed he was seeing distant waters. "I thought that would be my life forever—the boats, the nets, the endless rhythm of casting and hauling. But then John the Baptist began preaching by the Jordan."

"The Baptizer?" I studied his face, drawn by the change in his voice. "I have heard of him. How did you come to know the Baptizer?"

"I went to see him out of curiosity and stayed because I had heard no one speak truth with such power." Andrew's voice took on a quality of wonder. "Then one day, a man came from Nazareth to be baptized. Jesus is his name. The day after, John could speak of nothing else. He said the heavens opened and the Spirit of God descended like a dove to rest upon this man, Jesus. And then..." Andrew's voice dropped to barely a whisper. "A voice spoke from heaven itself."

My heart raced. "A voice?"

"The voice of Adonai." The words left him in a hush. "It spoke from heaven and said, 'You are My beloved Son; with You I am well pleased.' The Baptizer said it was the voice of the Lord Himself, claiming Jesus of Nazareth as His own. I wish I had been there to witness it. That moment changed everything."

The room seemed to hold its breath. "To hear the voice of the Lord would be..." I groped for a word broad enough. "Would be..."

"Life-changing," Andrew said. "Yes."

"It would change everything," I agreed, a strange ache filling my chest. "I have never heard Him speak. Not like that.

Not even a whisper." I looked down at my scarred hands. *Sometimes I wonder if He sees me at all.*

Andrew shifted, and for a heartbeat, I thought he might reach for me. Deborah cleared her throat, and he sat back.

"He sees you, Anna," he said.

Perhaps He does, I thought, though my heart was slow to be persuaded.

"The next day," Andrew continued, "my friend and I were still by the river. John was teaching again, and Jesus appeared." A faint smile touched his mouth. "John stopped mid-sentence. Just stopped. Then he said the words that changed my life."

I waited, scarcely breathing.

"'Behold, the Lamb of God, who takes away the sin of the world. This is the Chosen One of God.'" His voice steadied as he spoke it. "My friend and I had to know more, so we followed Jesus. He noticed us and asked, 'What do you want?' We were so flustered, we did not answer properly, and then we blurted, 'Where are you staying?' Can you imagine asking the Messiah where he was lodging?" Andrew shook his head, laughing.

"What did he say? Was he angry at such boldness?"

"Boldness? More like impertinence." He smiled. "He was not angry. He said, 'Come and see.' So we did. We went to where he was staying and spent the rest of the day with him. Afterward, I found my brother Simon and told him we had found the Messiah, the one written about by the prophets."

"The Messiah?" My hands trembled, and I laced them together to still them. "Like the one promised in Isaiah?"

"Exactly like in Isaiah."

The beloved words rose as familiar as breath: For unto us a child is born, unto us a son is given... and his name shall be called Wonderful, Counsellor, The mighty God, The everlasting Father, The Prince of Peace. I thanked Abba quietly for insisting I learn to read and write. The scrolls had kept company with me through hours that might have been empty.

"What happened then?"

"We returned to our fishing, but not for long. Jesus found us at our work and said, 'Follow me, and I will make you fishers of men.' Simon and I left everything that day—the boats, the business, our old lives. We have been with him ever since."

"You gave up everything you had built? So quickly?" Amazement lifted my voice. "You abandoned your entire life?"

"I did not abandon my life. I found it. When he spoke, I knew I was meant to follow."

He smiled, and anticipation stirred low in my chest. "Jesus is my Rabbi, my teacher, and I travel with him and others. I have witnessed him healing the sick, casting out demons, turning water into wine at a wedding feast. So many wonders, I would not have believed them had I not seen them with my own eyes."

"Does he truly heal people?"

"Yes, anyone who comes to him in faith. He does not ask if they are worthy or demand that they prove themselves first. He simply gives what they need because he shows the mercy of God to all who come to him."

I set my cup down with shaking hands. "Mercy," I whispered.

"Perfect mercy that sees past our wounds to the person God meant us to be." Andrew leaned forward slightly. "You do not need to earn his favor, Anna. You need only come to him as you are. As he said to me, 'Come and see.'"

"Come and see," I murmured.

The invitation lingered between us. *Come and see.* Could it be that simple?

The early evening light slanted through the windows, and Andrew noticed. He rose with reluctance, and disappointment swept through me, not ready for our time to be over.

"I should not intrude upon you any longer. May I return tomorrow when your father is here? I carry a message that concerns his welfare."

The message. In my fascination with his stories, I had forgotten entirely about his original purpose. "Yes," I said too quickly, then felt color rise in my cheeks. "If it truly involves my father's safety." I paused, studying his face. "This message —it comes from Jesus? From your teacher."

"It does."

"What does it concern?" I had to know. "You said it involves his welfare."

"That is a conversation for your father's ears," Andrew said. "I would not be faithful to my charge if I spoke of such matters to others, even one so ... " He paused, seeming to choose his words carefully. "Even one I respect as I do you."

He moved toward the doorway, then paused at the threshold, looking back, smiling. "I will return tomorrow, then. It has been an honor to meet you, Anna of Arimathea."

His dimples stole my breath. "And you, Andrew of ... ?"

"Bethsaida. Though these days I am more Andrew of the road."

I stood at the window and watched his figure diminish along the path, my heart beating faster than it should. This man had seen my scars and had not turned away. He had spoken of a Messiah who heals all who come in faith.

"He seems to be a man of integrity," Deborah said.

"Yes." I pressed my palm to the window frame. "Do you think what he said about his teacher could be true?"

"I think," she said, "that the Almighty works in ways we do not always understand. And I think there is reason to hope."

Hope. As night settled over Arimathea and still no word came from Abba, worry worked at me. He had promised to arrive by evening, and while the roads and his arrival times could be unpredictable, something about Andrew's message concerning his "welfare" made every shadow seem threatening. What if something had happened to him? What if the warning Andrew carried had come too late?

Yet despite my concern, I thought of Andrew's invitation: *Come and see*. For the first time in years, I wondered if such an invitation could be meant for me.

CHAPTER 3

ANDREW DID NOT RETURN, but Abba came three days later.

The clip-clop of hooves pulled me from my restless morning prayers, a hollow rhythm passing through the stone like a pulse. Dust lifted in small swirls as his donkey plodded to a stop. I reached for my staff and went out, my hip tight from nights that had been more waking than sleeping, filled with dreams of dimples and invitations to come and see.

Abba dismounted with the careful movements of a man who had ridden hard. Road dust dulled his cloak to the color of old parchment. When he looked at me, his smile came swiftly, yet I saw the quick shadow behind it, the measure he took of my limp. Worse than before, his eyes said, though his mouth did not.

"Anna, my girl." He met me halfway and gathered me into an embrace that startled me with its fierceness. For a heartbeat, I stood stiff, astonished by the nearness, then I let myself lean into him, greedy for the warmth I craved but rarely received. Affection was a rare currency between us but one I would exchange happily.

He smelled of ink, warm wool, and the scrolls I knew he bent over in the evenings. The scents carried me back to Jerusalem, to a study where lamplight threw shadows across walls, where his voice rose and fell in prayer while my mother knelt beside him, her hand on my small back. I caught a whiff of incense threading through his beard. The city clung to him like a second cloak. Longing rose sharp beneath my ribs, an ache for streets I could barely remember, for a city I knew only through scent and shadow and the shape of my father's life.

"It gladdens my heart to see you, little dove," he murmured, using the old endearment I had not heard in many years. His whiskers rubbed roughly against my temple.

Relief rushed through me. He was here. I blinked hard, the sudden sting behind my eyes sharp as a thorn. "I missed you, Abba. We expected you days ago. The roads were safe?"

"Safe enough," he replied. "Troubled times in the city delayed me, but I am here now."

He did not turn toward the villa or call for Ezra as he usually did upon arrival. He steered us into my garden instead, and I nearly stumbled from the shock of it. Lavender brushed our robes as we walked the main path. Mint sprawled rebelliously across the paths despite my attempts to contain it, and jasmine climbed the wall in cascades of star-white blossoms.

"Tell me everything," he said, sitting on the bench he had placed here years ago for me. The warmth in his voice startled me. "How is Deborah? Are you still learning from her?"

He faced me fully, hands still on the stone between us, waiting. The words came easier than they had in months. I spoke of the fever that had nearly claimed little Aaron, the burn salve I had perfected after weeks of trial, and the signs of infection I had learned. For these few breaths, his attention did not stray toward the house or the accounts waiting in his study. He sat with me as though we had all the hours in the world, and I drank in every moment.

"Abba, I am worried about Deborah," I said when the tide of talk ebbed. "She is thinner. She presses her side when she thinks I do not see. Her hands tremble with the needle. Pain is taking something from her."

His brows drew together. "Have you asked her plainly?"

"I have tried. She always turns it aside, as if keeping me from sorrow would keep sorrow from the house. I know she seeks to shield me from worry, but how can I not? I am not a child. I see it. I know when pain walks disguised as weariness." I knew it all too well.

Abba watched me intently. "Anna, you are correct. You are no longer a child. You are a healer now in your own right."

His words surprised me, and I could think of no response.

"I will speak with her," he promised, his arm settling around my shoulders. "Then my daughter, the healer, can see to her care."

Relief swept through me like wind through wheat, bending something in me that had stood rigid too long. Abba would help me. "Thank you, Abba," I said, laying my hand on top of his. He smiled, but I saw a sadness pass through his eyes.

"Your mother would weep with joy to see what you have become." His voice grew thick with memory. "Sarah was a gifted healer. She always hoped you would follow her path, you know. She taught you her ways, even when you were young."

A memory broke over me sudden as storm light, myself at five summers, watching Ima's steady hands clean a lamb's wounded flank, her voice calm and sure as she spoke of frightened creatures fighting the very help they needed. I remembered the way she had let me touch the lamb's head, praised my gentle touch, and told me I had the gift.

"I remember," I whispered. "The lamb with the torn leg. She let me help tend it."

His eyes softened. "You do remember. She was so proud that day. She said you had healing hands like hers."

The same healing hands that led me to another crying lamb, I thought, the familiar ache filling my chest. How different our lives might have been if I had stayed by her side that day.

He plucked a lavender stem, rolled it between his fingers, and held it beneath his nose. "Her favorite. She said it calmed both patient and healer alike. She rubbed it as she worked."

"It has many uses, to be sure," I said, crinkling my nose. "I only wish I liked the scent more."

He laughed before he could help it, washing away the melancholy. "You are always a delight, Anna." He rose and brushed dust from his robes. "Ezra will be waiting. We will talk later."

Too soon, the man of duty stepped back into him.

"Abba," I called after him, part desperation to delay his departure, part need to unburden the news I had carried these three days. "A visitor came, a man named Andrew. He carried a message for you."

"A message?" Concern moved across his face. "He came here rather than seeking me in Jerusalem? Why?"

"I do not know. He said the matter was important and that it came from his teacher. Jesus of Nazareth."

At the name of Jesus, Abba's expression shuttered as if a door had been closed within him. The warmth of our talk vanished. "Thank you for informing me," he finally said, turning to go.

"Wait, Abba!" I pushed myself off the bench, grabbed my staff, and started toward him. "Do you know Andrew?"

"Possibly," he conceded. "Our paths may have crossed."

Hope stirred suddenly. Abba might know Andrew! "He said he would return when you were here. Perhaps you know how to reach him?"

"No." The word struck too hard. I flinched, and he drew a breath, gentling his tone. "It would be best to forget his visit ever occurred."

Forget? As if a stone could forget it had been thrown. How could I forget Andrew with his gentle eyes and easy smile, the stories of a teacher who heals, the invitation to come and see? Andrew filled most of my thoughts. There would be no forgetting him.

"Abba, who is Jesus of Nazareth?" I tried one more time. "Have you met him?"

"I know him," he admitted, clipped and careful. "His name is not one to be spoken lightly in Jerusalem." He weighed me with a look full of things he would not set on my shoulders. "For your sake and mine, let us leave it there. Ezra expects me."

"Please, Abba," I begged. "Tell me what you know."

"Not now." He tucked my arm into his; our conversation clearly over. "This is not the homecoming I wanted. Walk in with me."

Questions crowded my mind and had no place to go. I obeyed.

When dusk softened the edges of the estate, he sought me again.

"Come," he said, and held out his hand. My frustration with him melted away as he grasped my arm and helped me to the garden.

We ate together under the low light of oil lamps. He surprised me with a feast: flatbread still crackling from the ovens, roasted lamb fragrant with rosemary, dates stuffed with almonds, thick yogurt drizzled with golden honey, and his finest wine, dark as garnets. The lamps breathed, stars opened small bright eyes above the wall, and the air held that moment between heat and chill. The light seemed to glow warmer, the stars above brighter, the wine on my tongue sweeter than any I had tasted before. We were truly together, father and daughter, for the first time in so long. I wanted the night never to end.

He spoke easily then, as he rarely did with me, and of things I knew little about. Tin traders in distant Hispania, merchant vessels that carried our wine to ports along the Great Sea, vineyard partnerships that stretched from Galilee to Egypt, a merchant family in Caesarea whose daughters had a quick wit and a mind for business. I reveled in every word and laughed more than I had in months. Each story felt like a gift laid in my hand.

When the lamps guttered lower, his voice dropped and roughened, the ease draining from it. "I must leave at dawn."

Cold rippled through my middle, spreading outward

until my legs felt weak. Dawn meant hours, not days. "Dawn? You have just come."

"A messenger arrived. The council convenes, and my absence would be noted." He reached for me as if to steady what he had unsettled. "Every moment away from you tears at my heart, Anna. But duty calls with a voice I cannot ignore."

What about duty to me? The thought came bitter and sharp, but I swallowed it down before it could reach my tongue.

"Take me with you!" I implored before fear could make me meek. "Please, Abba. I will keep your house as I do here. Deborah can come. Only for a short time."

I watched his gaze trace the familiar territory of my face, the raised welts that marked my cheek, and the white lines that webbed across my hands. I knew what he would say before he opened his mouth.

"Jerusalem is not safe," he warned. "Crowds, unrest, men eager for a spark. It is not the city you remember." His hand smoothed my hair as if I were still five. "Trust me."

"I was a small child when we left," I said. "I remember almost nothing."

"That is why you do not understand." He shook his head once, and the matter seemed closed. "I could not bear to lose you as I lost her. You must remain here, where you are protected."

"That will not happen again," I said. "I would be careful—"

"No, daughter." He pressed his lips to my forehead. "Not while such darkness gathers."

"Yes, Abba," I said, and the taste of the words was bitter in my mouth.

I did not sleep. I lay listening to the house breathe, ear turned to his chamber, hoping for any sound to prove he still dwelt within reach. Far too soon, I heard the small noises of a man preparing to go — water pouring, leather creaking, a chest closing softly so as not to wake me. When the world turned from black to ash, I rose, wrapping a cloak around my shoulders. He would not leave without a farewell from me.

The courtyard held the coolness of the hour before dawn. Saddlebags lay across the donkey's back. The animal shifted and blew steam into the dim air. I stepped out, and Abba turned with surprise on his face, then something like sorrow.

"I did not want to wake you," he said, though relief flickered across his face. He wanted the farewell too.

Words caught behind the knot in my throat, every plea dissolving before it could take shape. He was already cloaked for travel, ready to leave. Tears filled my eyes, so I lifted my face to the sky, where night wrestled with the coming day, the last stars clinging to their posts before surrendering to the dawn, their watch complete.

He crossed to me quickly and folded me into his arms. We stood without speaking, the jasmine stirring on the wall. My rooster announced the day, a reminder that time would not hold still for us.

"I love you beyond measure," he said at last, his arms tightening. "I am proud of you. Remember that, if the loneliness weighs heavily. I will return as swiftly as I am able, and we can talk more about everything."

"I love you too," I managed. I gathered what courage I had. "Are you sure I cannot come to Jerusalem with you?"

He smiled, and I had to look away before my face could betray what his tenderness cost me. "You have your mother's hands and her strong will." He laughed softly. "But the answer is still no."

I held onto him as though my grip alone could hold back the dawn. Nothing but memory and the lingering scent of incense in his beard would remain. "Did you speak with Deborah?"

"Not as I wished. There was no time," he said, and the line of his jaw tightened. "Promise me you will watch her closely. If she worsens, send word at once. Some things cannot wait for convenience."

"I will. Watch and send word."

Light grew along the stones. He looked toward the road and then back to me, as if his body had already departed while his heart asked for a little more time.

"Truly, I must go. There is no more time. Shalom, daughter."

He mounted, gave me one last look, and rode out through the gate. His hoofbeats dwindled, and then silence flooded back over the courtyard, almost drowning me with it.

I stood with my staff and watched the road until even the dust had settled, until there was nothing left but the empty curve of packed earth disappearing into the olive groves. The villa waited behind me with its ordered rooms and familiar tasks. The garden breathed its morning scents of lavender and jasmine, unchanged by my grief. Somewhere out there, the father I loved rode back to Jerusalem on the same roads he had traveled a hundred times before, and another man, the one my heart could not erase, walked roads I would never see.

CHAPTER 4

After Abba left, I sought refuge in my garden. Pain ground through my hip with each step, sharp enough to steal my breath by the time I reached the stone bench and lowered myself down with shaking arms. Bubbeleh, my old sheep, found me at the gate, her wool, once bright as a spring cloud, now the color of ashes.

"Come then, old friend." She laid her head on my lap, and I scratched behind her ears. My palms remembered the rest—reed and linen, straw and dust, a lamb's breath on my wrist while the crowd flowed past without stopping. Now she pressed against my leg, her welcome touch anchoring me to this moment. At thirteen, she had lived longer than most, and I could not yet face the day I knew was coming.

From the house, I heard Deborah set the day in motion, her measured cadence threading the rooms. From the outbuildings came Ezra's lower answer, quiet as a millstone turning. On my shelf, the jars of honey and oil, comfrey salve, and clean linen waited. Today's work would find me when it wished. The familiar rhythms rose around me, but my thoughts slipped beyond the estate walls.

I bowed my head. *God of Abraham, Isaac, and Jacob, are You here? Please see me. I am alone again. Why must I always remain behind? I stretch out my hands, but You seem far. Do not forget me, Adonai.*

A rooster's crow split the morning air. "I am coming!" I called and smiled even as the weight of Abba's departure still pressed against my heart. I opened the coop, and the hens tumbled into the yard, Goliath herding them like a little general. Delilah, broody and round, shouldered the others from the best kernels. Little Hannah, as always, was between my feet. Abigail found what the others missed even with her crooked toes and uneven gait. We understood one another, she and I.

Grain scattered, I lingered while the eastern edge of the world took on the color of apricot first, then the pale gold of almond's inner skin. The silver-green olives caught it, and the terraces below stirred as if the vines had heard their names in the stillness.

I patted Bubbeleh one last time and headed toward the villa. My hand went to the gate latch, and the wind rose. It carried a scent I did not know, like frankincense, but wilder, threaded with honey and cedar. The fragrance clung to everything, richer and stranger than any incense I had smelled in the Temple, though it held that same sense of the sacred, of spaces set apart for holy use. The hairs on my arms lifted, and my damaged nerves woke. Blossoms leaned—yes, leaned—toward an unseen light. Even Bubbeleh lifted her head, ears forward.

The wind circled me, wrapped around my shoulders, lifted my hair, and stirred my robe against my ankles. It seemed I stood in the center of something vast and holy, something that had come for me alone. My scarred hands tingled where they gripped the iron as the air swirled around me.

Then, as suddenly as it had come, the wind stilled completely. The birds stopped mid-note. Even the hens stopped their scratching and stood motionless, heads cocked as if listening with me. The silence stretched and deepened until it seemed the very air held its breath, waiting.

I did not hear it with my ears first. It came up through the ground, through the stone, through the bones that ache in the rain, until it reached the place where fear had made a tiny house inside me.

"I see you, Anna."

The latch slid from my fingers and struck the stone. My knees loosened and would have given way if not for the wall. Those four words moved through me the way floodwater roars down a dry streambed, finding every hollow place. They reached places loneliness had carved and washed them clean.

"I see you, Anna."

"Adonai? Is that You?" I whispered. The scent lingered around me, clung to my skin, my hair, my robe. A blessing I could not wash away. Bubbeleh stood, eyes fixed on empty air.

Color suddenly sharpened into focus. Myrtle ran up the lattice, each white star cut bright. Dew along the path flashed silver. On the terraces, flowers flared red and blue, and the pomegranate tips glowed ember-bright. Olive leaves turned their silver sides all at once, a quick shimmer. Above it all, the sky stepped from milk to true blue in a single breath. Something small and alive uncurled beneath my breastbone, tentative, hardly daring to take shape, but unmistakably there.

The pain in my hip quieted to a distant murmur, withdrawn as though behind a heavy door. I did not dare breathe, afraid the world would dim if I blinked even once.

But no other words came. The sounds and shades of morning slowly returned. My hands shook as I touched the stone wall, pressed my palms flat against its rough surface, desperate for something solid to hold me upright.

My pulse beat wildly in my chest, my wrists, and behind my eyes as I made my way to my chamber. I entered and pressed my back against the closed door, my legs trembling beneath me. The bronze mirror caught my reflection, and though I saw the same scarred face, the same uneven features, somehow, I looked different. My eyes held a light I had not seen there before, as if a capacity for wonder I thought long dead had awakened and lifted its head to listen.

I touched my cheek, my neck, my wrists where the fragrance still clung. The scent of frankincense and honey and cedar wound through my hair, into the fabric of my robe. I brought my hands to my face and breathed it in, and tears spilled hot down my cheeks.

My spirit confirmed what my mind could not process. I moved to the window, then back to the door, unable to settle, unable to be still. The words kept echoing through me. *I see you, Anna.*

Deborah's footsteps sounded in the corridor. I turned from the window as she entered with a tray, and when I saw her face, I began to weep.

"Anna!" She set the tray down and came to me. Her hands reached for mine. "What has happened? Are you hurt?"

I shook my head, but the tears would not stop.

"I cannot find words." My voice broke on the last syllable.

She led me to the low stool and helped me down onto it, her hands steadying my shaking shoulders. "Breathe, child. Breathe and tell me."

"After Abba left—I was in the garden—" I could barely get the words out. "The wind came."

"Breathe, Anna." Deborah held my hands between hers. "Start from the beginning."

My mind whirled. How could I put shape to what had no edges? The otherworldly fragrance still clung to my skin, my hair. The voice still rang in my memory, four words I could not stop hearing. I had no explanation for her. I could not even explain it to myself.

I drew a shaking breath and tried again. "There was a scent on the wind. Like nothing I have ever known." I touched my hair, my robe. "Can you smell it?"

Deborah leaned closer, and her eyes widened. "I do smell it. What is it?"

"I do not know. It was like the Temple, but not. Wilder. The wind wrapped around me, Deborah, and the world—everything became so bright. Too bright. The colors—I cannot explain it."

My hands would not stop shaking. I pressed them against my knees, but they trembled still.

"Then the wind stopped. Everything stopped. The birds, the hens, everything went silent, and then—" I gripped Deborah's arm. "Then I heard it. Not with my ears. It was inside me and outside me and everywhere all at once."

"What did you hear?"

"A voice." Fresh tears tracked down my face. "A voice that said—" I could barely force the words past my lips. "It said, 'I see you, Anna.'"

Deborah drew in a sharp breath.

"Twice. Twice, He spoke my name. 'I see you, Anna.' Deborah, I had just asked—I had just prayed and asked if He saw me, if He was even there, and He answered. He spoke my name."

Deborah's eyes shone with tears. "Oh, Anna."

"Do you think it was Him? Could the Holy One have spoken to me?"

"Who else could it be? Who else could make the wind smell of heaven and speak a name with such power?" She gazed out the window toward my garden, where the morning light fell golden on the herb beds. "Your mother used to say that God speaks to those who need to hear Him most," she said finally. "Perhaps He knows you have been lonely."

"Or perhaps I imagined it all. Perhaps loneliness has made me hear voices that were never there."

"Anna. Look at me."

I met her eyes, seeing in them the love that had sustained me throughout my life.

"I have known you since you were five years old," she said. "You are many things—stubborn, tender-hearted, too quick to blame yourself for things beyond your control. But you are not given to flights of fancy. If you say God spoke your name, then He spoke your name. I believe you."

Her certainty settled over me like a warm embrace, grounding me when I felt I might float away from the strangeness of what had happened. "But why? Why would He speak to me?"

"Why does the rain fall on both the just and the unjust? Why does the sun rise on the evil and the good?" She smiled, and for a moment, the pain lines around her eyes softened. "Because that is who He is. Because love poured out is His nature, not His obligation."

Love poured out. The phrase nestled deep inside me, a seed in good soil ready to root and grow into something I could not yet see but knew would remain a part of me.

"What do I do with such a gift?" I whispered.

"You treasure it. You let it change you from the inside out. And you wait to see what He does next."

The rest of the morning passed in a strange, shimmering awareness. Every task felt full of new meaning, from mixing remedies for the village women to tending my herb garden to eating the midday meal. It was as if the voice that had spoken my name had roused some capacity for wonder I had not known still lived in me.

When Martha arrived seeking salve for her cracked hands, I really saw her for the first time in months. I saw the exhaustion etched in the corners of her eyes, the way she favored her left shoulder, the resigned set of her mouth that spoke of burdens carried too long without complaint. I had seen it before, I thought, but this was different somehow. Now I saw more.

"How is young David?" I asked as I worked the healing ointment into her palms. "Is he still coughing?"

"Some better," she said, but her voice carried worry. "The nights are worse. He cannot rest properly."

I reached for a small pottery jar, measuring dried coltsfoot and honey into it with careful hands. "Brew this into tea before bedtime. It will ease the tightness in his chest."

"Bless you, my lady. You ask for nothing yet give so much." She held the jar tightly in her hands.

"The healing comes from the Holy One, not from me. I am only His hands in this moment."

When she left, her step seemed lighter. Something opened in my chest, spacious and bright, full of possibility I had not felt in years. Taking care of others had always been my work, but now it felt transformed, made holy by the voice that had spoken my name this morning, a gift I longed to share.

Evening found me in my garden again, kneeling among the rosemary and thyme. The sun hung low in the western sky, painting everything in its path. "I heard You," I whispered to the quiet air. "I heard You speak my name."

A faint breath of frankincense drifted on the evening air.

CHAPTER 5

Two weeks had passed since God had met me in the garden, and the calm stayed and steadied me when despair threatened to overtake me. I was not hollow now but sharpened. Even so, the days lengthened with waiting. No word from Abba, and hope that Andrew would return had dwindled to almost nothing. Deborah's condition continued to worsen, though she would not admit it.

I sought refuge in my garden as twilight settled over the estate. I kneeled in the damp earth and pulled stubborn weeds from around the lavender with more force than the task required, hoping to distract myself from the restlessness within me. The soil was warm beneath my palms, rich with promise.

"Help... someone... please!"

I froze, my hand still buried in the soil. A man's voice carried over the stone wall, desperate and weak.

"Help!"

The second cry came fainter. Something was wrong.

I pushed to my feet, brushed dirt from my palms, picked up my staff, and hurried along the path toward the call. Frustration rose with my slow progress. Each step sent familiar fire up my spine, but urgency drove me.

I reached the courtyard as a man pitched forward onto the paving stones with a cry. Dark stains had soaked through his tunic in spreading patches, and his hair clung to a gash across his scalp.

For one terrible heartbeat I thought it might be Abba, but when I dropped to my knees beside the fallen man, my staff clattering away across the stones, I realized it was not him.

"Please." The word emerged hoarse and weak. The man lifted his head a fraction toward me, and despite the swelling and bruises and the crimson streaking his face, I knew him.

"Andrew!" I cried, unable to believe what I was seeing. One eye had swollen completely shut, and his lip was split and bleeding.

"Anna," he gasped, reaching for me with one arm. "Remember me? I am sorry ... to come here ... like this."

"I remember you." I looked at those features I had memorized weeks ago, and my thoughts scattered like startled birds, pulled in a dozen directions at once—the blood soaking into stone, the strange angle of his arm, the rasping quality of his breathing that spoke of potentially damaged ribs. I closed my eyes for one heartbeat and made myself still, made myself think in the ordered way Deborah had taught me.

"Do not move," I said, though my voice shook. "You are badly hurt. Lie still." My mind began its counting: clean cloths, water, heated but not boiling, something to stop the bleeding. We must get him inside. I needed Deborah.

"Andrew, I am here. Listen to my voice." I touched his face lightly. My fingers came away red and sticky, but his skin was not fever-hot. "You are safe now."

I forced my hands to remain calm. His tunic was slashed in several places, the cuts deep enough to require stitching. Dark bruises pooled along his ribs where the cloth had torn, and his left arm hung at an unnatural angle that made my stomach clench. Dried blood matted his brown curls.

I pressed my palm to his side where the flow was strongest. Catching the hem of my robe, I tore a strip free. The sound carried sharply across the courtyard. My hands might be scarred, but they were strong. I twisted the linen into a tight pad and laid it firmly against the worst of his wounds. His good eye fluttered closed.

"No. Stay with me." I shook him gently. "Andrew, look at me." He groaned, barely conscious.

"Deborah!" My voice rang out into the night. "Deborah, come quickly! Bring Ezra!"

"Lady Anna?" A sharp clatter behind me. Tamar, one of our youngest servants, stood frozen in the doorway, eyes wide.

I twisted at the waist without lifting my hands from Andrew's side. "Go. Run and fetch Deborah and Ezra. I need help immediately. Hurry!"

"Is he —"

"Do not look! Go!" She stared for a heartbeat, then nodded and fled toward the house.

Andrew's eye found me again. "You are still here," he whispered.

"I am, and I have ruined my favorite robe for you, so you absolutely must live," I said, trying to keep my tone light despite the fear that shook my hands. I smoothed damp hair from his brow. "Who did this to you?"

"Bandits. Outside Bethel." The words came broken, separated by shallow breaths. "They were attacking ... a family with children. I could not ... could not just walk by." He took a breath that rattled in his chest.

"You fought them off?"

"Long enough ... for the family to escape." His eye drifted closed briefly. "Worth it. My arm ... is bad?" He attempted a smile that was more grimace than anything else.

Something inside me twisted painfully, pulled so tight I could barely draw breath. He had risked himself for strangers, for children he did not know, without thought for his own safety. His body, his life, offered freely. The kind of man who would do that was rare as gold, and he lay bleeding because of his own goodness. "Hush now. You can tell me everything later." My palm lingered on his cheek before I could snatch it back. "And yes, you have done something to that arm."

"I thought so."

Deborah dropped to her knees beside us, shawl slipping from her shoulders, her face pale with shock in the lamplight that spilled from the house. "Anna! Who is this? What has happened?" Her gaze cut to his face and widened. "The young man who brought your father a message."

"Yes. Andrew. He was attacked." I pushed to stand, fighting the catch in my hip. "He is badly injured. Where is Ezra?"

"Here," Ezra answered, already crossing the courtyard. He took in the scene at a glance. "Let me help."

Between the three of us, we carried Andrew into the main room where the lamplight was brightest. Every step sent fresh waves of pain across his features, sweat beading at his temples despite the evening chill. Fire shot through my hip with each step, the familiar grinding pain that spoke of bone meeting bone in ways it should not. But I pushed it to the edges of my mind where it could scream all it wanted. Andrew's pain was so much worse than mine, his need so much greater, and I would not let my body's limitations keep me from helping him now. I could not.

We eased him onto the wide couch.

"Deborah, what do you need?" I asked, my voice sounding much more steady than I felt. Her skill far exceeded mine, and Andrew's life might depend on that difference.

She was already assessing the damage with experienced hands, fingers probing gently but thoroughly. "Ezra, send Shira for my basket. Have her get the silk thread, the curved needles, and the jar of honey salve. Clean cloths and boiled water. Tell her to hurry."

Ezra nodded and disappeared. I lowered myself onto a stool, easing the fire in my hip.

Deborah grabbed the scissors from her sewing basket and cut away the bloodied tunic with precise movements, the bronze blades flashing in the light. Her hands did not tremble as mine did, and her breathing remained even as she took account of the full extent of his injuries.

"Three deep cuts," she murmured, more to herself than to me. "The arm is dislocated, not broken. I can feel it here, where the bone has moved from its proper place." She looked up. "He has lost blood, but not as much as it appears. This will take time, Anna. Are you prepared to assist?"

"Yes," I said, making an effort to control myself. "Tell me how to help."

I could do this. I knew how to do this. The certainty

surprised me. The next thought surprised me even more. I had treated wounds, though never on someone whose welfare mattered so fiercely to me.

I rested a hand lightly on his shoulder. "You will be well," I said.

Ezra returned with Shira, both of them carrying supplies. She set a basin of steaming water and clean cloths at Deborah's knee while he placed the salve and the silk thread within reach. The room smelled of warm oil, metal, and the faint sweetness of honey.

"This will cause considerable pain," Deborah warned, threading a needle with steady hands. In the lamplight, the silk gleamed.

I kneeled beside her and held the lamp so the light fell true.

"I know." Andrew gripped the edge of the couch with his uninjured hand. "Do what you must."

Deborah began with the deepest wound, the one that gaped across his ribs. Her fingers moved swiftly, and I watched every motion, trying to memorize her technique. She had taught me that every stitch must be exact. Too loose and the wound might reopen. Too tight and healing would be compromised.

I closed my eyes for a moment and prayed silently. *Be with Andrew, Adonai. Be with us all. Let these hands be instruments of healing.*

"Hold the lamp steady," she murmured, "and watch closely. If my hands tire, you will need to finish."

"I understand." I leaned in, noting every angle and pull, spacing and knot.

"Where were you traveling?" I asked Andrew, wanting to keep him conscious and needing to hear his voice.

"Returning ... with the message." His breathing was shallow but even. "Message ... is important."

He had been coming back to us. "What does it say?"

"Jesus ... wanted Joseph to know ..." His eye slid closed, and my heart nearly stopped beating.

"Stay with me, Andrew." The sharpness of my voice startled us both. "Tell me about the message."

"Trouble in Jerusalem. Religious leaders... watching Jesus closely. Some want him stopped." He stared into my eyes as though willing me to understand. "Joseph needs to be careful ... if they discover his sympathies. He is in danger."

His words threaded their way into my heart and threatened to rip it open. Trouble in Jerusalem. Abba in danger. The two thoughts circled each other, predators sizing up prey, and I could not tell which frightened me more: that my father was at risk, or that I had been kept ignorant of it until a bleeding stranger brought the news to our door. My hands began to shake again, and the lamp trembled in my grip, casting dancing shadows across Andrew's face.

Deborah's hands paused momentarily. Our eyes met across Andrew's body, and I saw my fear reflected in her gaze before she bent to finish her work.

"There." Deborah tied off the last stitch and stretched her back with a soft groan. Ezra brought water and insisted she rest, guiding her to a chair. I bathed Andrew's brow and wiped away the blood caught in the curls at his temple.

In the lamplight, I could finally see his face clearly. The full extent of the damage was worse than I thought. Cuts marked his temple and jaw, the left eye was swollen shut, and bruises bloomed purple across his cheekbone. Two weeks ago this man had walked into my garden with his easy stride and ready smile, had invited me to come and see, as though such a thing were possible. Now he lay broken on our couch, his strength stolen, his confidence replaced by the shallow breathing of someone whose body had taken more damage than it knew how to process. But his skin was warm but not burning, and I allowed myself a moment of hope.

"Your arm now," Deborah said, returning after a few minutes of rest. She examined his shoulder carefully. "As I thought—dislocated, not broken. We can set it. Ezra, I will need your help."

She placed Ezra's hands and demonstrated the proper angle and pressure needed. "Ready? Take a deep breath and hold it. Now."

They pulled swiftly and hard. Andrew's scream echoed against the walls and cut off as darkness enveloped him. His body went limp.

"Better this way." Deborah checked his pulse. "He will sleep now. Rest is the finest healer." Her eyes searched my face and saw the tears blurring my eyes. "This has shaken you."

"It has." I wiped my eyes with the back of my hand. "But I am well enough." I looked at her more closely. "And you? You look exhausted."

"It has been a long evening. Do not set your worries on me."

We covered Andrew with soft blankets. In sleep, the lines of pain eased from his face, and he looked younger than I remembered. A boyish curl rested against his brow.

"I can watch him if you would prefer to rest," Deborah offered.

"No." The word came before I could soften it. Protectiveness had awakened in me. "You should rest. I will stay."

Through the long night, I kept vigil. I counted his

breaths, changed his bandages when they needed changing, and coaxed water between cracked lips. The lamp burned low, and my hip ached from holding one position, but I did not leave him.

This was what it meant to be a healer, to stand watch between life and death.

At some point, the panic that had been driving me for hours let up. My shoulders dropped from where they had been hunched near my ears. My breathing slowed, deepened, found its natural rhythm again instead of the irregular dance fear had reduced it to. He would live. The certainty rose from somewhere I could not name, but I trusted it with everything in me. He would live. I would accept no other outcome.

Near dawn, his eye opened, confusion crossing his features as he tried to focus. When his gaze found mine, recognition broke through.

"Anna?" Barely a whisper, rough with pain and sleep. "Where ... How did I ..."

"You are safe," I said, leaning close. "You reached our estate. Do you remember?"

"Somewhat. The bandits." His voice gained strength as his memory returned. "I remember walking, trying to reach you. Blood ... my arm." He tried to shift position and winced. "Water?"

I held a clay cup to his lips and supported his head while he drank. "Thank you," he said when he had drunk his fill. "For the water and ...everything else."

"You would have done the same."

"Would I?" A weak smile tugged at the corner of his mouth. "I think you are braver than I am, Anna of Arimathea."

"You would," I said. "Rest now."

I rose, but his hand closed over mine on the blanket, his grip weak but deliberate, his calloused palm rough against my scarred knuckles. The contact sent heat up my arm, settling beneath my breastbone.

"Will you stay?"

"Yes," I said, surprised by how deeply I meant it. "Of course, I will stay."

His fingers wrapped around my hand with surprising strength for someone so injured, as though anchoring himself to something solid in a world that had turned violent and unpredictable. I felt the places where our skin met—his palm against mine, his thumb resting against my wrist where my pulse hammered too fast, too loud—and wondered if he could feel what his touch did to me, if he knew that I would have sat here holding his hand until the sun rose and set again if that was what he needed.

"I am happy I made it here," he murmured, his eye drifting closed again. "Happy I found you."

Me too, I thought, sitting very still with his hand in mine. Outside, the first birds began their morning songs, but I barely heard them. My pulse pounded everywhere at once. I knew then I would always remember the way the lamplight caught in his dark hair, how our hands fit together, the way he said my name, like it was something precious on his tongue. I would remember all of it.

Me, too, Andrew. Me too.

CHAPTER 6

GOLIATH'S CROW pulled me from the first peaceful sleep I had enjoyed in days. Sunlight streamed through my chamber window, laying golden rectangles across the stone floor. I stretched carefully, felt the familiar pull in my hip, then sat up.

Andrew was alive. I said it to myself like a prayer answered. The fever that had threatened him since his arrival had broken completely the night before. In the days in between, life had narrowed to small mercies and steady watches: cool cloths at the brow, clean linen at dawn and dusk, sips of watered wine, a few spoonfuls of barley pottage sweetened with honey when he could take it. He slept more than he spoke, and when he woke, he listened to Deborah's playful scolding or asked the names of my herbs. Ezra shaved a branch smooth to make a staff in case of need. Each morning, more color returned to Andrew's face, and each evening, I left his chamber humming, catching myself halfway down the corridor and not caring who heard.

I dressed quickly and made my way to the guest chamber where we had moved him after that first terrible night. The scent of fresh bread drifted from the kitchen, and I heard the servants already beginning their day. Everything felt ordinary again, except that there was a man, unrelated to me by blood or marriage, sleeping in one of our guest rooms.

He lay on his side, his injured arm supported by pillows. The swelling in his face had diminished, though purple bruises still shadowed his jaw and temple. His breathing was deep and even. Peaceful.

I kneeled beside the bed to check his bandages, as had become my ritual every morning for the past week. The deepest wound on his ribs showed no sign of infection, the edges pink and clean beneath Deborah's expert stitches. I had never seen the bare chest of a man before, and most certainly not that of a man like Andrew with his broad shoulders and arms corded with muscle from years hauling nets. I tried not to look, tried to keep my attention on the bandages, but my eyes kept straying to the curve of his shoulder, to the line of his collarbone.

"You are staring."

My hand stilled. His good eye was open, watching. He smiled as though he knew a secret he would not tell.

I bent my head, my face hot with embarrassment. "I am checking your wounds."

"If you say so." He shifted carefully, and the movement cost him. "And what is your professional assessment, Physician Anna?"

"Do not call me that." I ducked my head, smiling. "If you must give me a title, try Keeper of Clean Linen. You are healing remarkably well. This should close completely within a few days."

"Thanks to your skilled care." His voice was rough from sleep, deeper than usual. "How long have I been here? I have lost track."

"Eight days."

"Eight days." He closed his eyes with a soft groan. "Jesus will wonder what became of me. My brother is likely tearing through the countryside looking for me."

Each time my thoughts turned to Andrew's complete recovery, dread followed close behind. As soon as he could walk without aid, as soon as his wounds closed and his strength returned, he would leave. The road would call him back to his teacher, to a life that had no place for a healer who could barely walk herself. I pushed the thoughts away, but they crept back every time I looked at him.

I kept my expression calm and dipped my fingers into the jar of healing salve then smoothed it across the bruised skin of his shoulder.

"Where were you to meet him?" I asked, keeping my tone light.

"Capernaum. I left them to bring your father's message, and then I was going to Capernaum to check on my mother. We were to meet up there."

"The three of you? Jesus, you, and your brother?"

"Yes, Simon is with us, and others as well. Twelve of us follow him everywhere he goes, along with many who come and go as they are able. Women, too. We have become a family bound by more than blood." He studied my face as I worked. "Have you ever thought about leaving this place?"

The question startled me. I finished with the salve before I answered. "I cannot leave my father's estate."

"Of course. You have responsibilities here." I helped him sit against the pillows.

"This is my home." The words were true, though the road beyond the gate tugged at me. I gathered my thingsm, not meeting his eyes.

"It is a good home, and good homes are difficult to leave."

There was a gentle softness in his tone. "You sound as though you miss yours."

"I do, sometimes. Bethsaida is not much, just a fishing village on the Sea of Galilee. But my father's boats, the nets, the rhythm of the catch..." He shrugged with his good shoulder. "It was a simple life, and I was content with it."

"But you left it."

"Jesus called me. When someone like that asks you to follow, you do not hesitate." His expression lightened, distant and reverent. "At least, I did not."

"Do you ever regret it?"

"Never," he said without pause. "I am where I am meant to be, especially now."

"Bruised, stitched, and in pain?" I asked, smiling.

"Even so," he answered, as I drew a stool beside his bed and sat. "At least I am in Arimathea."

"What is your teacher like?"

Andrew's face lit despite the bruises. "Unlike any other. When he speaks, you feel he is addressing your very soul. There is something about his eyes. When he looks at you, you feel truly seen for the first time in your life."

"That is how you make me feel."

The words escaped before I could catch them. Andrew went still.

"Anna ..."

"I am sorry. I should not have said that." I started to rise, flustered, but his good hand caught my wrist.

"Do not apologize for speaking truth." Dimples softened his cheeks. "I feel the same about you."

We stayed that way, his fingers circling my wrist where my pulse beat wild and obvious. He had to feel it. His eyes darkened and held mine. Something had been planted between us, small but alive, already taking root.

A voice from the courtyard broke the spell. "Anna?" Deborah called. "Where are you, child?"

I slipped free. "I am coming!" I called, avoiding Andrew's eyes. "Rest now. I will check on you later."

At the threshold, his words stopped me. "Anna, we are not finished with this conversation. Come back when you can."

I nodded and eased the door closed, then leaned against the wood. My wrist still felt warm where his fingers had been. I touched the spot gently as if I could keep the feeling there.

I found Deborah grinding herbs in the kitchen. She looked up, and her eyes narrowed. "Has something happened?"

"Of course not. I was checking on my patient. Did you need me?"

She studied my face. "You look different."

"I do not know what you mean." But I did know what she meant. I could not stop smiling.

"Mm." She returned to her work, but her mouth curved. "He is growing stronger."

The smile faded. He was growing stronger. Each day brought more color to his face, more strength to his body. Each day brought him closer to leaving.

"Yes."

"And he will leave soon."

I took a handful of dried mint and crushed the brittle leaves. The sharp scent rose bright and clean. "Yes."

"That will be difficult for you."

It certainly would be now. I watched the mint crumble to dust in my palm. "I suppose it will."

"Of course it will." Deborah set down the pestle and fixed me with her steady gaze. "You care for him. I see it."

"I care for all my patients."

"Anna."

I looked away. "He has a calling. He follows Jesus of Nazareth. He gave up everything to do so."

"And that troubles you?"

"It means he will leave. And I ..." I could not speak the rest.

The lines around her eyes softened, and she looked at me the way she had when I was small and needed comfort. "Child, when did you stop believing you deserved happiness? This does not have to be all you ever know." I went to her and laid my head on her shoulder, breathing in the familiar scents of flour, thyme, and clean wool. Her presence steadied me. "Oh, Anna," she whispered, her arm tightening around me.

"He asked if I had ever thought about leaving this place," I whispered.

"And what did you tell him?"

"I said this is my home."

"And it is your home, but must it be your only home?" Deborah pulled away so she could see my face. "I cannot even bear the thought of you not being here every day, but Anna, if love calls, you must answer."

"Love?" I shook my head, afraid to let my mind wander in that direction. "It is impossible. For many reasons."

Deborah's mouth tilted in that mysterious way she had when a hard-won lesson was coming. "When it is the Father's plan, everything is possible. Keep your heart open to His whisperings and do not let worry be your guide. Fear builds the walls that love breaks through, and break through it will." With that, she went back to her herbs, and I headed to the olive grove to walk among the trees that knew nothing of love or plans or walls.

A few days later found me in my garden, trying to lose myself in familiar tasks. The late spring air was sweet with lavender and early roses. Bees droned among the blossoms, heavy with nectar and sunlight. Everything was green and rising. I finally lowered myself onto my stone bench, closed my eyes, and sought to quiet my heart.

"You missed the midday meal."

I started and opened my eyes. Andrew stood at the garden gate, leaning on the staff Ezra had given him. He had managed a clean tunic, his damp hair brushed back from his face.

"What are you doing up? You should not be walking. Your fever has barely broken."

"I am weary of lying abed." He made his careful way toward me, favoring his injured side. "May I join you?"

I nodded and shifted to make room. He lowered himself with a soft groan, his shoulder coming to rest against mine on the sun-warmed stone. I did not move away. Neither did he.

"Stubborn," I murmured, smiling. I could feel the muscle

of his shoulder against mine and found I could not think of much else.

"So I have been told, mostly by my brother. And maybe my mother." He chuckled, his gaze looking over the curved paths, the neat rows of herbs, and the flowers just reaching glory. "This is beautiful. Is it your work?"

"Most," I said. "My mother began it, but..." I brushed a leaf with my fingertips. "It is mine now."

He was quiet, then turned to study my face. "Tell me about her."

The question took me off guard. "What would you like to know?"

"Whatever you will share," he said. "Mostly, I would like to know the woman who gave the world such a daughter."

I bent my head to hide my smile and pulled a sprig of rosemary from a nearby bush to steady my hands. "She was a healer, like Deborah. But Deborah says she had a gift. She could look at someone and understand at once what was wrong, what they needed." The herb's peppery scent rose between us. "I remember her hands most. Gentle hands. She always smelled of growing things. She sang while she worked." I swallowed. "I wish she could have taught me everything. I was far too young when she died. Much of what I know is from Deborah's memory of her methods. And I have my mother's journal where she wrote of her treatments."

"Your mother kept a journal?" He shifted, searching for a comfortable position, and drew a sharp breath.

"Careful." I steadied him with a hand on his arm. "You are aggravating your injuries."

His jaw tensed. "I am fine."

"Here." I adjusted his position just enough to ease the

pull on his side. He let me guide him back against the warm stone.

"Better. You have gentle hands, like your mother."

"Thank you," I murmured. I tucked his words away, a gift I would turn over later in the quiet of my chamber. "Yes, she kept one. I found it years ago, and I treasure it above all things."

"A journal written by her own hand? And you can read it?" Andrew's voice softened. "In Bethsaida, even many men do not keep the letters. Who taught you?"

"Abba sent for a scribe from Jerusalem," I said. "He placed the reed pen in my hand and kept me to my lessons, though some called it foolishness. My mother learned the same way and used it to bind knowledge with ink."

"You are more remarkable than I even realized."

Silence settled between us. I worried the rosemary down to a bare stem, caught between excitement and nervousness. Andrew thought I was remarkable.

"I like Deborah," he said at last. "She makes me laugh, and it is plain how much she loves you."

"I love her too." I smiled, surprised they had spent much time together. "She raised me. I do not know what I would have done without her."

He shifted, his attention fully on me now. "Will you tell me what happened? The accident that marked you?"

Rarely did anyone ask me so directly. I paused without answering, debating whether to crack open that door and let him in. I did.

"It was in Jerusalem's marketplace. We were there while my father attended a council meeting. A dispute broke out between the merchants and Roman soldiers." I nodded toward my scarred hands and my damaged leg. "I was five. I do not remember many details."

"You were with your mother?"

"Yes, and friends of the family. I heard a lamb crying and wandered over to help it. She is still here somewhere. Her name is Bubbeleh. You will meet her. I have kept her all these years."

My hands found each other in my lap. These were difficult memories. "Fighting started. People ran in every direction. I had climbed into the animal pen to help the lamb, and Ima came to pull me out. That is when it happened."

I flung the rosemary stem onto the path. It bounced once, then settled in the dirt. "A centurion's whip struck us, hitting her first and then my face and hands. The metal studs tore my skin..."

"The Romans whipped you?" Andrew stiffened.

"Yes, though perhaps not intentionally. We were caught in the middle of it." I closed my eyes, remembering the sounds and smells of that day. "Then the horses came. Ima threw herself over me and shielded me with her body. She took the worst of it. The hooves shattered my hip. That is why I walk as I do."

He was silent for a long moment. "She died protecting you."

"Yes," I said, opening my eyes to the sky, though it was not the clouds over Arimathea I saw. It was my mother lying next to me, a pool of blood around her head. "If I had stayed beside her, as she asked... She need not have died. It is my fault."

"Anna," he said. "Look at me."

I turned my face to his.

"Your mother saved your life. That is not your fault. That is love in its purest form."

My vision blurred. I blinked hard, but the tears fell anyway. "But if I had not wandered—"

"You were a small child filled with compassion, and you tried to ease suffering. Even then, you had a healer's heart. You still do."

A tear escaped and then another. He reached over and laid his hand on top of mine. "Parents do not blame us for the mistakes of our childhood," he said. "I should know. I made many. What happened was not of your doing, and the same might have happened had you been at her side."

"I do not believe that, but..." I whispered. "I still dream of it—the shouting, the people, the horses. I wake gasping."

"I imagine you do, and I am sorry for it." He squeezed my hand. "I dream about my father."

"The fisherman who loved the sea?"

"The same. He died three years ago. Simon and I were away on a days-long trip, trying to bring in a large catch before storm season. When we returned, we found him collapsed in the house. He had been ill for days but was too proud to send word. Our mother was visiting family, so he faced it alone."

"Oh, Andrew." I turned my hand to lace my fingers with his.

"I always wonder if we had returned a day earlier, if we had not been so set on filling the nets..." He stared past the garden. "He always said we must work and provide. But we should have been there. Perhaps we could have saved him."

"Andrew, no." My voice was gentle. "You could not have known. It was not your fault. You did what you believed was best."

He gripped my hand tightly. "So did you."

We let the quiet hold us, our hands intertwined, our griefs side by side. A breeze moved the jasmine, and its sweetness drifted around us like a whispered prayer. In the olives, a dove called to its mate.

"Thank you," I murmured.

"For what?"

"For helping me see my mother's death differently. For not making it mine to carry." I met his gaze. "The way you speak to me, the way you look at me — it is as if you do not see my scars or my limp at all. You simply see me. That has never happened to me before."

"I do see you, Anna. You are so much more than the terrible things that happened to you." He lifted our joined hands and pressed a soft kiss to my knuckles.

"So much more," he said again.

The kiss was brief, barely more than a brush of his lips against my scarred knuckles. No one had ever kissed my scars before. His thumb traced slow circles against my palm. The breeze loosened a strand of my hair and brushed it across my cheek.

"Beautiful," he murmured, catching the strand around his finger, his eyes holding mine. "You are so beautiful."

"How can you think my scars are—"

"Anna!"

I jumped. Deborah stood just inside the gate, arms crossed, her expression carefully unreadable. I drew my hand from Andrew's and shifted down as far as the bench would allow.

"Yes, Deborah? Did you need something?" My voice sounded guilty even to my own ears.

"I came to ask if you would like the evening meal in the

courtyard, since the weather is so fine," she said, her sharp gaze taking in our nearness. "But I see you are quite occupied."

I turned my face away, though my burning cheeks would betray me regardless. Andrew cleared his throat and sat straighter, his expression carefully innocent in a way that fooled no one.

"We were only talking," I said, rising and brushing at my tunic, though there was nothing on it.

Deborah's mouth twitched, but she said only, "Yes, I saw that." She turned toward the house and called over her shoulder, "I will set two places, then, so you may continue your... conversation."

I waited until her steps faded before I dared look at Andrew. He was grinning despite the discomfort.

"Well," he said, eyes bright with mischief, "that was perfectly timed."

"She has an uncanny way of appearing at the worst moments," I muttered, still clutching the edge of my sash. "When I was ten, she found me halfway up the olive tree when I was supposed to be helping Ezra in the garden. When I was twelve, she caught me feeding the chickens a mixture of herbs that I was sure would help them lay better. I could not wait to surprise Deborah with all those eggs. I nearly poisoned them all."

"You nearly poisoned the chickens?" His grin widened.

"I meant to help them. I did not know rue could kill them. I had just gone into the chicken yard to give it to them when Deborah showed up, grabbed it out of my hands, and made such a fuss that the poor hens would not lay for a week for the fright of it all." I shook my head, my smile returning. "How she knew what I was doing is still a mystery to this day and one she will not clear up. Deborah made me scrub every pot in the kitchen and copy proper measurements until my hands cramped. The hens forgave me after a week, but Deborah took longer."

I looked toward the doorway where she had gone, and a sudden truth settled over me: She had mended more than my wounds in this house, and I loved her beyond telling. "She has taken care of me my whole life."

"Then I should thank her," Andrew said.

We looked at one another. Something had changed between us, named or not.

"I should see if anyone needs help," I said. "And you should rest before Deborah decides you are well enough for her to put you to questions."

"Questions?"

"Oh, yes. She will want to know about your family, your trade, whether you honor your father and mother." I paused at the gate. "Fair warning, she is formidable when she is protective."

Andrew laughed, and the sound made my head spin. "I will keep that in mind," he said. "I suspect she already has her opinions."

"She likely does. She sees far too much." I turned toward the house before he could answer. My staff struck the stones with a lighter rhythm than usual, happiness spilling through me with each step.

CHAPTER 7

Days slid one into the next. Andrew mended by small degrees, and I fell deeper by the day, though I would not name it even in the silence of my chamber. I tried not to think about the day he would leave Arimathea. The knowing pressed against my ribs, cold and constant. For now, I gathered each glance and word, stored them away against the famine I knew was coming.

Evening drew a soft blanket over the courtyard. Jasmine breathed its sweetness into the air as we sat at the stone table where Abba and I had shared our last meal, though that felt like another life, another Anna who had not yet tasted the joy of a fisherman's smile. The slab held the day's warmth beneath my palms, and my fingers found the places countless meals had worn smooth, each hollow carried a small history.

Deborah had set out bread whose crust murmured as it cooled. Roasted lamb gleamed with rosemary from my garden, and when Andrew's knife pressed through it, the herb released its pine-sharp breath. Olives shone in their dish, and figs gave way with the lightest touch, their flesh the color of garnets. Taking in the bounty spread before us, I caught myself grinning. The common things had turned uncommon, and the cause of that transformation sat close enough that I could see the lamplight dance in his curls.

He reached for bread, and I followed his hands, net-scarred, rope-wise, yet tender when they moved among my herbs or scratched behind Bubbeleh's ears. The hair on his forearm caught the glow with every motion, and awareness stirred low in me, unfamiliar and unsettling.

"I do not think I have eaten so well since Bethsaida," he said, tearing the loaf. "My mother cooks with a generous hand."

I heard the note that came when he spoke of home, a softness at the edges like a song's last chord. "Deborah loves by feeding," I said. My thoughts traveled to Bethsaida, to his mother's table, and I wondered what she was like. "She is forever placing one more slice on my plate."

His slow smile gathered at the corners of his eyes and carved that small hollow in his cheek. "Then she must love me greatly. I may never find the will to leave."

He spoke lightly, but the words rang true. My stomach flipped. I looked down into my cup before my face could tell him more than I intended. *Please do not leave.*

Our days had fallen into their own rhythm. Mornings, we spent in the garden where Andrew, who had once claimed to dislike chickens, now greeted them by name and argued softly with Delilah about her brooding moods. He knew mint from thyme at a glance, and could now tell by thumb and forefinger if the rosemary thirsted. The way he moved among my plants, careful not to bruise leaves, respectful of roots, told me things about his character that words might have hidden.

We kept to what was proper. Deborah shaped our days so that eyes were always upon us. When we walked, either Ezra or one of the boys from the press was nearby with a basket or task. Within the walls, doors stood open, and the household moved in and out like a gentle tide. If a stranger called, Deborah would set my head covering within reach, and Andrew would step back, an invisible boundary suddenly present. Abba would have required no less, though the physical distance sometimes made my heart ache with longing.

Afternoons, we explored the estate. My staff beat its small measure on the hard earth, and the branch Ezra had smoothed for Andrew answered it. Neither of us walked quickly. His side still pulled if he lengthened his stride, and I moved carefully as always. He never urged me on or showed impatience with my pace. We threaded between olives and vines, pausing over a promising cluster or simply to watch the way light moved through leaves. Words came, then easy quiet. In time, our steps learned one another.

But the evenings were gold. Lamps drew a small world around us, and the day's heat gentled until it felt sacred. We kept within Deborah's sight. She would sit in the doorway with her sewing or talking with Ezra, always keeping a watchful eye. Neither Andrew nor I wished to break the quiet hedge she wove about my honor, nor did we wish to spend time apart. The meals wandered long, and I prayed Abba would understand when he returned.

I lived for Andrew's accounts of the road with his rabbi, tales that painted pictures so vivid I could almost see them — the crowds hungry for hope, teachings that turned the inside of a heart outward, men who left boats and tables because something truer had taken hold of them. And the healings. I asked after them as a thirsty woman asked after a spring, needing to believe they were real, that such restoration was possible in a world that seemed so often bent on breaking what it touched.

The household had noticed, of course. Deborah's eyes grew kind when they lingered on us. The servants' talk folded closed when I entered, but not unkindly, more like women guarding a secret they hoped would bloom. Even Bubbeleh had attached herself to Andrew and trailed him like a devoted child, her ancient eyes bright with something that might have been matchmaking.

Only one shadow threatened my contentment: Deborah herself. In the doorway, I caught the small gasp that escaped her, and I watched her needle falter as she pressed a hand to her side before rubbing the cloth as if nothing had happened. I had been so wrapped up in Andrew that I had set my concerns aside. It felt like a burden too heavy to carry while my heart danced through happy days. Shame heated my cheeks. Deborah deserved my full attention. In the morning, I would ask, and her deflections would not put me off.

Andrew dipped bread into oil, chewed, then let his gaze drift past my shoulder toward the fig tree. Something in his face went far away, the leaves holding memories of another shore.

"What is it?" I asked, chin propped in my palm, ready to follow him wherever his thoughts had wandered.

He tilted his head toward me, that dimple flashing and vanishing like a secret shared. "The catch," he said. "I was thinking of the catch that almost sank the boats."

"Tell me everything." I sat back, eager to listen. I loved being present while he stood inside his memories.

"It happened on a night very much like this one." He set the bread down and shifted toward me. When he spoke of Jesus, his voice changed. Awe lived there and a reverence that made me sit straighter without meaning to.

"We had been out all night," he said, eyes gone distant with remembering. "Cold hands, sore backs, with nothing to show for it. Not a single fish. We were washing our nets when Jesus came to the shore, and the people followed as they always did. He stepped into our boat as though he had fished with us his whole life. He sat and taught from the water for a while."

"You must have been astonished." I set his cup nearer his hand. He did not notice.

"More than astonished. Breathless." He shook his head once, a small, helpless motion that spoke of wonder too large for words. "The Messiah seated in our poor craft. Holiness sitting where fish scales clung to old wood."

He drew a long breath. "The people listened from the shore, and I could not take my eyes off him. When he finished, he told Simon, 'Put out into the deep and let down the nets.' We had worked all night. We had taken nothing. Simon said as much, respectful but honest. Then suddenly, he looked at Jesus and said, 'At your word, I will let them down.' So we went further out and put them down."

The courtyard seemed to listen with me. Even the crickets held their chorus.

"Anna," he said, shaking his head in amazement, "the nets filled so fast I thought the lines would snap. Fish leaped at his command, and silver bodies filled the boat's bottom, packed so tight we could barely move. We hauled and shouted and Jesus laughed with us, throwing fish with both hands, joy written across his face like a child's delight."

I could picture the chaos and the wonder, the heavy slap of silver bodies on wet planks, the sweet ache of disbelief made real.

"Simon cried for James and John to bring their boat alongside. When they drew near, we filled both boats until they rode low in the water. The wood groaned, but we did not sink." His mouth eased at the memory, then sobered. "Simon dropped to his knees amid all those fish. 'Leave me, Lord,' he said. 'I am a sinful man.' I felt the same, small and unworthy before such power."

"What did Jesus answer?" My voice barely cleared my throat.

"He said, 'Do not fear. From now on, you will catch men.'"

The words rested between us like a blessing, heavy with promise. The lamp's flame bent and straightened in the evening breeze.

"You left everything after that," I said.

He nodded, with a single sure dip of his head. "Boats, nets, the richest haul of my life. None of it mattered after that. We pulled the boats to shore and walked away from everything we had ever known."

I traced the rim of my cup with one finger, feeling the smoothness the potter's wheel had left there. "I think I would have followed as well."

Andrew watched me for a long moment before speaking, his eyes searching my face as if looking for something precious he feared he might not find. "You still can."

I looked at my hands, scarred but faithful, these tools that had mixed poultices and laid cool cloths on weary brows. What could such marked things offer to a man who called fish from emptiness?

"Anna," he said, and the gentleness in how he spoke my name sent a thrill through me. "What if I told you he could heal you?"

The entire world narrowed to those few words. For a moment, the world spun, leaving me dizzy and breathless. "What do you mean?"

"I have seen it." He leaned forward, forearms on the table, the quiet fire in him drawing me closer. "A leper came pleading, and Jesus touched him, and the skin was made clean. In the synagogue at Capernaum, he rebuked an unclean spirit, and the man sat in his right mind. Simon's wife's mother burned with fever. At his word, she stood to serve us. They lowered a paralytic through the roof, and Jesus said to him, 'Rise, take your mat, and walk,' and he did. On the Sabbath, he told a man, 'Stretch out your hand,' and it opened whole. A centurion's servant was made well from a distance because his master's faith was strong. And more. So much more."

"It cannot be," I whispered, my voice breaking around the edges of hope I had never dared to hold. "How does any man say, 'Rise,' and the lame walk? How does flesh obey a word?"

"He is the Messiah," Andrew said as if that explained everything, and perhaps it did. "If he can open blind eyes and make the dead rise, would a damaged hip stand against him?"

He reached across the table and took my hand, his thumb tracing the old marks the whip had left. He lifted my fingers and kissed them tenderly. "And as for these," he murmured, "I have grown fond of them. They tell the truth of you."

A stool scraped in the doorway, and Deborah shifted. Andrew dropped my hand abruptly.

"You are kind," I said, though thoughts of being made whole rose and scattered, too fragile to hold steady. If all he said was true, and I believed him, then healing was not beyond reach. Whether it would be given to me was another question entirely.

"You know who he is. You said you would follow."

"That is not the same."

"Is it not?" His eyes searched mine, and I saw in them a reflection of my longing.

The thought shone before me, fierce and brilliant.

"Let me take you to him," he said, the words soft and full of promise.

I shook my head, not in refusal but in fear. "What if he does not?"

"Heal you?" Andrew held my gaze steadily. "What if he does? And if he does not, nothing changes that matters. You are still you, extraordinary in every way that counts."

"Andrew," I whispered, tears gathering and clinging to my lashes. "I could not bear it if he refused me. I would rather limp all my days than be measured and found unworthy."

He rose and drew me up with him, his hands gently framing my face. His thumbs chased tears I had not known were falling. "Anna of Arimathea, you will not be found unworthy, not by the Master and not by me. You have captured me, scars and staff and all. None of that changes who you are." He rested his fingers lightly over my heart. "He taught us to look within a person. What I see there is good and true. And mine."

I let his words flow through me, filling the cracks loneliness had carved. I leaned into his touch and allowed desire to stand for a moment.

"What do you say, Anna of Arimathea?" he whispered,

his palm gentle over the old wound on my cheek. "Will you seek healing? Will you come with me?"

A voice came from behind me before I could draw breath to answer.

"If the Master is truly healing," Deborah said, one hand set to the stone for balance, her voice carrying a tremor I had not heard before, "perhaps there is healing for an old woman as well."

We turned together. Light from the house framed her slight figure. Her eyes moved from Andrew's hands to my face, and there was no censure there, only a quiet understanding that said she had seen more than I had guessed and loved me still.

"I did not mean to intrude," she said, though her tone suggested she was not entirely sorry for it. "Night carries words farther than we intend."

"You are never intruding," Andrew said. I felt the way he shifted slightly away, his hand falling from me with obvious reluctance.

Deborah kept her gaze on me, and in her eyes, I saw years of watching my pain, of offering comfort when the ache grew too much to bear alone. "Anna, I know you suffer even when you try to hide it from me. I have asked the Holy One for your healing until the prayers wore grooves in my heart." She laid a hand on her side without thinking then steadied it against her robe. "But I also have pain, more with each dawn. I would not burden you with it, yet if God, blessed be His name, has sent this Jesus, and if healing walks with him, then perhaps even a woman with silver in her hair might be made well."

Guilt lanced sharply through me. "Deborah! Why did

you not tell me? I knew something was wrong. I should have made you —"

"If you go to him," she said, not letting me finish my self-recrimination, "take me with you, if you will." Tears brightened her eyes, catching the lamplight. "If there is a door to be opened, I will not remain on the threshold."

She turned and made her careful way toward the house, each step deliberate, leaving us with her words. I moved to follow.

"She has spoken her heart," Andrew said, his hand touching my sleeve. "Let her rest with it until morning."

I stared at the empty doorway, my throat tight with unshed tears. "I told Abba I feared she was unwell. Then I let myself be distracted by ... " I gestured helplessly between us. "If he is who you say he is — "

"He is."

"Then I want her healed," I said. "More than I want it for myself."

His face softened, and he smiled as if I had just proven something he had hoped was true. "There," he said quietly. "Do you see? Extraordinary."

"I thought I was remarkable." I dashed the tears from my eyes.

"You are. Both remarkable and extraordinary and every other wonderful quality a woman can have."

A shaky laugh slipped out, half-sob, half-delight. "You know that is not true."

"I know what I know. Come."

He took my hand and led me to the bench beneath the fig tree. We sat quietly, hand in hand, the warmth from his shoulder traveled across the small distance between us whenever the breeze lifted. Night folded close around us, making me feel as if anything and everything were possible.

CHAPTER 8

I SAW THE DUST FIRST, a golden plume beyond the olive groves rising into the afternoon sky. The sight pulled me to the terrace, where I raised a hand against the sun and counted the figures stepping out of the shimmer. Seven. Eight. More still coming over the road.

"A messenger?" Deborah's voice came from behind, and I felt her arrive at my side, her presence steadying me as it always did. The scent of herbs still clung to her from the morning's work, rosemary and mint threading through the warmer smell of bread from her ovens.

"I do not believe so." I watched their pace, the swing of arms, and the set of shoulders that spoke of men with purpose rather than urgency. "Far too many for that."

Travelers, I thought, yet I heard no bray of donkeys, no jingle of harness, and saw how they held together like a flock drawn to their shepherd. Understanding took root in my stomach, spreading cold tendrils through my chest. "It is the Rabbi," I breathed.

Andrew's halting footsteps announced him before his words. He moved with more urgency than I had seen since his arrival, as if something in the approaching dust had set his blood afire. When I looked at him, his face seemed lit from within, relief so fierce I could barely name it joy or grief.

"He is here," he said. "I should have sent word. He does not even know I am alive."

His eyes watched the road, then turned to the house behind me, then to the olive trees where we had learned one another's steps in these gentle days. I saw the knowledge strike him. Arrival meant leaving. I watched his hand tighten on the staff.

"When he goes on..." he began, and the word caught in his throat. "I must go with him." He stopped and looked at me, and in that look I felt the pull that took him in two directions at once, the terrible weight of choosing between love and calling.

"Then we shall make today long," I said, though my heart stumbled and nearly stopped. The words tasted brave on my tongue and were not. They were the bitter medicine of acceptance, swallowed because there was no choice. "He will be glad to see you healing."

"Anna." Andrew turned, and the earnestness in his eyes made me look away. "This is your chance. To meet him, to see what I have tried to tell you." I had just forced myself to accept his leaving, and now he wanted me to rejoice in the reason for it. I could not do both at the same time.

"And Simon is with them, my brother." His mouth tugged toward a smile, though worry shadowed it. "Try not to like him better than me."

The jest was so nakedly vulnerable that something in me twisted painfully. "That seems very unlikely."

We made our way down from the terrace together, my staff tapping against the stone steps as we descended to meet them. The courtyard filled with dust and voices as they passed through the gate, weariness lifting from their shoulders at the promise of rest.

"Andrew!"

Simon. The voice that rolled across the courtyard could belong to no other. It carried the born command of wind over water, the sound of a man used to being heard above storm and wave, and it came from one so like Andrew I blinked in the bright light. Same strong build, same dark hair catching the sun, yet larger somehow. Behind him came the others, mostly men with a few women among them, all wearing a coat of dust and a look of expectation.

And in their midst, walking as naturally as breathing, was the man who must be Jesus.

He was ordinary. That was my first thought. Plain linen, the road's grit upon him, a height unremarkable, brown hair falling to his shoulders, nothing to mark him from any companion who might share his path. Yet the way he moved held a quiet rightness, and the circle seemed to turn of itself around him. Heaven had chosen flesh and footsteps, and my soul bowed in recognition.

Andrew had already crossed half the courtyard, though slowly, his healing wounds setting the pace. Jesus's face lit up when he saw him. They met and clasped shoulders, voices low, fragments reaching me across the heated air — injury, healing, sleepless worry, unknown whereabouts.

Then Jesus lifted his gaze and found mine across the sun-white space, and everything between us seemed to hush. His presence filled the space. I found it hard to breathe, as if the very air had thickened around me.

"Shalom, Anna. Peace to you," he said, his greeting carried on the afternoon breeze.

His voice had a depth that hummed in my bones. I knew that voice. *I see you, Anna.* My hands shook, so I laced my fingers and hid them within my robe. "Shalom. Welcome."

Simon reached Andrew and caught him in an embrace that made him gasp, whether from pain or joy, I could not tell. The sound carried across the stones. "Fool! We thought bandits had done for you. James wanted to search every road between here and Bethel."

"I am well, Simon. A little battered but healing." Andrew's words muffled against his brother's broad shoulder, yet I heard the smile weaving through them.

"A little?" Simon held him away, his hands steady on Andrew's shoulders as he took stock of the fading bruises, the guarded way Andrew favored his left side. "You look as if you wrestled beasts and barely won."

"Close enough." Andrew's eyes found mine over Simon's shoulder. The ease between us was still there, but now it shared space with his other world, the one that had first claim on him. "Simon, meet Anna. She saved me."

Simon turned with a sunrise of a smile.

This family smiles easily, I thought and felt my mouth return his smile despite my nervousness.

"I am Simon, Andrew's elder. We owe you much."

Andrew raised his voice to the company, pride threading through his words. "I would not be standing but for Anna. She is a skilled healer."

Suddenly, every eye was on me. I felt the wood of my staff against my palm, the roughness of my scarred hands, my uncovered face with its old marks laid bare beneath the beating sun, the way I leaned for balance. My face grew hot. I looked to Jesus, and there was mercy in his eyes. I did not feel examined. I felt received. And now I understood: To be seen by Jesus is a holy homecoming.

"Anna of Arimathea," Jesus said, stepping forward, and the very simplicity of his movement drew every eye. His feet were dusty in worn sandals, his hem travel-stained, yet authority moved with him. "Your father is Joseph of the Council."

"You know my father?" Surprise loosened my courtesy.

"Yes. I know Joseph well. I have known him since boyhood." His expression grew thoughtful. "I have spent happy days at this estate."

I blinked. When? How often? Abba had never spoken of knowing Jesus, only of the trouble the Teacher caused in Jerusalem. How well did they know each other? And why did Abba not tell me, even when I asked him directly? I set my shoulders, tamping down the rising questions that threatened to spill from my lips. "He is away on Temple matters."

"Yes. He often is." Jesus studied my face as if reading words written in a language only he could understand. "May we rest here? It has been a long road."

I burned with embarrassment. I should have offered before he asked. "Of course. Forgive my poor manners. You are all welcome." I gestured to Deborah, who had arrived with her usual perfect timing as if summoned by need itself. "This is Deborah. She will see to all you require. Come, rest and have refreshment."

"Actually," Jesus said, stopping me with a single word, "I hoped we might speak privately, you and I."

Silence fell over the courtyard. Simon stilled. Andrew's expression turned cautious, and the muscle in his jaw jumped.

"I do not think that would be proper," I said, though my entire self leaned toward him, a flower tipping toward light after long darkness.

"Please." Only that.

The word broke through the last of my caution. Hope rose so sharply it ached. *He may heal me.* "Yes, of course." I left the gate wide and kept to the outer path where the courtyard voices could reach us like distant music. "This way."

He matched his pace to mine without comment, without the careful attention that made me feel fragile. I heard some followers go with Deborah into the house for water and bread, their voices bright with travel's end, while Simon and a few others settled on the benches. Their voices blurred and fell away as we stepped into my garden. My staff kept its small rhythm over stone, and leaves whispered their afternoon prayers in the breeze.

"Your mother planted this," he said, stating a truth as naturally as naming the color of the sky.

I stopped, my staff striking stone with a sharp sound. "How could you know that?"

"The order of it speaks her name, the herbs threaded among flowers, usefulness married to beauty." He touched a rose cane with gentle fingers, and I saw the work in his hands, calloused and nicked by honest labor. "Sarah had a gift for coaxing life from poor places, for seeing what could bloom where others saw only barren ground. The garden did not look this way the last time I was here."

"You knew her?" My voice barely rose above the dove-soft cooing in the branches overhead.

"Yes. And I grieved her passing. A great loss for you and for Joseph. She was a light in a dark place." He paused by the trellis and ran his thumb over the mortise and its peg, as if greeting the work of old friends. "Our families were close when I was young. Once, I cut my arm on a broken shard, and your mother tended it. She sang to steady me while her needle worked. It was just before you came into the world." His voice thickened with memory. "I remember the song."

"I cannot remember her songs anymore. They slip away like smoke, no matter how I try to hold them."

"They are not lost, only sleeping." He smiled at me. "The songs are tucked away in your soul for safekeeping, waiting for the moment when you need them most." Then he started to hum, low and gentle. The melody was unfamiliar at first, then something deep in me woke to it. My mother's face close to mine, her hand smoothing my hair as she tucked the blanket around me.

"She sang this to steady you," he said quietly.

I pressed my hand to my mouth and nodded, unable to speak.

"You remember her, and you honor her, Anna. That is what matters."

"Look." He opened a hand toward the beds where my life's work spread in careful rows. Water murmured through the little channels, and a lizard skimmed the warm stones. "This place blooms under your care. Andrew lives by your skill. You have your mother's hands and her heart." He glanced at me, eyes kind. "Your father speaks of you often. I am sorry we meet only now."

"Abba speaks of me to you?" *How is that possible?*

"Joseph and I have spoken many times. He loves you deeply." Jesus sat on the stone bench and patted the place beside him. "Come. Sit."

I sank gratefully onto the smooth seat, bark pressing my shoulder where the fig's low limb leaned over us. I shifted to ease my hip, and the familiar ache sang its small song of limitation. His eyes noted the motion and said nothing. I felt no judgment in his silence, only the patience of one who understands that bodies carry their own burdens.

Andrew's teacher knew my father. He knew my mother. He had been in this very garden. The words circled in my head, refusing to be still. Abba had never mentioned him. Not once. He had even lied to me when I asked him directly. Why would he hide this?

"Do you believe the Father has more for your life, Anna?"

The question startled me, and I hesitated to answer. Had I wondered? The question had lived in me for as long as I could remember, whispered in the dark, unspoken during the day. A light wind lifted pieces of my hair, fallen loose from their braid. "I ... I do not know."

"But you have wondered."

How could he know the night-whispered questions, the prayers pushed into darkness? How could he see the ache for something beyond these walls, more than the small circle of my garden and my healing work?

"Sometimes," I admitted.

"Tell me about Andrew." The sudden change of subject surprised me.

Courtyard voices drifted to us, warm with laughter that spoke of reunion and relief. "What of him?"

"He is different. More at peace than since his father died." A small smile traced his mouth, and the lines around his eyes told me he smiled often and well. "You have a hand in that."

"I did only what anyone would do."

"Yes, that and more." His gaze held mine until I blushed, heat spreading across my cheeks. "His peace told me before his mouth did, and the pride in his voice when he said your name spoke louder than any proclamation. That is more than common care, more than duty grudgingly given. You bring the barren to life and the living to health."

I looked at the worn grooves on my staff, feeling the smoothness years of use had worn into the wood. *Do I do that?* It sounded larger than poultices and herbs, grander than the small kindnesses I offered to those who came seeking help.

"It is a gift," he said, as if reading the doubt written across my face.

"You speak as if you know me," I murmured.

"I do."

I looked toward the gate where I had stood that morning, when the colors had blazed impossibly bright and the wind had wrapped around me carrying that strange fragrance. Could I ask him? Did I dare?

His hand gestured to the garden. "Something happened here."

"Yes," I whispered. "I heard a voice. It called me by name."

He was silent for a moment. "You were seen," he said at last. "The voice was real."

The garden around me seemed to sharpen the way it had that morning. I could hear the words again as if they were being spoken fresh: *I see you, Anna.*

Another thought rose. "Then why have we never met? If you and my father are close, why has your name not been spoken in our house?"

"Sometimes love demands difficult choices. Your father has needed to be careful, more careful than you know."

"Careful? What do you mean?"

The garden gate creaked as the wood welcomed the sun. "Andrew carried a message for your father. You should know it." He leaned toward me, voice dropping low. "Men on the Sanhedrin suspect Joseph's sympathies toward me. They watch him, how he speaks, how he votes, whom he receives in his house. The message was a warning. Some have questioned his loyalty, and that could be very difficult for your father. Even more so in the days to come."

Fear pricked at my skin. "You mean he is in danger?"

"He could be. He must walk wisely, each step measured against the consequences. If they learn the depth of his belief, or our kinship..." He let the words hang between us like a blade suspended by a thread.

"Kinship?" My mouth went dry. "What kinship?"

He only smiled, the kind filled with secrets. "When Joseph returns, tell him what I have said. He must be more cautious than he has been, must consider each word before it leaves his tongue. And Anna, do not speak of this visit beyond these walls."

Questions rose, scattered, too many to voice, but laughter burst from the courtyard, calling my attention there.

"It sounds as though my friends are content with your bread." He offered his hand to help me rise to my feet. "Shall we see how Andrew fares?"

I placed my hand in his, and a rush of sensation flooded my hip. I stood straighter, then shifted my weight fully onto my damaged leg, the one that had made me careful for so long. The ground held me steady without spike or punishment.

I took a step without thinking, without bracing, without the tiny calculation I made a thousand times a day. I walked in a small circle, my staff hanging forgotten in my other hand. I could run if I wanted to. I could dance. I could kneel in the garden beds without struggling to stand again.

A sound broke from my throat, half-laugh, half-sob. I looked at Jesus through tears. "Is this you?"

"Sometimes the Father gives small tastes of what is possible," he said, his voice gentle as a mother's lullaby. "Come. We will join the others."

I followed, walking freely for the first time in years, each step a small miracle. *Thank you, Father.*

We returned to a courtyard that had become a feast of fellowship, overflowing with bread and cheese and dried figs, benches full to bursting, disciples cross-legged on stone like children gathered for stories. Andrew sat at the center, telling the bandit story with a storyteller's cadence that painted pictures in the air.

"And then the largest came at me with a club the size of a tamarisk, so I threw myself to the ground."

"You tripped over your own feet," Simon said, grinning.

"I repositioned myself with some wisdom," Andrew corrected, wounded dignity in every syllable, and laughter rang through the air.

"He stumbled, he means," said a woman with kind eyes and silver threading her hair, raising a brow.

"Joanna, I am attempting to preserve what little dignity remains to me," Andrew protested, though he smiled despite himself.

A younger woman laughed, bright and musical. "Oh, Andrew, you look so serious, like a commander recounting a brilliant victory rather than falling face-first into the dust." Her dark hair was braided, her features lovely, and she had warm brown eyes that lingered on Andrew's face. The way she leaned toward him as she spoke started my scars to prickle, sharp as nettle stings. I smoothed my tunic to steady my hands and tried to smile. I liked her at once and not at all, and both truths hurt.

"Invaluable commentary, Tirzah," Andrew said. Did he not see how she bent closer when he spoke, how her smile softened when she looked at him, how her eyes held his a heartbeat longer than conversation required?

I noticed. I noticed her chosen place near his knee, the quickness of her laugh at his smallest jest, the warmth that colored her voice when she spoke his name. In all our talk of his life on the road, through all the stories he had shared, he had not once spoken the name Tirzah.

Someone had set out a stool, and I took it quietly to avoid disrupting the circle's easy flow. Jesus sat where he could see all, content to listen, to add a word or quiet correction without claiming the center for himself. The peace that surrounded him seemed to settle over the entire gathering like a blessing spoken in silence. I longed to leave the stool and go sit at his feet.

"So what truly happened?" Simon asked, his tone gentling beneath the thunder of his voice. "We were sick with worry when you were not there in Capernaum to meet us. We were delayed by some days getting there and then discovered you had never arrived."

Andrew's expression grew more serious, laughter fading from his eyes. "Just outside Bethel," he said, "I came upon a small family on the road, a man, a woman, and a child leading their little donkey. Three men had cornered them near the ditch, hands on the halter, voices raised in threats."

"Were they armed?" asked a younger man from the edge of the circle.

"Yes, they had clubs, and one had a knife." Andrew's hand drifted unconsciously to his side. "I told the father to take the child and go toward the town, to run and not look back." His voice dropped. "Then I stepped between."

Tirzah's fingers twitched as if to reach for him, comfort offered before thought could stop it. I glared at her.

"Did they follow the family?" Simon asked.

"No, they lost interest in pursuit once they had me to occupy them," Andrew said. "They took what they wanted from my pack and left. After that, memory becomes fog. I remember the taste of dust and the road's heat against my face. God gave me enough strength to reach Anna's gate — I mean, the estate's gate — though I have no clear recollection of the journey."

"You risked yourself for strangers?" the younger man asked.

Andrew's mouth tugged into a small, tired smile. "For a father, a mother, and a child. What else was there to do?"

"And then Anna found you," Simon said, turning to me with a smile. "He has spoken of your skill with much gratitude."

"When did he have time to say that?" I asked, genuinely baffled. "You only just arrived."

Simon laughed, the sound rolling across the courtyard like thunder over summer hills. "He told us the moment he could draw sufficient breath. 'She is the most amazing woman,' he said. 'She saved my life. She is the kindest woman I have ever met, and she --"

"I did not," Andrew began, color rising in his cheeks.

"'She is beautiful, and she makes the most delicious honey cakes,'" Simon finished cheerfully, his eyes dancing with brotherly mischief. "Several times, in considerable detail. Both the beauty and the honey cakes received thorough descriptions."

"Simon," Andrew warned, though his mortification was clear. I saw Tirzah look at me, eyes narrowed.

"Perhaps," I cut in, taking pity on him before Simon could elaborate further, "you would rather hear of the night his fever climbed so high I feared we might lose him." I made my voice light, though the memory still seared through me — his too-hot skin under my palms, my foolish panic, Deborah's calm hands and firm correction. "I thought his fever had spiked again, but it was only the stack of blankets I had piled on him. Sometimes, caring too much makes a woman overlook the obvious. My apologies, Andrew. I did not mean to almost kill you with wool."

"Graciously accepted," he said. "She is being modest. She did not leave my side for three days and nights. I would not be here to embarrass myself otherwise."

"Do not forget the honey cakes," Jesus said, and laughter shook the circle again.

"Those were Deborah's creation," I mumbled. "Though I may have helped with the mixing."

"Thank you for keeping our Andrew alive," Tirzah said sweetly, laying her hand for just a moment on his arm. *Our Andrew.* The words made my stomach churn, and I prayed, not very piously, for deliverance from the jealousy that clawed at my chest.

A clatter from the house and Deborah's sharp exclamation saved me from answering. I rose at once to see what had happened. As I stood, a quick twinge flickered in my hip, sharp as a wasp's sting, then passing. *Father, please, do not take this from me,* I prayed frantically, glancing at Jesus. If he knew the pain had returned, he gave no sign.

"Shall we see what troubles her?" he asked, accompanying me inside.

We found Deborah on her knees beside a shattered water jar, her face pale, hands trembling as she gathered the larger pieces. Sweat beaded her brow despite the kitchen's coolness, and her breathing seemed shallow.

"Deborah!" I went to her. "Are you hurt? Did you cut yourself?" This woman had mended my night-terrors and fevered winters, had been mother and teacher and dearest friend all bound in one beloved form. Seeing her falter woke a child's fear in me and a healer's resolve at the same time.

"No, child. Only clumsy old hands forgetting their business." Her voice was barely audible. "Pay me no mind."

Jesus kneeled without ceremony and lifted the larger shards with ease. "Allow me."

"There is no need, my lord," she protested, but he was already at work, hands sure and careful among the broken pieces.

I helped her stand, feeling how she leaned heavily against me, how her breath came too quickly. "You have done too much," I said, letting worry sharpen my voice. "The guests, the preparations. You should have called for help."

"Nonsense. I am perfectly fine," Even as she spoke the words, she swayed, and I braced her with my arm, feeling the tremor that ran through her frame.

Jesus looked up, meeting my eyes across Deborah's bowed head. He had seen it too — the tremor, the pallor, the way her hand pressed unconsciously to her side as if holding something in place.

"You must rest," I said firmly. "I will see to the kitchen and our guests. Shira and Tamar will help."

"You have visitors of importance."

"They are content with bread and fellowship," Jesus said,

the authority in his voice making protest impossible. "Go. Rest now."

She nodded reluctantly, and let me guide her to her chamber.

When I returned, Jesus had stacked the fragments in a neat pile on a wooden tray. "She is ill," he said quietly.

"Yes. She will not allow a proper examination, but I see the signs. She even admitted it once to me and Andrew, though she refused to speak of it after. I have been worried for weeks."

"Have you told your father?"

"I tried when last he was here. He left in such haste ..." My words frayed like old cloth, and I could not find the ends to weave them back together.

He nodded. "Those we love are often the hardest to help," he said. "They would protect us from their pain, as if love were a shield that could turn aside mortality."

Before I could say more, Andrew filled the doorway, concern creasing his brow. "What happened? Is Deborah well?"

"Only a broken jar and weariness," I told him. "She is resting."

He glanced between us, sensing the importance of what lay unspoken and choosing not to pry into matters that were not his to know. "The others ask if we might stay the night. They have come far, and tomorrow's road is long."

"Of course," I said, relief flooding through me. He would stay another night. "We have room enough, and Deborah would never forgive me if I sent guests away at dusk. I apologize. I should have offered already."

"Thank you." He smiled at me, and I realized he was not

yet ready to go either. *One last night. I will treasure every second with him.*

We walked back toward the courtyard with Jesus beside us, and I stole small glances at this man who knew my father, who had known my mother's song, who carried answers to questions I could barely frame. Andrew called him Messiah, and after today, I understood why. There was something about him that needed no trumpet or title, something that made trust rise unbidden. His very presence opened doors in my heart that I had not known were closed.

Tonight, it would be enough to sit in the circle and watch Andrew alive among his own people, to sit next to him, to listen to stories that painted the world in colors I was only beginning to see. Answers could wait. The questions would keep.

Yet one word would not leave my mind alone, circling like a hawk over a hidden nest. *Kinship.* Before he left my gate, I would have the truth of it, whatever the cost of knowing.

CHAPTER 9

THE EVENING STRETCHED LONG. Some disciples settled in our guest chambers, while others made their beds in the courtyard beneath the stars, cloaks bunched under their heads, the warm stones beneath them. I did not want the night to end. These people had welcomed me as if I belonged with them, and the feeling was strange and wonderful and hard to let go.

When the lamps finally burned low and voices dropped to whispers, I made my way to my chamber. I could still feel where Jesus had taken my hand, where the pain had vanished. What did it mean? I undressed slowly, my thoughts circling back to that moment again and again.

I had just unbound my hair when I heard voices from the courtyard below. Jesus and Andrew sat beneath the fig tree, directly under my window. Their words carried up through the lattice. I knew I should not listen. I listened anyway.

"She is unlike anyone I have ever known," Andrew said. "Everything I told you, and more. Her healer's skill, the way she kept me alive when death prowled the edges of the room, her love for Deborah. Rabbi, I care for her."

I froze, my fingers still tangled in my hair. He cared for me. Andrew cared for me.

"I can see that." Jesus chuckled softly. "And what troubles you about it?"

"Everything." Andrew's voice went tight. "She is Joseph of Arimathea's only daughter, heir to one of the wealthiest houses in Judea. I am a fisherman with no property, no standing, no house to offer. Even if Joseph considered it, which he would not, how would I meet a husband's duties? I cannot offer a bride-price, cannot prepare a home in a betrothal year, cannot remain in one place long enough to court her properly through her father."

I pressed closer to the lattice. Andrew had thought about this. About marrying me. About what it would require.

"You say that following me makes marriage impossible."

"Yes." A beat of silence. "No. I do not know. Master, you know the Law better than any of us. How does a man follow you and also keep a husband's vows? How do I ask for Joseph's daughter when I cannot promise her security or a settled life? How do I have her and you?"

My hands gripped the windowsill. *Ask me anyway*, I wanted to call down. *I do not need a settled life. I need you.*

"These are good questions, Andrew." Jesus was quiet for a moment, and I leaned closer to the lattice, my ear pressed against the wooden slats. "But perhaps you are asking the wrong one."

"What do you mean?"

"Perhaps the question is not whether you can offer Anna a traditional life, but whether the life I am calling you to is worth sharing with one who values its worth."

"But the practical matters—"

"Will find their way if this is truly from the Father. Pray. Wait. If it is meant, a way will be given."

Silence opened between them, heavy with unspoken hopes. Then Andrew said, quieter now, "I care for her too much to ruin her life with impossible dreams."

"Love is never an impossible dream, Andrew. Things are more complicated than you know, but you will find that it is wise to wait for the right time. Have patience, my friend."

I gripped the sill with both hands to steady myself, the rough wood biting into my palms. For a moment I just stood there, staring at the wooden slats as if I could somehow push the words back through them, send them back into the night where they belonged. But I could not unhear what I had heard. *He wants me for a wife.*

The thought kept repeating itself, refusing to give way. He had thought about bride-price, about a betrothal year, about speaking to Abba. These were not idle thoughts. He had considered what it would take to make me his wife.

And then decided he could not do it. Every obstacle he named was real. He had no property, no way to provide the traditional securities. He followed a wandering teacher and could not stay in one place. Even if he asked, Abba would refuse. Of course, Abba would refuse.

I should not have heard any of this. The knowledge sat wrong in my chest, and shame burned through me. Andrew had spoken in confidence to his teacher, and I had stolen words that were not meant for my ears.

I pressed my palms against my eyes. It did not matter now. I knew now, and I could not unknow it.

Let it be me, my heart whispered into the darkness. *Let*

me be his wife. Let me belong among these people who had welcomed me so completely.

He spoke of prayer and trust, of waiting for the Father's timing. To my aching heart, it sounded too much like "not yet," perhaps "not ever." The hope that had flared so bright went quiet, leaving only an ache. My entire future felt close enough to touch through the lattice, and still impossibly out of reach.

If there were a way, I could not see it.

When at last I lay down, tomorrow rose before me, unwanted and unavoidable. He would be gone with the light, and I would remain with a secret I should not have and promises I had not been asked to make.

Sleep would not come, and my thoughts would not calm. I climbed the outside stair to the roof, my staff marking each step softly. Night pressed cool against my cheeks, carrying the scent of jasmine and the promise of dew. Below, the courtyard lay quiet with sleeping forms wrapped in cloaks, while above me the stars pricked the dark like seeds from a scattered hand.

I sat by the parapet and opened my mother's journal where the ribbon marked her notes on fevers. The familiar sight of her careful script steadied me, as it always did. Her words were company in the lonely hours, a voice that still spoke comfort across the years.

Show me the way that is mine, I whispered into the night. The words rested on my tongue, half prayer, half plea. A jackal called from the hills, its voice thin and wild. The fig leaves moved softly somewhere below where Andrew and Jesus had spoken of love and duty, of dreams and impossibilities.

If Andrew is kept from me, let me yet be of use. Send me

those I may mend. And if there is truth in what the Rabbi meant by "more complicated than you know," let me find it without fear when the time comes.

The pages rustled beneath my fingers as if my mother knew my heartache and whispered encouragement from whatever place holds the righteous dead. Above me, the small cluster of kimah shimmered and beyond it the bright belt of kesil. *He who set the stars in their courses can surely order my steps*, I told my heart. After some time, I closed the book and returned to my bed, where sleep finally found me in the small hours before dawn.

I woke before the first light to quiet stirrings in the courtyard. When I rose and looked through the lattice, I saw them gathering their few belongings with the efficiency of those who live on the road, sharing bread and early fruit, passing a skin of water from hand to hand. A brief twinge tugged at my hip. The pain had returned as I had feared it would. I put my palm there and breathed a prayer. The ache eased to a manageable whisper. I dressed quickly and stepped out into the cool air.

The courtyard was full of purposeful movement. Tirzah counted dates into a travel sack, her lips moving with the numbers. Joanna checked the water skins, then tucked dried mint inside one. For the noon heat, I realized. These were people who knew how to care for one another on the road.

Simon showed one of the younger disciples how to coil rope properly, his big hands patient with instruction. I could see why Andrew loved his brother. Near the gate, Ezra stood watch as if they were treasure worth guarding. Perhaps to him, they were.

They were leaving. All of them. And I would stay.

"Take this," I said, setting a small pouch on the low wall

—honey wrapped in linen, comfrey salve still fragrant from yesterday's grinding, a sprig of hyssop tied with thread. "For blisters and small hurts along the way."

Joanna's eyes warmed as she accepted the gift. "You send us with good things, sister."

Sister. I had to look away before my face betrayed how much the word meant. "Bring the pouch back empty. That will please me most."

Andrew stood a little apart from the others as if he had saved a place for me in the morning's farewells. At the center of the group, Jesus spoke with two of the others about the road ahead and where they would rest when the sun grew too fierce. Someone had already gathered Andrew's few things. Ezra's smoothed branch leaned against the wall by the gate, waiting.

When Andrew saw me, his face lit up from within, and the sight made my steps falter.

"There you are," he said. "I was thinking I would have to wake you myself, which would have shocked Deborah beyond all recovery."

"You knew I would come." My voice carried everything I could not say aloud. *I heard you last night. I know you care. I know you mean to let me go. Losing you will hurt worse than keeping you ever could.* "I could not let you leave without a proper farewell."

We stood a breath apart. The others moved around us, but for a heartbeat, they might as well have been miles away. There was so much I wished to ask and could not. I tried to memorize every line of his face, every expression, to carry them with me through whatever days lay ahead.

"Will you ..." I began then faltered. What could I ask? To send word when he was able? To come back when duty allowed? To remember me when the road grew long and other faces filled his days?

"I will be thinking of you," he said softly. "And praying. For your father's safe return, for Deborah's strength, for your healing, for everything. You saved my life, Anna, in more ways than one."

"And I will pray for your safety. For all of you." I wanted to take his hand, to hold it fast against the coming separation. "And I liked Simon. Very much." I managed a smile that felt fragile on my lips. *Do not go. Stay. Stay with me.*

"How much?" His laugh came quick and bright, and the air between us lightened, but I saw the tears filling his eyes. "Anna, I—"

Jesus reached us then, and the moment ended before it could fully form. "Thank you for your welcome, Anna. Your kindness will not be forgotten. Nor will you."

"It was my honor to receive you all." I looked over at the people who had brought such light to my quiet house. "Thank you for letting me be a part of this, even for a little while. And for ... for all the rest." For confirming I heard God, for speaking of my mother, for taking the pain away. My tears threatened to have their way if I tried to say it all aloud.

"Peace be with you, Anna. We will meet again." He kissed my forehead tenderly and stepped away.

Andrew took my hand in his and drew a narrow cord from his wrist, its length worn smooth by salt and sun and countless days of handling nets. He looped it once around my wrist with careful hands and tied a small, neat knot I did not recognize.

"A fisherman's knot," he said, his voice low enough for my ears alone. "It holds when the pull is strong." The simple words carried the solemnity of a vow. I could not speak through the sudden tightness in my throat. "I wish..." He shook his head and cleared his throat.

"I know. I do too."

He smiled then turned toward the gate where the others waited. They moved with the unhurried pace of those who know the road will be long. "Shalom, Anna." He caught my hand in a quick, warm squeeze. "What we have is real. For me, it is real."

"For me as well," I whispered, a tear slipping free despite my efforts to hold it back.

"Coming, Andrew?" Simon called from the gate. "The road will not wait for us!"

"Anna of Arimathea," Andrew said, "my brave, beautiful, extraordinary and remarkable girl, do not forget me. I will find a way back to you. I promise."

I nodded, not trusting my voice to carry words. With one last squeeze of my fingers, he was gone.

I watched him take his place among the group and glance back once with a smile that held all our unspoken promises. *I will not forget you, Andrew. Not for a moment.*

They climbed toward the crest of the hill, their forms growing smaller with each step. When they reached the rise, Jesus turned and lifted his hand in farewell. Even at that distance, I saw him clearly, and his voice carried on the morning air as if the hills themselves bore his words to me.

"Shalom, little cousin."

CHAPTER 10

THEY WERE GONE, all of them, and Andrew was walking away from me, perhaps forever.

I braced against the low wall at the courtyard's edge, my hands gripping the sun-warmed stone. Grit bit into my palms. Already beyond the hill was the man who had looked at my scars and called me beautiful, who had spoken of healing and hope. His steps carried him down roads I would never walk, and Tirzah walked beside him.

My knees gave way. I sank onto the stone bench by the courtyard wall. My staff clattered against the paving stones, the sound sharp and final in the too-quiet courtyard. The tears I had been holding back since dawn came all at once. They dripped from my jaw onto my robe, left dark spots on the linen, and carried with them all the words I had not said, all the courage I had not found.

I had let him go. I had wished them well when every part of me cried out for him to stay, or better still, to ask if I might go with him. The words had been there, but I had swallowed them down and said nothing.

Now it was too late. He was gone. I wept until my ribs ached, until I could not catch my breath. The sound echoed off the walls and came back to me, broken and raw.

"Oh, Anna." Deborah's voice came from behind me. She sat beside me on the bench and drew an arm around my shoulders. "My sweet girl. Let it out. Tears are healing."

"I cannot—" I could barely speak through the weeping. "I cannot return to how things were. I cannot pretend I do not know what I am missing now."

The sun climbed higher, sharpening shadows across the courtyard until they lay black and distinct against the pale stone. A breeze lifted the grape leaves along the trellis, and I thought of evenings in the garden when Andrew and I spoke until the stars showed themselves. Now everything would remind me of him, from the bench where we had talked of healing and hope, to the herb beds where he had learned mint from thyme with the patience of a man who truly listened, even my bold hens who had claimed him at once and followed him about the courtyard.

"I should have asked to go with them," I said into my hands, my voice muffled and broken. "I should have been brave enough to ask."

"Would you have left?" Deborah asked.

Would I have? If Jesus had invited me, would I have found the courage to leave the only home I had known since childhood? To abandon the garden where my mother's memory lived in every planted row, the rooms where Deborah had raised me with such love? Even more, could I have? For Andrew, I might have.

ANNA OF ARIMATHEA

"I do not know," I admitted. "I wanted to. Oh, how I wanted to!" I wiped my cheeks with the back of my hand, tasting salt on my lips. "But look at me, Deborah. What use would I be to them? I can scarcely walk to the village without tiring, without my hip screaming its protest. How could I cross Judea, sleep under the open sky, walk mile after mile over rough roads?" I gestured at my staff, which lay fallen beside the bench. "I would slow them down. Andrew would come to despise me for my weakness."

"You might be surprised at what you can do when love gives you strength." Her hand rubbed comforting circles on my back.

Through my tears, I saw the empty road. I remembered Andrew's face when he spoke of the Rabbi's healings, the hope that had blazed in his eyes, the steady certainty in his voice when he said, "He could heal you, Anna." What if he was right? What if I had let wholeness pass me by because I feared reaching for it, because I had grown so accustomed to my limitations that I could not imagine life without them?

"They are gone," I whispered, the words falling into the silence between us, disappearing without echo. "It is too late now. I must learn to live with what I have chosen."

We sat without words while my weeping eased and the morning light warmed my face, though I felt none of it. Goliath crowed near the coop, his voice brazen and ordinary, announcing the day to anyone who would listen. From the olive grove came Ezra's voice, low and even, calling instructions to the workers. Life carried on as it always did, though mine felt shattered beyond all mending.

In that quiet space between grief and whatever must come after—if anything ever came after—the Rabbi's parting words rang in my memory. Something about them would not let go.

"Deborah," I said, my voice hoarse from weeping. "What did Jesus mean when he called me 'little cousin'?"

She went completely still. The color left her face. For a heartbeat, perhaps two, she simply stared at me.

She knew. She knew what those words meant, knew what they revealed, and knew why they mattered.

"Deborah?" I pressed, leaning forward, the bench hard beneath me. "You heard it. What did he mean?"

"I —" She stood abruptly, the shawl sliding from her lap to the stones in a whisper of fabric. "Anna, I cannot—your father—"

"My father what?"

But she was already moving toward the house, her steps quick despite the careful way she held herself, one hand pressed briefly to her side in that gesture I had learned not to question. "I must see to the midday meal. Ezra will be wanting—"

"Deborah, wait!" I grabbed my staff and pushed to standing, but she did not stop. She kept walking, pretending I had not spoken. "Deborah!"

I watched her disappear through the doorway, leaving me alone in the courtyard with nothing but questions and the terrible certainty that everyone in my life was keeping secrets from me. The sun climbed higher while I stood staring at the gate where Andrew had disappeared. How long ago now? An hour? Less? It felt like days, like years, like a lifetime had passed since I had watched him walk away.

Pressure built behind my eyes, and the courtyard felt too large, too empty. The stones where Andrew had stood still held his shape despite his absence. The gate through which he had walked seemed to mock me with its openness, its invitation to a world I could not enter.

I could not sit here in this space where every breath reminded of what would never be. The grief felt alive inside me, prowling, threatening to choke the life out of me.

If Deborah would not tell me, I would find the answers myself. I needed something to do other than sitting here drowning in what I could not change.

I moved through the house, my staff tapping sharply against the floor. Each strike rang out in the silent corridors, announcing my presence. Servants scattered from my path. The library first. My father kept records there, letters, documents from his travels to Jerusalem and beyond. I pulled scrolls from shelves, the parchment crackling under my fingers. My hands shook as I unrolled them, and I scanned lines of careful Hebrew script that swam before my eyes. The scent of old ink rose from the pages, musty and sharp. Council business. Trade agreements. Letters from Jerusalem about Temple taxes and tithes. Nothing personal. Nothing that spoke of family or blood ties or secrets kept.

I shoved them back and moved to his study. Olive harvests recorded in neat columns, wine production tallied with precision, household accounts balanced to the last lepton. Everything my father touched turned to order and control, every aspect of his world measured and managed and kept in its proper place.

My lungs felt tight, compressed, as though something heavy sat on my ribcage. Each breath came shallow, leaving me dizzy. There had to be something. Some letter, some record, some fragment of truth that would explain why Jesus had called me cousin.

Abba's private chamber. I was already moving down the

corridor before the thought fully formed, my hip arguing against the pace, but my need driving me forward. His door stood closed but unlocked. It had never needed a lock, not here, not in a house where every person had been chosen for loyalty and discretion. I pushed it open.

Cedar and old parchment. The scent hit me as I crossed the threshold, so familiar it made my stomach clench. His robes hung perfectly on their pegs, the fabric still holding the shape of his shoulders. Scrolls stacked in careful rows on the shelf beside his bed. Everything exactly as he had left it, waiting for his return.

I pulled open the chest at the foot of his bed. The hinges creaked in protest. Robes. More robes beneath, the wool rough under my palms, the linen smooth and cool. I pulled them out, dropped them on the floor in crumpled heaps, then dug deeper. The scent of lavender rose from the fabric. Nothing.

My hands were shaking. I moved to his writing table and touched the seal of the Council on the rolled parchments. Official business. Nothing that would give me answers. Nothing that would explain why Deborah had looked at me with such fear.

My breath came faster. There had to be something.

Then I saw it. A large wooden chest against the far wall, ornately carved with symbols I did not recognize. Unlike everything else in the chamber—the plain storage chests, the simple shelves—this one looked old, important.

I crossed to it and knelt before it. The carved surface felt cool beneath my fingertips, the wood ancient and dense, worn smooth in places where hands had gripped it for years. I traced the symbols carved into the lid. Flowers, I thought. Or stars. The grain of the wood ran dark and light, a pattern that spoke of age. When I tried to lift the lid, it would not budge. Locked, of course. Everything locked, everything hidden, everything kept from me as though I were a child who could not be trusted.

My hands shook as I pulled the pin from my hair, feeling the tug against my scalp as it came loose. The metal was warm from my body, slightly bent from years of use. Some distant part of my mind screamed that I should stop, that I had gone too far, but I kept working it free. My braid unraveled, heavy against my back. The need to know had become all-consuming. I could not stop.

I pushed the pin into the lock with trembling fingers. The metal scratched against metal as I worked it into the mechanism, probing, twisting.

"What are you doing?"

Deborah's voice cut through the chamber. I looked up to find her standing in the doorway, silhouetted against the corridor's light, her face pale with shock. Behind her, I could hear the household going about its work—distant voices, the clatter of dishes, the ordinary sounds of a day continuing without me.

"I am finding answers," I said, turning back to the chest, my voice steadier than my hands. "Since no one will give them to me."

"By breaking into your father's private things? By violating his trust?" She moved into the room. "Get away from that chest, Anna."

"No." I stayed where I was, kneeling before it like a supplicant before an altar, the hairpin still clutched in my fist like a weapon. "You will not tell me what I need to know. He is not here to tell me. So I will find out for myself."

"You will do no such thing." Deborah's voice carried an

authority I had rarely heard from her. "Do not do this. Stand up and leave this chamber."

"Or what?" The words came out sharp, ugly. "You will tell my father? He already keeps everything from me. What is one more betrayal?"

"Anna—"

"Do not 'Anna' me." I pushed to my feet, dropping the pin. I faced her across the scattered contents of my father's belongings—robes crumpled on the floor, scrolls rolled haphazard across the tiles, the evidence of my trespass laid bare between us. "I am tired of being kept in the dark. Tired of everyone deciding what I may know about my family."

"Then perhaps you should act with the wisdom your father has tried to teach you." The rebuke stung. "Look at what you have done here. You violate his privacy, destroy his things. Is this how you seek truth?"

"If you had simply answered my question—" My voice rose despite myself, cracking on the words. "What did Jesus mean when he called me 'little cousin'? You know, Deborah. I saw it on your face. You know exactly what he meant."

"It requires your father's answer, not mine." Her jaw set in a way I recognized. She would not be moved. "I gave him my word. I will not break it, Anna. Not even for you."

"So that is it? You will just leave me here with nothing?"

"I know your heart is broken right now, and that is why you are behaving this way. Go rest, Anna. We will talk about this later."

"Wait!"

Deborah turned toward the door. "No. I will not stand here and watch you destroy yourself." Her voice was quiet, almost gentle. "Or say things to me you cannot take back. Your father will return soon enough. Ask him then."

"Deborah! If you loved me, you would tell me!"

For a long moment she said nothing, her back still turned. "Loving you does not mean I must dishonor my word. I will come back later to clean this up."

She walked away. Her footsteps faded down the corridor, steady and even, and I was alone.

I turned back to the chest, fury driving me forward. I scanned the floor for the hairpin, found it near the wall where it had fallen, the metal glinting in a bar of sunlight. My hands shook so badly I could barely grip it. I kneeled before the lock once more, twisting, probing, trying to force something that would not yield.

Nothing. Nothing.

The lock would not yield. I threw the pin across the room. It struck the far wall with a small sound and disappeared into shadow. I stood up and kicked the chest. Pain exploded up my leg, radiating from my damaged hip through my thigh, my knee, down to my ankle. I kicked it again. The solid wood refused to yield, refused to break, refused to give me anything. I kicked it again and again, each blow sending fresh agony through my body, but I could not stop. All my grief and rage and helplessness poured into those blows—for Andrew walking away, for Deborah's silence, for my father's secrets, for this locked chest that would not open no matter how much I hurt it or myself. My eyes burned, and sweat ran down my back.

I did not choose to fall. My legs simply gave out, every muscle suddenly useless. My knees hit the floor hard enough to send pain shooting up my thighs. I caught myself on my hands among the scattered robes, palms flat against cold tile. Wool bunched under my left hand, linen under my right. The mess I had made surrounded me—Abba's carefully folded robes now crumpled and dusty, scrolls unrolled and askew, everything disordered, everything wrong.

The locked chest sat just beyond my reach, silent and unmoved and utterly indifferent to my pain.

What was I doing? What had I done?

The first sob broke from my throat before I could stop it, tearing its way out. Then another, this one worse, wrenching up from my chest. Then I was weeping, hard and helpless, my forehead pressed against the cool tile floor. The stone was hard against my brow, unforgiving. Everything poured out at once, tangled together until I could not tell where one torment ended and another began, until it was just pain, pure and overwhelming.

My hip ached in the position I had collapsed into, but I could not summon the strength to move. Tears soaked into my sleeves where my face pressed against my arms. The linen grew damp beneath my cheek, the fabric darkening with each sob.

"I am sorry," I whispered to the empty chamber, to the silent walls, to the absent God who seemed to have turned His face from me. "I am so sorry."

But there was no one to hear.

I owed Deborah an apology. The thought came through the fog of my grief. She had done nothing but keep her word, and I had thrown her love back in her face like something worthless. But I could not face her. Not yet. Not like this, with my face swollen from weeping and my hands still shaking and the evidence of what I had done scattered across my father's floor.

I do not know how long I lay there, curled around my pain. Long enough for my tears to dry in salt tracks on my face, pulling the skin tight, making my cheeks ache. Long enough for the wet patches on my sleeves to dry stiff. Long enough for my hip to go from agony to a dull, throbbing ache. Long enough for the light to shift across the wall. The bar of sunlight that had fallen across my father's writing table now slanted toward the door, steeper, moving as the sun climbed higher. Minutes or hours, I could not say. Time had stopped meaning anything.

Eventually, because there was nothing else to do and I could not lie there forever, I pushed myself upright. My hands shook as I groped for my staff, finding it lying near the doorway where it had fallen during my search. The wood felt solid beneath my palms, real and present in a way nothing else did, an anchor in a world that had come unmoored.

I looked back once at the chamber. I should gather the things I had displaced. I knew that. Should restore order to what I had disturbed, make some attempt to undo the damage I had wrought. But I could not bring myself to touch anything else in this room, could not face the evidence of what I had done. My hands felt unclean, my presence a contamination.

I made my way out, limping down the corridor, each step an effort of will rather than strength. The hall stretched long before me, longer than it had ever seemed before, and at the end of it lay my chamber, small and safe.

Behind me, my father's door hung open, the chaos within visible to anyone who passed. Deborah had said she would come back to clean it. I should have closed the door at least and hidden the sight of my violation laid bare for any servant who might wander past, the shame of it written in scattered fabric and displaced scrolls.

But I did not close it. I could not make myself turn back, could touch nothing more in that chamber, reeking of my poor behavior. Some things, once opened, could not be sealed again. Some wreckage could not be hidden, no matter how much we might wish it otherwise.

CHAPTER 11

I KEPT to myself for the next two days.

The villa felt too large and too small at once, its familiar rooms suddenly strange to me. Corridors held their own quiet conversations, doors opened and closed with purposes I could not fathom, and the very walls whispered secrets I could not hear. The house worked on without me, servants moving through their tasks while I drifted through mine, my presence marked only by uneven footsteps against stone floors I had known since childhood.

Deborah brought my meals to my chamber three times a day, though we did not speak beyond the necessary pleasantries that felt more like ritual than conversation. She would set down a tray, pottery scraping against polished stone with deliberate softness, and slip away before I could find words that might bridge the chasm I had dug between us with my cruelty.

I wanted to apologize. The words lived in my mind, formed themselves a hundred times as I lay in the dark staring at shadows that moved across my ceiling with the passage of the moon. *I am sorry. I should not have said those things. Please forgive me.* Simple words, true words, words that should have been easy to speak to the woman who had loved me my whole life.

But every time I saw her passing in the corridor or moving through the courtyard, shame rose up to choke me. How could I apologize for what I had said and done? The disorder I had made in my father's chamber had been cleaned away, the robes refolded, the scrolls returned to their proper places, but the damage between Deborah and me remained, sharp-edged and impossible to ignore, a wound that festered in silence.

So I stayed in my garden instead, seeking refuge among things that demanded nothing from me but water and weeding and the patient attention I could no longer seem to give to human souls. I worked from dawn until the heat grew too fierce to bear, until sweat soaked through my tunic and even the shade of the pomegranate tree could not cool the fever of activity I used to drown out thought. The air hung sharp with rosemary and thick with the green smell of sun-warmed fig leaves, a sweetness almost cloying in the afternoon heat. I breathed it in deep, desperate for anything but the sour taste of grief that lingered at the back of my tongue, no matter how much mint I chewed.

Bees drifted lazy and drunk between blossoms, their drone a constant backdrop that should have been soothing but only made the silence feel heavier. Underneath their humming came the liquid gurgle of irrigation channels carrying precious water from the cistern, and the dry rustle of leaves when the wind remembered to move. I listened for the soft cluck of my chickens as they scratched at the dirt and watched them tug at my sandals with their usual demands for attention and treats. Their feathers brushed my bare legs—soft and warm and grounding in a way I desperately needed. I talked to them as I worked, murmuring nonsense about Andrew and Deborah and the tangled mess I had made of everything. They listened with more patience than I deserved, heads cocked, bright eyes fixed on me as though they understood.

But every sound, every scent, every small pleasure brought Andrew back to me. I remembered his laughter over these same hens, his questions about feverfew and mint, his genuine interest in properties and harvest times as though healing herbs were matters of great importance. The way he made me feel important.

The way he had made this place feel less lonely simply by being in it.

His presence lingered in every corner, in every memory, filling even the smallest spaces with an ache I could not escape no matter how many weeds I pulled or how many irrigation channels I cleared of debris. He said he would find a way back to me. The words echoed in my mind, persistent as prayer, though whether they were promise or farewell, I could no longer say with any certainty. Perhaps it had been merely kindness, meant to soften a painful parting for a broken woman who had nothing to offer him but scars and limitations and a love that could never be enough. Perhaps by now he had already forgotten the healer who sent him away, his mind full of Capernaum and the ministry. And Tirzah. The thought of her and Andrew together on the road made me physically ill.

On the third day, unable to bear my brooding any longer and desperate for any human voice that was not my own, I went seeking Deborah. I still lacked the courage to apologize, but the isolation had grown unbearable, pressing in on me like grave clothes. She was the only person who had ever truly known me, who had seen me at my worst and loved me anyway, and I missed her.

I found her in the main room where she often worked in the afternoons, sunlight streaming through the tall windows to pool on the floor in bars of golden warmth that drifted across the tiles as the day aged. A faint thread of myrtle drifted in from the courtyard, mixing with the smell of beeswax from the freshly polished furniture. Servants moved through the rooms with their usual efficiency, so familiar I barely registered it. A boy balanced an amphora of wine from the storage chamber, the vessel nearly as tall as he was and heavy enough to make his arms tremble, and Tamar hurried by with an armful of folded linens bound for the upper chambers, her face set in concentration as she navigated the corridors. Their sandals whispered against stone in a rhythm as old as the house itself, their voices kept respectfully low in deference to the household's unspoken tension, to the thing that had broken between their mistress and the woman who had raised her.

Deborah looked up when I entered, and for a heartbeat, hope flickered across her face. Then her expression smoothed into neutrality, and she wore the mask she reserved for when my father entertained members of the council, when political allies came calling with their calculated words and hidden agendas. It was the face of a servant who knew her place, and seeing it directed at me hurt.

"Anna." She set down her mending. "Do you need something?"

The formality cut deeper than anger would have. I

wanted to beg her to stop, to drop the politeness and fight with me if she must, anything but this terrible distance that made me feel like a stranger in my home. But I could not find the words. What came out instead was, "I thought we might talk."

"About?"

About everything. About how sorry I am. About how I cannot breathe under the weight of what I said to you. About how the silence between us is killing me more surely than any fever ever could. But I could not force those words past the shame lodged in my chest, past the fear that any apology I offered would be too little, too late, too inadequate to mend what I had broken. "About nothing in particular. I have been alone with my thoughts for days, and they are poor company."

Something softened in her eyes, though she did not quite smile, did not quite let me off the hook I had impaled myself upon. "They often are when we are hurting."

The kindness in her voice nearly undid me, nearly broke the fragile control I had been maintaining over the chaos inside me. I sank onto the bench across from her, my staff striking the floor with more force than I intended, the sound harsh in the room. For a long moment we simply sat, the quiet between us heavy with all the things neither of us knew how to say, weighted with the history of eighteen years and the fresh wound of three days past.

"Deborah," I began, then stopped. Started again. "I—"

"You need not apologize," she said, her hands folded in her lap in that way she had when she was choosing her words with care. "You were in pain. You lashed out. People do when they are grieving."

"That does not make it right."

"No." She met my eyes steadily, and I saw no anger there. "It does not. But I understand it."

The forgiveness in her words felt unearned, a gift I had no right to accept, yet I grasped at it, desperate for solid ground, for anything that might keep me from sinking further into the mire of my making. "I should never have questioned your love. I know—I have always known—how much you care for me."

"Yes, well." She cleared her throat, looking away toward the windows where dust motes danced in the light. "What is done is done. We will speak no more of it."

We fell into an uncomfortable silence, broken only by the servants calling to one another in the courtyard about the evening meal, the cluck of chickens settling for their afternoon rest, the rhythmic creak of the olive press from somewhere beyond the walls where workers labored in the groves that had sustained my family for generations. Normal sounds, ordinary sounds, the sounds of life continuing its relentless march forward regardless of personal catastrophe, mocking the brokenness I carried like a second skin, like another layer of scars that could not be seen but were no less real for their invisibility.

"I miss him," I said finally, the admission torn from somewhere deep inside, trying to pretend it did not matter. "I keep thinking I see him turning a corner or standing in the garden by the fig tree where we used to talk. But it is only shadows."

Deborah's expression gentled, the detachment melting away. "It is not yet a week since he left. The ache is still fresh, still raw. Give it time."

"Will it fade? The ache, I mean." I needed to know, needed some assurance that I would not feel this way forever, this hollow emptiness where something vital had been torn away.

"I do not know." She folded her hands in her lap, and I noticed how thin they looked, how the bones stood out more prominently than I remembered, the veins visible beneath skin that seemed almost translucent in the afternoon light. "Some losses, we carry all our lives. Others--" She left the thought unfinished, her gaze distant, focused on something I could not see.

I wondered what losses she meant, what grief she carried in silence. I could not bring myself to press her further. She had already given me more grace than I deserved, more forgiveness than I had earned. I would not demand more nor pick at wounds that were not mine to examine.

As the sun began its descent toward evening, painting the courtyard stones in shades of coral and violet, Deborah rose to see about the evening meal. She moved slowly, and I saw again how carefully she held herself, pain clear in every movement, the brief pause before she straightened fully, one hand pressed to her side in a gesture I had seen too many times in recent weeks to dismiss any longer. Her cheeks looked flushed, and a faint sheen of perspiration covered her forehead.

"Deborah." I set down my cup harder than I intended, hitting stone with a sharp crack that made her flinch. "Please. You said that night in the garden that you had pain. Tell me what is wrong with your health."

"Anna—"

"I have been asking for weeks. You keep saying it is nothing, but you have admitted it is not. I can see—"

"It is nothing." Her voice carried an edge of finality I knew better than to challenge, the tone she used when a subject was closed and would not be reopened regardless of argument or pleading. "I am simply tired. That is all. It has been a long week."

She left before I could argue further, moving slowly, each step placed with the care of someone conserving energy, and I sat staring at the space where she had been, my hands clenched into fists on my lap.

The cold finger of fear traced down my spine, raising the fine hairs at the nape of my neck, and I knew with sudden, terrible conviction that I had been a fool.

The fever came three days later, swift and merciless.

I woke in the gray predawn to silence where there should have been sound. No footsteps in the corridor, no murmur of servants beginning their morning tasks, no familiar clink of pottery that meant Deborah was already up and about, ensuring the household ran smoothly before the rest of us even stirred. The wrongness of it pulled me from sleep, some instinct honed over years of living in this house telling me something was amiss before my conscious mind had fully grasped it.

I dressed myself with clumsy fingers, my hip stiff from the night, and made my way toward the kitchens to see what had kept her. The house felt too quiet, holding its breath, waiting for something I could not name.

Tamar met me in the corridor before I reached the kitchen, her face drawn with worry, her hands twisting in her apron in that gesture people made when they bore bad news and did not know how to deliver it.

"My lady," she said, her voice low and urgent, barely above a whisper though there was no one near enough to overhear. "It is Deborah. She fell ill in the night. She would not let us wake you, but—" She glanced toward Deborah's chamber, toward the door that suddenly seemed ominous in a way it never had before. "I think you should see her."

Fear cut through the fog of my morning thoughts. I pushed past Tamar without ceremony and hurried down the corridor as quickly as my uneven gait would allow. Deborah's chamber door stood ajar, and I could hear her labored breathing even before I entered, each inhale a struggle, each exhale rattling in a way that made my healer's training scream warnings I did not want to hear.

She lay on her pallet, face flushed with fever, skin shining with sweat in the dim morning light, her hair damp and clinging to her temples in dark strands. When she heard me enter, her eyes opened. They took a moment to focus, confusion clouding them before recognition finally came.

"Anna?" Her voice came out rough, barely above a whisper. "You should not—you should not be here. I will be fine by midday."

But even as she spoke, a violent shiver ran through her entire frame, her teeth chattering despite the heat radiating from her skin, and I saw how she curled into herself instinctively, seeking warmth that would not come no matter how many blankets covered her. The body's terrible contradiction—burning from within while feeling frozen without.

I dropped to my knees beside her pallet, ignoring the jabbing pain from my hip, and pressed the back of my hand to her forehead. My hand feel cold in comparison to the temperature of her skin and made the air between us shimmer like heat rising from sun-baked stones. This was not the mild fever of a simple illness. This was something else entirely.

"How long have you been feeling unwell?" I demanded, though I suspected I already knew the answer. I could read it in the hollows of her cheeks, in the way her collarbones stood out sharp beneath her shift. Days. Perhaps a week or more, dismissed as fatigue, ignored in the wake of everything else that had claimed our attention, hidden with the skill of someone who had spent a lifetime caring for others and had never learned to accept care herself.

"It is nothing," she insisted, but the words dissolved into a coughing fit that shook her, coming from deep in her chest. When it finally passed, she lay back against the cushions, her breathing shallow and as quick as a frightened bird's, each breath a visible effort.

"Tamar," I said, not taking my eyes from Deborah. "Bring me clean cloths. I need wide strips. And willow bark—there should be some in my workroom. Also feverfew and yarrow." I spoke in my healer's voice, calm and detached, the voice I used when panic threatened to overwhelm me and action was the only thing that might help. "And have Shira bring fresh water from the cistern and vinegar from the kitchen. Oil from the storeroom. Send someone to find Ezra. I do not know where he is this early, but find him. Tell him Deborah is ill, and I need his help. Quickly."

As Tamar hurried away, her sandals echoing against the floor in her haste, I took Deborah's hand in mine. It felt small and fragile. The pulse at her wrist fluttered fast and weak beneath my fingers. Sweat gathered at her temples, dampening the silver wisps of hair at her brow. This fever had taken hold with frightening speed.

Shira returned with water, and Tamar appeared with an armful of clean cloths. I plunged one strip into the basin and laid it across Deborah's burning forehead then placed another at her wrists where the pulse beat so rapidly. The fabric darkened almost immediately with the heat of her skin.

When Shira came back with the jars of vinegar and oil, I warmed the oil between my palms and stroked it into Deborah's arms, hoping to ease the tremor that ran through her body. I soaked another strip of cloth in vinegar, the sharp scent rising to catch in my throat, and laid it across her chest to draw out the fever's heat.

Before the second cloth had time to cool, I heard Ezra's approaching footsteps in the hallway. When he appeared in the doorway, his face had gone the color of old linen.

"Come," I said, gesturing him to Deborah's side. "Help me lift her shoulders while I arrange the cushions properly."

He nodded and moved carefully to support her, his hand steady at her shoulder, his voice dropping to the low, gentle murmur he used with sick animals.

The air in the chamber grew thick with the mingled scents of vinegar, oil, and fever heat until every breath felt heavy in my lungs.

Draw the fire out of her, I prayed, pressing the vinegar-soaked cloth more firmly to her chest. *Adonai, help me see what needs to be done. Please let this work.*

Tamar and Shira moved quietly in and out of the chamber, the soft slap of their sandals and the splash of fresh water the only sounds besides Deborah's labored breathing. Their presence steadied me. I was not alone in this fight.

"Anna," Deborah whispered. "You are right. I have a fever, I think."

"Yes, you do." I laid my hand on her forehead, testing the heat but also out of love. "But I am here, and you will be well."

"I am sorry to be so much trouble." She coughed, then closed her eyes, a tear falling down the side of her face.

"You are no trouble," I said. First Andrew had been taken from me, and now Deborah lay burning with fever. I could not lose her. I would not survive such a loss. My hands shook as I prepared a mild tonic of willow bark and mint, crushing the herbs until their fragrance rose sharp and bitter. Steam rushed up from the cup and stung my eyes.

These hands had been powerless to make Andrew stay, and now they fought desperately to cool a fever that might steal the only mother I had ever truly known.

The room filled with the competing scents of mint and vinegar, the air growing close and difficult to breathe. I bowed my head until my forehead touched the edge of the sleeping mat.

"Adonai," I whispered, the word catching and breaking in my throat. "Do not take her from me. Not her, too. I need her."

My voice was small in the lamplight, but it lingered in the silence. And in that silence, I waited.

CHAPTER 12

THE WILLOW BARK tea ran down Deborah's chin when I tried to make her drink, pooling in the hollow of her throat before soaking into the linen beneath her head. The bitter scent rose between us, mingling with the sour smell of fever-sweat. I wiped it away with trembling fingers, the cloth already damp and warm from previous attempts, watching the precious liquid waste itself. Each drop lost felt like failure made visible.

"Please," I said, holding the cup to her cracked lips again. "Just a sip."

But Deborah's eyes remained closed, her breathing shallow and rapid, each breath barely there. At times it came in a small rush, then faltered and paused long enough that I sometimes feared it would not come at all. The chamber had taken on the smell of prolonged sickness—sweat and herbs and the sour scent of bodies too weak for washing. The air hung close and damp despite the windows standing open, clogging my throat with each breath I took. Even the sharp bite of vinegar from the cooling cloths could not cut through it. The vinegar that had always drawn heat from fevers proved powerless against whatever consumed her from within. Six days of trying, and nothing I had done brought even the smallest relief.

And it was my fault.

The thought came fresh each time I looked at her wasted face. I had been worrying about her health for weeks before Andrew ever arrived, the way she moved more slowly through her daily tasks, how she had to rest between chores that had never tired her before. I let those signs pass by unheeded. I placed them on a shelf with other small concerns and left them there too long. When Andrew came, wounded and needing care, I set my worry for Deborah aside completely. I had been a healer who forgot to heal, a daughter who forgot to truly see.

I leaned closer to Deborah's still form and brushed a strand of damp hair from her burning forehead. Her skin seared beneath my palm, yet her hands lay cool and clammy on the coverlet. The fever drew all warmth to her head and left the rest of her body cold. "I am sorry," I whispered, the words barely audible even in the quiet chamber. "I am so sorry, Deborah. I should have acted sooner. I should have trusted what I knew instead of what I hoped to believe." *I should not have been so selfish.*

Her face softened at my murmuring. Perhaps she could hear me somewhere in the distant place where fever had carried her spirit. Her lips moved without a sound. The corners flaked and split from days of thirst, and when I moistened them with a damp cloth, she turned toward it, seeking comfort.

I had dozed fitfully beside her pallet these past nights, but proper sleep had abandoned me since she fell sick. My eyes felt gritty and hot, the lids heavy as lead each time I blinked. My back ached from kneeling on stone, and a dull throb had settled behind my temples that no amount of mint tea could touch. Ezra came and went through the hours, his face lined with worry. He would sit beside her for long stretches, holding her hand and whispering prayers in the old language our grandmothers had spoken. When she cried out in delirium, he would step into the courtyard and stand with his back to the house, as if distance might help him bear what he could not change.

"She keeps calling for Sarah," he had told me on the fourth morning, his voice thick with tears he refused to shed. "She calls for your mother. Sometimes she reaches toward the door thinking Sarah stands there, waiting to enter."

I set down the bowl of untouched broth and stared at him. "What does she say?"

"Mostly just her name, over and over. Sometimes she speaks to your mother like she is sitting right beside her, having a conversation I cannot hear." He rubbed his face with both hands, the gesture of a man trying to hold himself together. "Anna, I have never seen her like this. Even when the fever took half the village fifteen years ago, she kept her wits sharp and her hands steady. But this is different."

I looked down at Deborah, who lay so still I had to watch carefully for the slight rise of her chest. The hollows at her temples had deepened over these days, making her eyes seem to have retreated into her skull. A false bloom colored her cheeks, while the skin around her eyes had taken on a waxy appearance. When I lifted her hand, it felt weightless, fragile as dried leaves. She was disappearing before my eyes. Frustration filled me at the complete uselessness of my healing skills, and with it came fear so sharp it made my hands shake.

I knew with certainty that this was not a simple fever. I had seen fevers break and return in cycles, had watched them burn through the weak while somehow sparing the strong, and sometimes the other way around. But this was different entirely, devouring her from within. The way she had been growing thinner over the past months, the pain she tried to hide in her side, the bone-deep exhaustion that no amount of rest could touch — it all matched the wasting sickness I had witnessed in other households. The yellowing of skin, the slow but relentless consuming of flesh. I had no physician's learned name for it, only the terrible memory of watching it steal others. The time for gentle remedies had passed.

"Ezra," I said, making the only decision I could, "we need to send word to Jerusalem. To Abba."

He looked up at me with eyes made raw by sleepless vigil. "We can," he said. "Though I confess I do not know what he can do that you cannot." His voice cracked on the words. "But if there is any chance, any physician he might know, any remedy we have not tried..." He swallowed hard and laid his rough palm upon my head in a brief blessing, the gesture of a father offering what comfort he could. "Anna, you are doing everything that can be done. Deborah taught you well, and you possess skills that surpass your years. If anyone can save her—"

"But I cannot!" I stood so abruptly that my staff clattered to the floor, the sound harsh in the quiet chamber. "Can you not see? I have tried everything I know, and nothing touches this fever. She is all the mother I have ever truly known, Ezra. If she dies—" The words choked off, too terrible to finish.

Ezra studied my face with eyes that had witnessed six

decades of life and loss. "Do you believe your father will know how to help her?"

"I think Abba has connections beyond Arimathea that I do not. Physicians in Jerusalem, learned men who might have encountered this sickness before and fought it." I retrieved my staff and gripped it until my knuckles showed white through the skin. "And if not physicians, then perhaps he knows how to find Jesus."

Ezra's lined face shifted as understanding and fear warred within him.

"Jesus," he repeated, testing the name on his tongue.

I gestured toward Deborah, who shivered despite the heat that poured from her skin in waves. "Look at her, Ezra. Truly look. How much time do you think she has left?"

He was quiet for a long moment, his gaze fixed on her face with the unflinching attention of a man forcing himself to see the truth. "Not long at all."

"Then we send word today." I moved toward the door, my mind already racing through what would be required. "Benaiah can carry the message. He knows the Jerusalem roads well, and his loyalty is beyond question."

Benaiah was one of our younger servants, swift of foot and keen of mind, born on this estate and raised with the deep loyalty that comes from being treated as family rather than mere property. If anyone could be trusted with such a mission, it was he.

"What will you tell your father?" Ezra asked.

"The truth, plain and simple. That Deborah is dying, and I need him here immediately." I paused at the threshold, looking back at the woman who had been my anchor for so many years. "And Ezra? Tell Benaiah to travel as swiftly as possible. He should rest only when danger or the donkey's exhaustion demands it, but let nothing else delay his journey. This cannot wait for anyone's convenience."

He nodded, resolution settling over his features. "I will prepare Benaiah for departure immediately."

With Shira keeping watch at Deborah's bedside, I spent the rest of the morning gathering what the road would require—silver coins wrapped carefully in soft cloth, dried meat and hard loaves that would not spoil, and a waterskin filled with our finest wine for strength and bargaining. The familiar routine of preparation steadied my shaking hands.

When Benaiah appeared in the courtyard leading one of our most reliable donkeys, his calm demeanor reassured me. "My lady," he said, bowing respectfully. "Ezra tells me you have urgent business with Lord Joseph."

"The most urgent business possible." I placed into his hands the letter I had written, sealed with my father's signet ring. The wax still bore the clear impression of our family mark. "Find Joseph of Arimathea in Jerusalem. Give this message to no one else. Place it directly in his hands."

"And if he is not in Jerusalem when I arrive?"

"Then follow him wherever his duties have taken him. Tell him that Deborah lies dying, and his daughter needs him. Let nothing turn you from this task."

He tucked the letter securely into his tunic and swung himself onto the donkey's back. The animal shifted beneath him, restless, sensing the urgency. For a moment Benaiah met my eyes, and I saw my own fear reflected there. Then without further words, he kicked the donkey into motion and rode through our gates. I watched until he disappeared around the bend in the road, dust hanging in the air where he had been.

I returned to Deborah's chamber to find Shira carefully changing the water in our basins.

"Any change while I was gone?" I asked, though her expression had already given me the answer.

"None that I could see," she said.

"She managed a few drops at dawn," I told her, "but she has not truly woken since yesterday evening."

Shira lifted the bowl where I had steeped elderflower in cool water. "I have been trying, my lady, but she cannot seem to swallow more than the smallest amount at a time."

I kneeled beside the pallet and set my palm against Deborah's brow. The fever still burned there, as relentless as a forge fire. Her mouth had grown dry as old leather, her tongue slow and thick when I tried to give her water with a small spoon. When I pressed my fingers to her wrist, the pulse fluttered fast and weak beneath the skin. "Deborah," I said, hoping my voice would call her back to this world. "I have sent for Abba. He will come to us. You must hold on just a little longer."

Her eyelids fluttered at the sound of my voice, and for one precious moment, I thought she might wake and speak to me. Instead, she turned her head slightly and breathed my name, the sound no louder than air sighing through dried reeds.

"I am here," I told her, taking her cool hand in both of mine. "I am right here beside you."

The day dragged on, each hour feeling longer than the last. I tried everything my training had taught me and some remedies I only half-remembered—fenugreek and honey laid warm over her chest, elderflower given drop by careful drop, even the old practice of cupping with heated pottery bowls, though my hands shook so badly I could barely manage it. The red circles I raised on her back served only to mark my desperation and helplessness. Nothing worked. Nothing even slowed the fever's advance. Deborah continued slipping away from us, the pauses between her breaths growing longer before the small rush of air would return, leaving me to count and pray and count again.

Night brought no relief from our vigil, only the distant call of birds settling in the olive grove and the low sound of cattle being brought in from the hillsides. I dozed fitfully on a mat beside her pallet, waking each time the silence stretched too long, afraid she had stopped breathing.

Near dawn, Bubbeleh woke me with an urgent bleating outside the window. The old sheep had wandered close to the house and would not be quieted, her cries sharp and insistent in the darkness. I lifted my head, disoriented from the shallow sleep I had finally fallen into, my neck stiff from the awkward angle I had slept in.

I listened, and through the early morning stillness came the sound I had been praying for—hoofbeats approaching fast from the Jerusalem road.

I struggled to my feet, my body stiff after hours on the hard floor. By the time I reached the courtyard, the first gray light of dawn was touching the eastern sky, turning everything to shades of silver and shadow.

Two riders approached through the dim light, dust swirling in their wake like smoke. Even at that distance, even in the uncertain light, I knew the silhouette that could belong to no other man. The way he sat his mount, the breadth of his shoulders, the tilt of his head. Abba was here.

He dismounted before his donkey had fully stopped, nearly stumbling in his haste. The animal's flanks were dark with sweat and foam, its sides heaving. It had been ridden hard. Abba looked disheveled in a way I had never seen—his cloak askew, dirt coating his fine robes, his hair disordered.

Fear had stripped away his usual measured calm, leaving only a father who had ridden through the night to reach his troubled household. "How is she?"

"Dying," I answered, letting the word cut clean through the morning air. "Abba, I have tried everything I know, and nothing touches this fever."

He gathered me into a fierce embrace, his arms tight around my shoulders. He smelled of dust and sweat and donkey, of the road and exhaustion. I breathed him in, my face pressed against his chest. The tears I had been holding back for days finally came, hot and fast, soaking into the fabric of his travel-stained robe. I clung to him, grateful beyond words not to bear this weight alone any longer. My father had come.

"Show me," he said.

In Deborah's chamber, Abba stopped short in the doorway. I saw his face change as the smell hit him. His eyes adjusted to the dim light and found Deborah's wasted form on the pallet. Then he moved forward and kneeled beside her, his knees cracking with the movement. He placed his hand on her burning forehead, just as I had done countless times, and I saw his jaw tighten.

"How long has she been like this?"

"Six days," I said, my voice hoarse from sleeplessness and worry. "Perhaps seven now. The days have blurred together. Each one has been worse than the last."

"You have done well, Anna."

I nodded, unable to speak through the tears in my throat.

He remained quiet for a long moment, his hand still resting on her brow. His thumb moved gently across her temple. When he finally looked up at me, his face wore a panicked expression. He steadied himself with visible effort, but I had already seen it. My father, who never showed fear in council chambers, was afraid.

"Anna, there is... there is a man. Some say he has a gift for healing that goes beyond ordinary skill."

I waited, not wanting to reveal what I knew.

"Jesus of Nazareth," he said quietly.

I let out the breath I had been holding. "If he can help her, we must try."

"She is so weak," he said, his gaze moving back to Deborah's still form. "And even if we could reach him, there are no promises. The risks may outweigh any benefit."

For a heartbeat, I hesitated. Yet one look at Deborah's labored breathing burned away any doubt.

"And if we do nothing, Abba? She is the heartbeat of this house. If we lose her, the house may remain standing, but what good is it if those we love most are gone? A house without Deborah will be nothing but stone and silence."

He closed his eyes. In the stillness, I could hear Deborah's labored breathing, the sound that had become the rhythm of my days and nights. His hands clenched into fists on his thighs. A muscle worked in his jaw. Something held him back, though I could not name what.

"Please," I said, barely above a whisper. "I am asking you as your daughter. We must try."

He opened his eyes then, and I saw them bright with unshed tears.

"You are right," he said at last, his voice carrying new resolve. "We will find him."

"Thank you." I was no longer carrying this impossible hope alone. I took Deborah's hand in mine, feeling how light it had become, and silently promised her that help was finally coming.

CHAPTER 13

AFTER CALLING Shira to sit with Deborah, I went in search of Abba. I found him with Ezra in the main hall, their voices low as they bent over plans that had taken shape in the short time since his arrival. Neither man had slept. I could see it in the shadows beneath their eyes, in the way Ezra's hands trembled as he gestured.

"She will not last another day," Ezra was saying when I entered. "The fever burns too high. She keeps calling for Sarah."

Both men looked up, urgency written on their faces. Half-empty cups sat on the table. They had been talking over whatever food they could grab. A loaf sat between them, torn open but abandoned. Their focus allowed no room for hunger.

"Anna," Abba said, rising quickly, his movements stiff from too many hours bent over donkeys and scrolls. "How is she?"

"The same," I said, lowering myself carefully onto a

bench. Every muscle in my body ached from days of kneeling beside Deborah's pallet. My eyes felt hot and heavy, and my head thick with exhaustion.

"Anna, we need to discuss our plan," Abba said, his words carrying a seriousness I had never heard before, each syllable measured and found wanting.

"We have a plan?" I looked between the two men, hope stirring despite my exhaustion.

"We are going to find Jesus," he said quietly, the name spoken with the reverence reserved for desperate prayers. "All of us. Together."

My heart leaped. "You know where he is?"

"I do," Abba said. "The council keeps close watch on his movements, tracking him across Galilee. He has been teaching near Capernaum, by the great lake."

"How far? Can Deborah survive such a journey? She can barely swallow water."

"Three days of hard travel," Abba said, his voice carefully neutral. "Four or five if we take the easier paths and rest frequently."

"Four days?" I looked toward the doorway that led to Deborah's chamber, seeing in my mind's eye the fever's relentless claim on her body. "She may not have four days left."

"Then we travel as swiftly as we dare while being as careful as we can," Ezra said. "There is no other choice before us."

"There is no other choice. We must go and go quickly. If we meet trouble, I will do all the talking."

I nodded eagerly. I would be grateful for him to handle such matters. I would have more than enough to do keeping Deborah alive through whatever trials lay ahead.

"There is more to consider," he continued, his mind already working through dangers I had not yet imagined. "The roads north are not peaceful. Bandits prey on travelers, Roman patrols question anyone moving in groups, and there is anger in some villages against those who follow unusual teachers. Taking Deborah in her present condition will be difficult."

"We have to try," I said firmly, surprising myself with the steel in my voice. "She is worth any risk."

"Yes, she is. We will go," Abba said. "All of us together. We take the largest covered wagon, make her as comfortable as possible with cushions and blankets, and pray she holds until we reach him."

"So be it," I said. "We make ready."

"When do we leave?" Ezra asked.

"Today," Abba said without hesitation. "Before the sun reaches its highest point. Every hour we wait, she grows weaker. Let us gather what we need. Provisions for five days in case we face delays on the road."

Ezra nodded. "We will need flatbread, barley, dried figs, dried meat. A skin of oil for cooking. Water secured at all corners of the wagon."

"A spare strap in case one breaks. An extra pin for the axle. Blankets for warmth, thick cushions to soften the jolting," Abba added.

"The ridge road would be shorter but rougher," Ezra mused aloud. "The lower road has more patrols but gentler slopes."

"We take the lower road as far as the fig bridge," Abba decided. "Then cut up through the hills by the old mills. That should avoid the worst of both dangers. We will need men to help."

"Three should suffice," Ezra said.

"Benaiah, Simeon, and Joash," Abba replied without pause. "They understand discretion, and their loyalty runs deep."

"They will serve us well," Ezra said.

"I will tend Deborah throughout the journey," I said. "We will have to stop whenever necessary. Water when she can manage it. Cool cloths for her brow, and shade over her face at all times."

"Ezra, prepare the largest wagon with the leather covering," Abba said.

"I will see to every detail," Ezra answered. "Straps checked twice, blankets and cushions arranged properly."

"At once," Abba added, already turning toward action. "I will go see Deborah now. If she is awake enough to understand, I will tell her we journey toward healing."

Ezra inclined his head with the dignity of a man accepting a sacred duty. "All will be ready."

"Let us hurry," Abba said. "There is little time to waste. Anna, gather your things too. Whatever you need for yourself and to help Deborah."

They dispersed to their tasks, and the hall felt strangely hollow without their urgent murmurs. Only the familiar sounds of the house waking surrounded me now—the scrape of a broom across stone, the quick rush of servants' feet, the gentle sigh of a door closing somewhere in the depths of the villa.

The hours that followed were a blur of preparation and motion. The entire household moved with urgent purpose, everyone understanding without explanation that this day would change everything. A boy ran past carrying a waterskin, water sloshing with his haste. Tamar's shawl brushed the door frame as she hurried by with an armload of supplies.

I stepped into the courtyard for a moment of air before the work consumed me entirely. The morning sun warmed the stones beneath my feet, and for a heartbeat everything felt impossibly normal. My chickens clucked and pecked at the dust with their usual optimism, utterly unconcerned with fever or journeys or desperation. Goliath lifted his bright head to study me with one golden eye, his scarlet comb vivid against the pale courtyard stones.

"Keep order while we are gone," I told him, and he ruffled his wings, accepting the responsibility. Bubbeleh wandered over and nudged my palm with her soft nose. I stroked the rough wool between her ears and pressed my forehead against hers, breathing in the familiar scent of lanolin and sunshine. "Mind the house," I whispered, "and do not forget me." She huffed warm breath against my hands, and the smell clung to my fingers when I finally turned away.

I kneeled by the lavender bed, remembering the moment I heard God speak my name. I pushed my fingers deep into the soil, still cool from the night, the earth dark and crumbling beneath my nails. The lavender's sharp, clean scent surrounded me, mixing with the green smell of crushed stems. I breathed in its rich promise, letting it fill my lungs. "I will come back," I said to the bees that worked among the purple spikes, and they continued their labor as if they believed me completely.

While servants loaded the wagon with supplies, I gathered everything that might help Deborah survive the journey ahead. Glass vials settled into my palms with familiar weight, cool and smooth against my skin as I wrapped each carefully in soft cloth. The herbs whispered against the fabric, dried and brittle, each one a prayer I was carrying with me. I packed honey preserved in linen, hyssop for breathing, comfrey for pain, and thyme for strength. Reed splints, a needle, and thread in case of injury. Clean wool strips for bandages. The vinegar cloths sealed in a clay jar.

Tamar appeared at my elbow with an armful of traveling clothes.

"For the journey, my lady," she said, her young face serious with responsibility.

"What else will I need?" I asked, suddenly aware of how little I knew about travel beyond our estate walls. "I have never journeyed so far from home."

"Clean shifts for changing," she said. "Your warmest cloak. The nights can turn cold without warning. Sturdy sandals that will not fail you." She lifted my mother's silver bracelets from where they lay on the table. "These, for something of home to carry with you."

I packed the vials and pouches carefully beside my mother's journal, its leather cover worn smooth by years of faithful use. I ran my fingers over the surface, feeling the softness of the leather, warm from sitting in the sunlight that streamed through my window. Her handwriting was inside, waiting. Her voice captured in ink. If we fail — I pushed the thought away before it could take root and tied the satchel shut with determined hands.

Abba appeared in my doorway, his own preparations complete. "Are you ready?"

I looked around the chamber that had sheltered me for so many years. Everything appeared the same. I saw the bronze mirror, the simple furniture, and the window that looked out over my garden, yet I felt as if I were seeing it all for the last time.

"I believe so," I said.

"Anna." The way he spoke my name made me nervous. "There are things I must tell you during this journey. About our family. About Jesus. Choices I have made over the years."

My heart beat with the knowledge of my own secrets. "Abba, there are things I need to tell you as well." Andrew's face filled my mind, along with all the truths I had been holding back. And another truth, one that had been burning in me since that day in the courtyard. "About Jesus, the Teacher. When he was here—"

His head snapped up, his whole body going rigid. "Jesus was here? At our estate?"

I had not meant to reveal it like this, blurted out in haste before I had time to consider my words. But the words were out now, and there was no calling them back. "Yes. A few weeks ago. He came with his disciples, and he—" I stopped, unsure how to explain the moment, the way he had looked at me with recognition I did not understand. "He called me 'little cousin.'"

The color drained from my father's face. All of it, until he looked almost gray in the morning light. For a long moment he simply stared at me, and I watched him struggle for words that would not come. Fear flickered in his eyes, or maybe guilt, or some mixture of both that made my stomach clench.

"What did he tell you?"

"Nothing. He told me nothing beyond that." Frustration crept into my words, and my hands clenched at my sides. "I asked Deborah what it meant, but she said you had bound her to silence. Abba, what does it mean? How am I his cousin? Did he misspeak?"

"Anna—"

"Please. I need to know. If we are family to him somehow, if there is some connection to him—"

"We will discuss this later." His voice shifted, taking on the authoritative tone that brooked no argument. "Deborah is dying. That is our only concern right now. Everything else must wait."

"But—"

"Anna." He cut me off with a look that could have silenced the Sanhedrin itself, his voice dropping into the tone he used with recalcitrant council members. "I said later. We leave soon. Finish your preparations."

He turned and walked away before I could respond, his shoulders stiff with tension, his footsteps echoing down the corridor with the finality of a door closing.

The words tasted bitter. How many times in my life had I heard that? Wait, Anna. Not now, Anna. When you are older. When the time is right. Later. Always later.

I knew he was right. Deborah's life hung by a thread, and nothing else mattered in this moment. But knowing he was right did nothing to ease the questions I had, did nothing to fill the ache of not understanding my story.

I picked up my satchel and made my way toward the courtyard. We would save Deborah first. And then, perhaps, I would finally learn what everyone else seemed to know about who I was.

The courtyard was already full of activity when we emerged. Donkeys stood ready, their breath pluming in the cool air, forming small clouds that dissipated as quickly as they appeared. Oiled leather warmed under the strengthening light and released its rich, sweet scent, mixing with the smell of animal and nervous sweat. Men moved with purpose, checking straps and loads, speaking in low voices that carried the weight of what we were attempting. Dust motes danced where feet had disturbed the stones, settling back to earth in fine clouds. The great wheel by the olive press creaked once in the breeze and fell silent.

Ezra had prepared the largest wagon exactly as Abba had requested, its high sides covered against sun and rain. Blankets and cushions created a small sanctuary in the wagon bed, and there Deborah lay now, barely conscious, her skin as pale as old parchment in the morning light.

Three men stood beside their mounts—Benaiah, Simeon from the olive groves and Joash from the vineyard. The donkeys snorted and stamped their feet, eager to be moving.

"They understand the dangers we may face," Abba said, following my gaze. "And they know we must pass quietly, without drawing unwanted attention."

I climbed into the wagon beside Deborah, settling myself as comfortably as I could manage. The cushions would soften the worst jolts, and I could endure whatever else came.

Abba swung into his saddle and looked back at our small expedition. "Ready?"

I placed my palm flat against the wagon's planks and nodded once. We were as ready as hope and desperation could make us.

The wagon lurched into motion with a jolt that made Deborah moan softly. Wheels creaked in protest, wood groaning against wood. Dirt rose in golden clouds that tasted of clay and stone on my tongue, gritty between my teeth. I braced myself against the wagon's side, already feeling every rut and stone in the road through the boards beneath me. I looked back once at the villa that had been my entire world. The white walls gleamed in the morning sun. The olive trees cast their familiar shadows across stones I knew like my own hands. The garden where God first spoke my name. The courtyard where Andrew had fallen into my life and changed everything. All of it growing smaller behind me with each turn of the wheel.

At the outer gate, Shira stood waiting in her simple robe, both hands wrapped around the spindle Deborah had given her when the fever first took hold. She held it pressed to her breast, trying to keep our household together through the strength of a single thread. She did not wave or call out. She simply stood, small and still against the weathered stone, until distance and dust erased her from my sight. The thread she clutched was thin, but I felt it stretching from her faithful hands to mine across the growing miles. *I will see you again.*

As we took the road that led away from everything familiar, my thoughts flew ahead to Andrew. In a few days, if all went well, I might see him again. I remembered the way he had looked at me that last morning, the promise in his eyes. He said he would find a way back to me. Now I headed to him. Perhaps this desperate journey was the way God intended.

I watched Abba riding just ahead of our wagon, his back straight despite the weight he carried—Deborah's life, the dangerous journey, whatever secrets he had promised to reveal. The space between us felt wider than the few feet of road, filled with all the things we had not said to each other.

"There are things I must tell you," he had said. And I had my own truths to share—about Andrew, about what my heart had discovered in the weeks he had been with me. But those conversations would have to wait. For now, we had only one purpose: to reach Jesus before it was too late.

I turned my attention to Deborah, checking the dampness of the cloth on her forehead. The fabric had already grown warm, absorbing her fever-heat. I replaced it with a fresh one, my fingers gentle as I smoothed it across her brow. Her breathing remained shallow, rapid, each breath a small struggle. Whatever lay ahead between my father and me, whatever revelations would come on this journey, they would matter only if we kept this woman alive long enough to reach the healer who might save her.

CHAPTER 14

THE FIRST DAY of travel passed without incident, with steady miles covered, and Deborah's fever holding at the same dangerous level without worsening. We had made camp as darkness fell, eating cold bread and dried figs too quickly to taste them. I had managed perhaps three hours of fitful sleep on the hard ground before morning pulled me back to wakefulness, my body stiff, my hip a dull ache that promised to worsen with the day's travel.

The second day found us several milestones beyond the olive groves, the world washed in shades of unbaked clay under a sky gone white with heat. The donkeys blew into their feed bags, their breath stirring chaff and dust. Their ears flicked constantly at gnats, leather creaking as they shifted their weight from hoof to hoof. A breeze ran along the stones and carried the faint, clean bite of wild thyme growing in the cracks between rocks.

Deborah lay cushioned in the wagon bed with her head turned toward the light. Fever flushed the edges of her cheeks, but the rest of her had gone pale. I lifted her wrist and counted, letting the slight *thud* of her pulse settle my own. Too quick, too light.

Ezra rechecked the lashings by touch, tugging each knot once, then smoothing the strap as if gentling a skittish foal. Abba stood on the road and looked north, his cloak dark against the gray.

My hip had behaved through the night, much to my surprise. I set my palm over the cord at my wrist, where the little fisherman's knot rested against my skin. It held as Andrew had said it would. *Hold*, I told it. *Hold until I find you.*

We moved out quietly in the strengthening light. Ezra led the first donkey, one hand on the cheek strap, his smoothed branch in the other. Abba kept his donkey abreast of the wagon, angling his body to throw shade over Deborah whenever the road turned us toward the sun. I sat beside her, one hand on the sideboard, staff across my knees, counting the rhythm in my head. The servants spread around us—Joash walking ahead to pick the firmest track, Benaiah at the rear with staff and sling, Simeon leading the spare donkey and watching the ruts for trouble.

Fields opened on either side of the road, slick with dew that would burn away within the hour. Far off, a woman balanced two jars on a shoulder pole and watched us pass, her silhouette dark against the pale morning sky. She lifted her chin toward the east in greeting, the gesture of one traveler acknowledging another. The smell of damp earth and crushed mint rose from where our wheels had passed, green and sharp, waking hope in me that I would not name too soon.

Hours passed with the steady creak of wheels and leather.

The sun climbed, and the damp burned off the road. We halted once to rest the donkeys and cool Deborah's brow. She flinched at the first touch of water, then sighed and let her breath go.

"A shade farther," Ezra said, glancing at the sky. "Let us take the river crossing before the heat sits on us."

The fields gave way to low rock and scrub, the vegetation changing as water drew near. We followed the road as it curved toward the river, the air growing thick with the smell of mud and reeds and standing water. The temperature dropped slightly near the water, but brought with it a new humidity that made sweat bead on my forehead. By the time we reached the crossing, flies had begun their worrisome conversations with us, buzzing around the donkeys' eyes and landing on any exposed skin, and the heat rode along the bank in small waves that made the air shimmer.

The wooden bridge looked sturdy enough from a distance, but as we drew closer, I could see one of the support beams had shifted. The planks sagged at an angle that made my stomach clench, and the entire structure looked precarious and uncertain. Water rushed beneath it, brown and fast with spring melt from somewhere upstream.

"That will not hold our weight," Abba said, studying the bridge with the eye of a man who had built things.

Ezra climbed down from the wagon and walked to the water's edge, testing the ford with his staff. "Knee-deep here, but the bottom feels sound. We can cross, but we will need to be careful."

It was then that the wheel chose to betray us.

As Ezra guided the first donkey into the shallow water, the rear wheel caught on a stone hidden beneath the surface. The impact jolted through the entire wagon. I grabbed for the sideboard as we lurched hard to the left, tilting at a sickening angle. The crack of wood splitting came sharp and clear above the sound of rushing water—the unmistakable sound of something breaking that should not break. Deborah moaned as she slid against the wagon's side, and I threw myself across her to keep her from tumbling out of the wagon.

"Hold," Ezra called, but it was too late. The wheel had snapped two spokes clean through, and now wobbled uselessly, the rim scraping against the hub with each attempted revolution.

For a long moment, we all stared at the damage. No one spoke. No one moved. Water lapped around the donkeys' legs, the animals shifting nervously, sensing our distress. Somewhere downstream, a fish jumped and splashed back into silence. The sound felt impossibly loud in our stillness.

"Well," Joash said finally, "at least we are already wet."

Ezra waded to the back of the wagon, water darkening his robe to the knees, his face grim. He ran his hands over the broken wheel, testing each piece, his weathered fingers reading the damage. "The hub is sound, but those spokes--" He shook his head. "We cannot continue like this. First, we must get her to dry ground."

What followed was a struggle of ropes and muscle. The men unhitched the donkeys and repositioned them on the far bank. With careful coordination—Benaiah and Simeon pushing from behind while Ezra guided the front—they dragged the crippled wagon through the remaining water and up onto solid ground. The broken wheel scraped and complained with every turn, but it held together long enough to reach the muddy bank.

"Can you repair it?" Abba asked once we had settled.

"Perhaps. But I will need time, and proper materials." Ezra looked around at the reeds and scattered driftwood along the bank. "There is ash wood here, if I can find pieces straight enough. And we have rope."

"How long?" I asked, thinking of Deborah growing weaker with every hour.

"Half the day, if the wood holds and the Lord grants us no more troubles."

We made camp on the muddy bank while Ezra set to work. The servants scattered to help and gather materials. Joash searched for suitable wood while Benaiah collected stones to brace the wagon. Simeon kept watch on the road. I stayed with Deborah, bathing her face with river water and trying not to count her increasingly shallow breaths.

The repair work became a small miracle of craft. Ezra carved new spokes from the straightest pieces of driftwood he could find, testing each for strength and grain. He used hemp rope soaked in tree sap to join the wood to the hub. Where the wheel needed bracing, he wedged stones between the spokes and bound everything with strips torn from an old cloak.

"Will it hold?" Abba asked, wiping sweat from his forehead as Ezra emerged from beneath the wagon.

Ezra set his weight against the repaired wheel and rocked it gently. "It should. The wood is green but strong, and the rope will tighten as it dries." He paused, studying his handiwork with a craftsman's critical eye. "We will need to go slowly and avoid deep ruts, but yes, it should hold."

The sun had climbed to its highest point by the time Ezra pronounced the repair complete. Half the day was gone, just as he had predicted. We loaded Deborah back into the wagon with gentle hands, and I climbed in beside her once more.

We moved onward with careful attention at first, listening for any sign that our makeshift repair might fail. The wheel felt solid beneath the wagon's weight and followed the animals as it should. Dust rose and settled in veils behind us, and the road hummed beneath our wheels.

By noon, we had reached a village where we watered our team and replenished our supplies. We left with modest provisions and continued north.

Our repaired wheel struck a stone, then continued rolling. I maintained my grip on the wagon's sideboard and counted the rhythm beneath my breath.

Deborah slept suspended between worlds, where the soul hovered near openings without crossing them. I cooled her wrists and the hollow at her throat with water. The clean scent of thyme oil rose each time I smoothed the dampened cloth across her burning skin.

"Northern bend ahead," Joash called from his position. "I can see a place to rest."

We discovered a grove of trees where a narrow stream threaded through the stones, and poplar leaves clicked together in the breeze, the sound like distant rain. We drew our wagon into the shade, the temperature dropping immediately under the canopy. Ezra lifted Deborah onto a folded cloak with the tenderness of a man handling something infinitely precious, and I bathed her with light strokes, the old cloth moving over her fevered skin. Her parched skin drank in the moisture, and I watched color return to her lips, saw her throat work as if tasting the coolness.

She awakened gradually, consciousness returning in stages, awareness lighting different chambers of her mind one by one. First her fingers twitched. Then her eyelids fluttered but did not open. Her breathing changed, becoming less automatic, more intentional. The final lamp kindled behind her eyes, and for one clear moment, her gaze sharpened—present and entirely Deborah.

"Where am I?" she whispered, and the sound of her voice made tears spring to my eyes.

"On the Jordan road," I explained, hardly daring to hope this lucid moment might last. "We are traveling north toward the great lake, toward Capernaum."

"Why there?"

"You have been very ill with fever. Do you remember any of it?" I put my hand against her forehead. Still hot, but perhaps not quite as burning as before.

"No, I remember nothing." She closed her eyes and lay still for a moment, her chest rising and falling with the effort of speaking. I could see her gathering strength, pulling it from some deep reserve. "I have been dreaming constantly of your mother. She keeps speaking to me."

"Yes, you have been calling for her." I lifted the water cup and held it to her lips. "Can you manage a sip?" She took several swallows before sighing with exhaustion.

"Tell me truthfully, Anna," she said, with her old authority. "How serious is my condition?"

I paused, weighing how much to reveal. She deserved nothing less than honesty. "You have been burning with fever for more than a week now. Nothing I have tried has helped reduce it." Her eyes searched mine, and I saw the first stirrings of fear in their depths. "But you must not despair. We are traveling to find Jesus. We will reach him, and he will make you well again."

"That is good," she said, drawing a careful breath. "Anna."

"I am here beside you."

"You will tell me when we find him," she said, her voice barely audible.

"Yes, of course I will tell you," I promised. "We will find him."

"Do not let me die on this road, Anna." She spoke it not as a plea, but as an explicit instruction, in the same tone she had used when teaching me as a child to salt soup from a proper height so it would fall evenly. As though death were just another task that required proper management. "Do not leave me with strangers. Keep me with you."

"I will keep you safe," I vowed, gripping her hand more tightly. "You are mine to protect."

"If the one we seek finds me, but I am not aware of it happening, you will tell me about it afterward." Her grip on my hand strengthened with surprising force. "Every detail. Promise me this."

"I promise," I said. "But you will know, Deborah. I will not need to tell you anything." The cord at my wrist pulsed with warmth, and for a moment, the woven strands felt alive beneath my skin, responding to some distant heartbeat.

Her eyes clouded once more as the fever reclaimed her. She drifted back into those realms where consciousness goes during illness. I held a cup to her cracked lips and watched her manage a swallow.

We remained in that shelter until the heat released its grip on the road, then resumed our journey. I found myself eager to complete this traveling, knowing that each revolution of our wheels carried us closer to Deborah's healing and to Andrew.

. . .

By evening, we had covered more ground than I had dared hoped when the wheel first cracked. The repairs held. Deborah still breathed, though each breath seemed to cost her more than the last. And ahead of us, the road continued north toward Capernaum, toward Jesus, toward whatever healing awaited if we could arrive in time.

We made camp in a walled yard that offered protection from the wind. Abba broke our bread with tenderness. Simeon stripped the harness from the animals. Benaiah carried his sling to a patch of bare earth and practiced his throws while Joash kept watch.

Our supper consisted of barley simmered until it thickened. I crushed garlic and drizzled olive oil over our meal, the familiar ritual bringing small comfort.

Halfway through our eating, the quality of silence around us shifted. Joash lifted his head with every sense alert. "Someone approaches our animals," he whispered.

Simeon and Benaiah rose soundlessly to their feet. Ezra set down his bowl with care. Abba remained seated, but his stillness carried more weight than any movement could have achieved.

"Peace be with you," he called toward the edge of our camp.

A leather harness creaked in response.

"Come and sit with us," Abba called. "If you intend harm, we shall make you work considerably harder before you can accomplish it."

A young boy stepped into our lamplight's circle, his face half in shadow, half gilded by flame. His hand rested on the lead rope of our spare donkey, fingers already positioned to lead the animal away. Had we reacted one heartbeat later, he would have melted back into the darkness with our donkey in tow, and we would have woken to find it gone.

But then his eyes found Deborah's still form in the wagon, and he flinched visibly. His hand dropped from the rope as though it had burned him. For a moment he looked very young indeed, a child caught doing something he knew was wrong.

"Release the donkey and step away from it," Abba said firmly. He did, and Simeon moved quietly to secure the animal.

"Now come closer," Abba continued, his tone warming. "There is barley enough to share."

The boy hesitated momentarily, his eyes darting between us, calculating his chances. Then he approached with cautious steps, moving like a stray dog that had been kicked too many times. He lowered himself to the ground with his hands open on his knees, palms up. He was terribly thin. The bones of his wrists showed. Dirt darkened his skin, and his tunic hung in tatters.

"What name do you answer to?" Abba asked gently.

The boy attempted to deepen his voice beyond his years. "Who wishes to know?"

"A man who finds it unpleasant to eat while others go hungry," Abba replied, offering the bowl.

The child's defensive expression softened. "Yohanan," he said, accepting the bowl with both hands and obvious gratitude.

He ate with deliberate slowness, taking small portions and chewing each bite thoroughly, trying to make the food last as long as possible. Trying not to look desperate. When he finished, he returned the bowl with both hands and respectful care, his eyes downcast.

"Who instructed you to take our animal?" Abba inquired.

"No one," Yohanan replied.

"Then why were you attempting to steal our donkey? Where does your journey lead?"

"I need to go north," the boy answered. "To the lake. I heard there might be work available there."

Abba gazed thoughtfully into the empty bowl. "A young man with quick feet could be useful to travelers," he observed. "We often need help with the animals and supplies."

Yohanan glanced toward our wagon and Deborah's still form. "I possess little strength," he admitted.

"But you demonstrate considerable speed," Joash pointed out. "Swift enough to make off with the donkey and gain distance before a man with a sling could raise objections."

"I would certainly have raised objections," Benaiah said, fixing the boy with a stern stare.

"That much is obvious," Yohanan replied. "You have the appearance of someone who enjoys a good argument."

"We all enjoy arguing," Simeon said with amusement. "We simply choose different topics for debate."

"Would you consider walking with us when morning comes?" I asked.

The boy looked at me directly and nodded. "If you would accept my company."

"We would welcome it," Abba declared. "You will obey the men's instructions, assist the women as we direct, and cause no trouble for our party. In return, you shall have our protection and share our provisions fairly. Do you agree?"

The boy nodded gravely. "I agree to these terms."

"We are putting our trust in you. Do not make me regret it." Abba turned back to the fire, matter settled.

We organized our watch schedule and included Yohanan in the rotation. The men bunked down into their places around the camp, voices low as they spoke of the road ahead and what tomorrow might bring.

I lay down beside the wagon, close enough to hear Deborah's breathing over the normal sounds of the night—insects, a distant animal cry, the cooling of coals in our fire. My hand rested on the weathered wood, feeling its solidity, its faithfulness. The air carried the scent of dust and thyme oil and smoke, familiar and strange all at once.

When my eyes closed, I pictured the great lake, close enough now that I could almost taste its waters on the evening breeze. One more day. Perhaps two.

CHAPTER 15

THE NEXT DAY, the sun climbed as we drew near the Sea of Galilee. The air changed before we could see the water. It grew heavier, moister, carrying salt on every breath. Sharp and clean, it threaded through the dust that rose from our wheels in pale spirals and cut through the accumulated grit and sweat. The road widened here, no longer the narrow track that had tested our axles and our resolve. Other travelers joined us—merchants with laden donkeys whose bells chimed soft discord, pilgrims walking in small groups with staffs worn smooth by countless miles, families with children who ran ahead and circled back, restless and excited.

Deborah stirred as the wagon lurched over a stone, her hand reaching out to grip the sideboard for balance before her eyes even opened. When they did, they caught mine immediately, alert in a way they had not been for days. The fever still claimed her, painting her cheeks pink against the pallor of her skin, but her gaze had sharpened, aware and present.

"The lake," she whispered, voice cracking, dry from fever and thirst. "I can smell it."

I dampened a cloth with precious water and touched it to her lips, watching her throat work to swallow. "Yes. We are almost there."

Almost there. Almost to Jesus. Almost to healing. Almost to answers for the tangle my life had become.

Almost to Andrew.

My heart quickened at the thought. How many days had it been since he had left? How many nights had I fallen asleep counting them? I laid my palm on the cord at my wrist where Andrew's knot rested against my pulse, feeling it throb beneath my fingertips.

Ahead, Abba rode with his shoulders straight, but I caught the way his eyes swept the horizon, measuring distances and counting risks. I saw tension in the set of his jaw, in the way his hands gripped the reins just a fraction too tightly. Did something besides Deborah trouble him?

A group of travelers had paused beside a stone marker, their voices carrying on the morning breeze like smoke from distant fires. Their cadence made me lean forward, straining to hear over the creak of wheels and leather.

"—Paralytic walked again after years on his mat. When Jesus saw their faith, he said, 'Your sins are forgiven,' then commanded the man to rise and walk."

They spoke of Jesus, and their words fell on my ears, welcomed and desperately needed.

"And he did?" another voice asked, wonder threading through skepticism.

"Rose without effort, praised God, and walked out carrying the mat that had carried him."

Such healings were possible, I thought. Andrew had

spoken the truth when he described his teacher's power, and now strangers confirmed what my heart longed to believe. What I needed to believe. My hands trembled as I adjusted Deborah's blanket, pulling it higher over her chest, tucking it around her shoulders. The rough wool caught on my dry palms.

We rolled past them, but their words stayed with me. If Jesus could command paralyzed limbs to move, surely he could cool the fire that burned through Deborah's body. We just needed to find him.

The road curved, and suddenly the lake spread before us.

I had not been prepared for the size of it. Brilliant and vast, so much larger than I had imagined, stretching to the horizon like an inland sea. Its surface caught light and threw it back in scattered diamonds that made me squint. The water moved, restless with wind, deep blue near the center and turquoise where it met the shore.

The smell hit me next—fish and wet rope and water weeds. Along the nearest shore, men worked their nets, the hemp darkened with water, spread across the sand to dry. Their voices carried across the water, calling to one another in rhythms shaped by years of shared labor. Fishing boats dotted the surface, their brown sails full and straining. One was being pulled up onto the beach, four men heaving in unison, their backs bent to the work, feet digging into wet sand.

Gulls floated overhead, their cries sharp and insistent. The breeze off the water cooled the sweat on my face and carried the scent of reeds growing thick along the marshy edges where the shore gave way to shallows.

On the far shore, hills rolled green and gold toward distant mountains that stood purple against the sky.

It was beautiful. Achingly beautiful. And somewhere on those shores, Andrew walked.

"I see it," Deborah murmured, her gaze following mine, and I startled, not realizing she was awake. "Your mother always loved the water."

"Did she?" I had so few memories of her preferences, her joys. Each small revelation felt precious, drawn from deep waters I could not access on my own. I rested my hand briefly against Deborah's forehead. Still hot, but her eyes were clear.

"She said it reminded her that God's mercies are new every morning, washing clean what had been stained." Deborah's voice grew stronger as if the sight of the lake had awakened something sleeping in her spirit. "When you were little, she would take you to the pools near Arimathea and let you splash while she gathered watercress. You loved that. Do you remember?"

Tears blurred my vision until the lake became a shimmer of light and color, everything running together. I did not remember, but I could almost see it—a young woman, a child who knew no scars or limitations, small hands splashing without fear or pain. Water sparkling in afternoon light, bright and pure. Laughter. The life that had been before Romans and riots and blood changed everything. The life we should have had.

"You are feeling better," I said. "This is the most you have spoken in days."

"I have much stored up to tell you. Perhaps later." Deborah lay back and closed her eyes, a small smile playing at her lips. Her breathing steadied as she slept once more.

We passed more groups of travelers, their conversations filled with testimonies of healings and wonders that spread like wildfire through the common folk. Each story built the testimony higher, stone upon stone.

Near evening, we overtook a small caravan of several families traveling together for safety. An elderly man approached our wagon, drawn by the apparent signs of Deborah's illness.

"Peace be with you, travelers. I am Nathan of Bethsaida."

Bethsaida. Andrew's home.

My breath stopped. This man was from Andrew's village. Had walked the same streets. Perhaps knew his family. Perhaps had seen him as a boy, before he became a disciple, before he met me.

I leaned forward, my whole body straining toward this connection, this thread that led to him.

"We carry this woman to the Teacher," Abba explained, his voice carefully neutral. "She burns with a fever that will not break."

Nathan's face creased with sympathy, deeply lined from years in the sun. "You seek healing from the Prophet. A wise choice. I knew him as a boy, you know."

"You knew Jesus as a child?" I could not hide my eagerness, though I felt Abba's eyes on me like a physical touch.

"Indeed. A serious boy, always asking questions that made the scholars uncomfortable." Nathan chuckled. "I lived in Nazareth then, before moving to Bethsaida. Even as a child, he was drawn to the broken, the hurting."

"There was a fisherman's family in Bethsaida," I ventured, my voice carefully casual. "A man named Andrew. His brother is named Simon. Might you know him?"

The words felt dangerous leaving my mouth. A confession I had not meant to make, not here, not now.

I felt Abba's sharp gaze snap to me. His eyes narrowed

slightly, his whole body going still in that way it did when he was truly paying attention. I knew he had questions he could not ask in present company. I would answer them later.

Nathan's weathered face brightened with recognition. "Ah yes! Andrew bar Jonah. Good boy. Had a heart for the outcasts even then, always bringing home strays, human and otherwise—injured birds, homeless children, anyone who needed a meal or a kind word." He chuckled, shaking his head with obvious fondness. "The sons follow the Teacher now, both of them. Left everything to walk the roads with him."

"What kind of strays?" The question left my mouth before I could stop it. I needed to know. Needed to see the boy he had been.

Nathan's eyes warmed with memory. "Once, must have been ten years old, he brought home a beggar child—filthy thing, covered in sores. His mother nearly fainted. But Andrew had already promised the boy a meal, and you know how it is with children and promises. He would not be moved." Nathan shook his head. "Sat with that child while he ate, talking to him like he was a visiting dignitary. His mother fed the boy, of course. What else could she do?"

"And the birds?" I asked, remembering Nathan's mention of them.

"Any injured creature within a mile somehow found its way to Andrew's door. Sparrows with broken wings, a dove that had flown into a wall. Most died despite his care, but he tried." Nathan's voice softened. "That was Andrew. Always trying to mend what was broken. I lived nearby and spent much time with them then."

Longing rose in me so sharp it stole my breath and made my eyes burn with sudden tears. How I wished I had known that boy who gathered strays. I wished I had grown up on those same streets where Jesus asked uncomfortable questions and Andrew gave the broken and unwanted a place to belong.

Perhaps I would have been one of his strays. Perhaps he would have gathered me too, even then.

"These are dangerous times for those who follow unusual teachers," Abba murmured, his eyes still fixed on me with that penetrating look. His voice carried warning.

Nathan's expression grew serious, the levity draining from his face. "Indeed. Yet when the Messiah calls, can any righteous man refuse?"

Messiah.

It was spoken so naturally, as if the old fisherman did not doubt Jesus's identity any more than he doubted the sun would rise.

We shared the evening meal with Nathan's company, grateful for their fire and fellowship. As darkness fell like a gentle hand over the world, Nathan spoke more of Jesus, of teachings that turned the world upside down, of mercy extended to the undeserving.

"He says the first shall be last, and the last shall be first," Nathan explained, his voice dropping to match the intimacy of firelight. "It troubles the rulers, this talk of reversals."

"As it should," muttered one of the other men before spitting into the fire so it hissed. "Rome does not take kindly to talk of new kingdoms."

"Nor do the chief priests," added another. "There are whispers of orders to seize him, of plans to silence him."

Cold spread through me despite the fire's warmth. Andrew walked in the circle of that danger, following a man marked for destruction by both Rome and the Temple. One wrong word, one angry crowd, one Roman patrol in a foul mood, and he could be arrested. Beaten. Killed.

What had I hoped for? That I might somehow join that company, share that risk? The thought terrified me and drew me in equal measure.

I caught Abba watching me across the fire, fear in his eyes. He understood the gravity of what we were walking toward, understood it better than I did. Not just healing but a choice that could not be undone. A line that, once crossed, would change everything. It would make us targets and put us in that same circle of danger.

And still we kept moving north.

When Nathan's group headed for sleep, Abba rose and gestured for me to follow him away from the fire. We walked to where our donkeys grazed, far enough from the camp that our voices would not carry on the night air.

"Anna," he said quietly, his face grave, shadows pooling beneath his eyes. "We need to speak about things we should have discussed long ago. Things I should have told you years ago, but..." He stopped, seeming to search for words. "Come. Walk with me."

I followed him into the dark.

CHAPTER 16

HE STOOD in the starlight for a long moment, weighing his words. The night air had grown cool, raising gooseflesh on my arms, but I was not sure if I shivered from cold or nerves.

"You asked Nathan about Andrew specifically. Not just any fisherman from Bethsaida, but Andrew by name. Is this the same Andrew who carried a message to our estate weeks ago?"

I knew I blushed, could feel the color spreading from my cheeks down my neck. But I refused to look away. "Yes."

"What is this man to you, daughter?"

I could offer some deflection, some half-truth that would spare us both the awkwardness of this conversation. But standing here beneath the vast sky, with tomorrow's uncertainties pressing close, with Deborah dying and Andrew so near, I found I had no patience left for careful words. For pretending. For protecting my father from uncomfortable truths.

"He is the man I love," I said, my heart pounding. "And who loves me."

The words were said now, impossible to take back.

Abba's breath escaped him in a rush. His eyes closed, and his whole body went rigid.

"Anna— "

"He was carrying a message for you when bandits attacked him on the road. He reached our gate more dead than alive," I continued, the words flowing now that the barrier had broken. "I tended his wounds for weeks. During that time, we came to know each other's hearts." My fingers found the cord at my wrist, touching it without conscious thought. The gesture of a woman reaching for proof. "He gave me this before he left. A fisherman's knot, he called it. One that holds fast when the pull grows strong."

"Tell me about this Andrew," he said. "Not simply that you love him, but about the man himself. His character. His intentions toward my daughter."

So I told him everything. About the stranger who had collapsed at our gate, about his gentleness when he saw my scars for the first time, his stories of miracles witnessed, his patience with Deborah's fussing, even his delight in my ridiculous chickens. I spoke of conversations that stretched through afternoon heat, of hope stirring in my chest after years of dormancy, of the moment when he had asked if I had ever imagined leaving Arimathea behind.

Abba's expression darkened as I spoke, his jaw tightening. "Anna, you were alone with this man for weeks. Without proper oversight, without—" He stopped, clearly wrestling with how to voice what needed asking. His hands clenched at his sides. "Did anything happen that should not have? Did he take liberties with your gratitude, your inexperience?"

"No!" The word came out sharp with indignation, louder than I intended. Heat rushed to my face again, but this time from anger rather than embarrassment. "He was gravely injured for most of that time, barely able to sit upright without assistance. Deborah was always present when we spoke. And he —" I searched for words that would make him understand. "He was honorable, Abba. More honorable than he needed to be. He could have taken advantage of my gratitude, my inexperience, my isolation. I was grateful, and I cared for him deeply. But he never crossed proper boundaries. He would not."

"You are certain?" Abba pressed, his voice gentler now but no less insistent. "You have led a very protected life, Anna. You might not recognize subtle manipulation, or—"

"I am certain." I met his eyes directly, letting him see the truth there. "He kissed my hand once. Nothing more. If anything, he guarded my reputation more carefully than I guarded it myself. When he might have claimed more, he chose restraint."

Relief crossed Abba's features, quickly followed by fresh concern. "Yet his feelings are engaged, as you have said. What expectations exist between you? What promises were exchanged?"

"None," I admitted. "He said he would find a way back to me, but, Abba, I cannot be certain he meant it. It might have been merely kindness meant to soften a painful farewell."

"You fear he spoke from pity rather than love."

The words stung, exposing my deepest terror to the light. "I fear many things. That gratitude masqueraded as affection. That he will see me among his fellow disciples—among whole, beautiful women like Tirzah—and realize how impossible a match we would make. Maybe I built my hopes on shifting sand, and I will arrive tomorrow and see in his eyes that he regrets the words he spoke to me."

Abba studied my face intensely, searching for something. We stood there without speaking. Only the distant sound of night insects and the crackling of the fire at our camp filled the silence. "When he looked at you, Anna," he said finally, his voice soft, "truly looked at you, what did you see reflected there?"

"Love," I whispered. "I saw love. And the possibility of a future I never dared imagine could be mine."

"Love is a powerful thing to exist between two people." Abba looked up at the sky, and I suddenly remembered him doing this very thing, teaching me about the stars in the night sky.

We would lie on our backs on the roof after dark, the stones still warm from the day's heat. He would point to clusters of stars and tell me their names—Kesil, Kimah, Ayish—his voice low and patient as he traced invisible lines between points of light. I could never quite see the shapes he described,, but I would nod as though I understood, just to hear him keep talking, to feel his presence beside me in the darkness, to know I was safe under that vast sky because he was there.

Then he stopped coming to Arimathea as often, and those nights ended.

I looked at him now, his face tilted toward those same stars.

"What do you know of his background? His family circumstances?"

"They are fishermen from Bethsaida. His father died three years ago, and Andrew still carries guilt over being absent when it happened. His mother fears for her sons' safety but takes pride in their calling. His brother Simon holds a position of leadership among the disciples." I paused. "They possess no great wealth, but they are honest people who work with their hands."

"So he has no wealth to offer," he said at last, the words more observation than question. "No property, no established home. He follows a teacher who may face arrest at any moment. By every practical consideration, he represents an impossible choice for a woman of your station."

I nodded, unable to deny the stark facts. Disappointment rose up inside me, bitter and dark.

"And yet you love him."

"And yet I love him." My hand rose to trace the familiar ridges along my cheek. "He sees worth in me despite these marks. He called me extraordinary, and when he speaks, I almost believe I could live a different life than the one I have known."

Abba's expression changed, and I felt a spark of hope. "There is much I must consider," he said carefully. "But first, Anna, there are truths about our family you must learn. Things I should have told you long ago." He extended his hand toward me.

Finally, he was going to tell me.

Abba closed his eyes, and I watched the seriousness of this moment settle over him. "I knew this day would come. I have put it off for far too long." He drew a breath. "What did Deborah tell you when you asked her about Jesus of Nazareth?"

"Nothing." The word emerged bitter. "She refused. She said you had bound her to silence, that I would have to ask you myself."

He stood silent for a long moment, grief and regret

written in every line of his face. His mouth opened, then closed. Opened again. Whatever he was about to say, it was clearly difficult for him.

When he finally found his voice, it shook. "You deserve the truth. All of it." He took my hand in both of his, gripping it as though I might flee. His palms were damp. "When Jesus called you little cousin, he spoke truly."

"He did?" It was one thing to suspect a truth and another to hear it spoken so plainly.

"Jesus is Mary's firstborn child, and Mary is my niece. She is the daughter of my sister Anne—your aunt, though you have no memory of her. Your mother and Mary were closer than many blood sisters, despite the difference in their ages." His voice broke. He swallowed hard and continued. "They were devoted to each other."

Each word rewrote my understanding of the world. Rewrote my entire life.

Jesus was my cousin. We were family. The man whose name made Roman soldiers nervous and Pharisees angry. The man who healed the sick and raised the dead. The man Andrew followed across Galilee.

My cousin.

"When you were small, before your accident, you knew them all intimately," Abba continued, the words coming faster now. "Jesus played in our courtyard. He was a serious boy who knew much about many things. His younger siblings—James, Joses, Simon, Judas, and the girls Mary and Salome—they all called you cousin. You would run through the house together, leaving chaos in your wake." A smile briefly touched his lips, there and gone. "You and Salome were particularly close, always getting into mischief together. You were inseparable."

A memory flickered—sudden and bright and then fading. A girl with dark braids laughing. Small hands sticky with honey, reaching for mine. We were running through a courtyard, sunlight hot on our faces. She was calling my name, but I could not hear it, could only see her mouth forming the syllables. The smell of baking bread. Warm stones under bare feet. Her hand in mine, pulling me toward something I could not see.

I tried to hold it, this precious fragment. Tried to follow it back to more—to faces, to voices, to the feeling of belonging. But it slipped away like water through cupped hands, leaving only the impression of sweetness and laughter and a connection I had lost without knowing I possessed it.

Salome. My cousin. My friend.

Gone.

"I had a family," I whispered. "All this time, I had cousins. Brothers and sisters in all but name. People who knew me, who loved me. And I..." My hand went to my throat, where my breath felt trapped. "Why did you never tell me?"

"After your accident, after we lost your mother —" Abba's voice cracked. He closed his eyes, his face contorting with pain. "I could not endure seeing what our life had been. Mary's family was mourning too—her husband Joseph died shortly before your mother. The visits became too painful to bear for either of us. I convinced myself you needed peace to heal, that travel would prove too difficult for you in your condition." Shame filled his voice. "But truthfully, I was the one who could not bear it. Seeing Mary's children whole and running and continuing to laugh while you were broken and suffering—" He stopped, his jaw working. "I let the visits stop. I chose my own comfort over your need for family."

Cold spread through my chest.

"How do you know they were laughing?" The question came quietly, but every word was edged with ice. "After the visits ended, how would you know what they were doing?"

"Anna—"

"You kept visiting them." My voice sounded strange to me. "You went to see them. Without me."

He nodded, unable to meet my gaze. His shoulders sagged. "I did—many times. I would travel to Nazareth on business and call upon Mary and the children. They asked about you constantly. Every single time. Wanting to know when you would visit, how you were healing, whether you still remembered them. Jesus especially would plead with me." He paused, tears finally spilling down his cheeks. "He would beg me to bring you, saying he missed his little cousin terribly. That he prayed for you every night. That Salome cried because she thought you had forgotten her."

The betrayal hurt worse than any physical wound I had ever endured. Worse than the accident that had broken my body. This broke something deeper.

Nausea climbed up my throat. My vision swam. "They remembered me," I said, my voice shaking. "They wanted to see me. They missed me. And you told them what?"

"That you were too delicate for travel. That physicians advised against it. That your condition was too fragile, that you needed rest and quiet." He pressed his palms against his eyes as though he could block out the memory. "That perhaps when you grew stronger—" His hands dropped. "Lie upon lie, year after year. Mary would send gifts—small dolls she made with her own hands, honey cakes wrapped in linen, drawings from the younger children with your name written carefully at the top. I would accept them with gratitude and promises to deliver them." His voice went hollow. "But I never brought them home to you."

"Where are they? Do you still have them?"

"Yes." He looked at me then, forcing himself to meet my eyes, to let me see his shame fully. "In my chambers. In Arimathea. In a locked chest."

The locked chest. The one I had found that day when I searched his room in desperate grief. The one I had tried to open, pulling at the lock until my fingers ached. All that time, it had held pieces of my stolen childhood. Gifts from a family I did not know I had. Proof that I had been loved, had been remembered, had mattered to people beyond the walls of our estate.

And he had locked it away. Kept it from me. Year after year after year.

I gulped down a steadying breath, and my heart felt like it lost its rhythm. *How could he do this to me?*

"I told myself I was sparing you the pain of longing for what you could not have," Abba continued. "But I was protecting myself from having to face what I had taken from you."

"All those years," I whispered. "They were asking about me. Missing me. Praying for me. And I..." My voice failed. I laid my hand on my chest where the ache throbbed. "I thought I was alone. I thought no one beyond the estate walls cared whether I lived or died. I thought—" The tears came then, spilling over before I could stop them. "I thought I was forgotten. Unwanted. Too broken to be worth loving."

"No, Anna—"

"And all that time," I continued through tears, "all that time they were asking for me. Jesus was begging you to bring me. And you just... you just kept visiting them without me.

Kept accepting their gifts and lying about why I could not come."

He took a deep breath. "There is more. Mary has a cousin named Elizabeth. You might have heard of her son, John the Baptizer. He and Jesus grew up knowing each other, bound by blood and calling both."

I thought of the stories I had heard of the prophet in the wilderness. The stories Andrew had told me. "John the Baptizer is family to us as well?"

"Yes. The connections run deep, Anna. Deeper than I ever wanted you to know."

His shoulders sagged. "I should never have burdened Deborah with such a secret," he said. "She has carried it faithfully for years, watching you suffer in ignorance because I commanded her silence." When he raised his eyes again, they brimmed with fresh tears. "I always knew this day would arrive. Secrets have their own momentum. They always come to light eventually."

We stood in the vast silence, years of deception laying between us. Then Abba drew a trembling breath.

"Your mother would have wanted you to know your family. She would have wanted you to seek healing if such could be found. She would have wanted you to love and be loved, regardless of any scars or limitations." He began to reach for me but stopped. "I failed her. I failed you. I let fear rule me when love should have guided me. Anna, I have no right to ask this, but I must. Can you ever forgive me?"

Part of me wanted to rage at him, to list every year stolen, every gift hidden, every moment of loneliness that could have been filled with family. Part of me wanted to turn away and let him feel the full consequences of what he had done.

But then I looked at him and saw not the powerful councilman or the distant father, but a broken man who had made terrible choices from unbearable pain. Who had let grief poison love and had protected himself at my expense and now had to live with that knowledge.

"I forgive you, Abba." The words came out thick with tears. "I wish things had been different. I wish you had been braver. I wish I had known them, grown up with them, been part of that family. But I forgive you now."

His face crumpled. Tears came then for both of us, grateful and grieving all at once. I fell into his arms as I had not done since childhood, and he held me tight, my whole body shaking with sobs. He held me while I wept, and we clung to each other in the darkness, two people broken by grief, finding our way back to each other through honesty and forgiveness.

When the tears finally slowed, I pulled back, my breath still hitching with the aftermath of weeping. I wiped my eyes with the heel of my hand, and my fingers came away wet. The night air felt cool against my damp cheeks, against my swollen eyes. I felt wrung out, emptied, but also somehow lighter. As though a weight I had carried without knowing it had finally been set down.

We had spoken of so much lost, but perhaps something could still be found.

"Abba—Mary and the others. Could I meet them? When we return home, could you arrange it?"

"Yes." His face softened. "Of course. I will send a messenger as soon as we reach Arimathea." He paused. "Mary would be overjoyed, Anna. They all would."

Tomorrow loomed close, bringing with it uncertainties I could no longer avoid. I would see Jesus and ask him to heal

Deborah. And I would see Andrew and learn whether his promises had been real.

"I am terrified," I whispered. "What if Andrew's feelings have changed? What if he has grown to care for someone else? There is a woman who travels with their company. I saw how she looked at him, spoke his name with such tenderness. What if he has forgotten what we shared?"

"Then he will prove himself a fool unworthy of you," Abba said. "But you will know you possessed the courage to dream of love. That alone is more than many achieve."

"I hope Andrew is not a fool," I muttered, and Abba laughed. The melancholy of the evening broke, and we returned to the fire, walking hand in hand, father and daughter finally united by truth.

I returned to the wagon and checked Deborah's fever one more time, my fingers gentle against her burning skin. She stirred restlessly as the heat climbed with the darkness, her body fighting a battle she was slowly losing. I cooled her brow with fresh water and whispered prayers that felt desperate, cast into darkness with only faith to guide them.

CHAPTER 17

Dawn broke over Capernaum like an invitation written in gold and rose across the sky.

As our wagon crested the final hill, the sight before us stopped me cold. My hand tightened on my staff, and despair threatened.

The modest fishing village had transformed beyond all recognition, swollen into a sea of humanity that stretched from the stone houses to the water's distant edge. Hundreds of people pressed together in desperate hope—families with possessions bundled on their backs, merchants who had abandoned their stalls to seek something more precious than profit, pilgrims from distant provinces whose dusty robes spoke of journeys measured in weeks rather than days. Everywhere I looked, the sick were being carried on makeshift stretchers, loaded into carts, and supported on the shoulders of loved ones who had traveled impossible distances for this single moment.

The morning air thrummed with a symphony of need

and anticipation. Voices rose in a dozen languages, children wailed with exhaustion, donkeys brayed their complaints, and fishing boats splashed into the water despite the chaos that had claimed their shore. Smoke from countless cooking fires drifted across the scene, marking places where people had camped for days, unwilling to risk missing their opportunity. The very stones beneath pulsed with collective longing.

"My Lord Joseph," Ezra breathed, bringing our donkeys to a halt as we absorbed the magnitude of what lay before us. His voice sounded incredulous. "How are we to find him in this multitude?"

Panic fluttered in my chest. Three days of desperate travel, and now this. How could we possibly reach Jesus in such a crowd? How could anyone?

Abba urged his mount closer to the wagon, worry etching deep lines around his eyes. "The crowds stretch beyond counting, Anna. I fear we cannot get the wagon through so many people. And Deborah in her condition—"

I looked down at her still form in the wagon bed. The fever had climbed higher during the night—impossibly higher—and her breathing came in rapid gasps that barely moved her chest. Her lips had gone blue at the edges. Her skin had taken on a quality that I recognized from other patients, other deathbeds. We had traveled three days to reach this place, crossing dangers and difficulties that had tested us all. We could not turn back now.

But I also knew the truth: She was running out of time. Hours, perhaps. Maybe less.

"We carry her," I said, reaching for my staff. My hands trembled, but I forced strength into my voice. "However far we must go, whatever obstacles we face, we carry her to him." I would not fail her now.

Yohanan appeared at the wagon's side, his face set with the determination of someone who had survived by his wits. "I know how to move through crowds," he said. "I can guide us."

Joash and Benaiah exchanged meaningful glances, then nodded in unison. "We will fashion a litter," Joash declared. "Carry her between us."

Within moments, their capable hands had fashioned a stretcher from our spare cloak and two sturdy branches. I gathered my healing satchel, checking once more that the precious vials and herb pouches remained secure. These simple remedies seemed pitifully inadequate in the face of what was consuming Deborah, but they were all I had to offer.

As we lifted her from the wagon, her eyes fluttered open. For one precious heartbeat, awareness returned to them. The fever's fog lifted just long enough for her to see where we were and what we had done.

"We made it," she whispered. Wonder colored the words. Relief. "We made it."

"We made it," I confirmed, taking her burning hand in mine. "Hold on, Deborah. Just hold on a little longer." *Yahweh, help her hold on.*

Simeon remained with our wagon and animals while the rest of us formed a small procession of determination and desperation. We turned toward the crowd and entered the chaos. Yohanan darted ahead with the fluid grace of a fish navigating reeds, finding gaps in the crowd that my eyes could never have detected. Joash and Benaiah bore Deborah's litter with careful steps, keeping her as level as possible despite the uneven ground. Ezra walked in front of us, his walking stick moving people aside. Abba flanked our small group, constantly checking that we remained together.

I followed close beside the litter, my staff tapping out a rhythm that echoed in my heart: *Hold on, hold on, hold on.*

The density of people grew overwhelming as we descended toward the town center. Bodies pressed against us from every direction, some surging forward with desperate urgency, others sitting in patient resignation, and still others arguing in heated whispers about where the Teacher might appear next. The mingled odors of unwashed humanity, cooking food, and sick bodies created a suffocating atmosphere that made each breath a conscious effort.

A woman clutched at my sleeve as I passed, her fingers desperate with need. "Sister, have you seen him? The Nazarene? They say he will teach by the water when the sun climbs higher."

"We seek him as well," I managed, gently freeing myself from her grasp.

"He healed my neighbor's boy," she called after me. "Restored his sight with clay made from dust and holy spit! If you find him, tell him Rachel of Chorazin still prays for her daughter's eyes to open—"

The crowd swallowed her voice as we pushed deeper into the human river. Stories rose and fell around us. Each testimony added fuel to the fire that had drawn this multitude to a simple fishing village by the sea.

"There!" Yohanan's voice carried back to us above the noise. He pointed toward the water where boats bobbed at anchor like scattered leaves. "They gather by the shore!"

We pushed through the last wall of humanity and emerged at the edge of the crowd that ringed the sea. Here, people had arranged themselves in rough concentric circles on the sandy beach, all faces turned toward a single fishing boat anchored perhaps thirty cubits from shore. The morning sun glinted off the water, making me squint. In the boat's stern, a figure sat teaching, his voice carrying with miraculous clarity across the water and over the multitude.

Jesus.

My cousin.

The thought still felt impossible. Unreal. This man, who commanded such attention, who drew so many to a fishing village, who healed the sick and raised the dead, this was the boy who had played in our courtyard and had begged my father to bring me for visits.

Even at this distance, even when he was among hundreds of other men, I recognized him. The way he held himself spoke of quiet authority that needed no announcement, no decoration, no throne. When he spoke, the vast crowd fell silent as if his words carried their own commanding power. Peace radiated from him, washing outward in waves, touching even those of us at the crowd's edge.

He was here. We had made it. There was still time.

"Can you hear his words?" Deborah whispered.

I kneeled beside her litter, listening to what Jesus was saying. The natural acoustics of water and shore carried his voice with startling clarity. "Yes, I can. Can you?"

"The kingdom of heaven is like a merchant seeking beautiful pearls," Jesus was saying, his words reaching us across the impossible distance. "When he found one pearl of great price, he went and sold all that he had and bought it."

Deborah nodded. "He speaks of heaven."

"We need to get closer," I said, but even as the words left my mouth, I saw the impossibility of it. Between us and the water's edge, hundreds of people sat packed shoulder to shoulder. Many cradled sick loved ones, waiting for the moment when Jesus would return to shore and begin the healings everyone had come to witness.

"Anna."

The voice came from behind us, and I turned to see a familiar figure pushing through the crowd with purposeful grace.

"Joanna!" I rose, recognizing the woman who had traveled with Jesus to our estate. "You remembered me!"

"How could I forget Joseph of Arimathea's daughter?" Her eyes took in the litter and Deborah's condition with immediate understanding. "You have traveled far to reach us."

"We have," Abba said, moving closer with protective concern. "She hovers at death's threshold. We hoped—"

"He will see her," Joanna said with a confidence that calmed my racing heart. "Have no doubt of that."

Another woman approached, her bearing radiating competence. "I am Mary of Magdala," she said. "Bring her this way. There is shade available, and we have hands ready to help."

The two women led us to a cluster of trees where several other families had established small camps with their sick. Here, the crowd's intensity lessened, and we could spread a clean blanket for Deborah in the dappled shade. I dampened a cloth and laid it across her burning forehead. Mary knelt without ceremony, folded her traveling cloak, and slipped it beneath Deborah's head with gentle hands.

"Let your body rest now," she told her in a voice that carried years of experience with suffering. "We will keep watch over you." Then to me, quietly, she said, "Breathe deeply now. You have carried her far and well."

I nodded gratefully and looked toward the water where

Jesus continued teaching. "How long has he been speaking?" I asked.

"Since dawn broke," Joanna replied. "He will continue until the last person understands what they came to hear. Then he will heal until the last seeking soul receives what they need."

My eyes widened in amazement. "That could take a very long time."

"Yes," she said. "It may prove to be a very long day indeed."

Mary smiled at Joanna's words. "Long days are better with sustenance." She pressed a ripe fig into my palm. "Begin with this small strength."

Jesus's voice rose again from the boat, carrying another parable: "Again, the kingdom of heaven is like a net that was cast into the sea and gathered fish of every kind—"

A fisherman's parable, spoken from a fisherman's boat. I thought of Andrew and wondered if he stood in that vessel with his teacher. Wondered if somewhere in this vast crowd, he might find me.

"Anna." Abba's voice carried sharp concern. I followed his gaze, and my stomach twisted.

Moving through the crowd came a group of men wearing the distinctive robes of Pharisees and scribes. Unlike the desperate seekers pressing toward the water, these men moved with deliberate authority, their clean robes and carefully arranged phylacteries marking them as those who studied law rather than lived by the sweat of their brows. Their faces bore the pinched expression of those who had come not to learn but to entrap, not to witness miracles but to gather evidence for condemnation. Several carried scrolls tucked under their arms like weapons waiting to be drawn.

The crowd parted for them not out of respect but out of wariness, the way sheep give ground to wolves circling the flock. I watched mothers pull their children closer, watched men lower their eyes and turn away. These were the ones who could summon authorities with a word, who could declare a man unclean and destroy his livelihood, who held the power of the Temple and the ear of Rome.

"They follow him everywhere now," Joanna said wearily. "Searching for reasons to accuse him of wrongdoing. They count his words like coins and weigh his actions on scales of their own devising."

One of the religious leaders had stopped near our grove and was speaking in low, urgent tones to his companions. His gestures toward the crowd were unmistakably dismissive, and when a gust of wind carried his words our way, I caught fragments of his bitter complaints.

"Such fools," the man was saying during a brief lull between Jesus's parables. "Abandoning their trades and duties, chasing after signs and wonders like children pursue butterflies. What manner of kingdom could possibly be built on the hopes of fishermen and tax collectors?"

"A kingdom that will outlast your rules and regulations," said a voice behind him.

I could not see who had spoken through the crowd, but I knew that voice. I would have known it anywhere, had heard it in my dreams every night since he left.

The Pharisee turned sharply, and I gasped.

"Andrew," I breathed, and the fingers of panic I had lived with for days loosened their grip on my heart.

He stood with quiet dignity despite his travel-stained clothes. His face was fuller than I remembered, tanned darker by weeks on the road under an unforgiving sun, and his hair was sun-bleached at the ends. His eyes blazed with controlled anger as he faced down the Pharisee.

I took a step toward him before I could think. My staff caught on a root, and I stumbled slightly. Abba's hand steadied my elbow.

Then I saw her.

Tirzah. Beautiful Tirzah. She stood so naturally at his side, her body angled toward his, her face tilted up to watch him with obvious pride and affection, that they looked like they belonged together. Like a pair. Like two people who had found each other and would not be separated. Her hand lay lightly on Andrew's arm, resting there with easy familiarity.

A sharp shot of jealousy caught me so unprepared, I nearly staggered.

He has already chosen.

"Anna," Abba said quietly beside me. "Is that him?"

A sob caught in my throat. I turned, trying to push past him, trying to get away before Andrew could see me standing here watching them.

Abba's hand caught my arm, firm but gentle. "Wait—"

"Let me go," I managed through tears. "Please, Abba. I cannot—"

"Do not draw attention," he said, his voice low and urgent. "Not here. Not now."

I could not run. Not without drawing the Pharisee's eye and bringing attention to us.

I was trapped.

"You dare address me?" the Pharisee sneered with aristocratic disdain. "What could you possibly know of kingdoms, you who spend your days among nets and fish scales?"

"I know this," Andrew replied with even-tempered conviction. "I have seen the lame walk on steady legs, the blind receive perfect sight, the dead raised to new life. I have watched my teacher heal the sick with a word and cleanse lepers with a touch. I have seen him calm raging storms with a single word and cast out demons with a simple command. What signs have your laws and traditions produced? What lives have your countless rules restored to wholeness?"

Pride filled me at his words, not just at his courage in facing down a learned Pharisee but at the quiet dignity with which he defended his teacher and his faith. This was the man I loved, standing firm against religious authority without arrogance or fear, speaking truth with the confidence of one who had witnessed miracles firsthand. I longed to reveal myself and run to his side. Yet, seeing Tirzah there beside him, her eyes bright with admiration as she watched him speak, stopped me.

Beside me, Abba shifted slightly forward, and when I glanced at him, approval showed in his eyes as he watched Andrew speak. Here was a man defending his beliefs with reason rather than emotion, meeting scholarship with personal testimony, answering condescension with measured conviction. The councilman in my father recognized a worthy advocate when he encountered one.

The crowd around them took notice. Faces turned toward the confrontation, some nodding in agreement with Andrew's words, others watching nervously for the Pharisee's response.

"Blasphemy," the religious leader hissed through clenched teeth.

"Name another teacher whose word heals," Andrew called back, not shouting, but his voice carried clearly as the press of bodies quieted to listen. "If you doubt him, test him against the prophets you claim to teach. Isaiah promised that weak knees would be strengthened, and the stumbling made firm. Look around you with honest eyes. The signs are not merely ink on ancient scrolls. They are standing on their own feet."

The words rang out clear and uncompromising. Agreement rippled through the nearby listeners.

The Pharisee's face flushed deep red with rage. "You will answer for such words. Before the Council, before the authorities—"

"I will answer to God," Andrew said with unshakable calm. "And to my conscience. But I will not answer to men who strain out gnats while swallowing camels, who place heavy burdens on others while refusing to lift a finger to help bear them."

The confrontation might have escalated further, but at that moment Jesus's voice rang out from the boat, clear and carrying:

"Come to me, all you who labor and are heavy laden, and I will give you rest."

The words washed over the crowd like a cleansing wave, settling tempers and turning faces toward the water. The Pharisee shot Andrew a venomous look but moved away, muttering darkly to his companions.

Mary stepped closer to me. "Do not fear their words," she murmured. "They make much noise but possess little true strength."

I prayed for that to be true. For all our sakes.

Andrew remained standing where he was, breathing heavily as if the confrontation had cost him considerable effort. Tirzah's hand was still on his arm, and she said something to him in a low voice, her face full of concerned affection.

My stomach twisted at the sight. They stood too close. The easy intimacy of her touch on his arm sent cold through me. His body leaned slightly toward hers, accepting her touch, familiar with it.

I had been a fool to come.

I gripped my staff harder, preparing myself for the moment when his eyes would slide past me with polite recognition. But even knowing it was coming, I could not look away.

Then, as if sensing he was being watched, his eyes swept methodically through the crowd, searching.

Our eyes met across fifty cubits of humanity, and time stopped.

I watched recognition dawn on his face. First confusion, as if he could not trust what he was seeing. Then certainty. Then something so raw and unguarded I felt it in my bones.

Joy. Pure, uncomplicated joy.

The noise of the multitude faded to nothing, the heat of the day disappeared, and the mass of bodies around me became irrelevant. The ache in my hip, the weight of my staff, the exhaustion of three days' travel all vanished as though they had never been.

Everything narrowed to that single point of connection. To the way he looked at me—not with pity, not with obligation, not with the careful kindness one might show a wounded bird. But with the kind of seeing that reaches past skin and bone to the soul underneath.

He looked at me as if I were the only person in the world.

He looked at me like he had been drowning, and I was air.

In that moment, every doubt I had carried dissolved. The fear that I had imagined what we shared, that gratitude had masqueraded as love, that I was merely a story he told himself while wounded, all burned away in the light of that gaze.

He had not forgotten. He had been searching for me too.

Tirzah followed his gaze, her face changing as she realized who had captured his attention. The protective warmth in her expression shifted—understanding, perhaps, and unexpected sadness.

He said something brief to Tirzah, words that made her nod and step back gracefully. Whatever passed between them in that moment, it was clearly a farewell. He began moving toward us with the focused determination of a man who had found what he was seeking. People stepped aside almost instinctively, perhaps sensing the power of his purpose.

"Anna." He reached us in moments that felt like hours, stopping just close enough that I could see the gold flecks in his dark eyes, just far enough to maintain propriety before the watching crowd. "You came." He smiled at me, and his hands hung at his sides, clenched into fists as though he was physically restraining himself from reaching for me.

"You said you would find a way," I managed, tears falling that I had not realized were there. "I thought perhaps I should try to find one as well."

His smile widened impossibly further. "I would have come back," he said. "I was trying to figure out how, trying to find a way that would not—" He stopped, glanced at my father, seemed to remember where we were. "I was coming back to you, Anna. I promised I would."

"I know," I whispered. "I see it now. I see it in your eyes."

I felt Abba's presence at my shoulder, his protective instincts sharpening as he took in this reunion. Andrew remembered himself suddenly, tearing his gaze from my face to look at my father, and I saw him straighten with immediate understanding of who this must be.

"Sir," Andrew said, inclining his head respectfully while maintaining steady eye contact. "I am Andrew of Bethsaida. I was the one who brought you a message from my teacher some weeks ago."

Abba studied him with the careful assessment of a man who had spent years evaluating character in council chambers. "So you are the messenger." His gaze moved meaningfully between Andrew and me. "Though it seems you delivered more than just a message to my household. You have clearly won my daughter's heart."

Surprise crossed Andrew's face and then relief. A faint flush touched his cheeks, but he did not look away. "Yes, my lord. On all counts."

"We will speak of this matter," Abba said, his tone neutral but not unkind. "But first—"

Andrew's eyes had moved to the litter where Deborah lay, taking in her condition quickly.

"She is worse," he said, his voice full of concern.

"Dying," I whispered. "That is why we came. We hoped —" I could not finish.

Andrew kneeled beside Deborah's litter, his expression gentle as he studied her fevered face. "Deborah," he said. "Can you hear me?"

Her eyes opened, focusing with obvious difficulty on his face. "Andrew," she whispered, and the faintest ghost of a smile touched her cracked lips. "You found her."

"Actually, she found me," he said. He raised his eyes to mine, and my heart turned over in response.

"Good," Deborah breathed, her eyes drifting closed again. "That is very good."

Before Andrew could speak further, a woman's voice cried out from the crowd behind us.

"Anna? Anna, is that truly you?"

I turned to see who was calling my name. Running toward us through the crowd came a young woman with dark hair braided with colorful ribbons, her face radiant with joy and recognition. Though thirteen years had passed since we were children together in Jerusalem's marketplace, I would have known her anywhere.

"Miriam!"

She reached me in a rush of embraces and tears, her arms coming around me so tight I could barely breathe. I dropped my staff and wrapped both arms around her, clinging to her as though thirteen years could be bridged by the strength of our grip. We were both weeping and laughing at once, making sounds that were neither quite one nor the other.

My dearest friend. My companion in childhood games and secret whispers and dreams we had shared in the marketplace while our mothers bargained for cloth. She had become a lovely woman with clear brown eyes and the bearing of one who had found her place in the world. But underneath, I could still see the girl I had known. Could still recognize my Miriam. I picked my staff back up and regained my balance.

"I cannot believe it," she kept saying, holding my face in her hands as if to convince herself I was real. "When I heard Joseph of Arimathea had arrived with his daughter, I hoped, but I barely dared to believe—" She broke off, tears streaming down her cheeks. "Oh, Anna, I have missed you so."

Her fingers traced the air just above the scars on my cheek, not touching but acknowledging them with the tenderness of one who remembered their making. "That terrible day," she whispered. "I still dream of it sometimes—

the crowd, the soldiers, your mother..." Her eyes moved to my staff, to the careful way I balanced my weight. "I am so sorry for everything that happened. I wanted to find you, to see you, but my mother said it was too dangerous, that we must stay away from each other."

"And I longed to see you," I told her. "I have thought of you so often. I wondered if you remembered our friendship, if you were well, if you blamed me for what happened to us both."

A man approached, tall and kind-faced. He waited patiently for our reunion to run its course before stepping forward.

"Anna," Miriam said, turning with pride, "this is my husband, Philip. Philip, this is Anna, my dearest friend from childhood, the one I have told you so much about. And this is her father, Joseph of Arimathea."

Philip bowed respectfully to my father. "My lord Joseph, it is an honor to meet you. Your reputation for wisdom and justice precedes you throughout the region." Then he turned to me, clasping my hand with genuine affection. "Anna! I have heard your name spoken with such love and longing. Miriam has prayed for you so often, wondering how you fared, hoping for news of your welfare. And I know you from Andrew's stories as well—the skilled healer who saved his life."

My cheeks warmed as I glanced toward Andrew, who had stood at a respectful distance. "You spoke of me to others?"

"Only constantly," Philip said with a grin that made Andrew's color deepen further. "He could speak of little else for days after returning from Arimathea. 'There is this remarkable woman,' he would say, 'with hands that heal and a heart that—'"

"Philip," Andrew warned, glancing at my father, but his eyes held affection for his friend.

Miriam's gaze moved between Andrew and me, understanding on her face. "Oh," she breathed, then looked at our hands—for at some point during the reunion, Andrew had taken mine, and I had not pulled away. "Oh, Anna."

"We have much to tell each other," I said.

"Indeed, we do." She kneeled beside Deborah's litter, her expression growing serious as she took in the fever and labored breathing. "But first, let us see to this dear woman's healing. Philip, can you—?"

"I will speak with the teacher," Philip said, already moving toward the water's edge. "He will want to know that Joseph of Arimathea has arrived, and with such urgent need."

As Philip departed on his mission, Miriam came to stand beside me, her presence filling an empty place I had carried for thirteen years. "Tell me everything," she said simply. "Start from the day we were separated and leave nothing out."

"I will," I promised with a laugh. "As soon as Deborah is healed."

Around us, the great crowd continued to listen as Jesus spoke of kingdoms and seeds and harvests, of the mysterious ways of God made manifest in the world.

But I heard only the sound of my heart beating in rhythm with the gentle lapping of waves against the shore, keeping time until the moment when everything would change.

From the boat, Jesus's voice carried one final parable: "The kingdom of heaven is like a treasure hidden in a field. When a man found it, he hid it again, and in his joy went and sold all he had and bought that field."

In his joy. Whatever came next, whatever healing was

granted or withheld, I had found my treasure in this crowd of seekers, in this moment of recognition, in the love that had survived separation and would hold when the pull was strong.

The teaching was ending. Mary and Joanna moved through the clusters of people with the efficiency of those who had done this many times before, directing mothers where to wait, settling the weary, keeping hope from fraying into despair. Soon, Jesus would come to shore.

Soon, everything would be possible.

CHAPTER 18

"Soon" ended up taking longer than I expected. The midday heat pressed down on the multitude while Jesus continued teaching from the boat. My heart sank as his voice carried across the water with crystalline clarity, speaking yet another story to the crowds that kept arriving. *How much longer?* I thought, glancing down at Deborah's increasingly labored breathing. *Please finish soon.*

I sat beside Deborah in the dappled shade of the trees, one hand resting on her burning forehead. The vinegar cloth had grown warm against her skin. When I lifted it to dampen it again, her eyes fluttered but remained closed.

"How long can she endure this?" I whispered to Andrew, who kneeled on the other side of her.

He reached across Deborah and brushed my hair back from my face, his hand lingering on my cheek. "Not much longer," he said. "But Jesus will not let her slip away. I have seen him call back those who stood at death's very threshold."

Miriam sat close beside me, her hand a steady presence

on my shoulder. Every few moments, she would squeeze gently, a reminder that I was no longer alone in my vigil, that childhood bonds could bridge years of separation and still hold firm. Philip had not yet returned from the shore, and I scanned the crowd repeatedly for any sign of him approaching with word from Jesus.

"When will he finish teaching?" I asked Joanna impatiently. She had positioned herself where she could watch both Deborah and the boat.

"When the Father tells him to," she replied with the patience of one who had learned not to rush the divine. "He will not leave a single soul unfed."

Mary of Magdala joined us, a water skin slung over one shoulder, a small bundle tucked under the other. "Clean linens," she said. "And bread, if anyone can swallow." She took in Deborah's labored breathing and then looked at me. "You have done well to bring her here."

Around us, the great crowd continued to swell. Late arrivals came from all directions, and the air thrummed with anticipation as thick as honey. The needs of thousands falling on one man.

I caught fragments of conversation floating on the breeze: mothers worrying over feverish children who had not spoken in weeks, men speaking of limbs withered for twelve years, families who had carried loved ones all the way from Damascus on their backs. Each story was a thread in the vast tapestry of human need spread before Jesus. Though I grew frustrated with the waiting, I understood now why he would not hurry his teaching.

Abba stood near a cluster of olive trees, speaking in low tones with several men I did not recognize. Council members, perhaps, drawn by word that Joseph of Arimathea had arrived. I caught him glancing our way, his face unreadable.

"Your father takes a substantial risk by being here," Andrew said, following my gaze.

"I know." The seriousness of the situation weighed against my chest. "If the wrong people see him, if word reaches the high priest—"

"Then he will face whatever comes," Andrew replied. "A man does not travel so many days with a dying woman unless he has counted the cost and found it worth it. Love drives him."

Love drives him. The phrase wrapped around my heart like a prayer. "Is that what gave me the courage to come find you?" I asked.

Andrew's hand found mine, his fingers intertwining with my scarred ones. "Love," he said, "and the knowing that some things are worth any risk." His thumb traced gentle circles against my palm. "I would travel to the ends of the earth if it meant seeing you again."

I kept my hand in his. Here, where we were surrounded by thousands yet somehow alone in our small grove of trees, his touch felt like an anchor in a storm. "Andrew—"

"I know we must be careful," he murmured, glancing toward Abba. "I know there are proper ways to do such things. But, Anna, I need you to know that what I feel for you has only grown stronger in our time apart. If anything, it has become more sure, deeper, like roots finding good soil."

"My roots run deep as well."

A ripple ran through the crowd near the water's edge. Jesus had stopped speaking. In the sudden quiet, I could hear the gentle lap of waves against the boat's hull, the creak of wood, and the soft murmur of disciples preparing to row ashore.

"He comes," Joanna said, rising to her feet.

I watched with growing urgency as the boat began its slow journey toward shore. This was the moment we had traveled so far to reach, the culmination of days on dusty roads and nights spent praying over a woman I loved like a mother.

"Anna." Deborah's voice was barely a whisper, but it pulled me back to her side as surely as a rope.

"I am here," I said, taking her hand. Her skin felt like parchment, dry and fragile.

"Promise me something," she said, her eyes opening to find mine. For a moment, the fever seemed to release its grip. "Promise me you will not blame yourself if this does not end as we hope."

"Deborah—"

"Promise me." Her grip tightened with surprising strength. "I have lived long enough to see you grow into a woman of strength and compassion. I have seen you find love with a good man who treasures you as you deserve. If the Lord takes me home today, I go content."

"No!" The word tore from my throat.

"I have kept a list in my heart," she whispered, "of the times God surprised me. It is a long list, Anna. Add this day, whether I rise or rest."

Tears blurred my vision. "You are not going anywhere. Jesus will heal you, and you will live to see my children born and raised."

"From your mouth to God's ears. But promise me anyway."

"I promise," I whispered, though the words tasted like ashes in my mouth.

The boat scraped against the sandy shore with a sound that seemed to echo across the entire crowd. Disciples leaped out to drag it higher onto the beach, their sandaled feet splashing in the shallows. Then Jesus stepped onto dry land, and the crowd pressed forward like a tide.

"Make way!" Philip's voice carried above the noise as he pushed through the crush of bodies, clearing a path from the boat toward our grove of trees. "Make way!"

Andrew was on his feet at once, moving to help Philip carve a corridor through the crowd. Their combined efforts, along with several other disciples whose names I did not know, created a narrow lane from the water's edge to where we waited.

But the multitude was vast, and the sick were many. Between us and Jesus stretched a sea of reaching hands, crying voices, desperate faces turned toward the man they believed could change everything with a word.

"How will we reach him?" I asked, despair creeping into my voice as I watched the crowd close behind Philip like water filling a wake.

"We will not need to," Miriam said, putting her arm around me. "He will come to us. Do not lose faith."

And indeed, Jesus had moved deliberately through the crowd, not rushing but not pausing either. His hands touched heads as he passed, giving a blessing here, a healing there. I saw a hunched woman suddenly straighten, tears streaming down her face as she touched her spine in wonder. A man cast aside his crutch with a cry of joy and took tentative steps that grew steadier with each movement. A child blinked rapidly, then gasped and pointed at everything around him as if seeing the world for the first time.

Yet despite all the miracles happening around him, Jesus's gaze remained fixed on our small grove of trees. On Deborah's still form. On Abba. On me.

The crowd parted before him as if moved by an invisible hand. Perhaps it was the authority that seemed to radiate from him like heat from a forge, or perhaps it was the disciples working to clear his path, but somehow, miraculously, he drew steadily closer.

When he was perhaps twenty paces away, our eyes met across the crowd. A smile of acknowledgment crossed his face.

He reached our small sanctuary beneath the trees and stood for a moment looking down at Deborah, his face grave with compassion. The noise of the crowd seemed to fade to a whisper as if even the wind had stilled to listen.

A voice spoke from behind us, sharp with authority that cut through the grove's peace. "Joseph of Arimathea."

The words were full of accusation and danger.

Abba turned, and I watched his face change in an instant from the warm relief of reaching Jesus to careful neutrality, every line of his expression schooled into the mask he wore in council chambers. A man in fine robes approached through the grove, parting the crowd with the arrogance of one accustomed to making way. Young for a council member, perhaps in his fourth decade. His robes were finer than necessary and his phylacteries larger than most. Everything about him spoke of ambition.

His bearing marked him as learned, wealthy, powerful. But it was his eyes that frightened me most—hard with suspicion, already judging, already condemning. Already calculating.

I knew that look. The look of a predator who has found prey.

I stepped closer to Abba. Whatever this man represented, it was enough to make my father's face go blank with caution.

"Matthias," Abba said, his voice perfectly controlled. "What brings you here?"

"I saw you from the shore," Matthias said without preamble. "The Nazarene is present, spreading his lies to these ignorant masses, and I find a member of the Sanhedrin in conference with him, seeking an audience? Is there something I should know, Joseph? Are you a follower of this 'Teacher'?"

"Of course not. I am not among his followers," Abba said. His hands clenched briefly at his sides. "My daughter insisted we come. She believed this teacher might help her dying servant. I argued against it, but..." He gestured helplessly toward me. "You know how daughters can be. Stubborn. Irrational when emotion clouds judgment."

Matthias glanced at Deborah, pale and weak on her litter, not yet healed, and something like satisfaction crossed his face. "And clearly, your skepticism was well-founded. The woman still dies despite this charlatan's presence." His gaze sharpened, boring into my father's face. "Tell me plainly, Joseph. Do you believe this man has the power to heal? Do you think he speaks for God?"

The question opened its mouth to swallow my father whole. I held my breath and felt time slow as I watched Abba's face. This was the moment. The choice that would define everything.

ANNA OF ARIMATHEA

Around us, I could feel others listening. Disciples. Followers. Jesus himself, standing just paces away, his face unreadable as he waited to hear what his uncle would say.

"I believe in the God of Abraham, Isaac, and Jacob," Abba said carefully. He did not look at Jesus. Could not, perhaps. "Not in—" He paused, and I saw his jaw work. "Not in street performers."

The words fell like weapons. I felt them hit Jesus, though he did not flinch. Though I understood why he had to say them, those words hit me too.

"Good." Matthias stepped closer, his voice dropping. "Because there are those on the Council who wonder about your loyalties, Joseph. Your recent absences, some of your counsel, have been noted. I trust this foolish expedition has reminded you where your true allegiances lie?"

"My loyalty to the Council is unwavering," Abba replied.

"See that it remains so. You would be wise to consider your actions more carefully in the future." With a final dismissive glare at Jesus, Matthias departed.

For a long moment, no one moved in our grove. Jesus slowly turned to face Abba.

Abba could not meet his eyes. "Jesus, I—" he began then stopped.

"Uncle," Jesus said, and the single word held universes. No anger in his voice, no reproach, no wounded pride. Only understanding so deep it felt like mercy.

"I denied you." The words came out broken. "Called you a street performer. While you stood right here, listening to every word."

"You protected your family," Jesus replied simply. "And mine. There is wisdom in knowing when to speak and when to stay silent."

"How can you—" Abba's voice sounded incredulous.

"You were acting as a father. A man caught between two worlds, trying to keep those he loves safe." Jesus placed a gentle hand on Abba's shoulder. "The time will come when such choices become harder. But today, you did what love required."

Tears stood in Abba's eyes. "Can you forgive me?"

"There is nothing to forgive," Jesus said. "I know your heart, Joseph of Arimathea."

The two men embraced briefly, and I felt Andrew's hand tighten around mine as we witnessed grace in action.

Jesus turned to Deborah. "Peace, my daughter," he said, kneeling beside her. "I see your suffering."

Deborah's eyes opened, and when she saw who was beside her, such awe filled her face that she seemed to glow from within. "Lord," she whispered.

"You have served faithfully," Jesus said, his hand hovering just above her forehead. "You have been a mother to the motherless, a healer to the broken, strength to those who had none. The Father sees your love, and he is pleased."

"I have tried." Tears slid down her cheeks. "I have tried to be worthy."

"Worthiness is not earned, beloved. It is a gift given by the Father." His hand rested on her brow tenderly. "Be healed, daughter."

Deborah gasped.

I watched color return to her face, starting at her throat and spreading upward like dawn breaking. The waxy gray that had frightened me for days simply disappeared, replaced by the warm olive tone I remembered. Her lips, which had been cracked and blue-tinged, pinked. The hollows beneath her eyes filled. Her chest rose and fell, rose and fell, each breath deeper than the last. No more of that terrible shallow panting that had made me count each gasp and wonder if the next would come. She blinked, her eyes clearing as if a veil had been pulled away.

She turned her head and found Ezra. "Husband," she whispered, wonder in her voice.

Ezra's face crumpled. He dropped to his knees beside her, taking her hand in both of his, bringing it to his lips. "Deborah. My Deborah. Praise the Holy One!"

Then she sat up as if waking from an afternoon nap rather than fighting her way back from death's edge. Her free hand went to Ezra's weathered cheek, cradling his face with such tenderness that I had to look away from their intimacy. Then she turned to me, her eyes bright with tears and joy. "Anna," she said, her voice clear and strong. She looked at her hands in wonder, flexing her fingers. "I feel as if I could run to Jerusalem and back."

Ezra wiped his face on his sleeve, not bothering to hide his tears. "Run if you must," he said, voice unsteady, "but do not make me chase you. I am not built for speed."

Joy burst in my chest. I threw my arms around her, laughing and weeping at once, feeling the solid warmth of her embrace, the steady beat of her heart against mine.

"Thank you," I managed through my tears, looking up at Jesus. "Thank you." In his eyes, I saw such love that my breath caught. I stood and turned to him.

The plea rose from the deepest part of my heart, trembling on my lips before I could stop it. "Lord," I whispered, my voice barely audible even in the quiet that surrounded us. "Would you — could you—"

I could not finish. I could not bear to hear him say no. Fear bound my words and locked them up tightly.

But he knew what I could not say.

"Anna, your faith has brought healing to the one you love," he said. "That is gift enough for today."

"But—" The protest rose automatically. He shook his head slightly, and the words died on my lips.

Please heal me. Do not say no. Please.

His hand lifted toward my face, and for one wild moment, I thought he might change his mind.

His palm cupped my cheek, and I waited for the healing to come.

Nothing changed.

My hip still ached. My staff still bore my weight. My body remained as it had been, as it would always be.

"Have faith, little one," he said softly. "Your reward will come in its proper time."

But when? How long must I wait?

I could not say it aloud.

Why her and not me?

The thought came unbidden, and shame crashed over me immediately. What kind of person thought such things? Deborah had been dying. Dying. And I stood here wishing Jesus had chosen me instead, as if my limp mattered more than her life.

Heat flooded my face. I could not look at Andrew, could not bear to see if he had read the ugly thought written on my face.

I felt Andrew's hand find mine, and the shame burned hotter.

I should be grateful. Deborah is alive. That is what I prayed for. That is what matters.

But the disappointment still clawed at my chest, the wanting still ached in my bones, and I hated myself for it.

I blinked tears away as fast as they came.

"Anna, you think it is selfish to want wholeness. It is not. It is human." He paused, and something passed across his face—grief and longing tangled together. "Even I want things I cannot have."

I looked at him. For one moment, I saw past the miracles and the crowds to something I had not expected.

He understood.

Heaven had learned what it meant to ache.

I had told Andrew I would rather have Deborah healed than be healed myself. So be it. I was content for it to be so.

Across the small grove, Abba stood with tears in his eyes as he watched Deborah rise with renewed strength, while I remained as I had always been. Ezra had one arm around his wife, his face bright with wonder at her transformation, yet his eyes kept drifting to me with sorrow. This man had lifted me countless times when my hip would not bear my weight. He knew what I had just been denied.

Jesus's hand touched my cheek again briefly, a blessing and a promise combined.

I bowed my head in acceptance. "As you will, Lord."

His eyes held a hint of humor. "Now go help Ezra. He looks like a man who has forgotten what to do with a healthy wife."

Despite everything, I felt my lips twitch.

Jesus turned back toward the crowd, toward the next person waiting for healing. Around us, the crowd pressed closer, drawn by the miracle they had witnessed. Voices rose in praise and petition.

"Teacher, heal my son also—"

"Lord, if you would only touch her—"

"Please, Master, we have come so far—"

Jesus took in the sea of need surrounding us. "Bring them," he said to his disciples. "Bring them all."

Mary and Joanna helped organize the people, saying, "You are next," and somehow making the words ring true.

What followed was the kingdom of heaven unfolding on earth.

They brought the sick and injured forward one by one then group by group. Jesus moved among them, shepherding his flock, his hands touching every fevered brow, his voice speaking words of healing that seemed to remake the very air they traveled through.

Beside me, Deborah rose as if the wasting illness had been nothing but a bad dream. She moved with the grace I remembered from my childhood, when she had seemed capable of anything. Her eyes were bright with awe as she took in the miracles happening around us.

"How long since I have felt this strong?" she marveled, stretching her arms toward the sky. "How long since pain did not live in my bones?"

"I cannot say," I replied, smiling, still hardly able to believe what I was witnessing. "You would never admit weakness." I hugged her fiercely. "But I am so grateful, Deborah. I have you back."

"You see?" Andrew said softly, his eyes shining with emotion as he watched Deborah move through the crowd with renewed energy. "Did I not tell you he would not let her slip away?"

"You did." I squeezed his hand. "Thank you for believing when my faith faltered."

"Faith is not the absence of doubt," he replied. "It is choosing to believe despite doubt. You did that. Your love for

Deborah, your willingness to make this journey, that was faith in action."

I caught sight of Abba across the grove, watching the healings with an expression of profound amazement. This was perhaps the first time he had seen his nephew's power displayed so openly, so undeniably. The sheer magnitude of what he was witnessing swept away whatever political calculations had been running through his mind.

As the crowd thinned, Abba approached our small group. When Jesus saw him coming, he stepped forward, and they embraced quietly, briefly but warmly, the councilman and the teacher, kinsmen who were careful not to draw too much attention.

"Thank you," Abba said, his voice barely above a whisper as he looked at Deborah, radiant with new health.

Jesus's hand rested briefly on Abba's shoulder. "Love finds its way. Even when fear would silence it. And, Uncle, think no more of what happened earlier. It is forgiven and forgotten."

The use of the family term was for our ears alone, an acknowledgment of bonds that had to remain hidden from the world.

Jesus looked at us slowly, his eyes moving from face to face—resting on Deborah with a smile, meeting Abba's eyes with understanding, nodding at Andrew's protective stance beside me, and finally settling on me with such warmth that, despite my lack of healing, I felt somehow remade.

"Go in peace," he said, his words falling over us like a benediction. "And remember that love is the greatest miracle of all."

Jesus moved back into the crowd, and the disciples followed, guiding the next group of seekers forward. The grove felt suddenly emptier despite the number of people all around us.

I watched my father's face as he stood apart from our small group, his eyes tracking Jesus's movement through the people. Something had changed in him during the confrontation with Matthias. Some mask had cracked that could not be easily repaired.

"Anna." Abba's voice was strained and carried an urgency that made Andrew glance between us. "Walk with me a moment. Andrew, please stay with Deborah and Ezra."

Andrew turned to me, his eyes questioning. I nodded to reassure him, though uncertainty coiled in my stomach.

Abba led me away from the grove, toward a cluster of rocks that offered a small measure of privacy from the crowd. When we were far enough that our voices would not carry, he stopped and turned to face me. The lines around his eyes seemed deeper than they had been that morning.

"You saw what happened with Matthias," he said.

"I saw you deny Jesus to protect us." The words sounded harsher than I had intended. "I saw you call your own nephew a street performer while he stood right there."

"Yes." He did not flinch from the accusation. "And I would do it again, Anna, because the alternative is far worse than wounded pride or family shame."

I waited, my staff planted firmly in the dirt between us.

Abba drew a breath and glanced back toward where Jesus continued his work. "Do you understand what it means that Matthias saw me here? That he questioned my loyalty to the Council?"

"He threatened you," I said. "He said your absences have been noted."

"More than that." Abba's voice dropped lower. "The

Council has been watching Jesus for months now. They debate constantly about what to do with him—whether to arrest him, silence him, discredit him. Some want him killed, Anna. They call him a blasphemer, a threat to everything they have built."

A chill ran through me despite the afternoon heat. "But you are on the Council. You can protect him."

"Can I?" His laugh held no humor. "I am one voice among many and a suspect voice at that. They already question my loyalty because I have been too moderate in my counsel, too willing to consider mercy. If they discover our family connection—" He stopped and stared at the ground.

"What would happen?" I asked, though part of me already knew the answer.

"They would accuse me of conspiring against them. Of supporting a blasphemer who claims authority that belongs only to God. Of betraying my oath to the Council." His hands clenched at his sides. "They have the power to strip me of my position, Anna. To confiscate our properties, our wealth. To destroy everything I have built."

A wave of foreboding swept through me. "But surely they would not—"

"They would." The certainty in his voice silenced my protest. "I have seen them do it to others they deemed threats. Men who spoke against the high priest's decisions. Families who were deemed too sympathetic to Roman rule or not sympathetic enough. The Council's reach is long, and their memory is longer."

I thought of our estate in Arimathea, of the olive groves and vineyards, of the servants who depended on us. Of Deborah and Ezra who had nowhere else to go.

"If they strip me of everything," Abba continued, his voice rough with fear, "what becomes of you?"

I had no answer, but his eyes told me he did.

"You would be alone, Anna. A young woman with no male guardian, no protection, no means of supporting herself." He stepped closer. "Do you understand what that means? They could declare you unfit to manage your own affairs because of your condition. Appoint a guardian—some stranger who sees you as nothing more than access to whatever assets remained. Marry you off to whoever would take you. Some elder councilman looking for a young wife. Someone seeking control of what little fortune remained. Someone willing to overlook your limitations in exchange for the status of your name."

"No!" My hand tightened on my staff until pain shot up my arm. "Andrew would—"

"Andrew has nothing," Abba said, with brutal honesty. "No property. No wealth. No standing with the Council that would give him the right to protect you. They would crush him. He is a good man, an honorable man. But in the world we live in, love is not enough to protect a woman alone."

The full magnitude of what Abba was saying settled over me like a shroud. I thought he kept me hidden in Arimathea out of shame or grief. But there had been this too. A very real danger I had never imagined.

"How long have you lived with this worry?" I whispered.

"Since Jesus began his public ministry. Since his name became known throughout Judea and the Council began monitoring everyone connected to him." He rubbed his face with both hands. "Every day, I walk a knife's edge. I do what I can to protect him, to speak against those who would move against him immediately. But there are members who watch me, who have suspicions about me."

"The man today. Matthias..."

"Is one of them." Abba's voice was grim. "He will report what he saw to the others. That I was here seeking an audience with the 'Nazarene.' They will question me when I return to Jerusalem. They will demand I explain myself, prove my loyalty."

"What will you tell them?"

"What I told Matthias. That my foolish daughter dragged me here against my better judgment. That I argued against it but came anyway because Deborah was dying." His eyes met mine, and I saw how he struggled with what he was about to say. "That I was proven right in my skepticism."

"You will tell them Jesus refused to heal me," I said slowly.

He looked away. "If they believe I came here seeking miracles and left disappointed, they will stop looking so closely at why I really came. They will see me as a father who indulged his daughter's hope and learned his lesson." His voice dropped. "I hate it, Anna. But if it keeps them from discovering our true connection to Jesus—"

"Then do it," I said. "Use whatever you must."

Neither of us spoke for several moments. I could hear Jesus's voice raised in teaching, could see the people crowding close for healing. My cousin. My family. The man who had just saved Deborah's life and told me my reward would come "in its proper time."

The man whose ministry might cost my father everything.

I looked at Abba and saw not just my distant father, but a man who had been fighting a lonely battle I had not known existed. A man who had just denied his own nephew to keep his daughter safe. A man who would use her greatest pain as a shield if that was what survival required.

"What do we do now?" I asked.

"We go home to Arimathea. We keep our heads down. We do not speak openly of our connection to Jesus." He glanced back toward where Andrew stood with Deborah, clearly resisting the urge to come check on me. "And I must remain on the Council. It is the only way I can continue to protect him."

"Protect Jesus?" I asked.

"Someone must speak for him in those chambers," Abba said. "When they debate arresting him, I will counsel patience. When they demand immediate action, I will remind them that moving against a popular teacher could spark unrest among the people. When they plot against him, I will know of it, and perhaps I can delay their plans, plant doubts, convince others that wisdom requires caution." His voice grew firm with purpose. "If I am stripped of my position, Jesus loses one of his only advocates in the Sanhedrin. There are one or two others who question the rush to condemn him, but they are cautious. They will need someone willing to speak first to give them courage."

I had not considered this. My father was not just protecting our family. He was fighting for Jesus from within the very institution that threatened him.

"But that means you cannot openly follow him," I said. "You cannot be seen at his side."

"No." The word held resignation and grief. "I must remain in the shadows, playing the part of the skeptical councilman who tolerates his nephew's eccentricities but does not endorse them. It is a lonely position, Anna. But it may be the most important work I can do."

He put his hands on my shoulders and leaned close. "And you must decide what you want your future to look like. Because loving Andrew, joining yourself to Jesus's disciples, will put you directly in the path of the council's scrutiny."

"I have already decided," I told him. "I love him. I will not give him up out of fear."

"Then you must understand the cost." Abba's grip on my shoulders intensified. "The danger is real. It will only grow as Jesus's ministry continues. One day, the Council will move against him. And when they do, everyone connected to him will face consequences."

"Including you."

"Including me. And you." He managed a faint smile. "But perhaps by then, you will be safely married to a good man who will take you far from Jerusalem and the Council's reach."

We stood together in the fading afternoon light, father and daughter bound by love and fear and secrets that could destroy us both. In the grove behind us, Deborah laughed—the sound clear and joyful and impossibly alive. Beside her, Andrew waited for me, his steady presence a promise of the future I wanted despite all that came with it.

"We should go back," I said finally. "They will wonder what we are discussing."

"Let them wonder." But Abba released my shoulder and turned toward the grove. "Anna?"

"Yes?"

"I am proud of you. For making this journey, for your courage in seeking healing for Deborah, for choosing love despite your fears." He cleared his throat. "Your mother would be proud too."

Tears pricked at my eyes, but I blinked them back. "Thank you, Abba."

We walked back together, and I thought about everything he had told me. About the knife's edge he walked every day. About the danger that lurked in shadows I had never seen. About the price that love might demand from all of us before the story reached its end.

Andrew's eyes found mine as we approached, questions written clearly on his face. I shook my head slightly. I would tell him later. He understood, and his expression shifted to acceptance. He knew, as he always seemed to, that some conversations took time to unfold.

"Ready to go?" Andrew asked.

"Yes," I said. "I am ready."

CHAPTER 19

THE CROWDS SCATTERED as evening shadows stretched across the shore, families gathering their belongings and their newly healed loved ones for the journey home. Yet for all the miracles I had witnessed, for all the joy of seeing Deborah restored to vibrant health, my heart carried a heaviness. I had not admitted it to anyone, even myself, but I had come seeking healing for myself as much as for her, and I would return to Arimathea unchanged.

"Anna." Philip appeared at my elbow. "Simon Peter has invited your family to share his home tonight. His wife has prepared a meal, and there is room for all of you to rest properly before your return journey."

I glanced toward Abba, who was speaking with Ezra near the water's edge. "That is generous of him," I said. "But we do not wish to impose—"

"Nonsense. After what you have done for Andrew, they consider you family. Besides, Rachel has been cooking since she heard you had arrived. If you refuse, she will take it as a personal affront to her hospitality."

Mary appeared behind me. "Rachel keeps a generous table," she said. "And she has a keen eye for the weary. Go."

Andrew moved closer, picking up my satchel of healing supplies. "It would honor us to have you stay," he said. "And I confess, I am not ready to say farewell so soon after finding you again."

His words made something in me ache. One more evening. One more chance to sit beside him, to hear his voice, to memorize everything about him. I was not ready to say farewell either.

"Yes," I said. "We would be grateful."

Deborah, who had been bustling about since her healing with the tireless energy of a woman given a second chance at life, clapped her hands. "Wonderful! I am eager to meet this wife of Simon's. Any woman who can manage a household of fishermen and traveling disciples must have reserves of patience I could learn from."

"More than patience," Philip said. "Rachel has the gift of making twelve hungry men feel like beloved sons rather than burdens to be fed. You will see."

Abba and Ezra collected the last of our provisions, and the servants left to fetch Simeon and the wagon. I walked beside Andrew, our pace naturally slowing to accommodate my staff.

"Tell me about her," I said. "Simon's wife."

"Rachel?" Andrew's face softened with affection. "She is everything you would hope for in a sister-in-law. Kind, practical, with a laugh that can fill a room and a tongue sharp enough to keep Simon humble when his confidence outgrows his wisdom."

ANNA OF ARIMATHEA

"Which happens often?" I asked, smiling at the fond exasperation in his voice.

"Daily." He shook his head. "My brother has many gifts, but quiet reflection is not among them. He speaks first and thinks later, acts first and considers consequences after. Rachel has learned to smooth the wake of his enthusiasm."

We walked through Capernaum's narrow streets as the day's heat eased with Deborah close behind us. Children played in doorways, their voices bright with laughter. Women called to neighbors across courtyards, sharing news of the day's miracles. The scent of baking bread and roasting fish drifted from open windows, reminding me how long it had been since we had eaten a proper meal.

"Andrew," I murmured, mindful of Deborah's presence but needing to voice my thoughts. "The healings and power I witnessed today were beyond anything I had imagined."

"And yet you seem troubled," he observed, his eyes searching my face.

Deborah, with the intuition that had guided her through years of caring for me, touched my arm lightly. "Oh, look at that pomegranate tree," she said, nodding toward a courtyard wall where the fruit hung heavy and red. "I wonder if the variety grows as well in Arimathea. I need to take a look." She moved closer to examine it, giving us the privacy we needed.

"You are happy for Deborah and sad for yourself all at the same time?" Andrew asked.

I was quiet for a moment, choosing my words carefully. "Yes," I said finally. "I rejoice for Deborah. Yet I confess I had hoped—" I tapped my staff against the stone, the familiar click echoing my uncertainty.

"For your own healing."

"Yes. I know I should be content with what was given. I

know Deborah's healing is miracle enough for any lifetime. But I cannot help wondering why the Lord passed over me. I feared this would happen, and it did."

We stood in the shadow of a grape arbor, momentarily sheltered from curious eyes.

"I remember," he said. "Your lack of physical healing does not diminish your worth in God's eyes. Or in mine."

"I know that," I said. "Truly, I do. But—"

"Do you?" He stepped closer, his voice soft but earnest, and reached out to touch the cord at my wrist with one finger. "I know you wanted to be healed."

"I did. The scars for vain reasons, but my hip for more practical ones," I admitted, the words coming easier than I expected. "I am disappointed that it did not happen. Walking without pain would be a blessing."

"I wanted it for you, and I am sorry. But, I love you as you are, Anna of Arimathea." He grasped my hand. "Staff and scars and all. I will help carry your pain as I am able."

Tears gathered on my lashes. "You say that now—"

"I will say it when we are old and gray, when my own body fails and yours has carried you through decades of service." His hand moved as if to touch my face, then fell back to his side as he remembered where we were. "Your healing will come in God's time, if He wills it. But even if it never comes, you are complete to me."

A door opened nearby, spilling lamplight and voices into the street. We stepped apart, the spell broken by the reminder that we were not alone.

"Come," Andrew said, gesturing ahead. "Simon's house is just there, with the blue door. Rachel will scold us both if we are late for her meal." We waited for Deborah to join us before continuing on.

ANNA OF ARIMATHEA

The house was modest but welcoming, built in the practical style of fishermen who needed space to mend nets and store gear. Stone walls, whitewashed and weathered by lake winds. A small courtyard opened beyond the blue door, its packed earth swept clean, with a main room that could accommodate the occasional crowd of Andrew's fellow disciples. Oil lamps flickered from simple clay holders set in niches along the walls, their flames dancing in the evening breeze. The air was rich with the aroma of roasted fish, fresh bread, and herbs from Rachel's kitchen garden—rosemary and mint, sharp and green beneath the heavier scents of cooking.

"Andrew!" A woman's voice called, warm with pleasure. "You bring them at last!"

Rachel appeared in the doorway, and I liked her immediately. She was perhaps ten years older than I, with dark hair braided sensibly back and eyes that sparked with intelligence and humor. Her hands were dusted with flour, and she wiped them on her apron as she approached.

"You must be Anna," she said, taking my hand in hers with no apparent notice of the scars, "and Deborah!" She released me to embrace my second mother with genuine warmth. "Andrew has spoken of nothing but your skill as a healer, Anna, and your kindness in saving his life. And Deborah, he has told us how you raised Anna and taught her your healing arts. And how well you fed him!"

"He has spoken of us both?" Deborah asked with pleased surprise in her voice.

"Andrew's stories," Rachel said, laughing. "According to him, you are part healer, part ministering spirit, and part taskmaster when it comes to ensuring proper rest for patients."

"That sounds about right," I said, earning myself a playful swat from Deborah.

Before we could speak further, Abba appeared in the doorway with Ezra and our servants, having made sure our animals were properly settled for the night.

"And you," Rachel said, turning to him with a respectful bow of her head, "must be Joseph of Arimathea. My husband speaks of your wisdom in the council and your discretion in matters of faith with great respect. We are honored to host you in our home."

"The honor is ours," Abba replied. "Your kindness to strangers speaks well of your household."

"Strangers?" Rachel laughed, the sound bright. "Your daughter is Andrew's beloved, and that makes you our family too. Now come, all of you! The fish is perfectly cooked, and I will not have it ruined by ceremony."

Andrew's beloved? She had said it as easily as breathing, as if the whole world already knew what I had barely dared hope for myself.

She led us into the main room, where a low table had been set with more food than I had ever seen one woman prepare alone. Roasted fish gleamed with oil and herbs, its skin crisped to perfection, steam still rising from the flesh. Flatbread still warm from the oven was stacked in neat piles, each piece golden-brown and fragrant. Bowls of olives—both green and black, glistening with brine—sat alongside dates still on their stems and soft cheese that had been drizzled with honey. Pitchers of wine and water stood ready, their surfaces beaded with condensation in the warm evening air.

Faces turned as we entered, some familiar from this morning, others newly met. The sons of Zebedee, James and John, had claimed the far corner, all quick glances and shared grins, their energy barely contained even at rest. Matthew sat nearer the lamp, trimming figs with the tidy, precise care of a man who once counted other men's coins for profit. Simon the Zealot spoke in low tones with Nathanael, the tension that usually lived in his shoulders easing as conversation and laughter filled the room. Thomas lingered near the doorway, watching everything with the careful assessment of a man who trusted slowly. Mary of Magdala had already found Rachel's side, sleeves rolled up and ready to help, with Miriam beside her carrying a platter of bread.

I scanned the room once more. Tirzah was not here. Relief and guilt washed through me in equal measure.

Simon Peter rose from where he had been reclining near the head of the table, his large frame unfolding with surprising grace. Even in his own home, he filled the space around him.

"Joseph!" he boomed, clasping Abba's hands in both of his. "Welcome, brother. Your reputation for wisdom precedes you."

"Simon," Abba replied, and I heard genuine warmth in his voice. "I have heard much of your leadership among the disciples."

"You are kind to say so," Simon said with a grin. "Though I confess, leadership often means learning from my mistakes as much as from wisdom. Andrew here is the thoughtful one, the one who notices what the rest of us miss. I am better at charging ahead and asking questions later. Come, sit."

"As Rachel knows well," said a voice from the doorway. Jesus entered, followed by several other disciples I recognized from our estate. At the sight of him, we all rose, but he gestured for us to remain seated.

"Peace," he said simply. "We are all family here."

The easy intimacy of it struck me. The way he moved through Simon's house as if it were his own, the casual affection between him and his followers, the sense that this unlikely gathering of ordinary people had indeed become something like a family bound by more than blood.

At the table, I found myself placed between Andrew and Miriam, with Abba across from me next to Jesus. The conversation flowed as naturally as wine, touching on everything from the day's healings to the practical concerns of feeding multitudes to playful teasing about Andrew's cooking skills during their travels.

"He burns water," Simon declared, his voice carrying above the general conversation, earning laughter from around the table. Even Jesus smiled, his eyes lined at the corners. "Give him the simplest task—boiling barley, toasting bread—and somehow it becomes charcoal."

"I do not burn water," Andrew protested, his cheeks darkening with color. I could feel the heat radiating from him where he sat beside me. "That was one time, and there were other matters demanding my attention."

"What other matters?" I asked, unable to hide my smile at his discomfort.

"A beautiful girl washing her father's nets nearby," Philip said with a grin. "Andrew became so distracted watching her work that he forgot he was supposed to be tending the fire."

"That was years ago!" Andrew protested. "And she was not that beautiful."

"She was," Simon corrected. "But not as beautiful as some." His gaze flicked meaningfully between Andrew and me, causing me to lower my eyes.

"Simon," Rachel warned, but her voice held laughter. "Leave the poor man in peace."

"What peace?" Simon asked with mock innocence. "He has been wandering about like a man lost for weeks, sighing at clouds, staring at sunsets with that foolish expression. We all know what ails him."

"I do not wander about," Andrew said with dignity. "Or sigh at clouds."

"You wrote verses," Philip added helpfully. "Truly terrible verses about eyes like stars and voices like music."

"I did not—" Andrew stopped, looking mortified. "Did you read my letters?"

"Only the ones you left lying about," Simon said cheerfully. "Which was all of them. You have no discretion when your heart is involved."

I laughed despite my embarrassment, delighted by this glimpse into Andrew's private feelings. "Verses?" I asked, raising an eyebrow.

"Leave the poet his dignity," Mary said, smiling. "Bad verses are only seedlings. Some of them grow."

"These did not. They *were* awful verses," Andrew muttered, covering his face with his hands.

"I would like to hear them sometime," I said, and his hands dropped to stare at me in surprise.

"I would not subject you to such torment," he said. "They were truly dreadful."

Simon grinned. "Oh, they were, Anna. The worst. He once wrote, and I quote, 'Her eyes did sparkle like two startled fish.' Dreadful. He speaks the truth."

Jesus had been listening to this exchange with obvious amusement, but now he raised his hand for attention. "Before we embarrass Andrew further," he said, his eyes twinkling, "perhaps we should ask the blessing."

Around the table, heads bowed. James and John quieted

at once, Matthew's fingers stilled on the knife, and Simon the Zealot's hands lay open on either side of the platter as though giving up every sharp thing he had ever carried. I closed my eyes.

Jesus spoke the familiar words over bread and wine, and I felt the magnitude of the day settling around us. The conversation resumed, but the tone had shifted subtly. Jesus spoke of the journey ahead, of cities where they had been invited to teach, of growing opposition from the religious authorities.

"The Pharisees grow bolder in their accusations," he said, his voice carrying a note of sadness. "When I healed the woman with the withered hand, they questioned my authority. When I cast out a demon from the mute man, they claimed I do it by the power of Beelzebub."

"Fools," Simon muttered. "They have eyes but will not see, ears but will not hear."

"They see clearly enough," Jesus replied calmly. "They see that the kingdom of heaven threatens the kingdom they have built for themselves. They fear losing their place, their authority over the people."

Abba leaned forward. "What will you do when they move beyond accusations to action?"

Jesus met his eyes across the table. "What I have always done. Obey the Father's will and trust in His protection."

"And your followers?" Abba's gaze moved to Andrew, and I saw the concern of a man contemplating giving his daughter to someone who lived constantly in danger. "What of their safety?"

"I have told them what following me requires," Jesus said. "I have not hidden that the way is narrow. Each one must count the cost and choose their path."

"And no one has chosen to leave?" I asked.

ANNA OF ARIMATHEA

"Some have," Jesus admitted. "When the teachings grew difficult, when the way became harder, some decided it was not for them. I do not condemn them. The kingdom requires a sacrifice that not everyone is prepared to make."

Andrew's hand found mine under the table, his fingers intertwining with my own. The message was clear: He had chosen his path and would not be swayed from it, regardless of the cost.

Deborah, who had been quiet through most of this exchange, suddenly said, "My lord, may an old woman ask a question?" The silence that fell was immediate. Every conversation stopped mid-sentence.

Jesus turned to her fully, his expression open. "Of course."

She drew a breath, and I felt my stomach clench with anticipation and dread. "You healed me today. You brought me back from death's very door when I was hours from my last breath. Yet you did not heal Anna." Her words were plain, without accusation, but filled with a mother's fierce love. "Why?"

My cheeks flamed. "Deborah—" I began, horrified that she would speak so boldly in front of everyone, yet simultaneously overwhelmed by the fierce love that drove her to advocate for me even before the Lord himself. She would fight for me with her last breath, would challenge God himself if she thought it would win me healing.

No one moved. No one breathed. Part of me wanted to disappear into the floor, but the other part of me—the part that had wondered the same thing all evening—leaned forward, desperate for the answer.

Andrew's hand tightened on mine. Abba's eyes were on me. The entire table's attention focused on the exchange.

He was quiet for a long moment. The silence stretched, grew heavy. His eyes held mine across the table, and I could not look away, could not breathe, could not do anything but wait for his answer to the question that had haunted me since the beach.

"There are healings that smooth the skin," he said at last, his voice, "and there are healings that set a heart toward its work. Do not despise one for the other. Both are mercy."

We waited. The answer felt incomplete, like a door opened only halfway.

"Sometimes," he continued, his gaze never leaving mine, "healing comes in ways we do not expect. Anna's healing has been happening for weeks—in finding love where she thought none existed, in discovering family she did not know she had, in learning that her worth is not measured by the straightness of her spine or the perfection of her skin." He paused, and I waited. "For Anna today, it was the inward healing that was given. The outward healing..." He stopped. "The outward healing will come in its season."

"But surely," Deborah persisted, "physical restoration would be a blessing as well?"

I held my breath, my fingers tightening around Andrew's hand so tightly that he winced slightly, though he did not pull away.

"Indeed, it would," Jesus agreed. "And it may come, if it be the Father's will. But consider this, Deborah—" He leaned forward slightly, making sure she heard not just his words but his heart. "Would Andrew love Anna more if she were made whole in body? Would you treasure her more if she walked without aid? Would I?"

"Of course not," Deborah said immediately. "We love her exactly as she is."

"Then you see the truth," Jesus said gently. "Her worth is not diminished by her limitations. Her value is not measured by her wholeness of body." He turned his gaze toward me, and even I began to see.

"Her healing in the flesh, if it comes, will be a gift of grace, not a condition for love. She is already loved just as she is." His smile was radiant, filled with such warmth that I felt it like physical heat. "You are loved, little cousin. Never doubt that."

The meal continued with lighter conversation, and I memorized as many details as I could, knowing this night would become a treasure I would carry with me always. The way lamplight flickered across faces around the table, the sound of Rachel's laughter mixing with Simon's voice, Matthew's quiet chuckles from across the table, James and John finishing each other's sentences as brothers do, and the steady pressure of Andrew's hand in mine. Even Simon the Zealot, whose very name suggested fierceness, spoke with fondness about the day's events. This was belonging. This was family.

As the evening grew late, Rachel began clearing the table. "Anna, Deborah," she said, "I have prepared a room for you where you can rest comfortably. The men can sleep in the courtyard. It is warm enough, and they are accustomed to sleeping under the stars."

"Let me help," I said, beginning to rise, but she waved me back down.

"You are guests," she said firmly. "Besides, I have helpers."

Joanna, Miriam, and Mary moved with Rachel as if they shared one mind, stacking bread, trimming lamps, and clearing tables. They worked together, moving around each other without need for words, bodies angled to make room, hands reaching for what was needed before being asked. The ease of women who had done this many times before, in many different houses, with many different crowds, and would continue until the room was at peace.

I watched them work together and felt a sharp pang of longing so intense it almost hurt. What would it be like to be part of this? Not just for one night but always—to travel the roads with this group, to serve alongside them, to be one of the women who followed Jesus and cared for his disciples? To belong fully to this fellowship rather than standing at its edges?

But even as the thought formed, reality crashed down on it. I could not walk the distances they walked. Could not sleep on hard ground night after night without my hip seizing up. Could not keep pace with their constant movement from village to village, always staying ahead of trouble, always following Jesus wherever he led. My body would betray me within days, would slow them down, would make me a burden rather than a help.

My place was elsewhere. In Arimathea, tending my garden, healing those who came to me. However much my heart might wish otherwise, my limitations were real. Unchangeable. At least for now.

Andrew seemed to read my thoughts. "What is it?" he asked as the activity swirled around us.

"Nothing," I said, then caught myself in the deflection. "That is not true. I was thinking how much I would love to be part of this—" I gestured around the room. "This fellowship, this purpose. But I know my limitations."

"Do you?" he challenged.

Before I could answer, Jesus appeared beside us. "Anna," he said, "may I speak with you?"

I followed him to a quiet corner of the courtyard, where grapevines grew thick over a wooden trellis, their leaves rustling softly in the night breeze. The noise from inside was muted to a pleasant murmur—laughter and conversation blending into a sound like distant water. Stars had begun to appear overhead, bright and clear in the darkening sky. The air had cooled, carrying the scent of jasmine from somewhere nearby.

"You are wrestling with something," he observed, turning to face me in the dim light.

"Not wrestling," I said carefully, choosing my words. "Wondering, perhaps. Hoping for things that may not be possible."

"About your future," he said. "About whether you belong with us. Whether there is a place for you in this work."

His directness startled me into honesty. "How did you know?"

"Your heart is written on your face, little cousin. And your questions are wise ones." He sat down on a stone bench and gestured for me to join him. "You see this company and wonder if there is a place for someone whose body cannot keep pace with their spirit."

I nodded, not trusting my voice.

"What if I told you that belonging is not about what you can or cannot do? That the kingdom of heaven values the heart above all else, and measures worth by love rather than ability?"

I sat, grateful to take the weight off my hip. "I would say that sounds like comfort meant to soften disappointment, but not an actual answer," I replied, unable to hide the hurt in my voice. "Beautiful words that do not change the fact that I cannot follow you the way the others do."

Jesus smiled. "The Father's timing is not ours, Anna. He sees what we cannot see, knows what we do not know. Your heart's desire to serve matters deeply to Him. Trust that He will make a way when the time is right."

"But what if the time is never right?" The question burst out, raw and desperate. "What if I am meant to watch from afar while others do the work I long to do? What if my healing never comes, and my limitations never change, and I spend my whole life wishing I could serve you the way they do?"

"Then you would discover that love serves wherever it is planted," he said. "But I do not think that is your story."

"What do you mean?"

His eyes held mine with deep compassion, and in the starlight I could see the truth there. "I mean the Father delights in the desires of His children's hearts. What you long for—to serve, to be part of this work, to use your gifts for the kingdom—those desires matter. They were placed in you for a purpose." He smiled. "Be patient, little cousin. Your season will come. Perhaps not in the way you expect, perhaps not on the timeline you would choose. But it will come."

Relief flooded through me. My season would come. Not a maybe. Not a hopeful possibility. A certainty. "Thank you."

"For what?"

"For helping me see that being different does not mean being less."

He stood and extended his hand to help me rise. "True wholeness of the body can only follow the healing of the spirit. Remember that, Anna. In the days to come, you will need to hold fast to that truth."

As we returned to the house, I found Andrew waiting near the doorway, clearly having watched our conversation from a distance.

"Better?" he asked.

"Much," I said, meaning it completely.

Inside, the disciples were unrolling sleeping mats and arranging cloaks as blankets. Rachel led Deborah and me to a small chamber where a pallet had been prepared with clean linens and soft pillows.

"Sleep well," she said, handing me a small clay lamp. "Tomorrow will bring new challenges, but tonight, rest knowing that you are among friends."

Deborah lay down beside me and reached for my hand in the darkness. "A very good day," she said.

"One of the best days," I agreed, thinking not just of her healing but of all that had been revealed, of finding Andrew and reuniting with Miriam. It had been a perfect day. I fell asleep holding Deborah's hand and slept more soundly than I had in weeks.

CHAPTER 20

THE FIRST LIGHT of morning spilled through the narrow window of our chamber, pale gold touching the white-washed walls, and waking me with its warmth on my face. A cock crowed from the roof beams, his call sharp and insistent, answered by another somewhere down the street. The house stirred to life around us. Footsteps on packed earth, the scrape of pottery, voices rising in greeting. I could hear Rachel already at the ovens, her words rising and falling in cheerful rhythm.

Yesterday we had observed the Sabbath in rest—a gift after days of travel. Andrew and I had walked along the shore in the afternoon, while the household kept the holy day in quiet peace. But now the Sabbath had ended, and a new week had dawned.

I lay still for a moment on the pallet, my body heavy with the exhaustion that follows days of travel and high emotion. But my thoughts would not be still. Questions circled endlessly. What now? Will Abba insist we leave soon? Will I watch Andrew walk away again, disappearing down the road while I return to Arimathea, not knowing when I might see him next? Not knowing whether the promises made in starlight will hold in the harsh light of morning?

The smell of yeast and ash drifted in, mingled with the sharper tang of salt air. My body ached in its familiar places, but the ache seemed quieter this morning, softened by memories of the previous day. I remembered the laughter around Rachel's table, Andrew's fingers finding mine beneath the board, and Jesus's words spoken into the marrow of my bones: *You already belong. You are loved as you are.*

Deborah stirred beside me and sat up with a vigor that startled me. Her color was high, and her eyes clear. She smiled when she caught me staring at her.

"Do not look at me as though I am a marvel," she said. "I told you already. I have been restored. Thanks be to the Lord, and thanks be to the hands that carried me here."

"Then do not run yourself to ruin on the first day of health," I teased.

She reached over and patted my cheek, her palm warm. "Anna, you sound like me."

By the time I laced my sandals and made my way into the courtyard, the household had found its rhythm. Rachel's words set the measure, and even Simon kept time to it, though he would never admit to following anyone's lead but his own. Mats rolled, cloaks shaken out and refolded, sandals strapped tight. The small rituals of people who had learned to live on the move, ready to leave at a moment's notice.

But not today. Simon had said they would fish this morning.

Andrew worked near the well with the others, his hands moving through the familiar motions of checking rope. He looked up as I stepped into the courtyard, and whatever he had been saying died on his lips. His eyes found mine and held, and for a heartbeat the busy morning fell away.

He had looked at me as if I were the reason morning came.

Heat bloomed under my skin, spreading from my chest to my cheeks. I knew that look now. And I felt the same.

James and John had arrived from their dwelling just as the first light touched the walls, and they quarreled amiably over the mending of a torn strap on John's sack. Their words carried the easy irritation of brothers who had weathered a lifetime of minor disputes and emerged closer for the wear.

Matthew sat apart near the pomegranate tree, scratching careful notes on a parchment with the concentration of a man who knew that words, once lost, rarely returned unchanged. His stylus moved with precise strokes, capturing something—a saying of Jesus from the night before, perhaps, or simply the details that would help him remember this morning when years had dimmed its colors.

Simon bellowed orders that no one obeyed. "James, leave that strap alone. The rope will hold! John, stop helping him. You are making it worse! Matthew, come help!"

Mary moved through the chaos with calm purpose, her hands sure as she helped Rachel distribute the morning meal. I watched with growing admiration the way she anticipated needs before they were spoken and the grace with which she settled disputes with a glance or a quiet word. She was someone I could grow close to if given the chance.

Rachel appeared at my side with a tray of steaming bread, the crust golden and split with heat. "Eat before you scatter to the winds again," she said, placing a warm loaf into my hands. "You will need strength for what lies ahead."

"You heard her," Simon called. "Eat, then to the boats. The fish will not catch themselves. In this house, no one goes hungry."

Andrew set a jug of watered wine by my elbow and leaned close, his shoulder brushing mine as he settled beside me on the stone bench. "He always says that," he murmured, his breath warm against my ear, "but it is Rachel who makes it true."

Rachel overheard and snorted. "That is true enough."

Simon threw back his head and laughed, bread crumbs scattering into his beard. "A wise man marries above himself. Rachel is the best of us."

She flushed at the praise but did not contradict him, merely patted his shoulder before moving on to ensure that everyone had received their portion.

Andrew's shoulder pressed warm against mine on the stone bench. I could feel him breathing, could see the way his fingers broke the bread with care before offering half to James beside him. The gesture was unconscious, generous without thought. He listened to Philip's story with his complete attention, and when Philip finished, Andrew's laugh came full and genuine.

I wanted to be this for him. I wanted to be the one who made him laugh like Simon made Rachel laugh, who steadied him when the way grew hard, who knew his thoughts before he spoke them. I wanted to be the best of him, the way Rachel was the best of Simon.

I wanted to be his.

With the meal finished and the men prepared to head to the lake, Andrew found me near the doorway where my staff leaned against the wall, still holding a piece of bread from the table.

"Sleep well?" he asked.

"Well enough," I replied, though the truth was I had woken with my pulse pounding, torn between the joy of the last few days and the terror of parting from him. "I am worried about what happens now. I am not prepared to be without you again."

"Nor am I. I do not know what happens next, but I do know that our future lies together." He studied me for a moment. "You have looked lighter since you have been here. As though a burden has lifted."

"Perhaps it has," I admitted. "Though not the one you think."

His brow furrowed.

"Andrew," I said, "I am still lame. I am still scarred. But for the first time, I believe that does not make me unworthy. Jesus helped me see it. And that perhaps I have a story still yet to be written."

"I already knew all of that." Andrew's expression softened, and he reached out to touch the cord he had tied around my wrist so many weeks before. That simple fisherman's knot had become something sacred between us. "Then it holds," he whispered.

Before I could respond, Abba's words carried from the far side of the courtyard. He stood with Simon and Ezra near the well, their heads bent together, his features grave even in the softening morning light.

"Too many watchers in Capernaum," he was saying, his words clear enough to catch despite his lowered tone. "Too many questions are being asked by the wrong people. We must move on soon, before curiosity becomes accusation."

Jesus stepped into the courtyard just then, emerging from the guest chamber where he had spent the night in prayer. The morning light caught on his simple linen tunic, and his presence seemed to hush the air. Conversations stilled and movements slowed. Without a word spoken, every eye in the courtyard found him.

"You are right, Joseph," he said. Had he heard the entire conversation though he had only just arrived? Or perhaps he had simply known, the way he always seemed to know what was in people's hearts before they spoke. They way he always knew what was in mine. "The time has come to leave Galilee behind, at least for now. The authorities grow too curious. Too bold in their accusations."

"Where will you go?" Abba asked, straightening from his conversation with the other men, his mind already working through logistics and dangers. "My family will leave for Arimathea."

I darted a glance at Andrew. I could not leave for Arimathea now.

Jesus's gaze traveled over the assembled company—disciples, followers, family. It rested on Simon, on Andrew, on Mary and Joanna. On Deborah, standing strong and whole, still marveling at her restored health. On Abba, whose face showed the strain of secrets kept and risks taken.

And finally, on me.

His expression changed. A decision made. A path chosen. A piece falling into place in a pattern only he could see fully.

"Not Arimathea. Not yet. It is time for Anna to be baptized."

The bread in my hands suddenly felt too heavy. I set it down, my fingers leaving damp imprints on the crust. My name. He had said my name in front of everyone, as if I were one of them instead of someone watching from the edges. I could feel Andrew beside me, could hear Deborah's sharp intake of breath from across the stones.

His eyes held mine across the distance. "Prepare yourselves. We leave tomorrow."

Andrew turned to me with an excited smile. "John," he said, wonder and memory mixing in his voice. "We are going to see John. We are going to the Jordan."

The Jordan. Where heaven had opened and God himself had spoken, where Jesus had stepped into the current and risen with the Father's blessing. Where Andrew's journey had begun.

And now he would take me there.

John the Baptizer. My cousin. Family bound by blood I had never been told of, kinship I could never openly claim. Would he know me when he saw me? Would he see something in my face that marked us as kin? Or would I be just another seeking soul come to the river, one face among thousands?

But first, I would have to reach him.

"The Jordan?" My hand went automatically to my hip, already aching at the thought of such a journey. "But Andrew, I am not sure I can make so long a journey. Days of walking—I will not be able to keep up. I will slow everyone down."

Jesus had already turned toward the gate, his purpose complete. He did not wait for protests or questions, did not linger to explain or reassure. "Be ready," he said over his shoulder, and then he was gone, disappearing into the street before anyone could ask more, before I could voice all the fears suddenly crowding my throat.

The courtyard burst into conversation. Disciples turned to one another, already calculating distances, debating routes.

How many days to the Jordan? Which roads were safest? What supplies would we need? Simon's voice rose above the others, making plans, while Andrew remained at my side.

"We will go slowly," he said, taking my hand. "We will stop and rest when you need. Jesus would not suggest we all go if he did not have a plan in mind."

I nodded, but the pain in my hip did not agree. The Jordan. Perhaps a week or more on the road depending on the route.

"Do not worry, Anna," Andrew said, smoothing out the lines between my brows. "You can ride a donkey if needed or a cart. We will make it work. I will be with you every step of the way."

The day passed in a blur of planning and preparation. Instead of fishing, the disciples gathered what they would need for the trip, and the women put together enough food to feed us all on the road. I stood near the doorway where the afternoon air was slowly beginning to cool, my shoulders against the sun-warmed stone. My hip had stiffened from the day's activity, and I welcomed the support of the wall. Lamplight spilled from the interior, casting long shadows across the courtyard, and the smell of cooking drifted in the air—roasted fish and herbs. Mary moved to my side, her presence quiet.

"The Jordan calls to you," she observed.

"Does it show so plainly?" I asked, surprised by her perception.

"To one who has experienced her own washing," she replied, and her smile held knowing and memory both. "There is something about the promise of being made clean, of starting fresh, that speaks to the soul in ways we cannot always explain. It calls to the deepest parts of us—the parts that long to be free of what we have been, to step into what we might become."

"You sought John's baptism?" I asked.

"No." Her expression grew thoughtful. "My cleansing came through different waters, through tears of repentance and the Rabbi's healing touch. Through seven demons cast out, and a life given back to me that I thought was lost forever." She met my eyes again, and I saw what she was not saying, the darkness she had walked through to reach this light. "But I understand the longing for transformation, for the moment when everything changes. For the before and after."

She paused, choosing her words carefully. "The woman I was before Jesus found me is not the woman who stands here now. You would not know her if you met her. You would not recognize her at all, though we wear the same face, carry the same name. We are not the same person. That woman died. I live." Her voice dropped. "Whether by water or by word, true cleansing is death and birth in the same moment. It is the ending of one story and the beginning of another. And Anna —" She touched my arm lightly. "There is nothing else in this world quite like it. Nothing that compares to the moment when you realize you have been made new."

Death and birth. The ending of one story and the beginning of another.

I was still turning Mary's words over when a voice cut through the air from the courtyard. Sharp, formal, carrying authority. I turned toward the doorway and saw heads lift, hands still on half-packed bundles. The pleasant warmth faded.

A man stood in the doorway. A Pharisee, his robes marking him as clearly as if he had announced it.

"I seek Joseph of Arimathea." The words came out flat, formal. "I am told he lodges here."

I stepped back into the shadow beside Mary, my fingers finding the cool stone of the wall.

Abba had gone out earlier with Ezra to settle accounts with a merchant. He was not here.

Simon rose from where he had been checking rope, positioning his body to block the Pharisee's view of the rest of us. He scratched his beard as if thinking, his face taking on the pleasant confusion of a simple fisherman confronted with names too grand for his understanding. "Joseph? Ah, yes. The councilman from Jerusalem. He was here earlier, seeking directions to Caesarea. Business with Roman officials, I believe he said."

The lie came so easily that I almost believed it myself.

The Pharisee's mouth thinned. His gaze swept the room, lingering on each face. When his eyes found mine, I forced myself not to look away, not to give him anything he could use against us.

"Left this morning." Simon gestured vaguely south.

"Strange that a member of the Sanhedrin would visit a house known to harbor followers of the Nazarene." The words carried accusation beneath their surface.

"Is it?" Simon's voice held nothing but the bewilderment of a man who could not imagine why anyone would think such a thing odd. "He asked directions as travelers do. We answered as neighbors should. Unless the Council now forbids simple kindness to strangers on the road?"

"If Joseph of Arimathea returns," he said tersely, looking over Simon with open disdain, "tell him Malchus seeks him. I wish to speak with him."

"I will tell him if I see him." Simon's smile never wavered, though I saw the tension in his shoulders. "Though I doubt our paths will cross again. We are simple fishermen. Councilmen do not often seek our company twice."

The Pharisee turned to leave, then paused at the threshold. "You do follow the Nazarene, do you not?"

"We follow Jesus of Nazareth," Simon said, and something in his voice changed. "As do many in Galilee. Is that what brings you north? To count his followers?"

"To warn them." The Pharisee's eyes moved to me again, then away, as if I were beneath his notice, as if women always were. "The Council's patience wears thin. Those who attach themselves to false prophets often share their fate."

He left, his sandals sharp against the stone.

No one moved. No one spoke.

Simon broke the silence. "Well," he said, attempting lightness that did not quite land, "that was unpleasant."

Rachel appeared from the back room, her face pale. "Simon—"

"He believed it." Simon's voice held relief. "He is heading south to find Joseph in Caesarea. Do not worry."

Mary touched my arm, her fingers comforting against my skin. "Are you well?"

I nodded, though my hands shook. This was what Abba had warned me about. The Council was watching, tracking, asking questions.

Andrew appeared at my other side. He did not speak, but his hand found mine, steadying me against the trembling that wanted to claim my limbs.

When Abba returned a short time later, dusk was settling over the courtyard, painting the whitewashed walls in the colors of evening. Simon met him at the door and spoke in low tones, their heads bent together. The evening meal preparations had stopped. Rachel stood motionless by her cooking fire, a wooden spoon forgotten in her hand. I watched my father's face go still and glance toward me. Andrew's hand tightened on mine, his palm warm against my cold fingers.

Abba crossed to where we stood. I could smell the dust and produce from the market on him and the sharp tang of metal from the merchant stalls.

"Everything is well, Anna. Malchus found me in the market. He is a Pharisee from the local synagogue. Apparently, he had heard of my reputation on the Council and wanted to meet me, to seek my counsel on a legal matter. I told him I was bound for Caesarea. He accepted it and went on his way."

"But Abba, they know you were here. What if—"

"This time it was nothing." His hand found my shoulder. "But it could have been. We were fortunate. Still, we cannot stay here for long. We finish what we came here for, and then we leave."

I exhaled and willed my stomach to stop its rebellion. I turned to Andrew and laid my head on his chest. His arms came around me and held me tightly.

I thought of Mary's words. Death and birth. The ending of one story and the beginning of another.

My story was about to change.

CHAPTER 21

WE STOOD in Simon's courtyard, packs shouldered and ready for the road to Jordan. The morning sun shone through the grape arbor, warming the stones beneath my feet. I could taste anticipation in the air, sharp on my tongue. My first meeting with John, the promise of baptism, the beginning of something new.

Simon kissed Rachel in farewell and headed to the gate. We fell in behind him, Andrew smiling encouragingly at me. I prayed my body would cooperate on the trip.

Then Jesus raised his hand. "Wait."

We all stopped, confused. He tilted his head as if listening to something only he could hear. The disciples exchanged glances. Andrew stepped closer to me, his brow furrowed. My fingers found the smooth wood of my staff, gripping tighter as unease prickled along my spine.

Footsteps pounded on stone outside the courtyard wall —urgent, purposeful, moving fast. Coming closer. Everyone turned toward the sound.

The gate burst open with enough force to make it slam against the wall.

And there stood John the Baptizer.

The air itself changed. Thicker, charged, as though lightning had struck nearby and left the taste of copper on my tongue. Heat rolled off him in waves despite the morning coolness—the heat of a man who had walked far and fast under the climbing sun.

I knew him instantly, though I had never seen his face, had never heard his voice except in my imagination. But this could be no one else. No one else carried such presence, such wild holiness barely contained in human form.

He was tall and lean, all muscle and sinew and bone, his skin burned dark by sun and wind and years in the wilderness. A cloak of camel hair hung from his broad shoulders, rough and primitive, bound with a leather belt worn soft from constant use. His tangled hair fell well past his shoulders in dark waves. His beard was untamed, wild as a prophet's beard should be.

But it was his eyes that marked him as more than a man. Fierce. Direct. Burning with an intensity that made my breath stop in my chest, made me unable to look away even though I wanted to. The look of a man who had seen visions that would break lesser souls, who had spoken with God face to face and survived the encounter.

My cousin. Standing here in Simon's courtyard, looking at me with recognition I had not earned.

"Jesus," he said, and his voice matched everything else about him—rough, scraped raw from years of preaching repentance to thousands, from calling Israel back to God. The single word filled the courtyard, seemed to make the very air vibrate.

Jesus smiled and nodded, a greeting between kinsmen who understood each other without need for many words.

His keen stare swept over the assembled group, taking measure of each person present with his piercing gaze. And then his eyes found me and stopped.

"I have come for the daughter of Joseph."

Silence followed, and every eye in the courtyard turned toward me. My palm grew slick with nervous sweat against the smooth wood of my staff.

"How do you know—" I began, but my voice came out barely a whisper, cracking on the words. How did he know my name? How did he know to come here?

"The Spirit spoke of one who waits," John said, stepping closer, his sandaled feet sure on the courtyard stones. Each step seemed deliberate, weighty. "One who has borne much and seeks to be made new. One marked by suffering but called to purpose." His eyes held mine, unflinching. "Anna of Arimathea. Daughter of Joseph. Cousin to the Messiah. Beloved of God."

My breath stopped, and shock crashed over me in waves.

My knees went weak, and the staff trembled in my grip, the only thing keeping me upright. The Spirit—the Spirit of the living God—had shown this prophet my face, had spoken my name, had sent him across Galilee for this moment.

Andrew's hand found my elbow, steadying me, and when I glanced at him, his eyes were wide with wonder. He looked between John and me as though trying to comprehend what he was hearing, his grip on my arm tightening. Tears burned behind my eyes.

The certainty in John's voice left no room for doubt, no space for questioning. This was divinely ordained.

Jesus moved forward. "Cousin, welcome." He grasped John's forearms in greeting. "It is good to see you."

"And you," John said, returning the embrace. "You received my message, then? That I was coming to you?"

"I did, and your timing is excellent." Jesus's glance swept over our shouldered packs with what might have been amusement. "Though perhaps my instructions were less clear to them than they might have been."

I turned to Andrew, realization washing over me like cold water. "He knew," I whispered, my voice tight with wonder. "Jesus knew John was coming. That is why he told us to prepare."

Andrew's eyes widened, then a slow smile spread across his face, dimples deepening. "And we all thought—"

"The Jordan," I finished, feeling foolish and amazed at once. My packed supplies suddenly felt absurdly heavy on my shoulder. "We assumed the Jordan."

A laugh bubbled up in my chest, surprising me. All that worry about the long journey, about keeping up, about my hip lasting the distance had been pointless. Jesus had known all along that John would come to us.

John's gaze moved briefly to Abba. "Uncle," he said with a slight nod, acknowledgment and respect in the single word.

"Herod grows bolder, cousin," John continued, turning back to Jesus. "The authorities watch the river crossings with hungry eyes, making the journey dangerous for seekers. When the Spirit showed me her face and called me north, I knew I should come to her rather than have her come to me." His attention shifted back to me, and I felt pinned beneath that fierce gaze. "If she is to be baptized, it should be today, while the way is clear."

My throat went dry. The words scraped past my lips. "You came all this way for me?"

"The Lord of Hosts does not send His prophets on meaningless journeys." Something in John's expression softened slightly, like sun breaking through storm clouds. "Besides, you are family. It is time we met."

All these years, I believed I was alone, and now cousins had emerged from every corner of Judea, appearing like stars at twilight, one by one until the sky was full.

"Did you have somewhere in mind?" Jesus asked.

"The springs above the town," John replied. "Hidden waters, sacred ground. I know a place." He looked at me again, and this time his gaze held something almost gentle. "Can you walk that far?"

"I can," I answered, though my hip already ached from standing.

Andrew moved to my side, his presence solid and steadying. "I will help her."

"We all will," Simon Peter added gruffly, stepping forward with the others.

"No." John shook his head, the movement decisive. "Too many travelers draw attention. Jesus, myself, the girl." He looked at Abba. "And her father, if he wishes to witness what the Lord does this day."

"I do," Abba said immediately, his voice firm.

"And I," Andrew said. His tone left no room for argument. He was coming.

John studied him for a moment, eyes narrowing as if measuring Andrew's determination. Then he nodded. "The one who would be her husband has the right."

My eyes widened, heat flooding my face. How did he know? But John continued without pause, already turning to

Mary. "The woman as well. She who has been cleansed understands the need."

Mary stepped forward, her expression serene. "I would be honored."

"Then we go now," John declared. "Before the sun climbs higher."

Within moments, our small group had formed—Jesus and John leading the way like twin pillars of purpose, Abba and Mary following, and Andrew matching my slower pace. The others would wait at Simon's house, their faces a mixture of curiosity and concern as we departed.

We left Capernaum by a shepherd's path that wound up into the hills above the town, narrow and worn smooth by generations of feet. My hip protested the climb almost immediately, the familiar ache sharpening with each upward step. But Andrew's steady arm and my staff made it manageable, and I refused to slow our pace. Behind us, the Sea of Galilee spread wide in the morning light, beautiful and distant.

The sun beat down on my head and shoulders, and soon sweat trickled between my shoulder blades, dampening the back of my tunic. Dust rose with each footfall, coating my sandaled feet, drying my throat until I could taste it—gritty and bitter. The stone path was rough beneath my palm when I steadied myself, sun-heated and sharp-edged. My staff tapped a rhythm against rock worn smooth by countless flocks, and with each step upward, my hip joint ground and ached, sending sharp bolts of pain down my leg.

"Would you tell me of this place?" I asked John as we climbed, needing to fill the silence that stretched between us like something alive.

"A pool fed by springs in the hills above Capernaum," he said without turning, his voice carrying back to me over the whisper of wind through dry grass. "The water runs cold and clear, a place where shepherds have brought their flocks for generations. Hidden, peaceful. A place fit for divine purposes."

Divine purposes. My pulse quickened with more than exertion, and I felt my palm grow damp against the wood of my staff.

After we had endured perhaps an hour of climbing, the path finally leveled. We crested a small rise and there, spread before us, was a hidden valley cupped between two hills, sheltered and secret. A place that felt untouched by the world below.

The air changed immediately. Cooler here, cleaner, carrying moisture that kissed my sun-heated skin and soothed my dust-dried throat. Sound softened, muffled by the embrace of the hills. Even our footsteps became hushed. The breeze moved differently in this place, gentle and constant, carrying the green scent of growing things and the mineral-sharp smell of cold water rising from stone.

Ancient olive trees dotted the slopes, their gnarled trunks speaking of centuries of growth, their leaves shimmering silver-green in the breeze that whispered through the valley. And there, in the valley's heart like a jewel set in stone, lay a pool of water so clear it looked almost unreal.

We descended, and the path down was easier than the climb had been, though every jarring step still proved difficult. When we reached the valley floor, John stopped.

"Here," John said, and the single word resonated in the valley like a bell struck in silence.

I stood at the pool's edge, staff planted in the soft earth. I stared down into water so pure, so crystalline, I could count every pebble on the bottom, see every grain of sand, and every blade of water grass waving in the gentle current. Springs bubbled up from the depths, sending ripples across the surface that caught and scattered the light in a thousand directions. The sound whispered gentle and constant, singing an invitation I could not refuse.

Holiness hummed through the valley, tangible and present, settling into my bones and lungs with each breath. This was hallowed ground where heaven touched earth.

Abba touched my shoulder, and when I looked at him, his eyes were bright with unshed tears. "Your mother would be so proud."

Andrew stepped closer, his hand finding mine. "I will be right here when you come out."

Mary smiled, and in her expression I saw understanding. She who had been cleansed knew what I was about to receive.

John's rough voice cut through the air, through my thoughts, through everything.

"The water waits."

I turned to see him standing waist-deep in the pool, the spring-fed current swirling around him. Water darkened his camel-hair cloak, and droplets glittered in his beard. Jesus stood nearby on the bank, his manner expectant, waiting.

"Come, Anna," John commanded. "Your old life ends here."

With trembling legs, I took my first step into the pool. The water was shockingly cold. Bone-achingly, breath-stealingly cold. I gasped at the first touch of it against my ankles, felt gooseflesh rise instantly on my arms, felt my whole body trying to reject this sudden immersion. The sandy bottom shifted beneath my feet, soft and yielding, so different from the hard stone path I had just left. Small pebbles pressed into the soles of my feet as I stepped deeper.

The cold climbed my body with each step—calves, knees, thighs—a rising tide of ice that made my muscles tighten and my skin prickle. My soaked tunic clung heavily to my legs, dragging with each movement forward.

I could see my feet on the sandy bottom. I watched the small clouds of sediment that rose with each step and then settled again. The water was so clear it created the illusion of walking on air, of being suspended between earth and sky.

Each step felt monumental. Filled with meaning beyond what I could fully grasp. But I kept going.

John steadied me as the pool deepened, his hands firm on my arms, his grip strong and sure. When I reached his side, standing in water that came to mid-chest and made every breath shallow and difficult, he looked at me and spoke.

"Do you confess that you have sinned against the Father in Heaven?" he asked, his voice carrying over the water, echoing off the hillsides, filling the valley with those sacred words.

"I do." My voice came out stronger than I expected, clear and firm despite my shivering.

"Do you repent of these sins?"

"I do." I meant it with everything in me.

"Do you choose to die to the old Anna—" His grip on my arms tightened slightly. "—to the woman who believed herself unworthy, who hid behind walls, who measured her value by her scars and be born as a new creation?"

Tears mixed with the spring water already on my cheeks, hot against the cold. "I do. With all my heart, with everything I am, I do."

"Do you believe in the One who has brought the Kingdom of Heaven to earth? I baptize with water, but he will baptize you with fire and the Holy Spirit. What begins in these waters will be completed in his hands. Do you believe in Him?"

My eyes met Jesus's across the water, and in their depths, I found my home. My heart swelled with love so profound and deep it felt like something breaking open inside my chest, unfurling, and I stumbled with the force of it.

"I do," I whispered, then louder, "I believe."

John nodded, satisfied, his fierce expression softening into tenderness. "Then I baptize you, Anna of Arimathea, that your sins may be washed away and your heart turned toward the Lord. Die to what was. Rise to what shall be."

His hands pressed me backward into the water with surprising gentleness. First came the icy shock, sharp and startling. Then my head went under, and the world changed completely.

Silence. Absolute silence that muffled everything—the voices above, the wind, my own racing heart. Only the rush of water in my ears, the pressure building as I sank deeper. Cold enveloped me entirely, pressing against my closed eyelids, seeping through the fabric of my tunic to touch every inch of skin. I felt the current moving around me, pulling gently, as though the water itself was alive and welcoming me into its depths.

My hair floated free, streaming upward. My garments billowed and swirled. For a moment, suspended between one breath and the next, I was weightless, held in a greater purpose. The cold stung my scars, sharp and cleansing. Then John's hands lifted me, strong and sure, and I burst through the surface. Water streamed from my hair, my clothes, my very skin. I was forgiven.

When I found my footing and stood in the chest-deep water, shivering but strangely warm from within, I knew I had changed. My teeth wanted to chatter, but I held them still. The water lapped at my chest with each movement, and my soaked garments dragged heavy around my legs. Yet beneath the physical cold, beneath the shaking and the gooseflesh and the wet fabric, warmth bloomed. The shame I had carried for so long, the burden of guilt, the loneliness, the hollow ache inside me that never seemed to be filled, had all washed away in these sacred waters.

I looked to the shoreline, blinking water from my eyes. The first thing I saw was Andrew's face, bright with delight, his smile so wide it showed his dimples. The second was Jesus stepping into the water toward me, and when he spoke, his words carried the weight of eternity.

"Daughter of sorrow, daughter of joy." Jesus's voice carried clearly across the water, and though he spoke at normal volume, every word reached me as though he stood beside me, as though he spoke directly into my heart. "Today you have chosen the narrow gate that leads to life. Well done."

He waded toward me until he stood close enough to touch.

"What was hidden shall be revealed," he continued, his eyes holding mine with such intensity I could not look away. "What was lost shall be found." He took in my scars, my staff floating beside me in the water, the tears on my cheeks. "What was broken becomes the very place where light enters. Your wounds will be your ministry, Anna. Your scars will be your testimony."

He reached out and touched my wet hair, smoothing it back from my face so tenderly it made fresh tears come. Then he leaned down and kissed my forehead, his lips warm against my cold skin, and grace poured into me.

"You have seen the Father's face in mine, and you have not turned away. You have believed when others doubted. You have loved when others feared." His hand moved to rest over my heart. "Because of this faith, mysteries will unfold before you that you cannot yet imagine. You will walk in places you have never dreamed of going. You will speak words you do not yet know. And you will heal others in ways that will astonish even you, little cousin."

His voice dropped to barely above a whisper, yet every word rang clear and true, seemed to echo in my very bones. "The last shall be first. The broken shall be made whole. The despised shall be exalted. Remember this in the days to come, when the path grows dark and the way seems impossible. Remember that I have called you. Chosen you. Set you apart for purposes beyond your understanding."

He smiled then, and the love in his eyes held me captive. "You are mine, Anna. And I am yours. That will never change."

I bowed my head, water still dripping from my hair. "I am yours, Lord. In every way, I am yours."

He smiled at me, then turned to return to shore, each step deliberate. I followed, making sure my staff kept me stable on the shifting bottom, feeling the pull of the current around my legs. The water resisted my movement, dragging at my waterlogged tunic, making each step an effort. My hip still ached, and my bad leg wanted to buckle with the added weight of soaked fabric and the instability of the sandy bottom. But I moved forward, staff planted firm, until the water grew shallower. My baptism had not healed my hip. The familiar ache was still there, the hitch in my gait unchanged. But somehow, it mattered less now.

"How do you feel?" Mary asked as I waded toward shore, reaching out to steady me as I found my footing on the bank.

I paused, taking inventory of my heart, my spirit, my very bones. "Clean," I said. "For the first time in my life, completely clean."

John followed me from the pool, water streaming from his camel-hair cloak in rivulets, darkening the earth where it fell. "It is done," he said with satisfaction.

Andrew came forward with his traveling cloak and wrapped it around my shoulders. The wool was warm from the sun, and I pulled it close, my teeth beginning to chatter.

"I am not the same woman," I told him.

He smiled, his dimples deepening as his hands lingered on my shoulders. "I was counting on it."

CHAPTER 22

I SAT on a low stone bench in Simon's courtyard, my hair now dry from the walk back, but still carrying the scent of water. The memory clung to me as I watched Andrew pace near the grape arbor. I felt like pacing, too. My future hung in the balance like fruit not yet ready to fall.

Deborah emerged from the house carrying a tray with cups and a pitcher of wine, her movements still full of that miraculous vigor that made me want to weep with gratitude every time I saw it. She set the tray on the table with deliberate care, then looked at Andrew with motherly concern.

"Enough pacing, young man," she said. "You will wear a groove in Rachel's stones, and she will have words with all of us." Her tone held warmth beneath the worry. "Come, sit with us. Some conversations require stillness to begin properly."

Andrew stopped mid-stride, his cheeks flushing. "I am not—I was not—" He ran a hand through his hair, leaving it even more disheveled than usual. "I know your father wishes to speak with me, but I confess I am—"

"Nervous," Deborah supplied kindly. "As any man would be in your position."

Abba approached from across the courtyard, his expression thoughtful but resolute. "Andrew," he said, lowering himself onto the bench across from us. "I believe we have matters to discuss. Anna, you and Deborah can — "

"Abba," I said quickly, before he could continue. "I wish to remain for this conversation."

Both men looked at me with surprise. Abba's eyebrows rose. "Anna, this is not—"

"It is my future you will discuss," I interrupted, then immediately softened my tone. "Please, Abba. I know this is not customary, but these are not customary times. If my life is to change, should I not have a voice in how it changes? I have learned what happens when decisions about my life are made without me knowing. I would not have that happen again."

Andrew looked between us uncertainly, clearly torn between respect for tradition and his own desire to have me present.

"The girl speaks sense," Deborah said. "She has a wise heart, my lord. Perhaps her voice would bring clarity to the discussion."

Abba considered this for a long moment, his gaze moving between Andrew and me. "Very well, Anna. Stay." He glanced toward the house where voices drifted from the main room, then looked around the courtyard. "Such matters deserve privacy. Would you ask the others to give us the courtyard for a time?" he asked Deborah.

She nodded and disappeared briefly into the house. I heard her speaking, then the sounds of people moving deeper inside or perhaps to the roof. She returned and took a seat.

"Deborah?" Abba asked. "I thought this conversation would be between Andrew, Anna and me."

"And her mother," Deborah said. "Since she cannot be here, and I have spent years loving this child, it is only fitting that I am part of this too. I will only listen." She smoothed her tunic and waited. I dipped my head to hide my smile.

My father sighed. "Fine, though I sincerely doubt that last part."

"I will do my best," Deborah said. "Continue."

"As Anna has pointed out, these are not ordinary times." Abba said, "So ordinary customs may not serve us well." He cleared his throat and stood. "But I believe we all know why we are gathered here. Andrew, you have something to ask me."

Andrew straightened his shoulders, gathering his resolve. "My lord Joseph," he began, his voice strong. "I wish to speak with you about your daughter's future. About her future with me, if you will permit it."

"Speak then," Abba said.

The words seemed to catch in Andrew's throat for a moment. He glanced at me, and I saw vulnerability there that made my heart ache. This man who had stood firm before the Pharisees, who had left everything to follow Jesus, now looked as uncertain as a boy.

"I love her," Andrew said finally. "I love Anna fully, and I want to marry her, to be her husband, to build a life together in service to our Lord." He paused, swallowing hard. "But I must be honest about what I can offer."

"And what is that?" Abba asked, his tone neutral.

You know what he can offer, I thought, irritation flickering through me. *You are making him say it.*

Andrew's hands clenched in his lap. "Little, by the world's standards. I am a fisherman's son with no property, no permanent home, no wealth beyond what I can earn with these hands." He held up his palms, marked by years of labor. "I follow a teacher who owns nothing but the clothes on his back, who warns his followers to count the cost of discipleship because the way is narrow and the end uncertain."

I wanted to reach across the space between us, to stop the words that wounded him even as he spoke them.

"I cannot offer Anna a fine house or servants or the luxury she has known," he continued. "I cannot promise her safety, for those who follow Jesus draw the attention of dangerous men. I cannot even promise her a settled life, for our teacher goes where the Father sends him, and we follow."

"So what can you offer my daughter?" Abba asked.

"My heart," Andrew said without hesitation. "My protection, such as it is. My faithfulness, for as long as breath remains in my body. I can offer her a love that sees her scars and calls them beautiful, that values her wisdom more than her wealth, that will never ask her to be anything other than exactly who she is."

"And if that is not enough for my daughter? Anna is the daughter of a member of the Sanhedrin. There are expectations about whom she should marry."

Not this. Not now. Do not make this about your position, Abba.

I felt Deborah shift beside me, her disapproval almost tangible.

"If it is not enough, then I will accept your decision,"

Andrew said, though I saw his jaw clench. "But know that I will not stop loving her. That is beyond my power to change."

"Enough." The sharp word came from Deborah, not Abba. She leaned forward, her eyes blazing with protective fire. "My lord, you speak as if Anna is goods to be bartered, as if her happiness matters less than maintaining your family's standing."

Abba's eyebrows rose at her boldness, but Deborah was not finished.

"I have watched these two together," she continued. "I have seen how he looks at her—not with pity for her limitations or greed for her inheritance, but with the kind of love that sees straight to the soul. I have seen her bloom under that regard like a flower that had been waiting all her life for the sun."

She turned to Andrew, her expression softening. "And you, young man, stop speaking as if you bring nothing to this match. You bring honor. You bring kindness. You bring a faith so strong you left everything to follow it. Love is not measured in denarii, and a woman's worth is not measured by the size of her husband's purse."

"Deborah," I began, overwhelmed by her advocacy.

"No, Anna, let me finish. I raised you from a child. I know your heart better than anyone in this courtyard, perhaps better than you know it yourself."

My eyes burned. She was fighting for me. Deborah was standing between me and disappointment with the fierceness of a lioness.

She looked at Abba. "Your daughter does not need luxury. She needs purpose. She needs to be valued for her mind and her skills, not just her beauty. She needs a man who will stand with her, not in front of her."

She stopped abruptly, as if suddenly hearing her own words. Color rose in her cheeks as she looked at Abba. "Forgive me, my lord. I have spoken too boldly. It is not my place to—"

"Peace, Deborah," Abba said, raising his hand. "You have spoken from love, and words spoken from love are always welcome in my hearing."

The courtyard fell quiet except for the distant voices of Simon's neighbors preparing their evening meals.

Finally, Abba spoke. "You speak truth, Deborah, as you always have." He looked at Andrew with respect. "You offer honesty where others might offer flattery. That has value." He paused, then continued, "But let me be equally honest. Anna is my only child and the heir to everything I have built. That brings both responsibilities and privileges. Her security is of utmost importance to me."

"Abba," I said, finding my voice at last, "may I speak for myself?"

He turned to me with surprise, as if he had forgotten I was present for this conversation about my future. "Of course, daughter."

I stood, needing to be on my feet for what I had to say. "I understand the honor of our family name, the importance of inheritance, and the expectations that come with wealth and with your position. But I also understand love. Real love, the kind that changes both the giver and receiver."

My voice grew stronger as I continued. "Andrew, you speak of what you cannot offer, but you do not understand what you have already given me. Before you came to our gate, I believed I was unworthy of love. I watched other girls my age receive marriage offers while none came for me." My voice caught slightly, and I winced at the sound. "I had convinced myself that the best I could hope for was to be useful, perhaps needed, but never truly desired."

Andrew's eyes filled with tears, but he did not speak. Could he ever understand what he had given me?

"You changed that," I said. "You looked at me and saw not a broken woman to be pitied, but a whole person to be treasured. You made me believe I was extraordinary, not despite my wounds but complete with them. You loved me." I touched the cord at my wrist, the fisherman's knot that had become a symbol of promises held fast. "That is not a small gift, Andrew. That is everything."

I turned to Abba. "And you, Abba, speak of protecting the family honor and ensuring my security. But what good is security without happiness? What honor is there in a life lived safely but without love?"

Abba's face softened at my words, but he still looked troubled. "Anna, I want your happiness. Truly, I do. However, I also want to ensure that you are provided for and that you will not face hardship. Love is precious, but it does not put food on the table or shelter over your head."

"Then let me ease your concerns," Andrew said. He had stood as well, and now he faced Abba with new resolve. "I may not have wealth, but I am not without resources. My brother Simon owns fishing boats, nets, and a house. Those of us who follow Jesus are like family to one another. No one among us goes hungry, goes without shelter, faces danger alone." He paused. "And there is this—Jesus has spoken of the kingdom coming, of rewards for those who sacrifice earthly things for heavenly treasures. I do not know what form those rewards will take, but I trust him completely."

"That is all well and good," Abba replied, "but trust does not—" He stopped mid-sentence. He sat down, and his fingers tightened on his knees. I watched him struggle with something, saw the way he looked from Andrew to me and then away, as if seeking an answer in the middle distance.

The silence stretched. A bird called from Simon's roof. Someone laughed in a neighboring courtyard. I counted my own heartbeats, afraid to breathe, afraid to break whatever was happening in my father's mind.

Please say yes, Abba. Please. I willed him to look at me, to see what this meant, but his eyes remained fixed on some distant point.

"If the council discovers what I am considering—" He stopped and shook his head slightly. "Supporting a man they consider dangerous—" Another pause. When he spoke again, his voice was quieter. "But I have watched Deborah rise from her deathbed. I have seen my daughter walk into the water for baptism and travel for days to save someone she loves. My niece Mary chose faith over the easier way years ago. Perhaps it is time I did the same."

He stood to join us. "I do not know whether this is wisdom or madness. But here is what we will do." His voice grew warmer. "We need to plan wisely. Son—for if you marry my daughter, you will be my son—that inheritance is not a burden but a blessing. Used judiciously, it could support not just you and Anna, but the work you do in Jesus's name."

Andrew blinked in confusion. "My lord, I do not understand."

Abba smiled, the first genuine expression I had seen from him all evening. "Andrew, you speak of having nothing to offer, but you offer something I am only now beginning to understand my daughter needs—a calling beyond the confines of a safe, quiet life. I confess that I have been too absent from Anna's life to know her heart as I should. But seeing her determination to bring Deborah to healing, watching her courage today at the baptism, listening to her speak tonight — "He paused, his gaze moving between us. "I see a woman who needs more than comfort and safety. The resources she brings to this marriage could support whatever work the Lord calls you both to do."

"You mean—" Andrew stopped, as if he could not trust what he was hearing.

"I mean that Anna's inheritance is substantial enough to support a household, to fund travel, to provide for the practical needs of ministry," Abba said. "I have been setting aside funds for her future since she was born. With your agreement, Andrew, we could arrange the ketubah so that Anna receives income from the estate, income that you both could direct as the Lord leads you. It is not the usual way, but these are not usual times."

My legs nearly buckled with relief and wonder. "Abba, you would structure the marriage contract this way? To allow us both to decide how the funds are used?"

"My daughter, I have spent years on the Sanhedrin watching religious leaders accumulate wealth while ignoring the poor, building their own kingdoms while claiming to serve God. My nephew brings the true kingdom of heaven to earth, and his work is clearly from the Father. What better use for earthly treasure than to support such a purpose?"

He moved to where Andrew remained frozen in shock. "Son, I am not giving you my daughter as charity, but as my most precious treasure. Her inheritance is not my generosity but God's provision, not your need but His abundance. Can you accept this?"

Andrew looked from Abba to me, his eyes wide with disbelief. "I — I never imagined — My lord, I fear I am not worthy of such generosity."

"None of us is worthy of the gifts we receive," Abba replied. "But that does not mean we should refuse them." He extended his hand. "Will you take my daughter as your wife, love her as she deserves, and use the resources God has provided through our family to serve his kingdom?"

Andrew gripped Abba's hand, his voice unsteady as he spoke. "I will, my lord. Yes, I will."

"Good." Abba turned to me. "And you, daughter? Will you take this man as your husband, knowing that the life he offers is uncertain, dangerous, and far from the comfort you have known?"

I looked at Andrew. Surely my heart would burst out of my chest at any moment. "Yes, Abba. A thousand times, yes."

Deborah rose from her bench and embraced us both, her face wet with tears that caught the lamplight. Her arms, strong again with life, held us fiercely. "Oh, my dear ones, if your mother could see this day — "

"She does see it," Abba said softly. "I am certain she does."

"So what happens now?" I asked, overwhelmed by how quickly everything had changed.

"Now we plan a betrothal," Abba said with growing enthusiasm. "It must be soon. In a few days if it can be managed. As we all know, these are dangerous times, and I would see you properly wed before— " He trailed off, but we all understood. Before the authorities moved against Jesus, before following him became even more perilous than it already was.

"How soon?" Andrew asked.

"Within days," Abba replied. "But first, your mother

must be invited, your family properly consulted. These may not be ordinary circumstances, but we will honor what proprieties we can."

"The betrothal in a few days," I said, my mind spinning with the speed of events, "and the wedding?"

"Soon after," Abba said. "Perhaps we could travel to Arimathea for the ceremony itself. I would like to see you married in your mother's garden, if you are willing."

The image rose in my mind. Standing beneath the fig tree where I had first met Andrew, in the garden where I had first heard God speak my name, surrounded by jasmine and lavender and all the growing things that had comforted me through years of waiting. "Yes," I breathed. "Oh yes, I would love that."

Andrew's face brightened at the mention of his family. "Anna, I want you to meet my mother before we are betrothed. I want to tell her everything—how we met, what you mean to me, how you saved my life in more ways than one. She should know the woman I am going to marry."

"I would like that very much." Nervousness crept through me. Meeting his mother felt suddenly daunting. What if she did not approve?

"Then that settles it," Abba said. "We will travel to Bethsaida, make the proper introductions, and then return for the ceremony."

Andrew's hand found mine, our fingers intertwining, the fisherman's knot at my wrist pressing between our joined hands. "Anna," he said, "are you certain? Once we take this step, there will be no returning to the safety of your father's house, no protection from the dangers that follow those who walk with Jesus."

I thought of the morning's baptism, of sinking beneath

the waters and rising clean, remade, ready for whatever came next. "Andrew, I am certain of this beyond all doubt. Where you go, I will go. Where you lodge, I will lodge. Your people will be my people, and your God,"—I smiled—"well, your God is already my God."

"Ruth," Deborah murmured, recognizing the echo of the ancient words.

"Yes," I said. "Like Ruth, I choose to follow where love leads, whatever that path may hold."

Andrew lifted our joined hands and pressed his lips to my knuckle, a lingering kiss that trembled slightly, warm breath ghosting across my skin. A promise and a prayer combined, sealed in that single gesture.

As oil lamps flickered to life around us and the last light faded from Simon's courtyard, I felt the rightness of this path we had chosen. Soon, I would be betrothed to the man I loved and be his wife.

"Tomorrow, then," Abba said, rising and embracing us both. "Tomorrow we go to Bethsaida and meet our new family."

"Finally!" Simon's voice boomed from the doorway. He strode into the courtyard with his arms spread wide, grinning like a fool. "I thought you would talk until dawn."

"Simon Peter!" Rachel appeared behind him, swatting his shoulder. "Must you announce that you were listening?"

"Why pretend otherwise?" Simon said unapologetically. The rest of the household spilled out behind him—Mary, James, John, the other disciples, all wearing various expressions of delight and poorly suppressed curiosity. "Joseph asked for privacy, not that we go stone deaf."

"Brother," Andrew said, laughing, "you have no shame."

"None whatsoever." Simon clapped Andrew on the back

hard enough to make him stumble forward. "Welcome to the family, Anna of Arimathea. You are marrying the second-best fisherman in Galilee."

"Second-best?" Andrew protested.

"Obviously. I am the first." Simon winked at me. "But he is far prettier, so you made the right choice."

CHAPTER 23

THE COASTAL PATH to Bethsaida wound along the Sea of Galilee like a thread spun from dust and hope. Our small party had left Capernaum behind with the morning mist, and now the lake stretched beside us, its surface catching fragments of light that danced and shifted with each ripple. Gulls flew overhead, their sharp cries cutting through the rhythmic calls of fishermen checking nets. The morning air held wildflower sweetness, with chamomile and wild thyme rising from the terraced hillsides where goats crushed the fragrant stems underfoot.

I had barely slept. Excitement and nervousness jostled for space in my thoughts as I considered how swiftly my life was changing. Yesterday I had been Anna of Arimathea, the councilman's scarred daughter. Today I walked beside the man I would marry, traveling to meet the woman who would become my mother—for surely that was what she would be, this stranger whose approval had suddenly become as precious as breath itself.

"You are quiet," Andrew observed, matching his pace to mine with the careful attention that still startled me.

"Yes, I am." I paid close attention to the road, watching where I stepped. "There is much to think about. Your mother does not even know we are coming."

"She likely does by now. I sent a local boy early this morning to tell her we would be there by noontime," Andrew told me. "I thought it unwise to show up unannounced with my future wife, her father, and Deborah. You will love her, and she you."

"Are you certain? I am terrified," I admitted, then immediately wished the words back. "What if she finds me wanting? What if she thinks you could have chosen better than a lame woman with a marked face?"

Andrew stopped so abruptly that Abba and Simon, walking ahead, had to pause and look back with raised brows.

"Anna," Andrew said. "My mother will love you because I love you, but more than that, she will love you for who you are." His hands framed my face with gentleness. "You saved my life, opened your home to strangers, followed your heart all the way to Capernaum. Trust me when I say a woman who is baptized and agrees to marry a fisherman all in the same day will impress her greatly."

My face flushed. "You mean to tell her all that?"

"Eventually." His grin held boyish mischief. "She deserves to know what kind of woman has captured her son's heart so completely."

Simon had ambled back to us, clearly enjoying our exchange. "She has been praying you would find someone worthy of you," he said to Andrew. "Though she may be surprised by how spirited your choice proves."

"She will think Andrew deserves better." Anxiety twisted in my belly, refusing to relent.

"Stop." Abba's voice carried gentle authority as he approached. "Why do you borrow trouble that may never come? If you believe in the love you share, then the welcome you will receive will be a happy one. Andrew's mother will have you as a daughter and be glad of it."

His words brought relief. Behind us, Deborah kept an easy pace with Ezra and two servants. She had insisted on coming, declaring that a prospective daughter-in-law should not meet her intended's mother without another woman to vouch for her character.

"What is your mother like?" I asked Andrew as we crested a rise that revealed Bethsaida spread below like a handful of pearls cast along the shore.

"Naomi is her name. Have I told you that already?" His voice softened as most do when we speak of our mothers. "Ima is small but mighty, a wren that has learned to order eagles. She kept us in line when my father was on the water, managed household accounts better than most merchants, and could mend a net so the repair proved stronger than the original weave."

"Your mother sounds formidable."

"She is. Yet she has the sweetest spirit."

The path curved downward through terraced gardens where olive trees cast shade over barley and young wheat. As we approached the village, people emerged from houses and workshops. Children ran alongside our small procession, faces bright with curiosity, while women paused at their tasks to lift hands in greeting. Men straightened from their nets and boats, calling to Andrew, who answered with easy warmth.

"Andrew!" called a voice from the harbor. "You bring guests to your mother!"

"The finest guests," Andrew called back with a grin. "Tell your wife I said her bread smells sweeter than ever."

The simple exchange pleased me. This was Andrew's world. These were the people who had known him from boyhood, who welcomed him home with genuine gladness.

"There," Andrew said, pointing toward a row of stone houses that rose from the water's edge. "The one with the green door and climbing roses. She painted it green the year I was born and planted those roses too. She said every child deserved to come home to beauty."

Roses bloomed wild over the modest doorway, their pink petals dropping onto the threshold with each gust of lake wind. A woman who planted flowers for an unborn child would surely find room in her heart for a daughter-in-law with scars.

The green door opened before we reached it.

Naomi stepped into the sunlight, and I understood at once where Andrew had inherited his warm eyes and gentle smile. She was small, barely reaching her son's shoulder, with silver-streaked hair and hands that spoke of useful work faithfully done. But it was her face that caught and held me. On it was pure joy at the sight of her son, tempered by a keen intelligence taking measure of the woman beside him.

"Andrew," she said, and her voice carried music threaded with tears.

He crossed the space between them in three strides and swept her into an embrace that lifted her clear off the ground. She laughed and scolded and wept all at once, small hands patting his shoulders as if to prove he was truly there.

"And my Simon!" she said as Andrew set her down,

turning to embrace her elder son with equal fervor. "I am so happy to see you both. It has been too long."

"Peace, Ima," Simon said, laughing. "We are well, and we bring happy tidings."

"Foolish boys," she said, stepping back to study both sons. "Riding off to follow teachers, never coming home for a proper meal. I will not even bring up the bandits. Your poor mother's hair has gone white with worry."

"Your hair has had silver since I was twelve," Andrew protested, but he pulled her closer as he said it.

I watched them together—the easy teasing, the devotion between them—and felt the loss of my mother anew. I had been too young to have this with her, this blend of exasperation and love that only years together could build.

"Hush." She tapped his chest with one finger, then turned her attention to our group. Her eyes moved to Abba with the respectful curiosity befitting a councilman, then to Deborah with polite interest, before settling on me.

I felt the weight of that examination like a physical thing. This woman had shaped the man I loved through countless acts of daily nurture and correction. Her judgment mattered to Andrew more than he perhaps realized.

"So," she said, approaching me. "You are Anna."

"Yes, my lady." I managed a respectful bow despite my staff. "The honor is mine in meeting you."

She stopped directly before me, close enough that I could see laugh lines around her eyes, the small mark on her chin that spoke of a childhood mishap, the way she looked at my scars.

"I am told you saved my son's life," she said.

"Deborah and I tended his injuries, but the healing came from the Almighty."

"Hmm." She reached out and took my free hand before turning it palm-up in both of hers.

Every instinct told me to pull away, to hide what she was seeing, and to tuck my hands back into my sleeves where the damage stayed hidden, but I held still. Her fingers traced the pale lines left by Roman leather and bronze, lingering on the deepest scars as if reading a language written in damaged skin. I did not move, bracing for what she might say.

"These are part of you."

I nodded.

"My sister has lived in Jerusalem for many years, and once wrote of a tragedy involving Joseph of Arimathea's wife and daughter." Her thumb traced one pale line across my knuckles. Then her gaze lifted to my face, to the scar that marked me from temple to jaw.

"Yes," I said. "My mother was killed, and I was injured. It was a long time ago."

"You bear the story still." She released my hand and stepped back, but her expression had softened like wax near a flame. "Such stories live in a woman's heart."

Tears threatened, but I held them back with effort. "Yes, they do."

She turned to Andrew. "You chose wisely, my son. A woman with scars understands the value of healing. One who has known loss recognizes treasure when she finds it."

I gripped my staff harder. She had looked at my worst parts and called me treasure. She had seen the scars and named them wisdom instead of shame.

I had prepared myself for questions about dowry, domestic skills, and my ability to bear children despite old injuries. Instead, I found an understanding that went deeper than surface concerns.

"Come," she said, gesturing toward the house. "We have much to discuss, and these old bones need shade. All of you, please—honored councilman and companions alike."

We followed her into the main room of her modest home, and I studied every detail — the furnishings were worn but well-tended, mended yet clean linens, and the mezuzah I glimpsed on the doorpost as we entered. This was where Andrew had learned to become the man I loved.

Naomi brought out cups and a pitcher of cool water, along with dates and figs arranged on a simple wooden platter. She served us, distributing food with the insistence of a woman accustomed to feeding hungry fishermen.

"Now then," she said when all held cups. She sat on a low stool with the authority of a queen upon her throne. "Tell me how this courtship proceeded. I confess curiosity about such swift arrangements."

"Swift but certain," Andrew said, his eyes finding mine across the small room.

"And you, Anna? You are content with such haste?"

"I am," I said. "When something rings true, waiting only invites doubt or danger."

Naomi considered this. "Wise words. Practical ones, given these times."

We spoke for a time about the betrothal plans, about when we would return to Capernaum, and about the wedding itself. Naomi asked questions about my father's estate and about the time Andrew had spent there. Then, as the conversation grew easier and the formality between us softened, she studied Andrew with the look of a mother who had stored up years of embarrassing stories to share.

"I hope my son has conducted himself properly. He was not always so dignified in matters of the heart."

Andrew's face colored. "Ima, please—"

"Should I not tell Anna about the time you practiced declaring love to the fishing nets? You were fourteen, convinced no one could hear you from the harbor."

Simon burst into delighted laughter. "You practiced on nets? Andrew, you never mentioned this!"

"Because it was private!" Andrew protested, glaring at his brother. "And I was a boy!"

"How did it go? Oh, yes. 'You are the most beautiful catch in all the sea,'" Naomi quoted with devastating accuracy. "And 'My heart beats for you like waves upon the shore.' So earnest about it too, bowing to the nets and everything."

Even Deborah hid her mouth behind her shawl, though her eyes sparkled with mirth.

"I was preparing for the moment I met the right woman," Andrew said with what dignity remained to a man thoroughly embarrassed by his mother. "It seemed — practical."

"Very practical," I said. "And did those skills serve you well?"

"I never practiced on nets again," Andrew said, looking at me with eyes that held both mortification and love. "But I did tell a certain healer that she had captured my heart completely."

"What did she say?" Naomi asked, clearly relishing this turn.

"She agreed to become my wife," Andrew said.

"Indeed." Naomi's expression grew serious as she addressed Abba. "Joseph of Arimathea, your reputation for wisdom precedes you. My husband is gone, so it falls to me to speak for my son's interests. What are your intentions regarding this match?"

"My daughter's happiness," Abba replied. "Your son offers that in abundance."

"And you understand he will travel, following his Rabbi, living a life of uncertainty?"

"I do. We have discussed practical arrangements."

She nodded approvingly. "Good." She looked at me. "And you, Anna? Are you prepared for such a life? The road is hard, the welcomes uncertain, the dangers real."

"I am," I said. "I would rather face uncertainty with Andrew than be without him."

"Well-spoken." She rose and moved to the wooden chest in the room's corner. "Then it is time for serious business."

She returned carrying a small bundle wrapped in faded blue silk. With careful hands, she unwrapped it to reveal a delicate silver bracelet, its surface etched with symbols I could not decipher.

"This belonged to my grandmother and her grandmother before her," Naomi said, holding it to catch the light. "Not valuable by worldly measure, but blessed by generations of faithful women. I always hoped to give it to Andrew's bride."

She reached for my wrist, lifting it gently. I felt the pressure of her fingers against my pulse, felt the cool metal slide against my skin. My hands had gone damp with sweat. We had met only hours ago, and she was giving me something that had been in her family for generations, fastening it beside my mother's bracelets as if I had already earned the right to wear it.

"May it remind you that you belong to our family now and that you are part of a story larger than yourself."

The silver was warm from her touch as it settled into place. Three bands now instead of two. My mother's silver that I had worn alone for so many years, and now this—Naomi claiming me as her own daughter, binding me to Andrew's family.

I thought of my mother, who would never meet the man I married, who would never fasten a bracelet on my wrist or whisper advice about marriage. But she would have loved Andrew. She would have loved Naomi. And perhaps from wherever the faithful go, she rejoiced that her daughter had found a family again.

My vision swam with tears.

"Thank you," I whispered. "I will treasure it."

"See that you do. And treasure my son as well. He is worth a dozen handsome boys with full purses and empty hearts."

"I know," I said. "I see his worth clearly."

"Excellent." She clapped once, somehow declaring formal business concluded. "Now, who hungers for the midday meal? I have fish stew simmering and bread rising, and I will not send my future daughter-in-law away unfed."

As she bustled about, I found myself drawn to the doorway. From there, I could see the harbor where Andrew had learned his trade, the nets he had mended, the boats he had sailed before Jesus called him to a different kind of fishing.

"Are you well?" Andrew appeared beside me.

"Yes," I said, watching the children play between beached boats while their fathers worked nearby. "I think about how different my life might have been growing up here, with roses over my door and a mother who fed half the village."

"A different life, perhaps. Not necessarily better." His hand found mine. "Your scars taught you compassion. Your loneliness taught you to value love, and your father's means will let us serve others. Every piece of your story prepared you for what comes next."

"Even the painful pieces?"

"Especially those." He turned me to face him, expression earnest. "Anna, I need you to know something before we return to Capernaum, before we stand among witnesses and make our vows. I am asking you to marry me because of who you are. For I am captivated by every part of you, and I am thankful for every moment that shaped you into the woman that will be mine. I treasure all of it."

"Andrew—"

"Let me finish." His hands framed my face. "When I lay broken in your garden, barely breathing, do you know what I thought when I first saw you clearly?"

I shook my head.

"I thought, 'This is the woman who will take care of me.' And when I lay bruised and hurting in your guest chamber, I thought, 'This is the woman who will change my life.' Not because you were beautiful, though you are. Not merely because you were kind, though you proved so. It was because I looked into your eyes and knew I had found her. There could be none other for me ever. There could only be you."

Tears came then, and I let them fall.

"I love you, Anna of Arimathea. Will you be my wife and my companion on whatever road the Lord sets before us? Will you let me spend my life proving you are the most precious gift I have ever received?"

"Oh, Andrew, yes," I whispered. "Yes."

He kissed my hand, lips warm and lingering on my knuckles, sealing the promise in the doorway of his childhood home. Behind us, the lake threw back the sun in blinding sheets of light, and from within, Simon called that the stew was ready.

When we parted, Naomi stood watching, eyes bright with tears and approval.

"About time," she said briskly, linking her arms in both of ours. "I thought you would stand there making speeches until the food burned. Come, eat. Tomorrow you return to Capernaum for betrothal planning. Today, we are simply a family sharing a meal."

Family. The word wrapped around me like an embrace as we gathered at Naomi's table, where she forced second helpings upon everyone, scolded Andrew for eating too quickly, and asked Deborah about healing arts, all while treating me as though I had always belonged.

As the afternoon wore on and we prepared for the return journey, Naomi drew me aside one last time.

"Anna," she said, voice serious, "the life my son has chosen is difficult. Following the Teacher means sacrifice, danger, and uncertainty. There will be times when you wonder if the cost proves too high."

"I know."

"Do you? Truly?" She searched my face. "Because I need to know that when dark hours come, and they will, you will not blame Andrew for choices made before he knew you. I need to know you will stand with him, not against him."

I understood what she was asking. This was more than a mother protecting her son's happiness. Naomi knew that following Jesus meant walking toward suffering, not away from it, and she was asking me to promise I would not flinch when that darkness came. To bind myself to whatever fate awaited Andrew, closing the door on safety, on comfort, on the peaceful life I could have had.

"I will stand with him," I said, meaning it with everything in me. "Whatever comes, I will not leave him."

She studied me a moment longer, then nodded. "Then you have my blessing, and you have my prayers. Now go, before day grows too late for safe traveling."

We left for Capernaum with both a bracelet and a blessing.

CHAPTER 24

My hands would not keep still. They fluttered from my hair to my sleeves to the wooden spoon stirring the morning porridge until Deborah finally took the spoon away with a gentle but amused sigh.

"Anna, child, you will turn the barley to butter if you keep stirring it like that," she said, her eyes alive with shared excitement. "Sit. Rest. Tonight will come no sooner no matter how much you pace."

Since our return from Bethsaida, the reality of what was coming had filled me with such joy I could barely contain it. There would be no grand ceremony tonight. We would have only the essential elements of a proper betrothal: witnesses, wine, and words spoken before God.

"Simple is better," Rachel had assured me yesterday while kneading bread. "Save your energy for the wedding feast at Arimathea. Then there will be flowers and fine clothes and everything else." Tonight would be an intimate affair.

"This day does not feel real," I confessed, sinking onto the stool beside Deborah. "By tomorrow morning, I will be Andrew's betrothed wife. Truly and legally bound to him."

"You glow like a lamp," Deborah observed. "I have not seen you this happy since you were a small child chasing butterflies in the garden."

Rachel appeared in the doorway, wiping her hands on her apron. "The wine is ready," she said, satisfied. "And I managed a small honey cake. It is nothing elaborate, but it is sweet enough to mark the occasion properly."

"Rachel," I said, rising and crossing to her, "I cannot thank you enough. For your home, your kindness, for making this possible—"

"Hush." She waved away my gratitude, but her eyes were bright. "What else would I do for my new sister?"

The word stopped me short. "Sister?" I had not expected that.

"Of course." Rachel's smile grew warm. "Andrew is Simon's brother, which makes you my sister. I have always wanted another sister, and now I have one." She laughed and took my hands in hers. "Simon already says Andrew is the luckiest man in Galilee."

"What does Andrew say about that?" I asked, gratitude flooding through me at the simple acceptance.

"That Simon finally speaks wisdom," Rachel replied with a grin. "Come. Let us see if the men have arranged the benches without breaking anything."

After arriving back from Naomi's, we had gathered in the courtyard, travel-worn and wind-blown, still tasting the dust of the road between Bethsaida and Capernaum. Jesus had looked up from his conversation with the inner circle of disciples, and something in his expression told me he already knew what had transpired with Naomi.

"Uncle," he had said to Abba, rising with fluid grace. "How fared your journey?"

"Well," Abba had replied, clasping Jesus's forearms in greeting. "Very well indeed."

Andrew had stepped forward, his hand finding mine. "We found blessing, Rabbi. My mother gives her consent."

A murmur of approval had rippled through the small group. Nathanael had smiled and nudged Matthew. James and John had exchanged knowing glances. Thomas had nodded and clapped Andrew on the back. Judas, who had just arrived, looked at me appraisingly.

"Then we shall witness your betrothal," Jesus had said. "Tomorrow evening, when the day's work is done, the ones who love you most will attend as befits the gravity of the covenant you undertake."

Now, as the sun began its descent toward the lake, the women excitedly swept me into the house. In Rachel's chamber, hands worked with swift efficiency, loosening my travel-stained robe, bringing a basin of heated water scented with rose petals, combing my hair until it fell in dark waves past my shoulders.

"Your mother would weep with joy to see this day," Deborah murmured as she fastened my mother's silver bracelets prominently at my wrists, adding Naomi's bracelet beside them. The three pieces caught the lamplight. "Sarah always said you would marry for love, not arrangement."

"She had those thoughts about me even though I was a small child?" I asked.

"Yes," Deborah answered. "Your mother was a dreamer, and this time, she dreamed right."

Rachel returned bearing a robe of deep-blue linen, simple but finely woven. "This belonged to my sister," she said, shaking out the folds. "She would be honored to see it worn for such a purpose."

The fabric whispered against my skin as they dressed me, the rich color bringing warmth to my olive complexion. When I caught my reflection in the still water of Rachel's washing basin, I barely recognized the woman looking back. My hair was unbound and gleaming, the blue robe made my dark eyes seem deeper, and my familiar features almost looked beautiful. There was happiness on my face. I was happy.

Then it was time. The courtyard held the quiet warmth of the evening as we gathered.

Rachel had set oil lamps in the niches, but only enough to see by, not enough for spectacle. Perhaps fifteen people sat on benches arranged in a loose circle: the closest disciples, Mary of Magdala and Joanna, Philip and Miriam, Deborah and Ezra, and of course, Jesus and my father.

The lake sent a soft breath through the open gate, and Rachel's ovens gave a clean warmth to the air. Someone had stretched a length of woven branches above the central stones, and myrtle brushed my shoulder when I passed beneath it.

Andrew stood near the center, and the sight of him set my pulse racing. He wore fresh clothes—a white tunic that threw his sun-darkened skin into relief against the lamplight, and a blue sash the exact shade of my robe. His hair had been combed back from his face, revealing the strong bones and gentle eyes that had first captured my heart. When he saw me, his expression moved from nervous anticipation to one of awe.

"Anna," he whispered, my name shaped by wonder and disbelief that sent heat through me.

"She is beautiful," Miriam murmured, and others voiced agreement—soft blessings that wrapped around me like a cloak.

I crossed the courtyard to stand beside him, my staff tapping softly against the stones. When I reached his side, he offered his arm, and I took it, feeling the strength and warmth of him through the linen.

Jesus rose from his chair, and all eyes turned to him. The courtyard fell silent except for the distant calls of night birds.

"Shalom to you," he said. "Peace to this house, and to all who have come under its roof and branches."

He paused, and when he spoke again, his voice carried easily to every corner. "Friends, we gather this evening to witness the joining of two hearts, the beginning of a new household, the blessing of love recognized and sanctified. Marriage is the first covenant, established in Eden when the Creator declared it was not good for man to be alone." His gaze moved from face to face, including all in his words. "We give thanks for life, for bread, and for wine, and for the mercy that has brought us to this hour. Blessed is He who keeps His people, and who makes joy in the presence of bride and bridegroom. May the Lord bless what is undertaken here tonight."

He gestured toward Abba with respectful deference. "Joseph, as Anna's father, the ceremony is yours to conduct."

I felt every eye upon me, but strangely, the attention did not burden. Instead, it felt like being held and supported by the good wishes of this unlikely family we had found in following Jesus.

Abba stood, his years on the Council evident in the

dignity he wore as naturally as his own skin. "I, Joseph of Arimathea, declare before these witnesses that my daughter Anna is of age and free will, that no betrothal exists to bar this union, and that I give my blessing to this covenant." He paused, his voice growing warmer. "Andrew, son of Jonah, you have proven yourself a man of honor and faith. I entrust to your care the most precious treasure of my house."

Andrew stepped forward, his face grave with the solemnity of the moment. "I accept this trust, my lord, and swear before God and these witnesses that I will cherish her, protect her, and cleave unto her alone as long as breath remains in my body."

"Then let the ketubah be read," Abba said.

Matthew stepped forward, carrying a scroll of parchment. His voice rang clear as he read the marriage contract Abba had prepared.

"Be it known that on the tenth day of Tammuz, in the sixteenth year of the reign of Tiberius Caesar, Andrew bar Jonah of Bethsaida takes to wife Anna bat Joseph of Arimathea. The bride price agreed upon is twenty silver denarii, paid by the groom. The bride brings to this union her father's blessing and a portion of the estate of Joseph of Arimathea, to be managed jointly by husband and wife for their sustenance and for the work of the Lord as they are called. Should death dissolve the marriage, the surviving spouse shall inherit all jointly held property. Should divorce dissolve it, the bride's portion shall be her original inheritance, to remain hers alone."

My throat constricted at the humble amount. Andrew had so little to offer in coin, yet he gave it without reservation. I noted Abba had been generous in the contract's language, ensuring I would never be left destitute, regardless of the circumstances.

"The conditions are accepted," Andrew said formally. "I pledge these things before God and this assembly."

"And I accept," I replied, my voice steadier than I had expected. "I pledge my heart, my loyalty, and my person to this covenant."

Abba nodded approvingly. "Then let the pledge cup be shared."

Rachel appeared with a clay goblet filled with wine, its surface gleaming in the lamplight. Andrew took it first, his eyes holding mine as he spoke the ancient words: "Blessed are You, Lord our God, King of the universe, who creates the fruit of the vine."

He drank, his throat moving with the swallow, then passed the cup to me. My hands trembled as I lifted it to my lips. The rim was still warm from his mouth, and the wine tasted of honey and pomegranate, clinging sweet on my tongue.

"The covenant is sealed," Abba declared formally. Then he turned to Jesus with deep respect. "Jesus, would you bless this union?"

Jesus turned to us, his presence filling the space between Andrew and me. When he spoke, his voice carried the authority of heaven itself.

"There is a cord that runs through a house," he said, "from old roots to new branches, from fathers and mothers to sons and daughters. It is not pride that keeps a house. It is kindness, and truth, and the fear of God that steadies the hand. A home is built stone upon stone, loaf upon loaf, day upon day. God takes small things into His hands and makes them more. Andrew, Anna—your house will have trials. The work to which you are called is not easy, and the days ahead will test you. But if you hold fast to each other and to the Father who made you, you will stand."

He paused, his eyes moving between us with affection. "Love each other well. Love each other through sorrow and joy, through plenty and want. Let your marriage be a witness to the faithfulness of God, who does not abandon His children even in the darkest valleys."

Then Jesus took both our hands in his, joining them together, and spoke the ancient blessing with quiet power: "What God has joined, let no one separate. Be fruitful. Be faithful. Walk in peace."

The words settled over us like a benediction, and I felt Andrew's fingers tighten around mine. This was real. This was happening. We were bound now, truly bound, by law and custom and sacred covenant.

He lowered his hand and looked at us as if we were both seen and sent. "Andrew, my friend, be strong and gentle. Anna, my cousin, be wise and unafraid."

Naomi drew a soft breath, and Deborah's eyes shone. Andrew squeezed my fingers and then let go with care.

"This is the betrothal," Jesus said quietly to us. "The first binding. Tonight, you return to your own doors. The wedding will have its day. May the Lord bless you and keep you. May His face shine upon you and give you peace. May your love be a light in the darkness and a shelter in every storm."

The courtyard erupted in celebration with voices raised in blessing and hands clapping, then someone began to sing the ancient wedding songs. But I heard none of it clearly, for Andrew had stepped close enough that I could see the lamplight reflected in his eyes, smell the clean scent of his freshly washed skin.

"Wife," he whispered.

The word washed over me, strange and wonderful and mine. I was his wife. He was my husband. The reality of it made me lightheaded.

"Husband," I replied, and a thrill shot through me to say it aloud.

He reached into his sash and withdrew a small object. In the lamplight, I saw it was a simple wooden carving, no longer than my palm, shaped like a small boat.

"I made this during the days of waiting," he said, putting it into my hands. "When I feared I might never see you again, when doubt told me you were beyond my reach." The wood was as smooth as silk beneath my fingers, worn by hours of patient carving. I could feel where his knife had shaped the hull, where his thumb had rubbed the edges until they rounded perfectly. It fit in my palm as if made to rest there. "It is only wood and time, but it carries my heart. Even if storms come, even if the way grows dark, remember that I chose you and you chose me, and that is anchor enough for any sea."

"Andrew, it is beautiful." The tears I had been holding back spilled over. "And you are wrong. This is the most precious thing I have ever owned. I will cherish it always. It is perfect."

"As are you." His thumb brushed away the dampness from my cheek. "My beautiful wife."

The celebration swirled around us. Music and laughter, toasts and blessings, the joyful chaos of love shared among friends. I found myself passed from embrace to embrace, receiving kisses on both cheeks and whispered wishes for happiness. Deborah wept openly, not troubling to hide her tears. "My little girl," she kept saying. "My dear little girl, a bride at last. And here you were all concerned about never marrying. I always knew you would."

"You did not," I said, laughing. "If Andrew had not come with his message, we would still be in Arimathea with me moping about and you telling me to stop."

"Maybe," Deborah said. "But he did come, and here we are." One more hug, and I returned to Andrew's side.

The disciples all offered words of blessing. Simon's hands engulfed mine as he spoke of the good fortune of brothers who marry wisely. James and John, the sons of thunder, promised to keep Andrew in line during his travels, to which Andrew rolled his eyes dramatically. Thomas, ever practical, advised me to pack light and learn to mend nets.

But it was Mary of Magdala who touched me most deeply. Drawing me aside during a lull in the festivities, she took my scarred hands in her own.

"You wonder if you are strong enough for the life ahead," she said. "I see the question in your eyes."

I nodded, unable to speak. She always somehow knew what troubled my heart.

"Let me tell you what I have learned," she continued. "The road with Jesus is not what people expect. There will be nights when you sleep on hard ground, days when crowds are so close you can barely breathe, times when the authorities watch every move you make." She squeezed my hands. "But there will also be moments when you see the lame walk, when you feed hungry children, when you know with absolute certainty that you are part of something eternal. The hardships are real, Anna, but so is the joy. More joy than you can imagine." She smiled, her grip tightening slightly. "And you are strong enough for all of it. I see it in you. I see the same strength that carried you through years of pain, that brought you here to seek healing for Deborah. That strength will serve you well on the road ahead. I will be with you if you need me."

I stepped away from the center of the gathering for a moment, needing air and space to absorb the magnitude of what had just happened. Betrothed. To Andrew. I turned the thought over and over in my mind, marveling at it.

"Anna."

I turned to find Tirzah approaching, her dark braid swinging over one shoulder. She had arrived with James and John earlier, but I had been too caught up in the ceremony to greet her properly. She smiled, and I felt an old unease stir—the memory of watching her at our estate, how familiar she had seemed with Andrew.

"I wanted to offer my congratulations," she said. "Andrew is a good man. You are well matched."

"Thank you." I returned her smile, though it felt uncertain on my lips.

"I hope—" She paused, seeming to gather her thoughts. "I hope we might become friends. It can be lonely sometimes, traveling with the disciples, and there are so few women."

The vulnerability in her words surprised me. I had imagined her confident, secure in her place among Jesus's followers. "I would like that," I said.

She glanced past me toward where the disciples had gathered, and a softness entered her eyes. I followed her gaze and saw James standing with his brother John, both of them listening as Simon Peter told some animated story that had them laughing.

When I looked back at Tirzah, she had turned away quickly, but a blush colored her cheeks.

Understanding came slowly. "James?" I asked.

Her eyes widened. "Is it so obvious?"

"Only to someone watching you." I felt a knot loosen in my chest, one I had carried since that day at Arimathea. "How long have you— ?"

"Months," she admitted, her voice dropping. "Since we first began traveling together. But he has never— I do not think he sees me as anything more than another follower of the Rabbi."

"He and Andrew have been friends since childhood," I said. The words came more easily now. "Perhaps I could speak to Andrew about him? Learn if James might be open to such attention?"

Her expression brightened. "You would do that?"

"Of course." Then, emboldened by her kindness and my relief, I confessed, "I must tell you something. That day at our estate, when you called Andrew 'our Andrew'— I thought you meant something different than you did."

Her brow furrowed in confusion, then she smiled. "You thought I had an interest in him."

"I am sorry. I should not have—"

"No, I am sorry." She shook her head. "I can see now how it must have sounded. When I said 'our Andrew,' I meant he is part of our family. All of us who follow the Rabbi are bound together as kin. Andrew is our brother, as Simon Peter is, as James is." A small smile touched her lips. "Though I confess I think of James rather differently than I think of Simon Peter."

I laughed, and the sound surprised me with its lightness. "I am glad we have spoken plainly."

"As am I. We are family now, are we not? Sisters in this strange and wonderful life."

"Sisters," I repeated, and knew it was true. "Yes, we are."

She embraced me briefly, and when we parted, the last shadow of my old jealousy had vanished entirely. In its place was the beginning of what I sensed would become a genuine friendship, one I would need in the uncertain days ahead.

As the evening deepened, Jesus approached where Andrew and I sat together on a bench. The carved boat rested in my lap, my fingers tracing its smooth lines while Andrew's arm encircled my shoulders.

"Rabbi," Andrew said, rising, but Jesus gestured for him to remain seated.

"Stay," he said, sitting on the bench across from us. In the lamplight, his face held a gravity that stilled me. "I have a gift for you both, though it is not one you can hold in your hands."

"Lord, your blessing is gift enough," I said.

"Even so." He leaned forward, and his voice dropped so that only we could hear. "The road ahead will test you in ways you cannot yet imagine. There will be times when following me costs more than you thought you could bear, when the price of discipleship seems too high for any heart to pay."

Beside me, Andrew's hand found mine, our fingers interlacing.

"Anna, your healing gifts will be needed in dark places, among people who have lost all hope." His eyes held mine with such intensity I could not look away. "Andrew, events that shake the very foundations of what you believe will challenge your faith."

My stomach turned cold. What did he mean? What

events? I wanted to ask, but his expression told me he would say no more.

He paused, letting the weight of his words settle over us like a mantle. "But if you hold fast to each other, if you remember that love is the greatest commandment and the highest calling, you will find strength you did not know you possessed."

The certainty in his voice both comforted and terrified me. He was not speaking of possibilities but of things he knew would come to pass.

"We understand," Andrew said, though I heard the tremor beneath his steady tone. His grip on my hand tightened.

Jesus reached out and covered our joined hands with both of his own. His hands warmed mine, and I drew strength from the touch. "Then hear this. What you build together in faithfulness will outlast kingdoms. It will outlast empires. It will outlast even the stones of the Temple itself." His voice grew softer but more intense. "Love is the only thing that endures beyond death, beyond destruction, beyond all the powers of darkness. And in that truth, you are rich beyond measure."

For a long moment, none of us spoke. His blessing wrapped around us, both promise and warning. My eyes stung with tears—not from sorrow but from the overwhelming sense that something eternal had just been spoken over us.

"Thank you," I whispered, not trusting my voice to say more.

He patted our hands once and rose. "Now, I believe there is more celebrating to be done. Rachel has been guarding a special honey cake with the determination of a Roman sentry."

We stood and returned to the center of the gathering, where laughter rippled through the crowd, breaking the solemn tension that had held us. Rachel appeared with a small round cake crowned with dripping honeycomb, her face bright with pleasure at being part of this moment.

"For the bride and groom," she announced, setting it before us with ceremony. "May your days be as sweet as this honey."

Andrew broke off a piece and lifted it to my lips, the ancient gesture that sealed our betrothal as surely as any contract. The honey melted warm on my tongue, clover-sweet with an undertone of beeswax and wildflower, thick enough to coat my throat as I swallowed. When I fed him in return, his lips brushed my fingertips as he took the cake, and warmth spread through me at the intimate gesture, this act that bound us together before witnesses. His eyes never left my face, and I saw in them a future I had never dared imagine.

"Sweet," he murmured, and I knew he spoke of more than cake. "Just like my wife. Sweet as honey cake."

I shook my head and laughed. "I thought you were done with the bad verses."

He just shrugged and grinned, his dimples deeper than ever.

"I have seen many betrothals," Simon said to us during a quiet moment, his arm around Rachel, "but there is something special about this one."

The last guests departed near midnight, still speaking in hushed tones about the simple beauty of what they had witnessed. As the women cleared away the remnants of the celebration and the men banked the lamps, I found myself oddly reluctant to see the evening end. This night had brought not just betrothal, but also the sealing of bonds that would carry us through whatever trials lay ahead.

I approached Jesus to bid him goodnight, and he looked up with a smile. I had to shift my weight carefully on my staff, my hip aching from the long evening of standing, but the pain seemed distant, unimportant compared to the gratitude flooding through me.

"Thank you," I said simply. "For being here. For blessing us. For everything."

"Remember that the Father delights in the desires of His children's hearts," he replied, his eyes knowing. "And He makes all things beautiful in their time."

Something in those words stopped me, a promise wrapped in patience, but before I could ask what he meant, Andrew appeared at my side.

Jesus grasped each of our hands, put them together, and laid his on top. "You are no longer two people, but one flesh. Let no one split apart what God has joined together. Go in peace."

And with that, he disappeared into the house, leaving Andrew and me standing together in the lamplight.

"Come," Deborah said gently, touching my shoulder. "Bride or no bride, you need rest. Tomorrow begins a new chapter, and you will want strength for the writing of it."

"Goodnight, husband," I said, the word still strange on my tongue, still wonderfully new.

"Goodnight, wife," he called back, his voice warm with promise.

I walked carefully toward the house, one hand on Deborah's arm, the other gripping my staff. Sharp twinges shot down my leg with each step.

In our small chamber, I lay awake despite my exhaustion, turning the carved boat over in my hands. The wood was smooth and warm, worn by Andrew's careful attention. From the courtyard came the gentle sounds of the household finishing its day. Quiet conversations, the banking of lamps, footsteps on stone growing fewer and more distant.

I set the little boat carefully on the table beside my pallet and blew out the oil lamp.

CHAPTER 25

THE HILLS LEANED close as we left the lake country and turned toward home. Terraces stepped down the slopes with their gray stones warm from the sun, and the olives stood with their leaves turned bright side out to the wind. The road narrowed, the land drawing closer around us with each bend.

After our days of travel, the vineyards of home rose before us like a psalm written in green ink, their leaves catching morning light and holding it like cupped hands. We had rested for the Sabbath in a wayside inn, adding another day to our separation. Four days without Andrew felt like four months, and the ache of his absence wove its way into every part of me. But this was the way of betrothal—the proper separation that made the wedding sweeter for the waiting.

Joash, Simeon, and Benaiah rode behind us, with young Yohanan on the donkey he had once tried to steal, now given freely into his care. Andrew had asked if the boy might come to Arimathea to stay, and Abba had agreed without hesitation. A child should have a home, he had said, and so Yohanan had packed his small bundle and joined our household. The journey back had been peaceful, free of the desperate urgency that had marked our outward travel with Deborah's life hanging in the balance.

"Look how the vines have grown," Abba said as our wagon wound up the familiar slope, Ezra guiding the donkeys with the same steady hands that had brought us safely to Capernaum and back. Abba's voice held the satisfaction of a man returning to a well-tended work. "The spring has been kind to us."

I nodded, though my eyes found not the vines but the places where Andrew and I had walked together. The olive grove where he had first spoken of love. The garden where we had shared quiet evenings talking until the stars appeared. In four days, he would return to me as my husband.

Our gate stood open. Goliath loosed a grand crow, then flapped away in scandal at his own noise. The fountain still sang its familiar melody, and the grape leaves had deepened to new green.

"My lord!" Tamar's voice carried across the courtyard as our small procession rounded the last bend. She dropped her basket of fresh herbs and ran toward us, her face bright with welcome. "My Lord Joseph, Lady Anna! Blessed be the Name, you have returned safely!"

The sight of her familiar figure, the sound of her voice calling me home, brought tears to my eyes. Other servants appeared from every direction, young men straightening from their work in the press, women emerging from the kitchen with flour still dusting their hands. They hurried forward with welcoming smiles.

I got down from the wagon. "Tamar," I said, crossing to

her carefully, my staff tapping against the stones. "It is good to be home." She embraced me warmly.

Her eyes fell on Deborah walking unassisted beside Ezra, and wonder spread across her weathered features. "Deborah — your strength has returned!"

"The Lord has been generous with His mercies," Deborah replied, her voice thick with emotion at this homecoming. "More generous than we dared hope."

"Deborah," came Shira's voice from behind Tamar, soft and hesitant. She stepped forward, her hands holding something familiar—Deborah's spindle, the one she had clutched like a lifeline when we departed. "I — I kept this safe for you. I knew you would return."

Deborah's eyes filled with tears as she took the spindle, her fingers closing around the smooth wood. "Dear Shira. You held the thread that bound me to home." She embraced the younger woman gently. "Thank you for keeping faith when mine faltered. Now we have a wedding to get ready for. Our Anna is now betrothed."

As servants scattered to complete the morning's work, already buzzing with excitement about the wedding preparations to come, Deborah turned to young Yohanan, who had dismounted and stood uncertainly next to his donkey.

"Come here, boy," she said. "Let me look at you properly."

Yohanan approached shyly. "Your tunic is filthy from the road, and your hair —" She shook her head with affectionate exasperation. "We will get you cleaned up and fed. But first, take the donkeys to Ezra so he can see them properly watered and settled."

"Yes, ma'am," Yohanan said, clearly relieved to have a

task. He gathered the lead ropes and headed toward the stables, the donkeys following obediently.

"That boy needs a proper home," Deborah murmured, watching him go. "And I intend to see he gets one."

Abba joined us, and we all made our way into the house. The familiar scents of beeswax and dried lavender surrounded me. These walls had been my whole world for so long. Soon they would be only a part of it. How strange that this place should feel both perfectly familiar and utterly changed. *I am the one who changed*, I thought.

"This house will feel different when you are gone," Deborah said beside me.

"I know," I said, taking her arm. "But love does not end when we step beyond these walls. It only grows larger."

She patted my hand. "Your mother would say the same thing."

"Anna," Abba said as we crossed the main hall. "Before the day takes us in its current, there is something I must give you. Something I have kept far too long."

"Go with your father. I will see to the unpacking. You two have words that need speaking." Deborah headed off toward the stables, and I hoped Yohanan was ready for some mothering.

I followed Abba through corridors that seemed smaller than memory painted them, past windows that framed views I had memorized in lonely childhood hours. When we reached his chambers, my steps faltered. The last time I had stood here, I had torn through his belongings like a thief, desperate and reckless. Blood rose, stinging my cheeks. I swallowed hard and followed him in.

He closed the door behind us and stood with his hand on the latch, as if gathering courage.

"Abba?" I asked. "What troubles you?"

He turned, and I saw tears standing in his eyes. "Not trouble, daughter. Healing, I hope."

He moved to the heavy chest beneath the window, the one I had desperately tried to open. Now he drew a key from his belt and kneeled before it with the reverence of a man approaching an altar, unlocking it with hands that trembled before lifting the lid.

The scent that rose was cedar and time, the sharp green of the wood mingling with dust and dried flowers, the smell of things carefully preserved against the day they would be needed. "Anna, come and sit." I lowered myself next to the chest, trying not to think about how many times I had kicked it in frustration.

Abba reached within and withdrew a small wooden sheep, its painted fleece faded but its carved legs still sturdy, still ready to graze across a child's imagination.

"This came when you turned seven," he said. "Your Aunt Mary sent it after I told her about the lamb you saved in Jerusalem, how you nursed her back to health. She thought you would enjoy having another little sheep to care for."

The sheep was warm in my palms, smooth from long storage, its painted wool faded to the color of cream. I could feel the carved ridges where Mary's knife had shaped each leg, the slight hollow where a child's thumb might rest. I could see the careful love in every detail—the alert ears, the woolly texture carved into the body, the sweet expression that reminded me so much of my dear Bubbeleh. My vision blurred.

"There is more," Abba said. "So much more."

He handed me a small cloth doll, its black wool hair braided, one braid mended with a thread that did not quite match. The face had only eyes and the neatest line for a mouth. The seam that ran along the shoulder had been tugged and sewn again by a patient hand. I let my finger rest on that place.

"Mary made it," Abba said. "She made a pair when you and Salome played at mothers. After the accident, she sent this again."

One by one, he placed more treasures in my lap. Another doll, this one grass, woven with patient fingers. A child's clay cup, lopsided but charming, with my name pressed into the soft clay before firing. A leather pouch filled with smooth stones from Galilee's shore. A packet of dried flowers, their colors long faded but their shapes still recognizable—roses, jasmine, mint.

Another bundle held a sheaf of papers. Charcoal drawings softened by years slid into my lap. A rooster with a large red comb. A boat with oars too many for any sea. A house with a tree that leaned like a friend. Across one page were the letters of my name in a hand that had learned its shapes not long before. I touched the strokes with my fingertip and felt the roughness of the fibers under the dust.

"James drew that rooster," Abba said, and a brief, surprised sound rose from him, almost a laugh.

A single strip of wool lay folded under the papers, dyed a soft red and bordered with pomegranates in tiny, tidy thread. A spindle whorl came next, as smooth as a river stone from many turns in another woman's fingers. A small twist of frankincense slept in papyrus with Mary's name in the same tidy hand. There was even a pouch that had once held dates, kept long past sweetness for love of the sender.

"There is so much, Abba," I said. "I am overwhelmed. And I am filled with sorrow that I did not receive these as they came. They would have meant so much to me during those years."

"I cannot change the past, Anna, but know that I regret keeping these from you."

"I know you do, and I forgive you," I said. "I struggle to believe I have people in the world who care about me. People I do not know."

"They loved you. They love you still," Abba said. "Every year, Mary would send something, some token of remembrance, sometimes from her, sometimes from the younger children. They never forgot you, Anna. Never stopped hoping they would see you again."

At the bottom, in finer linen, something waited. I lifted it. A head-covering lay across my palms, an even weave that held like good cloth does, with a border of myrtle leaves stitched in thread only a shade darker than the linen, so that the pattern lived when the light touched it and hid itself when the light moved away. I smoothed one corner as if to make it breathe.

"Mary sent it for the day you would stand as a bride," Abba said. "She wrote that a covering should be light. A cloud before it was cloth." His voice faltered for a moment but then found its path again. "If you wish it."

I did not speak at once. It lay across my hands, carrying love that had spanned years. I set it on my head with shaking hands. The linen fell with unexpected weight, not heavy, but substantial. The fabric settled across my hair and shoulders like a blessing, and the stitched myrtle leaves brushed my brow with their quiet shadow. I could smell the cedar it had rested in, could almost feel Mary's fingers in every careful stitch.

"I wish it," I said. "I will wear it."

Abba's shoulders eased, a knot he had carried too long slipping free. He put his hand on the edge of the chest and bowed his head. "That will make all of us very happy," he said.

A soft step sounded and halted at the door. Deborah had come without knocking. She took one look at the covering and at my face beneath it, and her expression changed, brightening. She crossed the room without speaking. Her fingers lifted the edge of the linen, testing the weave, tracing one embroidered leaf. She studied it as she had once studied my fevered face, with the same intensity of love. Then she nodded once, satisfied.

"Mary's work," she said. "I would know her hand among a hundred." She set the covering more firmly, straightened the lay of it at my temple, and kissed that place with the confidence of a mother who trusted her own blessing. "It is right. It is yours."

We put each gift back into its cloth. I slipped the spindle whorl into my pocket for its comforting weight and folded the covering. Abba closed the chest and rested his palm upon the lid.

"I took too much from you," he said. "I cannot give back the years. But I can give this, and all that follows, if you will let me."

"You have given me truth," I said. "I will carry it."

Deborah tucked her hand into the crook of his arm as if such tenderness had always been their habit. "Come," she said, bright with life. "There is work enough to tire good hearts, and still more for those who shirk."

We laughed, all three, and the laugh sat well in the room.

∼

The rest of the day passed quietly as we settled back into the rhythms of home. Deborah threw herself into household tasks with renewed vigor, directing the kitchen preparations and organizing linens with the energy of a woman half her age.

I found her in the kitchen that afternoon, Yohanan at her side as she taught him to knead bread dough. His hands worked the mass with determined concentration while Deborah kept up a steady stream of instruction.

"Not so hard you will tear it, not so soft it will not rise. There. Feel how it changes under your fingers?" She glanced up and saw me watching. "The boy needs to learn a useful trade. Wandering around the countryside alone has no future in it."

Yohanan's ears went red, but he did not stop kneading.

"He is doing well?" I asked.

"Very well. Quick to learn, willing to work, and has been a tremendous help since we arrived." She patted his shoulder. "He will make a fine addition to this household."

Yohanan looked up at her with something like worship in his eyes, and I understood. Deborah had that effect on people. She could be gruff and demanding on the surface, but underneath, she had a heart that gathered in strays and made them family. I walked away, chuckling. Yohanan had definitely chosen the right donkey to steal.

Ezra supervised the servants as they began the early preparations for the wedding feast. I helped where I could, but mostly, I walked through the rooms of my childhood, seeing them with fresh eyes that belonged to a woman about to become a wife.

That evening, we supped together in the main hall, our small family reunited and whole. Abba spoke of the estate's affairs, the harvest that would come in the fall, and the repairs needed before winter. Normal things, peaceful things, the kind I had longed for during all those years when we sat in careful silence.

"Abba," I said during a lull in the conversation, "have you sent word to Mary about the wedding? I should very much like her to be there, and all the family too. It would mean everything to me to have them present."

"I sent a messenger. Mary and the family will arrive the day before the ceremony, along with Jesus and his disciples." He paused, smiling at me. "I thought you would want your whole family here to witness your happiness."

Tears of gratitude threatened to fall. "Thank you, Abba. Thank you for understanding."

"It is past time for our family to be together again," he said.

The next days brought their own quiet joys. I walked through the vineyards with Ezra, learning what I had missed during our absence. Deborah worked beside the other women, her hands steady as she kneaded bread for baking. The house hummed with purposeful activity, but there was no urgency yet. That would come later, when more guests arrived and the final preparations began in earnest.

When the household had settled into its rhythm, the knock came. "My lord?" Tamar's voice carried excitement. "Visitors at the gate. Naomi of Bethsaida and Rachel of Capernaum have arrived."

Joy rose in me. Andrew's family had come to help with the wedding preparations.

Abba's face lit up. "They have come. Let us welcome them properly."

We made our way to the central courtyard, where I could

see two familiar figures standing near the gate, travel-worn but smiling. Naomi, small and silver-haired, stood beside Rachel, both of them looking around the estate with the pleased expressions of women who had come with purpose.

"Naomi, Rachel," I called, stepping forward with arms outstretched. "How good it is to see you again!"

They turned at the sound of my voice and hurried towards me. Rachel reached me first, her embrace fierce with sisterly affection.

"Anna!" she said, holding me tight. "We could hardly wait to come help with the preparations."

"And I bring a mother's blessing on this house," Naomi added, drawing me into her own embrace when Rachel released me. "What joy to see you again, dear daughter."

Abba approached with genuine pleasure. "Naomi, Rachel. The journey from Capernaum was peaceful?"

"Very peaceful," Naomi replied. "And how wonderful to see this beautiful estate. Andrew described it to us, but his words could not capture how lovely it truly is." They had left Capernaum, she said, with a basket tied so well to the pack-beast that not a single honey cake had leaped to its death on the road.

"The guest chambers are prepared," Abba said. "You must both be weary from travel."

"Thank you, my lord," Rachel said. "Tonight we rest, for there is much to do in two days, and I have brought my best recipes for wedding bread."

As we walked toward the house, servants appeared from every direction. Tamar materialized with basins of heated water and soft cloths. Others emerged with food and drink, with fresh linens and welcoming smiles. The household welcomed Andrew's family with open arms, and their faces showed this felt different from hosting ordinary guests. These women were family now, part of the great joy that was about to unfold.

"Your home is even more beautiful than Andrew described," Rachel said as we passed through the main hall with its tall windows and polished floors. "He spoke of your gardens especially."

"They were my mother's design," I said. "I hope to show you tomorrow, when the light is best."

"I would love to see them. Andrew said you grew the herbs there that saved his life."

I took them to the finest guest chambers, the ones that caught the afternoon light and overlooked the garden where the wedding would take place. After their journey, they needed rest, and there would be time tomorrow for all the things we wanted to share.

"I will see you in the morning," I promised as I bid them goodnight. "We have much to plan and prepare together."

That night, I lay awake longer than usual, thinking of Andrew somewhere with Jesus and the other disciples, knowing that tomorrow would bring us one day closer to our wedding. In two days, I would be his wife.

When morning came, bright with promise, I gathered the things I wanted to share—my mother's wedding dress which Deborah had carefully preserved in cedar and lavender, the pearls that would encircle my throat, the veil from Mary, the simple sandals that would carry me to Andrew's side.

Naomi and Rachel joined me in my chamber after

breaking their fast, and I spread these treasures before them like an offering.

"Oh," Rachel breathed, lifting the fine linen of the dress with reverent hands. "This is exquisite. Your mother had beautiful taste."

"She died when I was five," I said. "I have only fragments of memory. Her voice singing, her hands in the garden." I gestured helplessly. "For this, I need women who have walked this path before."

Naomi set down the dress and took my hands in hers. "Sweet Anna, you shall have all the guidance you need. Marriage is not a destination but a journey, and the best counsel I can give you is to choose love again each morning. When the road is hard and shelter scarce, choose love. When words come sharp from tiredness, choose love."

"Did you choose love? With Andrew's father?"

Her face grew soft with memory. "Every day for many years, until the sea called him home. Andrew has his father's heart. Faithful, generous, constant as the tide. You could not have found a better man to share your life with."

"And now," Rachel said, "let us see how this dress fits. A bride should know her gown is perfect before the great day arrives."

The next hour passed in a blur of laughter and tears as they helped me try on the dress, adjusting the drape of the linen across my shoulders and pinning the veil to catch the light just so. Their voices filled my chamber with stories of their own wedding days, of the joy and terror that comes with stepping into a new life.

"There," Naomi said, securing the last pin in my veil. "You look like a bride blessed by heaven itself."

I turned to the bronze mirror and stared at it. Was this

truly me? My dark hair flowed beneath the delicate veil, the fine linen making my olive skin glow as if lit from within. The scars were there, would always be there, but they no longer looked like damage. They looked like part of a story that had led somewhere beautiful.

"Do you think Andrew will be pleased?" I asked.

Rachel's reflection appeared beside mine in the mirror, her smile bright with certainty. "My dear sister, he will take one look at you and know he is the most blessed man who ever lived."

A commotion in the courtyard drew our attention to the window. Through the lattice, we could see servants moving with purposeful energy, arranging tables, testing the ovens that would bake tomorrow's bread, checking linens and vessels for the feast to come. The entire household buzzed with cheerful industry of wedding preparations.

"They are eager for this celebration," Naomi observed, watching Tamar direct two young women toward the storerooms.

"It has been too long since this house has known such happiness," I said, thinking of all the quiet, lonely years. "They deserve to celebrate."

As the servants went about their work, their voices carrying fragments of excited conversation about flowers and feast preparations, we turned away from the window.

"You will be a stunning bride," Rachel said, beginning to unpin the veil.

Later that afternoon, we went into the courtyard to take in the wedding preparations. The light had shifted to that hour when every color deepens and shadows are kind. Ezra had the boys tie lamps high along the trellis so the taller men would not bump against them later. The servants had arranged the benches in a wide semicircle, with a space left clear at the center, marked by the stones. When I passed beneath the fig, a leaf brushed my shoulder as if it had been waiting all day for me to notice it.

I sat on the stone bench near the fountain and dipped my hands into the water. Rachel brought me a crust with steam still in it. "Eat," she said. "You will forget if someone does not put bread in your mouth." I did as I was told, and the first bite made me sigh with pleasure. She watched my face with satisfaction and went to check the wine jars.

As the lamps took fire one by one, the garden gathered its own sky. Olive leaves shone. The trellis cast a net of light upon the path. Voices softened to the tone people use in places they love. Deborah moved from task to task with a hand on a shoulder here, a word there. Ezra stepped back at the gate and measured the whole with his eyes, promising himself and his master that the house would not disappoint us.

When I retired to my chamber for the night, I sat with the wooden sheep in my palm. Tomorrow, Rachel and Naomi would teach me the secrets of being a wife, and we would prepare the feast that would celebrate not just a wedding but the joining of two families, two hearts, two futures made one.

Outside my window, jasmine perfumed the night air with sweetness, and somewhere in the house I could hear Rachel's voice mingling with Deborah's as they planned. The sounds were ordinary—women talking, footsteps on stone, the distant lowing of cattle settling for the night. But to me, they were home.

CHAPTER 26

THE SOUND of approaching voices carried across the morning air, drawing me from my restless pacing in the garden. I had been awake since before dawn, too excited to sleep, too nervous to sit still. Every sound from the road made my heart leap with anticipation. Yesterday, we had observed the Sabbath in quiet rest. The household moved through prayers and reflection as we prepared our hearts for the celebration to come. But now, with the holy day ended and a new week begun, anticipation thrummed through my veins like honeyed wine. Today, Andrew would arrive, and tomorrow would be our wedding.

"Travelers approaching!" Ezra called from his watch post near the gates, and a burst of adrenaline rushed through me.

"Lady Anna!" Tamar's voice rang out from the courtyard, bright with excitement. "The Teacher and his disciples come! Your bridegroom is here!"

I abandoned all pretense of dignity and hurried toward

the courtyard, my staff moving quickly over the cool stones, pure happiness propelling me forward. I could hear the low murmur of men's voices approaching our gates. *Andrew was here!*

The household came alive around me—servants rushing past, water basins, voices calling. Deborah appeared from the kitchens, Rachel and Naomi behind her.

"They are here!" I called.

"Anna, child, try to contain yourself!" Deborah caught my arm. "You will startle the poor man if you greet him like a runaway donkey."

I pulled free, moving toward the gates. Yohanan appeared in my path, carrying a tray of cups that looked almost too large for his small hands. I swerved around him without stopping.

"Lady Anna!" he called after me, but I was already at the gates as they swung open, my heart dancing for joy as they came into view.

Jesus entered the courtyard first. His presence reached me before he did, and I stilled. When he saw me waiting by the gates, he beamed.

"Cousin," he called, approaching with arms outstretched.

Tears pricked my eyes. "Jesus! Welcome back. Welcome to my wedding!"

He embraced me tightly. He smelled of sun-warmed linen and the road. "How beautiful you look," he said, pulling back to study my face. "Marriage suits you well."

"Even though we have not had our wedding feast yet?" I asked, laughing through my tears, which fell despite my attempt to stop them.

"The feast is just the celebration. You became his wife when you shared the cup."

Behind him, the disciples were setting down their packs and walking sticks. Simon shaking road dust from his cloak, John and James stretching after their journey, Matthew carefully protecting his ever-present scrolls from the morning breeze. Philip, Judas and Simon the Zealot were there, and Nathaniel, and several others I recognized from our time in Capernaum.

And then finally, I saw him.

He had taken care with himself. His dark hair was combed back from his forehead, still showing the damp tracks of water as if he had washed at a stream that morning. The tunic he wore was his finest, one of undyed linen that fell clean and unpatched across his shoulders. Even his sandals looked freshly oiled.

The instant he caught sight of me, elation blazed across his face. It started in his eyes, then spread to his mouth, curved in a smile so broad I thought I could count every tooth. His dimples carved themselves deep into his cheeks, and I forgot to breathe.

He took two quick steps toward me, then checked himself. Stopped. Glanced at the watching crowd. I saw him draw a breath, square his shoulders, clearly attempting to approach with dignity befitting the occasion, then emotion won out, and he broke into a run.

He caught me around the waist and pulled me close, lifting me slightly so my toes barely brushed the ground. I laughed, dropping my staff as I threw my arms around his neck. My head covering went askew, and my carefully arranged hair came loose from its pins, but I did not care. His arms stayed locked around my waist, holding me against him tightly as though anything else might let me slip away, and supporting my weight so my hip bore no strain. The rapid beat of his heart pounded against me through the linen of his tunic. He smelled of dust and male sweat and the sharp green scent of rosemary his mother must have packed among his clothes.

"Anna." My name came out rough, almost broken. He loosened his hold just enough to look down at me, and what I saw in his face stole what little breath I had regained. "My beautiful wife," he said. "Did you miss me?"

"What do you think?" My fingers found the front of his tunic and held on.

One corner of his mouth quirked up, that half-smile I loved. His right hand released my waist, rising with deliberate slowness until his palm settled against the side of my face. The calluses on his fingers rasped slightly against my cheek. His hand was warm, and the heat of it seeped into my skin like a brand.

I turned in to his touch without thinking, letting the weight of my head rest in his palm. My eyes closed of their own accord. In the darkness behind my lids, every other sense sharpened — the slight tremor in his fingers, the quickened rhythm of his breathing, the way the air between us seemed to hum with everything we could not say in front of witnesses.

When I opened my eyes again, he was studying me, memorizing every detail.

We stood there, rooted in place. The courtyard moved around us, but it all blurred to nothing. Somewhere nearby, Deborah was undoubtedly shaking her head at my impropriety. I did not care. I saw only Andrew.

"Well," Simon Peter announced loudly, his arm around his wife, "if you two are quite finished gazing at each other like lovesick fools, some of us would appreciate water for our animals and perhaps a cup of wine for our throats."

I flushed, but Andrew just laughed. "Always the practical one, Simon."

"Someone has to be, since you have been walking around in a daze ever since we left Capernaum."

"No, I have not."

"You walked into a tree yesterday," John pointed out helpfully.

"It was a low branch!"

"It was noon, Andrew. The sun was directly overhead. There were no shadows. You should have seen it."

"You cannot deny you have been useless for days." Matthew waggled an eyebrow at me, laughing.

"Untrue," Andrew protested.

"Yesterday you put your sandals on the wrong feet," John said cheerfully. "We had to point it out twice."

"And you missed your mouth while eating bread," James added with a grin.

"That was one time, and I was distracted—"

"By thoughts of Anna," Matthew finished. "We know. You told us. Repeatedly."

"Ignore them," Andrew said to me, taking my hand in his. "They are just jealous."

"Jealous?" James scoffed. "Of what?"

"Of the fact that I have a wife as wonderful as Anna," Andrew replied without missing a beat, "while the rest of you are still stumbling around unmarried. Well, except Simon."

Laughter broke over the courtyard, and I had to bite my lip to keep from joining them.

"Poor man," I said, patting Andrew's arm. "Have they tormented you throughout the entire journey?"

"Every step," Andrew replied with mock suffering. "They have no appreciation for the trials of a man in love."

"We appreciate them," Simon said. "They are highly entertaining."

"Perhaps we should move this conversation somewhere with shade and refreshment," Jesus suggested with amusement, "before Andrew thinks of new ways to embarrass himself."

As the laughter subsided, Yohanan stepped forward hesitantly, still clutching his tray of cups. "Andrew?" he said, his voice small but hopeful.

Poor Yohanan. I had forgotten all about him.

A grin sprang across Andrew's face. "Yohanan!" He ruffled the boy's hair affectionately. "Deborah must be feeding you properly. You look like a different person."

"She has been teaching me to make bread," Yohanan said proudly. "I am really good at it. And Ezra is teaching me about the vineyards, and —" He stopped, suddenly self-conscious.

"And he has not stolen anything," Deborah added tartly, appearing beside him. "Not once." She looked at Yohanan the way she looked at me when I told her the proper herb to use for an ailment. They would have each other when I left, and the thought made me glad.

"Well, that is an improvement," Andrew said with a wink at the boy. "See? I told you Arimathea would be good for you."

"And that it has." My father had been hanging back, Naomi at his side, allowing us our reunion, but now he stepped forward. "Jesus, my friend. Andrew, my son. Be welcome here. All of you, welcome."

He embraced Jesus cordially and then clasped Andrew's shoulders with paternal affection. "How are you, son? Ready for tomorrow's celebration?"

"More than ready," Andrew replied firmly. "Though I may not survive the teasing."

"The teasing is part of the tradition," Abba assured him. "If they did not love you, they would not torment you."

Andrew moved to his mother and gathered her into an embrace. She held him tight, and I saw her hand come up to cup the back of his head the way mothers do, even when their sons are grown men. "Ima, thank you for coming early to help with the preparations. I am glad to be here now."

"I am sure you are," she said. She held him at arm's length to study his face with a mother's critical eye, then touched his cheek, satisfied.

I watched them. This woman would be my mother now. And she already loved me—I had seen it in her eyes in Capernaum, felt it in her welcome here.

"Everyone grab a cup and relieve young Yohanan of his heavy burden," Abba announced and took the first one. "Come. We will get everyone settled."

As we moved toward the house, I walked beside Jesus. "How was your journey? Any trouble on the roads?"

"Peaceful. Though we encountered some interesting travelers near Sychar. A merchant caravan from Damascus, carrying news from the north. Interesting times, Anna. The world is changing more quickly than most people realize."

His tone made me glance at him sharply, but his expression was untroubled. Still, I caught an undercurrent of something. Worry perhaps, or the knowledge of hard days ahead.

"Should I be concerned?" I asked.

"Not today," he said. "Today is for joy. Tomorrow is for celebration. The future will take care of itself."

At the main hall, Jesus paused. "I will walk in your olive grove for a while, if I may. The road has been long, and I find I need some quiet before evening comes."

"Of course," Abba said at once. "You know these grounds as well as anyone. Take whatever time you need."

Jesus smiled gratefully. "Thank you. The hills here have always been a place of peace for me." He clasped Andrew's shoulder briefly. "Enjoy this time with your wife, my friend. We will speak more later."

As Jesus walked away toward the grove, Andrew shook his head in wonder. "Even when crowds come from every side, calling out for healing and teaching, he does not seem bothered. He always steps away to pray. It is as if he draws strength from solitude the way we draw strength from food."

"That must be overwhelming, though," I said. "All those people, all those needs."

"It would be for us," Andrew agreed. "But when Jesus is with someone, they receive his full attention, as if they were the only person in the world. He is not like the rest of us. He is more."

"More what?" I asked.

"More everything."

The disciples were fed and given rooms to rest in after their journey, and the house settled into a peaceful rhythm. I found myself alone with Andrew for the first time since his arrival. We strolled through my mother's garden while the afternoon sun slanted gold through the olive trees.

"Tell me about Capernaum," I said, my hand resting in the crook of his elbow.

ANNA OF ARIMATHEA

"I missed you," Andrew replied with a rueful laugh. "Every moment felt longer when I could not share it with you. The crowds were larger than ever, but all I could think about was how much I wanted to tell you everything I was seeing."

"That must have been distracting."

"Completely. Simon had to grab my arm twice to keep me from walking into the lake because I was thinking about something you would have found interesting." He smiled sheepishly. "The other disciples made fun of me."

"I am sorry I caused you to be so absent-minded," I laughed.

"You did. Everything reminded me of you, Anna."

We paused beside the fountain where we had first talked as more than healer and patient. The water sparkled in the sunlight, and a thrush sang from the cypress nearby.

"Andrew," I said carefully, "after we are truly married, what are our plans? I know we will go to Bethsaida first, but then what? Do we travel with Jesus immediately, or do we have time to settle into married life?"

He turned to face me fully, his hands coming up to frame my face. "I have been thinking about that constantly. Jesus has given us his blessing to take time in Bethsaida, perhaps a month or two, to establish our household with my mother and for you to know the community there."

His thumbs brushed across my cheekbones, and his voice grew quieter. "But Anna, I want you to know that whatever we do, wherever we go, you will not only follow along. Jesus values your healing skills. You will have your own role in the ministry, not only as my wife."

"What do you mean?" I asked, intrigued.

"The women who travel with us—Joanna, Mary of Magdala, Tirzah, the others—they are not only supporters. They minister to people Jesus cannot easily reach. Women, children, families who need care." His eyes grew earnest. "You will do much good, Anna. Your knowledge of herbs, your gentle way with the wounded and frightened will all be needed."

"I had not thought about it that way. I was worried I would be unnecessary."

He laughed softly. "Unnecessary? Anna, you will be invaluable. The question is not whether you will be useful. It is whether you are ready for how many people will need you."

"That is both exciting and terrifying," I said, though thoughts of how I would keep up with everyone crowded my mind.

"Good," he said, smiling. "That means it matters." He rested his brow against mine. "Tomorrow we celebrate properly."

"Tomorrow we celebrate," I agreed. I would think about my hip and what it meant to my future later. Not now.

We walked through the garden for some time, talking about everything and nothing, simply enjoying being together once again. We had just returned to the fountain when footsteps approached. Jesus emerged from the shade of the olive trees.

"Am I interrupting?" he asked with mild amusement.

"Never," I said quickly, stepping back from Andrew yet keeping hold of his hand.

"Good. Because I hoped we might talk before the rest of the family arrives."

"The rest of the family?" Andrew asked.

"My mother and siblings should arrive by evening," Jesus

explained. "Anna has not seen them since she was very young."

"How are they? Your mother especially. How is Aunt Mary?"

"She was well the last time I was with her. I am sure she is very much looking forward to seeing you again."

Jesus sat on the stone bench beside the fountain, gesturing for us to join him. "Before they arrive and the house fills with celebration, I would speak with you both about what lies ahead."

"What do you mean?" I asked, tightening my grip on Andrew's hand.

Jesus said nothing for a long moment. When he finally spoke, dread coiled in my stomach.

"You remember what I told you both in Capernaum, after your betrothal, about the cost of following me?"

We nodded.

"That cost is coming sooner than I had hoped. The religious authorities grow bolder in their opposition, and Rome watches every gathering with suspicion. My own followers —"He paused, choosing his words carefully. "Many still believe I will raise the sword against our oppressors. They do not yet understand that my victory will come through suffering, not conquest."

"What are you saying?" I felt cold despite the afternoon heat.

"I am saying the time is approaching when simply knowing me will be dangerous. When that day comes, and it will come soon, you must decide what matters most." His eyes moved between us with deep compassion. "Your safety or your faithfulness to what you know is true."

Andrew tensed beside me, and fear shot through me.

"But know this," Jesus continued, his voice strengthening. "Whatever darkness comes, whatever trials you face, I will never leave you. Even when you cannot see me—" his voice grew more intense "—even when it seems I have abandoned you to your fate, I am with you. Always. That is my promise to you both, sealed before the Father. My love will never abandon you. It is eternal, unbreakable, stronger than death itself. It is forever."

The garden had gone silent around us. Even the birds seemed to have stopped singing.

"Jesus," I said carefully, "are you warning us about our marriage?"

He looked at me and smiled. "Not at all. You marry with the Father's blessing and mine. Your love is a gift from Him, and your union will be a source of strength for the dark days ahead. I am simply ensuring you understand what you have chosen."

"We understand," Andrew said firmly. "And we choose you. Both of us."

"We do," I said, squeezing Andrew's hand.

"Then I am content. Love will carry you through whatever storms may come. Remember that in the difficult hours." He rose from the bench, brushing dust from his robe, and left.

"He has a lot of advice and warnings for us," Andrew noted.

"Everyone does," I said. "Every time I turn around it seems someone needs to speak to me privately."

Andrew laughed and grabbed my hand. "Perhaps they are squeezing a year's worth of talk into a few days. We have moved quite fast from betrothal to wedding."

"Maybe," I said. "I do not mind, truly. At least they care.

And we should pay close attention to everything Jesus tells us. He does not speak just to hear his own voice. He speaks with purpose."

As we walked back toward the house, I felt Andrew's arm tighten around me.

"Are you frightened?" he asked.

"Yes," I admitted. "Not of the future we will face together. Only the one we might face apart."

"Then we will not face it apart," he said.

"Andrew, there is something I need to tell you. It happened shortly before you arrived injured at our gate."

He turned to face me fully, giving me his complete attention.

"I was in this very garden, and I was so broken. Lonely. I asked whether God even knew I existed." I looked toward the place I had stood that morning. "I heard a voice. Clear as yours is now. It called me by name. 'Anna,' it said, 'I see you.'"

Andrew's eyes widened, but he remained silent, and let me speak.

"I thought I had imagined it, but Jesus confirmed it was real. God called me by name. Before I knew about our family connection, before I knew anything about Jesus's ministry, the Father saw me. Called me." My voice steadied. "So whatever trials come, I am not following Jesus only because I love you, though I do. I follow because He called me first. I am His, and He is mine."

Andrew's face glowed with pride. "Anna," he breathed. "How blessed I am to marry a woman whom God calls by name."

"We are both called," I said firmly. "And we will both answer."

"We will," he agreed, and the words sealed our resolve.

I stood at my chamber window as the sun sank toward the western hills, taking a moment from the preparations to watch the road. Dust rose in the distance. I watched a small party of travelers moving at the relaxed pace of people who had journeyed far but were almost home. Finally!

"They come!" Tamar called from the courtyard below, her voice ringing with delight. "Mary and the family of Jesus approach!"

I joined the welcoming party. This was the reunion I had dreamed of since learning the truth about my extended family — meeting the aunt who had sent gifts through the years, the cousins who had grown up knowing my name when I had forgotten theirs.

The gates swung open. Mary of Nazareth entered first, her face glowing with happiness as she looked around the estate. She was a woman in her forties with a round, open face and sun-browned skin, her eyes holding a brightness that had nothing to do with youth.

Jesus moved forward to greet her, and she reached up to touch his face. He bent to kiss her forehead, murmuring something I could not hear. Then she turned her attention to the courtyard, and her smile widened.

Behind her came her children — young men and women I had never met but who shared my blood. One young woman broke from the group and rushed toward me.

Salome.

She was near my age, with Mary's dark eyes.

"Anna!" she cried, and before I could respond, she had closed the distance between us and pulled me into an embrace that smelled of travel and jasmine oil. Her arms were strong, and her grip fierce. "I am Salome. I have wanted to meet you again for so long." She pulled back to look at me, then her eyes caught on the fig tree. "There it is! We hid in that tree. Ate figs until our stomachs hurt and our mothers had to call us down three times."

I looked at the fig tree. Sticky fingers, leaves rustling, someone laughing beside me. "I remember," I breathed.

She pulled back to study my face. "Look at you! You are radiant. You are brimming with good things. Tomorrow you will be the most beautiful bride in all Judea."

"Tomorrow I will be the happiest," I said, glancing toward Andrew, who was receiving enthusiastic embraces from Jesus's brothers. "And you?" I asked. "Are you married? Do you have children?"

"Married two years now, to a good man from Cana. No children yet, but the Lord willing…" She touched her hand to her heart in hope.

Mary approached more slowly, her eyes drinking in every detail of my face. When she reached us, she opened her arms, and I fell into her like a child coming home.

"Anna, my darling girl," she whispered against my hair. "You look so much like your mother."

"Aunt Mary," I whispered, holding her tight. After a moment, we stepped back to look at each other. "I have my mother's wedding dress. Deborah preserved it for me. And I have the veil you sent — the one with the myrtle leaves. I will wear them both tomorrow."

"Oh, Anna." Mary's eyes filled with tears. "Your mother would be so proud to see you wear her dress, and I am honored that you will wear my gift as well. You will be lovely." She glanced back toward her children with a touch of regret. "My daughter Mary wished desperately to be here, but she is near her time with her first child. The journey would have been too difficult."

"I understand," I said. "And I hope all goes well for her. Perhaps we will meet when the babe is safely born."

"I hope so as well. And now," she said, wiping her eyes and looking around the courtyard, "where is the young man who has won our Anna's heart?"

"Here, Aunt Mary," Andrew said, approaching with a mixture of confidence and nerves that made me want to laugh. "Andrew bar Jonah, at your service."

Mary studied him with the keen eye of a woman who had raised many children. Andrew shifted his weight, and I saw him swallow. Finally, her face broke into a smile. "You have good eyes," she said. "And you make our Anna happy. That is enough for me."

Abba moved to Mary's side. "Welcome to this house, all of you. Mary, it has been far too long since these walls heard your laughter."

"Joseph." Mary embraced him, and he returned it with the ease of old friendship. "Your home is as welcoming as I remembered. And your daughter—" She turned to look at me, and I felt the weight of her attention. "She has your eyes. But something of her own, too. A strength that bends rather than breaks."

Abba's hand found my shoulder. "Life has demanded much of her. She has not broken. And she had Deborah to guide her."

As if summoned by her name, Deborah appeared with a tray of wine cups and honey cakes still warm from the ovens. "The guest chambers are prepared, and supper will be ready soon. But first, you must be thirsty from your journey."

Rachel and Naomi flanked her, carrying additional trays laden with fresh bread and olives.

Jesus accepted a cup with gracious thanks, then raised it toward the assembled company. "To family reunited," he said. "To love that endures all separation."

"To tomorrow's joy," Andrew added, his eyes finding mine.

"To Anna and Andrew," Mary said, lifting her cup higher. "May your marriage be blessed with a long life, many children, and the peace that passes understanding."

We drank, and the wine was sweet on my tongue, but sweeter still was the sound of family voices filling the courtyard, the sight of people I loved standing together in the place where I had grown up so lonely.

As the evening deepened and we moved toward the dining hall, Salome slipped her arm through mine. "Tell me everything," she whispered. "How did you meet? When did you know you loved him? What is he like when he thinks no one is watching?"

"Everything?" I laughed. "That could take all night."

"Perfect," she said, grinning. "I was not planning to sleep anyway."

Before we entered, I caught Rachel's eye. She nodded knowingly, and I saw her exchange a meaningful glance with Naomi. The evening would hold more than family stories and wedding excitement. There would be wisdom shared, the kind passed from woman to woman, mother to daughter, across generations.

Mary approached us with warm amusement. "I suspect the women will gather tonight while the men talk of fishing and ministry. There are things a bride must know that only married women can teach."

"Things Deborah could not tell me?" I asked.

"Things Deborah would be too modest to share," Rachel said with a knowing smile. "But we take our duty to you seriously, Anna. We will tell you everything you need to know."

Anticipation coursed through me. Tonight I would finally learn what it truly meant to become a wife. Tomorrow I would put that knowledge to use.

CHAPTER 27

Hushed laughter drifted through my chamber window and pulled me from a restless sleep. My wedding day. Joy rose in me, bright and disbelieving. Today, our covenant would be witnessed and blessed before everyone we loved.

I rolled over and listened. Voices rose from below, footsteps on stone, the household already awake and preparing.

The door to my chamber opened quietly, and Salome's head appeared. "Are you awake? Please tell me you are awake, because I have been lying in bed for an hour listening to the women bustling about downstairs, and I am about to burst."

I sat up, pushing hair from my face. "I am awake. What brings you here so early?"

"Your wedding day preparations." She slipped into the room, followed by Rachel, Naomi, Aunt Mary, and Deborah, all of them carrying baskets and wearing identical expressions of barely contained mischief.

I stared at them. All five women, here in my chamber, ready to prepare me for this day. I had never imagined this—a wedding, a family gathered around me, women who cared enough to make this morning special. Emotion rose in my throat. "What are you planning?"

"Everything," Rachel announced, setting down her basket. "We have brought breakfast, because brides who faint during their ceremonies make for poor family stories."

Salome laughed and pulled white rosebuds from her basket, their petals still damp with morning dew. "Flowers for your hair. My mother insisted."

"And oils," Naomi added, producing small clay bottles that caught the morning light. "Every bride should smell beautiful."

Mary moved closer. "And if you would like, I have stories to tell you about your mother on her wedding day."

I could not speak. Every detail about my mother was like gold, every memory a gift I had been denied too long. "More than anything."

Deborah came to my side and brushed my hair back from my face, her touch familiar and sure. "And we love you."

They gathered around me, passing food, combs, and bottles of precious oils. Salome broke off a piece of warm bread, still fragrant from the oven, and held it out to me while Rachel poured wine into a cup. "Eat," Naomi insisted. "You will need your strength."

I ate, though I barely tasted the food, too aware of the hands working in my hair. Deborah's fingers were gentle as she combed through the tangles, while Salome wove white rosebuds among the strands, each one releasing its perfume as she secured it with pins. The scent filled my chamber—roses and bread and the sharper note of lavender oil that Rachel warmed between her palms before rubbing it into my hands.

"Your mother was so nervous she could barely speak the responses," Mary said, laughing at the memory. "She kept whispering to me, 'What if I say the wrong thing? What if I trip? What if I forget the words?' I finally had to remind her that Joseph had been watching her with complete adoration for months, and that even if she recited the names of every goat in Judea, he would still think it was the most wonderful sound he had ever heard."

"Did it help?" I asked.

"Not at all. She was still nervous. But she was glowing with joy. Just as you are." Mary reached for something folded carefully on the bed. "And now, I think it is time."

She shook out the veil, and it caught the lamplight - fine linen embroidered with delicate myrtle leaves along the border, each leaf rendered in thread so pale it seemed to shimmer.

"May I?" she asked.

I nodded, unable to speak.

She set it over my hair, arranging it so the myrtle leaves framed my face. Her fingers lingered at my temples as she adjusted the drape. "Your mother wore my veil when she married your father. And now you wear this one. The myrtle is for love, for marriage blessed by God." Her voice caught. "You are beautiful, Anna." She stepped back, her eyes wet. "Sarah would be so proud. She is here with us, I think. Watching her daughter become a bride."

I blinked hard and could only nod.

Deborah stepped back, her hand pressed to her mouth. Rachel's eyes shone with tears. Even Salome had gone quiet.

"There," Mary whispered.

I turned to the bronze mirror. The veil was sheer enough to see through - fine linen that softened but did not hide.

Through it, I could see the white roses woven throughout my hair, pale against the dark strands. The myrtle leaves embroidered along the border framed my face, drawing attention to my eyes, my cheekbones. The white linen of my mother's dress caught the morning light, and against it my skin looked warm. The scars were still there, visible even through the veil's softness, but somehow they mattered less.

I turned to Mary. "Do I look like my mother?"

Mary's eyes filled. "Oh, Anna. You could be her reflection. The same eyes, the same proud chin. When she wore that dress..." She touched the sleeve gently. "She was radiant. Just as you are now."

The bracelets at my wrists caught the light - gold and silver, old and new, circling my arms.

"Oh," Salome breathed. "Anna, you are the most stunning bride I have ever seen."

"Andrew is going to weep when he sees you," Rachel predicted with satisfaction.

"Good," I said, laughing nervously. "I want him to remember this moment for the rest of his life."

"Trust me," Naomi said dryly, "he will."

Noise in the courtyard drew our attention to the window. Below, we could see Jesus directing the placement of an arbor woven with olive branches and white roses. Andrew stood nearby, clearly trying to help but mostly just getting in the way, his nervous energy making him pace.

"Someone should rescue him before he wears a path in the stones," Mary said.

"Let him pace," Deborah said. "Men need something to worry about on their wedding day, or they feel useless."

I turned to Deborah with sudden urgency. "I need to speak with you in private, if I may."

The other women gathered their baskets and left, murmuring about checking on the preparations for the feast. When we were alone, I took Deborah's hands in mine.

"I cannot leave you," I blurted. "I know I am supposed to go to Bethsaida to establish my household with Naomi. But you have been my mother, my dearest friend, for all of my days. How can I simply walk away?"

Her eyes filled with tears, but her smile was steady. "Child, you cannot hold on to the past when the future calls. I have known this day would come since you were a little girl, even when you declared you would never marry because then you would have to leave me."

I pressed my forehead to our joined hands. "I meant it then, and I mean it now."

"Anna." Her voice was firm but kind. "One of my greatest joys has been watching you grow from a broken child into the woman you are now. Do you think I would keep you from your happiness to ease my loneliness?"

"But what will you do? Who will—"

"I will do what I have always done. I will serve this household, tend the gardens, and thank God every day that He allowed me to raise you." She brushed a tear from my cheek. "I do have my husband, after all. He is good company. And I will visit. Often. Bethsaida is not that far."

"Promise me."

"I promise. And you must promise me something in return."

"Anything."

"Promise me you will be happy. Completely happy. You have carried sorrow long enough. Let it go. Let yourself have this joy."

I pulled her into my arms, breathing in the familiar scent

of herbs and sunshine that always clung to her clothes. "I love you, Deborah. More than words can say."

"And I love you, Anna. You have been the daughter of my heart since the day I first held you." She pulled back, her eyes shining with unshed tears. "Now go. Your future husband is probably wearing holes in his sandals by now."

It was time. The garden had been readied into something like a dream made honest. Garlands of myrtle and garden roses bridged the posts, rosemary tucked in for luck. Linen streamers, plant-dyed in soft madder and woad, stirred from the olive branches overhead. The fig tree where Andrew and I first spoke wore a ribbon of undyed linen that caught the afternoon light.

When I appeared wearing my mother's dress and my aunt's veil, I felt a warmth like sunlight on my shoulders, a presence as real as breath. My mother was here, somehow, in the linen against my skin, in the veil brushing my face, in the scent of roses that had been her favorite. The knowledge wrapped around me like her arms once had: *You are loved. You are blessed. You are seen.*

My dress whispered against my legs with each step. My hands trembled so badly I had to clasp them together to still them, and my breath came quick and shallow. This was truly happening. After all the years of believing I would live and die alone, unwanted, unlovable, I was walking toward a man who had chosen me.

The garden had filled with guests—family, disciples, friends from both our households. I saw Miriam and Philip,

Mary of Magdala, and Tirzah. All of them gathered here to witness this moment.

Andrew stood waiting beneath the arbor, and when his eyes found mine, everything else fell away. The garden, the guests, even my nervousness dissolved into the background of this moment. His face changed. His eyes widened, his lips parted, and color rose in his cheeks. He clenched his hands at his side, as though he, too, fought to hold himself steady.

He is as overwhelmed as I am, I thought, and somehow, that made it easier to breathe.

The women who had prepared me gathered at my sides for the bride's procession. Miriam rose from her place and joined us, while Philip went to the men. Together, we walked down the garden path toward the start of the rest of my life.

Abba stood beneath the arbor with Jesus at his side, both of them waiting to officiate this covenant. When we reached the arbor, Abba stepped forward. The sun caught the silver in his beard, and I saw moisture glinting at the corners of his eyes. He had never been demonstrative with affection, my father, but in this moment, his love for me was plainly written on his face. We had come so far in the last few months.

The arbor Ezra had built, olive wood posts wound with grapevines and draped with linen, breathed and shifted in the gentle breeze, casting moving shadows across the space. A hush fell over the garden, broken only by the whisper of wind through leaves and the distant call of a dove.

"Friends and witnesses," Abba said, and his voice was strong and clear, reaching every corner of the courtyard, "we rejoice in what God has already joined. Anna bat Joseph and Andrew bar Jonah entered covenant at their betrothal. Today we bring them into that covenant before the faces who love them, and we ask God to bless the home they will make."

The formal words washed over me, familiar and ancient, spoken at countless weddings before mine and countless more to come. But hearing them now, knowing they were for us, made them new.

Ezra brought the ketubah, and I watched Abba's hands unroll the parchment with care. The scribe's work was beautiful, with neat lines of careful script recording the promises Andrew had made, the provision he would give, the honor he pledged—my bride-price, such as it was. My security, written in ink and witnessed by law.

"Witnessed," Abba said, showing the document to the assembly, and James and Joses nodded their affirmation. Then Abba rolled the scroll and placed it in my hands. The parchment was warm from the sun, surprisingly heavy. "It belongs to the bride."

Mine. This record of promises, this proof of covenant, was mine to keep. I clutched it to my chest, feeling the crackle of the parchment against my heart.

Jesus lifted the cup then, and the entire garden seemed to draw breath. His hands cradled the simple clay vessel with reverence. When he spoke, his voice carried a depth that made the words resonate in my very bones.

"As you share this wine, you vow to share all that comes in the future. May this cup bring you joy in your days and a heart sweetened from sorrow. May all your days be hallowed by respect, companionship, and love."

God creates. God makes new. God brings forth life from nothing.

Andrew lifted the cup to his lips and drank, his eyes never leaving mine. Then he turned and offered it to me.

The cup was still warm from his mouth. I drank, and the wine was sweet on my tongue. It tasted of promises kept and promises yet to be fulfilled. Of celebration and covenant. Of the life we would build together, cup by cup, day by day.

When I lowered the cup, I found I was crying. Silent tears slipped down my cheeks and wet the edge of my veil. Andrew's eyes were bright with answering moisture.

Abba broke bread next, and the sound of the crust cracking seemed impossibly loud in the stillness. "Blessed are You, who brings forth bread from the earth."

He placed a piece in Andrew's hand, and Andrew held it as though it were precious, which it was. Daily bread. The staff of life. The thing that sustained us when nothing else remained.

When Andrew brought the bread to my lips, his fingers brushed my mouth, and the intimacy of it made my breath catch. I took the piece he offered, chewed slowly, and tasted the wheat and salt and yeast. Then I fed him in return, my thumb grazing his lower lip, feeling him tremble at the touch.

We are sharing food, some distant part of my mind observed. *We are making a household. We are becoming one.*

"Before God, and before those who love us," Andrew said, and his voice was low but steady, "I will shelter you, honor you, and keep a table for those He sends."

He took the cord from my wrist, the fisherman's knot he had tied there so many weeks ago, and retied it with careful precision. His fingers worked the rough hemp with skill, and I watched, mesmerized, as the knot took shape. Loop and tuck, pull and tighten, each movement deliberate.

"What holds in a storm will hold in calm," he said, and pulled the knot secure.

I touched the cord, feeling the texture of it against my

skin, the slight pressure where it encircled my wrist. A binding. A promise. A physical reminder that I belonged to someone now, and someone belonged to me.

"Before God, and before those who love us," I said, though my voice shook, "I will keep your peace, speak truth, and go where we are sent, beside you."

I touched the knot again, and it felt like a seal. Like a door closing on one life and opening onto another.

"Let the seven blessings be given," my father declared.

Jesus stepped forward again, and the garden grew impossibly still.

"Blessed are You, Adonai our God, Ruler of the Universe, the Creator of the fruit of the vine."

The first blessing washed over me like cool water.

"Blessed are You, Adonai, our God, the Creator of the universe, who has created everything for Your glory."

The second blessing. I focused on breathing, on staying present in this moment even as my body struggled to stand. This was my wedding day. I would not let pain steal this joy from me.

"Blessed are You, Adonai, our God, the King of the universe, the Creator of human beings."

The third blessing. I shifted my weight on my staff, trying to ease the ache in my hip.

"Blessed are You, Lord our God, King of the universe, who has fashioned human beings in Your image, according to Your likeness, and has prepared for them from their own selves an everlasting bond. Blessed are You, Lord, Creator of humanity."

The fourth blessing spoke of being made in God's image, and unbidden, tears welled in my eyes. Made in His image, even with my scars. Even with my twisted spine and aching hip. Andrew had taught me that.

"Blessed are You, Lord our God, King of the universe, who gladdens Zion through her children. Blessed are You, Lord."

The fifth blessing. I tried to move discreetly, easing the weight onto my good leg. Andrew noticed, as he always did, and moved closer, offering silent support without making it obvious to the gathered witnesses.

"Gladden the beloved companions as You gladdened Your creatures in the garden of Eden. Blessed are You, Adonai, Who gladdens this couple."

The sixth blessing. I looked at Andrew standing beside me, his hand steady on mine, and gratitude rose in me so strong it nearly took my breath. This man who had chosen me, this moment I had never dared dream of, this joy that had found me when I had given up all hope.

"Blessed are You, Lord our God, King of the universe, who created joy and gladness, groom and bride, mirth, song, delight and rejoicing, love and harmony, peace and companionship. Lord our God, let there soon be heard in the cities of Judah and the streets of Jerusalem the sound of joy and the sound of gladness, the voice of the groom and the voice of the bride, the sound of the groom's jubilance from their canopies and of the youths from their feasts of song."

The seventh blessing flowed over me like honey. The words painted pictures in my mind of joy and harmony and peace. Everything I had never dared hope for, now mine. Ours.

Jesus lowered his voice, speaking words that seemed meant for Andrew and me alone, though all could hear them.

"Anna. Andrew." His gaze moved between us with such

love that I felt my eyes fill with tears. "Today you become one household, one flesh, one purpose before the Father. In the seasons to come, when the world presses in and the way seems unclear, remember this moment. Remember that your union was sealed this day, witnessed by those who love you, blessed by the One who formed you both."

He paused, and something shifted in the air, a thickening of presence that made the hairs on my arms rise.

"The Father delights in the desires of His children's hearts," Jesus continued.

I knew those words.

"And He makes all things beautiful in their time. Anna, you have learned that your worth is not measured by the physical. You have learned that you are beloved as you are. Andrew's love has proven that to you, as has the love of all those gathered here today."

My hand trembled on my staff. My heart was pounding so hard I thought surely everyone could hear it.

"And now," Jesus said softly, his eyes holding mine, "your season has come."

He stepped forward and placed his hand on my shoulder. Warmth flooded through me, not the heat of fever but something living, something holy. It moved down through my body—my chest, my ribs, my spine—pooling at last in my twisted hip where it gathered and waited.

And then, deep in the place where bone had broken and healed wrong all those years ago, something moved. Warmth concentrated there, intense and focused, and I felt pressure building like water behind a dam. Then it released, and my leg lengthened. My pelvis leveled, weight that had always borne down wrong suddenly distributing itself evenly across both feet. My spine straightened, vertebra by vertebra finding their proper place, and the muscles that had clenched for thirteen years to hold me upright released their desperate grip.

I gasped and drew breath deep into my lungs. The pain was gone. All at once, completely, as if it had never been at all.

I stood in the silence of it. That great, stunning silence where constant suffering had always been.

Time seemed to stop. I stood frozen, hardly daring to believe. I shifted my weight from one foot to the other—evenly, easily, with no grinding protest. I turned my hips, first left, then right. Nothing. I bent forward slightly, testing. Still nothing. My body held me without complaint.

My fingers went slack. My staff clattered to the stone pathway. The sound echoed in the stunned silence.

I stood straight. Truly straight, for the first time in memory.

A gasp rippled through the witnesses. Andrew's hand flew to his mouth.

"Anna?" His voice broke on my name.

"The gift," Jesus said, his hand still warm on my shoulder, "comes not as a condition for love, but as a celebration of it. You were already enough, Anna. Already worthy and beloved. The Father, who loves His children, chooses this moment to give you back what was taken all those years ago. This is from the Father who loves you, who sees you and has always been with you."

"I—" My voice broke. I looked at Jesus, standing there with his hand on my shoulder, and saw such joy in his eyes. "Jesus — " I whispered. No words would come.

He smiled and stepped back. "Walk, Anna."

"Walk," Andrew said, and I could hear the wonder in it.

I took a step. My foot lifted, swung forward, set down. The movement flowed like water, like breathing, effortless and whole. My weight shifted from one leg to the other in perfect rhythm.

I looked down at my feet, watching them move beneath me as though they belonged to someone else—someone who had always walked this way, whose body knew how to carry itself. Another step. Another. The ground rose to meet each footfall with steady assurance, and my legs answered in kind, matching stride for stride.

I turned to Andrew. His arms came around me and pulled me close. He held me as though he would never let go. After a moment, his head lifted, looking past me toward Jesus, and I saw his lips move. Thank you perhaps, though no sound came.

Around us, voices rose—some crying out in wonder, others praying, still others simply standing frozen. I heard Salome's laugh, filled with disbelief and joy. Someone started singing a psalm of thanksgiving, and others joined in, the melody rising over the garden.

Deborah reached us first. She pulled me from Andrew's arms and held me at arm's length, her hands gripping my shoulders as her eyes traveled the length of my body, taking in my straight spine, my even stance. "Walk for me," she said, her voice fierce. "Let me see it again."

I walked. Three steps forward, three steps back. No staff. No hesitation.

"My girl." She pulled me close. "He has given you back what the Romans took."

Then Abba was there, one hand on my face, the other reaching for Deborah, and for a moment the three of us stood together in the knowledge of what had been lost and now restored. Over his shoulder, I saw Mary watching with her hand pressed to her heart, and Naomi with both hands raised in prayer. Rachel had grasped Salome's hands, and they were both weeping, but James and Joses simply stared, their faces full of wonder.

Andrew's hand found mine, and he led me into the garden where the noise faded behind us. My veil caught the breeze, the myrtle leaves brushing my cheek. Each step I took still felt like a small miracle. He stopped beneath the olive trees where dappled light fell across the pathway and turned to face me.

"I would have loved you forever exactly as you were," he told me. "You know that, do you not? This changes nothing about how I see you. You were already perfect in my eyes, though I am grateful you will not be in pain."

"I know," I whispered, lifting my free hand to his face.

He pulled me close, and I went easily, without wincing, without having to adjust my stance to accommodate pain. The movement's simplicity brought fresh tears to my eyes. *I was healed.* We stayed that way for a few moments, letting the overwhelm of it all calm down in our hearts.

As we walked back to the courtyard, I turned to look at Jesus. He was speaking with Simon and my father, but as if sensing my gaze, he glanced toward us. Our eyes met, and he smiled the gentle, knowing smile of one who delights in doing good things for those he loves.

"Thank you," I mouthed, though I knew no words could hold the magnitude of what he had done. I laid my hand on my heart and bowed.

He inclined his head slightly, then returned to his conversation, leaving Andrew and me to marvel at the miracle that had turned our wedding into something beyond imagining.

Yohanan appeared at my elbow, his small face solemn. In his hands he carried my staff. He held it out to me, uncertain.

I looked at it, that constant companion worn smooth where my palm had gripped it ten thousand times. I would never need it again.

I knelt down so I was level with Yohanan's eyes. "Keep it," I said. "For when you are old and your legs grow tired."

His eyes widened. Then he nodded, solemn as a priest receiving a sacred charge, and tucked the staff under his arm.

When I stood, Andrew was watching me with that half-smile I loved. He offered his arm. "Shall we?"

The feast was waiting. Our guests were waiting. This day had held so much already, and it was not yet finished.

CHAPTER 28

THE TRANSFORMATION from ceremony to celebration happened in the space of a breath. We had been solemn beneath the arbor, bound by vows and witnesses, and now embraces, laughter, and congratulations swept us toward tables laden with food.

They overflowed with roasted lamb that fell from the bone in tender shreds, and meats seasoned with cumin and coriander. The scent alone made my mouth water. Fresh bread, still warm, the crusts golden and crackling, sat in great baskets alongside clay pots of olive oil infused with herbs from our garden. Honey cakes glistened in the sunlight, their sweetness cut with the bright tang of preserved lemons. Bowls of olives, green and black, some crushed with garlic, others swimming in brine, crowded against platters of soft cheese and bunches of grapes still dewy from the vine.

Wine flowed freely, deep red and robust from my father's vineyards, catching the evening light until it glowed like liquid rubies in the cups. A few musicians from the village—

men who had played at my mother's wedding, Deborah told me—had brought their instruments: a flute whose clear notes could pierce the heart, double pipes that sang like birds, a lyre whose strings hummed with ancient melodies, and a hand drum that spoke in the language of heartbeats.

I sat beside Andrew in the place of honor. The bench beneath me was hard, but I barely noticed. My back pressed straight against it without the familiar compensating curve. My feet rested flat on the ground, both of them bearing weight equally.

I could not stop smiling. My face actually hurt from it, muscles unused to such sustained happiness protesting the unfamiliar expression. But I could not help it. Every time I looked at him—my *husband*, bound to me now forever—joy bubbled up fresh. Not to mention the wedding gift from Jesus. I could not quite comprehend I had been healed.

Andrew kept leaning close, his breath warm against my ear, to murmur observations that were meant only for me. "See how Simon is trying to convince Matthew that fishing is superior to tax collecting? This argument has been going on for months." Or, "John just ate his third honey cake. I am taking bets on whether he makes it to four before his stomach fights against him." Or simply, "My wife." As if he too needed to say it aloud to believe it was real.

"You realize," he murmured as the servers brought out yet another platter of lamb, "that I am the most fortunate man who ever lived."

I turned to look at him fully, taking in the way the lamplight made his dark hair shine and his eyes dance, the small scar on his chin, his dimples deeper than ever before. "Truly?" I asked, pretending to weigh the matter with great seriousness. "What of Solomon? He had seven hundred wives."

"Ah, but did any of them save his life with healing herbs and a clear head?"

"I do not know. Scripture is silent on that point."

"There, you see?" His grin was infectious. "Clearly inferior wives, all of them."

I laughed so hard I nearly lost my sip of wine and had to set the cup down quickly before I spilled it down the front of my mother's dress. "Andrew bar Jonah, you are ridiculous."

"Ridiculously in love with my wife," he replied, so pleased with himself that I could not even pretend to be exasperated.

Across the courtyard, I caught sight of Deborah sitting with my aunt, their heads bent together in conversation. Whatever Mary was saying made Deborah throw back her head and laugh, a full-throated sound of pure delight I had not heard from her in too long. Before long we would leave for Bethsaida, and Deborah's days would grow quieter. Too quiet, perhaps.

But she will visit, I reminded myself. She promised.

The sun continued its slow descent toward the horizon, painting the sky in shades of gold and rose. Shadows lengthened across the courtyard, and the lamps were lit one by one, their flames dancing like tiny prayers ascending.

When the worst of the hunger had been sated and the tables looked pleasantly ravaged rather than abundant, the drummer picked up his instrument and began a rhythm. Simple at first, just a steady pulse like the beating of a heart. Then more complex, syncopated, calling to something primal in the blood.

The women heard it first. They always did. One by one they rose from their places, setting aside their cups and their conversations, drawn by that ancient summons. They formed a circle in the open space near the tables, and I watched them move—not quite dancing yet, just swaying, finding the rhythm in their bodies.

Salome caught my eye and beckoned, the invitation clear.

My heart stumbled. I had longed to dance all my life, had imagined what it might feel like to move freely in time with the music. But imagination was one thing. Actually doing it was another.

"Go," Andrew said softly, reading my hesitation. "You can now."

I rose. For a heartbeat I hesitated, my hand reaching for the staff that was no longer there. Then I stepped forward, feeling the ground solid beneath both feet, and walked toward the circle of women, who parted to make space for me. Deborah's face was bright with encouragement. Tirzah smiled and reached out a hand.

The drum found a steadier beat. The pipe joined in, and its clear notes wove through the rhythm.

And then I was moving.

I was actually moving.

My feet knew the steps somehow, though I had never danced them. Perhaps they were written into my bones, passed down through generations of women who had danced at celebrations since Sarah first laughed at impossible news. Step and turn. Arms raised. Skirts swishing around my ankles, the linen whispering against my calves with each pivot.

I was dancing. Each turn felt like reclaiming something that had been stolen from me.

I wanted to laugh. I wanted to weep. I wanted to throw my head back and shout my gratitude to the sky.

The women surrounded me, their faces glowing in the lamplight. Salome grinned at me over her shoulder, her cheeks flushed pink with exertion, her hair escaping its careful braid to curl damply at her temples. Mary of Magdala's laughter rang out.

Deborah clapped time with her hands, her eyes shining with tears she refused to let fall. "You are dancing, Anna! Look at you!" I gave her a little wave as I whirled by.

We stepped and turned, shawls flicking out like wings, skirts whispering secrets to the stones beneath our feet. The circle moved as one, each woman both individual and part of the whole, separate and united, singular and plural all at once.

Across the open space, the men had formed their own circle. Looser than ours, less disciplined, but no less joyful. Simon Peter's steps had the confidence of a man who believed he could do anything with his feet. He could not—I could see that even in my peripheral vision—but believing was half the battle with dancing. The others followed his lead with varying degrees of success. Some were graceful, while others were merely enthusiastic.

And there was Andrew, his eyes never leaving me. His gaze was a physical touch against my skin, warm and steady and full of awe. He had stopped even pretending to dance. He simply stood there at the edge of the circle, hands loose at his sides, watching me dance.

When the drummer gave the smallest nod—some signal I did not understand, but the other dancers clearly did—the two circles moved together. Not merging exactly but allowing for brief passes through the middle where partners could meet for a heartbeat before being swept back into their respective groups.

The drum quickened. The pipe soared higher.

And then Andrew was there, directly across from me,

and we came together in the center of it all. Not touching but close enough. The pulse beat visibly in his throat. Wine lingered on his breath, mingling with the faint scent of rosemary tucked into his belt. His eyes held mine with an intensity that made the rest of the world blur and fade. For three heartbeats we stood there, the music swirling around us, and the dancers circling like waves around stones.

Close enough for everyone could see the joy that passed between us.

Then the circles swept us apart again, and I was back among the women, breathless and exhilarated, my heart racing. My legs trembled slightly. When had I last used my body so fully? The linen of my dress clung damply to my back, and I could feel my pulse everywhere.

"I cannot believe I just did that," I said when the music finally paused and I found myself beside Andrew again, both of us sweaty and grinning. "I have dreamed of dancing so many times, wondering what it would feel like to move without pain, and now — "

I could not finish the sentence. There were no words adequate to describe the magnitude of what I had just experienced. The freedom. The simple, profound gift of a body that did as it should.

Andrew's face softened with understanding. "How does it feel?" he asked, though I suspected he already knew the answer.

"Like flying," I whispered. "Exactly like—look over there."

He turned to where Naomi and Abba stood together near the herb garden, deep in conversation. Their heads were bent close as they examined some plant, Naomi's hands gesturing as she explained something. Abba listened with the

ANNA OF ARIMATHEA

same careful attention he gave to matters of law, nodding thoughtfully at her words.

"Your mother and my father seem to get along well," I observed.

Andrew's eyebrows rose as he watched them. "Very well indeed. Look at how he stands closer than politeness requires." His voice held amused speculation. "And she is smiling. Mother does not smile that readily with strangers."

"They are both alone," I said. "Both have carried grief for many years."

"And both have raised children who found love despite the odds," Andrew added. He squeezed my hand gently. "Perhaps watching us has reminded them that hearts can begin again, even after sorrow."

As we watched, Abba plucked a sprig of something and offered it to Naomi. She accepted it with a laugh that carried clearly across the courtyard.

"Well," I murmured, "that is interesting."

"Very," Andrew agreed with a grin. "Perhaps there will be more than one new family bond to celebrate."

The thought surprised me, but watching Abba smile with such unguarded happiness, I found I hoped it might come true.

Gifts came, not fine but exactly right. Simon approached first, grinning as he pressed a small knife into my palm, its bone handle smooth from use. "For scaling fish," he said. "Every fisherman's wife needs one."

Rachel came next with a spindle of dark wood, and Naomi brought a good needle wrapped in soft cloth. The women's gifts piled in my lap—dyed wool, soft as lamb's fleece. From the men, a float carved from olive wood and a net-mender's bone. Miriam stepped behind me and settled a shawl across my shoulders as the evening cooled, her hands gentle as she smoothed the fringe. "Eat, drink, dance," she murmured. "Then sleep. The morning will come without your help."

Later, when the drum rested, Andrew and I slipped no further than the fountain. Lamps had taken their places along the wall, creating pools of light. Water lifted and fell, a sound like a calm breath. The fig limb threw its old shade, but tonight it felt dressed for company. I caught sight of Tirzah speaking with James. He listened intently, his expression interested rather than merely polite, and when she laughed at something he said, I saw him smile in return. Perhaps Andrew's encouraging word to his friend had borne fruit after all. I hoped so.

I leaned against Andrew, his arm warm around my shoulders. "Is this real?" I whispered. "Sometimes I fear I will wake and find this was only a dream."

"It is real," he murmured, pressing a kiss to my temple. "You are my wife, and I am your husband, and nothing will ever change that."

We stood there for a long moment, wrapped in each other and the joy of the evening, before I noticed Abba approaching across the courtyard.

Andrew kissed me once more, then stepped away to rejoin the men clearing tables, leaving me to speak with my father alone.

"A beautiful wedding, daughter."

His face was relaxed in a way I rarely saw.

"It was perfect. Thank you, Abba. For everything—the celebration, your blessing on our marriage, your kindness to Andrew's family."

"He is a good man," Abba replied, nodding toward where

Andrew helped clear tables with the other disciples. "I see why you chose him."

"He chose me as well," I said. "Despite everything."

"And he loves you deeply. That is all a father can ask for his daughter."

"And I love him," I replied. "More than I thought possible."

"Then I am content. And I hope you will be as happy in Bethsaida as you were here."

"I will miss this place," I admitted. "But I have seen tonight that a home can be built anew." I glanced toward where Naomi stood speaking with Mary. "As you may discover as well, if you are willing."

Something softened in his expression. "She is a remarkably capable woman."

"She is," I agreed. "And kind. And alone, as you are."

He cleared his throat. "Perhaps we shall see what time brings."

"I hope so, Abba. You deserve joy too."

He kissed my forehead. "Go to him, Anna. Begin your new life with my blessing."

As I crossed the courtyard toward Andrew, gratitude filling me, I heard approaching footsteps on the road beyond our gates — multiple sets of feet, steady and deliberate in the night air.

Andrew looked up from his work, frowning slightly. "Who comes at this hour?"

"I do not know," Abba replied, his voice suddenly sharp with concern. "But they come with purpose."

Everyone gathered, drawn by the sound of the footsteps and the tension in our voices. The disciples moved closer to

Jesus, while the women instinctively stepped toward each other, sensing danger.

Fear replaced the joy I had carried all evening. I reached for Andrew's hand and found it already reaching for mine.

The footsteps grew closer, accompanied now by the soft glow of torches visible through the gate, and the rustle of multiple cloaks. Not the casual approach of late-arriving guests. Not the eager pace of those drawn by music and celebration. Whoever approached moved with the precision of soldiers or officials, with the authority that turned weddings into interrogations and joy into fear.

Jesus appeared beside us as if materializing from the shadows, his face grave. "Joseph," he murmured, "you must prepare yourself."

"For what?" Abba asked, but even as the words left his mouth, I could see he already knew.

CHAPTER 29

THREE MEN in the dark cloaks of Temple officers appeared at our gate, carrying staves and torches that cast dancing shadows across the courtyard stones. They stopped at the threshold without entering, observing the proper boundary, but their presence alone was violation enough.

The lead officer stepped forward, holding the torch high. The flame threw a harsh light across his face, making the angles severe and the shadows deep. When he spoke, his voice carried the weight of authority that brooked no argument.

"Joseph of Arimathea. Peace to your house. We are officers of the Temple, sent by the chief priests and elders."

Moments ago, the courtyard was filled with the warm hum of celebration, laughter, music, and the clash of cups being raised in blessing, but now it fell silent. Not the comfortable quiet of people listening, but the terrible stillness that comes when fear steals the breath in your throat.

My lungs simply stopped. Refused to work. The edges of

my vision went gray, then black, creeping inward until I saw the world through a narrowing tunnel.

Andrew's hand found mine, his fingers lacing through my own with gentle pressure. The touch steadied me, but it was not enough to stop the spinning sensation that had overtaken me.

Abba stepped forward, his bearing that of a man accustomed to speaking before hostile councils. His face looked composed, but I saw the slight tremor in his hands before he clasped them behind his back. "I am Joseph of Arimathea. How may I serve the council?"

The officer produced a scroll from within his cloak. Even from where I stood, I saw the official seal, the dark wax pressed with the mark of the Sanhedrin. He did not approach, and he did not cross our threshold, but held the scroll where Abba could see it.

"You are requested to appear before the council at dawn to answer questions concerning your kinship with Jesus of Nazareth."

Someone drew a sharp breath. The disciples shifted and tensed, their hands moving instinctively toward their belts, where weapons might hang, though none of them were armed.

But all of that seemed distant, muffled.

"Kinship with Jesus of Nazareth."

They knew. Of course, they knew. The Pharisee who had questioned Abba in Capernaum had made sure of that. And now my father had hosted a wedding attended by Jesus himself, his mother, and his brothers, as well as his followers. We had made no secret of it. Had not tried to hide. Perhaps we should have been more careful. Perhaps — but no. There was no hiding kinship when it ran through blood and bone.

But knowing they knew and hearing it spoken aloud in official tones were two entirely different things. The honey cake Andrew had fed me now sat heavy and sickening in my stomach.

"We are charged with escorting you to Jerusalem tonight," the officer continued, his tone officially neutral. "The council wishes to speak with you immediately."

"Tonight?" Abba's voice remained steady, but I heard the steel threading through his words. "This is my daughter's wedding day."

A flicker of discomfort passed over the officer's face. "My lord, I understand, but our orders—"

"Your orders can surely allow a father to finish celebrating his daughter's marriage," Abba said. "I give you my word as a member of the council that I will leave at dawn."

The three men exchanged glances. In the torchlight, I could see the lead officer considering, weighing the respectability of a council member against whatever instructions he had been given. The silence stretched as taut as a bowstring.

"We will wait on the road and return at first light," he said finally. "But we are charged with ensuring your arrival in Jerusalem."

"That is unnecessary," Abba replied. "My word is sufficient."

"Perhaps, my lord. But these are our orders." The officer's tone remained respectful as but immovable as stone. "We will return at dawn."

The men withdrew into the darkness beyond our gates, taking their torches with them. But threat clung to the air, acrid and choking.

For several heartbeats, no one moved. No one spoke. The

lamps flickered along the walls, their flames guttering in the breeze. The courtyard stood unchanged. The arbor where we had spoken our vows. The faces of the people I loved. But the ground had shifted underfoot, and nothing would sit quite right again.

My legs gave out. The strength drained from them. I sagged, knees buckling, and would have hit the stones if Andrew had not caught me. His arms came around me instantly, taking my full weight, one hand cradling the back of my head, the other banded across my waist.

"Anna." His voice rumbled through his chest, low and urgent. "Breathe. You need to breathe."

I tried. Drew in air that felt thick and insufficient. My hands trembled against the fabric of Andrew's tunic. I could not make them stop. My ears roared.

"Inside," Deborah's voice cut through the chaos, sharp with command. "Everyone inside. Now."

Bodies moved, flowing toward the house like water seeking lower ground. I let Andrew guide me, his arm firm around my waist, but my feet felt disconnected from my body. Each step required conscious thought: lift foot, move forward, set down, repeat.

The threshold. The doorway. The familiar smells of olive oil and herbs and the lingering sweetness of the wedding feast. All of it exactly as it had been, and nothing like it at all.

Ezra slid the bolt home with a sound that seemed impossibly loud in the sudden quiet. The heavy wooden beam fell into its brackets. A barrier between us and what waited in the darkness outside.

Silence.

I stood in the entry hall, Andrew's arm still around me, and felt the weight of that closed door like a physical presence. We had just locked ourselves in. Or perhaps we had locked the danger out. I could not decide which interpretation was correct, and the uncertainty left me hollow.

Around me, others moved into position. Deborah gave orders, her voice steady, the tone of a woman who had weathered storms before and knew how to prepare for the next one.

But I could not focus on her words. I could not concentrate on anything except the terrible truth. They had come for Abba. On my wedding day, in my home, surrounded by everyone I loved, they had come for him.

And he was going to go. I gasped.

"Anna." Andrew turned me gently to face him, his hands on my face. "Look at me. Stay with me."

I tried. His face swam before me, features blurring and sharpening. Brown eyes dark with concern. The jawline I had traced with my fingers earlier. The mouth that had shared the cup with me.

He pulled me close. "Breathe," he murmured against my hair. "Just breathe. I have you."

I focused on the steady rise and fall of his breathing, letting the rhythm become an anchor. Slowly, so slowly, the roaring in my ears quieted. The darkness at the edges of my vision receded. The world came back into painful focus.

We were standing in the entry hall. The lamps burned along the walls. Abba stood near the doorway to the main room, his shoulders square despite the blow he had just received. Jesus was whispering with the disciples, his face grave. My aunt was moving among the women, offering quiet words and steady touches.

This was my wedding day.

The wave of emotion nearly buckled my knees again.

Grief and rage and terror all tangled together until I could not separate one from another.

"I know," Andrew murmured against my hair, holding me tighter. "I know."

And somehow, impossibly, that helped. Not because it changed anything or made the situation less terrible but because he understood. I was not alone in this moment, even though I felt desperately, crushingly alone.

Abba's voice cut through my spiraling thoughts. "Friends," he said, and the room quieted to listen. "Forgive us. The celebration is ended."

The words were final. Irrevocable.

Around me, people shifted, gathered belongings, murmured quiet words to each other. The sounds came muffled, distant, wrapped in wool.

Abba continued giving instructions and setting the house to order. He assigned men to watch the gate, arranged for a donkey to be ready at first light, and established order in the chaos.

Amid the chaos, Deborah appeared with Yohanan at her side. The boy's face was pale, his eyes wide with fear. He had lived alone long enough to know what authority looked like when it came with violence behind it.

"Come," Deborah said to him, her hand firm on his shoulder. "There is work to do in the kitchen. I need your help."

The boy nodded and followed her. Even now, with everything falling apart, Deborah was still gathering in the lost and frightened. I took a deep breath and felt a kernel of courage take shape inside.

"You will stay," Abba said to Andrew, and though the

words were kind, they held the force of command. "You will stay with Anna and keep her safe."

Andrew bowed his head in acceptance. "As you say. I will not leave her side."

Then Abba crossed to where I stood, still propped against Andrew like a sapling that would fall without support. He took both of my hands in his.

"Daughter," he said, and his voice was gentle now, stripped of its public polish. "There is no cause for fear, and no cause for noise. We will meet the morning with our heads high."

"I am afraid." The words came out small, childlike. The weakness they revealed made me hate them, but I could not unsay them, especially since they were true.

Abba's expression softened. "Courage is not a grand thing," he said. "It is simply taking one step, then the next. First, you will sleep if you can, and you will pray if you cannot."

Sleep. The word was laughable. How could anyone sleep with dawn approaching like the hour of judgment?

But I nodded anyway, because what else could I do?

Jesus's voice cut through the murmur that had filled the room. "Joseph, I would speak with you. And with Anna and Andrew."

We moved to the inner chamber, the small room where Abba kept his private scrolls and conducted business away from public eyes. The lamplight threw soft shadows against the plastered walls.

Jesus settled onto one of the low stools, gesturing for us to sit. I lowered myself carefully onto a cushion, my legs still unsteady, and Andrew sat beside me, his hand finding mine immediately.

Jesus looked at us with a long, searching gaze that seemed to see every fear, every desperate hope, every unspoken prayer. Then he turned to Abba.

"What will you tell them, Uncle?"

"The truth." Abba's voice was steady. "I will declare my kinship to you. I will declare my duty to the Sanhedrin. But I will not resign my seat."

I watched Jesus's face, trying to read his reaction, but he gave nothing away.

"They will press you," he said quietly. "They will demand you choose between your loyalty to me and your position on the Council."

"Then I will choose both." Abba's jaw set with determination. "I will withdraw from any case involving you or your followers. I will leave the chamber when your name is raised. I will keep my seat because my seat is a trust. I will not abandon the poor and the widows to win favor with men."

"And if they force you to choose?"

"Then I will let them say the law by which they do it." Abba met Jesus's eyes directly. "If such a law exists, I will submit. If it does not, they will have revealed more about themselves than about me."

Silence followed. Would Jesus judge Abba's strategy as cowardice or compromise?

Instead, he nodded slowly. "Wisdom and courage are not always incompatible. Sometimes the bravest thing is to remain where you can still do good. Your plan is sound."

The relief left me dizzy.

"But know this," Jesus continued, his voice taking on a weight that made the small room feel suddenly smaller. "The cost of walking this path will be high. They will watch you.

Question your every word. Use your relationship with me as a weapon against you."

"Let them." Abba's voice was firm. "I did not accept my seat to win popularity. I accepted it to serve justice."

Jesus's expression gentled. He reached out and gripped Abba's shoulder with the easy affection of family. "Then serve it well, Uncle. For as long as they allow you."

The qualifier hung in the air like a sword suspended by a thread. "For as long as they allow you." Not forever. Not even for long, perhaps. But for now.

It was not enough. It would never be enough. But it was what we had.

Jesus turned his attention to Andrew and me. His eyes held such compassion that it made my throat close with unshed tears.

"I told you the cost was coming," he said. "It is here now. Sooner than I hoped, but not unexpected." He looked between us. "What comes will test you. But it will not break you. Love is stronger than law. Truth outlasts councils. And the Father's purposes cannot be turned aside by the fear of men."

His gaze held mine. He looked straight through all my careful defenses and saw the trembling, frightened woman beneath.

"This house will stand," he said, and the words carried the force of prophecy.

"This house will stand, Anna. We will stand," Andrew said, his hand tightening on mine. "Whatever comes, we face it together."

I wanted to believe him. Wanted to take comfort in that promise. But fear had sunk its claws deep, and I could not shake the terrible conviction that everything was about to fall apart.

"Sleep now," Jesus said, rising. "Morning will bring what it brings, but tonight, you are safe."

Safe. The word felt hollow. We were locked in our own house, guards waiting outside, dawn approaching with the weight of judgment. How was that safe?

But I did not say it aloud. Just nodded and let Andrew help me to my feet.

One by one, people drifted away. The disciples headed to their chambers, still tense with the desire to fight but accepting that there was no enemy they could physically engage. Mary and her sons murmured quiet blessings in the hall, while others prepared to keep vigil through the dark hours.

Deborah caught me as I passed and pulled me into an embrace. "Be strong, child," she whispered against my hair. "This is not the end."

"It feels like it," I whispered back.

"I know. But feelings lie sometimes. Trust what you know is true instead."

What did I know to be true? That I loved Andrew. That I believed Jesus was who he claimed to be. That Abba was a good man trying to navigate impossible choices. That danger was real and present and coming with the dawn.

Those truths would have to be enough.

Andrew and I went to my room, prepared now for our wedding night. We entered it like the lost seeking shelter, exhausted and afraid.

I stood in the center of it, my mother's wedding dress still clinging to my body, and my veil crooked from the evening's chaos. Someone had prepared the room with care. Fresh linens were on the bed, so white they seemed to glow in the lamplight. Sprigs of hyssop and mint tucked between the folds. I could smell them from where I stood. A small table near the bed held two cups of wine, untouched, and a plate of honeyed dates. Three oil lamps burned instead of one, casting the room in golden warmth.

All of it prepared for joy. For celebration. For a wedding night that should have been nothing but happiness.

The scent of the herbs made me choke.

This morning I had been so happy. So full of hope and joy and anticipation for the day ahead.

Now I felt empty.

Andrew came up behind me, his arms encircling my waist, his chin resting on my shoulder. We stood like that, swaying slightly, drawing what comfort we could from simple proximity.

"I am sorry," he said after a time. "This should have been a perfect day for you."

"It was perfect," I said. "Until they came. And that is not your fault."

"Still. Your wedding day, and now—" He could not seem to finish the thought.

I turned and lifted my hand to his cheek. "We are married, Andrew. That is what matters. Not the guards. Not the summons. We spoke our vows, and they are binding. Nothing that happens tomorrow can undo what we did today."

His eyes searched mine, looking for certainty, for signs of regret. I hoped he found none, because I meant what I said. I would not trade him for safety. Would not trade the truth I had found for comfortable lies.

He kissed me then, gentle, reverent, tasting of salt and sorrow and stubborn hope.

"We should try to sleep," he said, though neither of us moved toward the bed.

"I cannot imagine sleeping."

"I know. But we should try anyway."

"I should—" I gestured vaguely toward the basin in the corner, toward the bed that had been prepared with such care. Heat flooded my face despite everything. Even with fear paralyzing me, even with guards waiting outside and my father facing judgment at dawn, my body still remembered this was my wedding night. That I was alone with a man for the first time in my life. That Andrew was my husband now, with all that implied. That I would need to — that we would —

My face burned. I could not finish the thought, much less speak it aloud.

"I need to change," I managed finally, the words coming out barely above a whisper.

"Take your time," Andrew said. He turned his back to give me privacy, moved to the window, and stood looking out at the darkness.

I fumbled with the dress, my fingers clumsy with nerves and fatigue. The fabric had grown heavy after wearing it all day, the weight of it pulling at my shoulders. When it finally fell away, I stood in just my undershift, suddenly aware of how thin the linen was. I felt exposed even with Andrew's back turned.

The night shift Deborah had prepared lay folded on the chest. Fine linen, softer than anything I owned, with delicate embroidery at the neck and sleeves. My wedding night garment. I pulled it over my head, feeling the whisper of fabric against skin that felt too sensitive, too aware.

The basin held cool water scattered with rose petals—another careful preparation, the petals releasing their scent as I dipped my hands. I washed my face, my neck, the simple acts feeling impossibly intimate with Andrew mere steps away. I cleared my throat softly.

Andrew turned. His eyes found mine across the dim room. He had removed his outer tunic. I had never seen him like this—barefoot, his tunic unlaced at the throat, his arms bare. The lamplight caught the curve of muscle in his shoulders, the line of his collarbone. *My husband.*

He was beautiful. And I was terrified. And somehow both things were equally true.

We both understood this was not how either of us had imagined this night.

He moved to the basin himself and washed quickly. When he turned back, we looked at each other.

"Come," he said finally, sitting on the bed and holding out his hand.

I went to him, and we lay down together. I curled against his side with careful modesty, my head finding the hollow of his shoulder. His arm came around me, holding me close but chastely. The linens smelled of mint. His skin carried the scent of the basin's rose water mixed with something distinctly him—warm and clean and male. His heart beat strongly beneath my ear.

We fit together as if we had been made for this. As if my body had been waiting to learn the shape of his.

And all I could think about was the Temple officers waiting in the darkness. My father leaving at dawn. Everything unraveling.

"Andrew?"

"Hmm?"

"What if they do not let him come back?"

The silence stretched before he answered. "Then we will meet it. I will not leave you. I will keep you safe. Try to rest."

But sleep would not come. I lay there in the darkness, Andrew's arm warm and heavy across my waist, his breath stirring the hair at my temple with each exhale. His breathing gradually deepened and slowed as exhaustion finally claimed him, but my mind refused to quiet. Every small sound made me tense. The creak of a shutter. The distant call of a night bird.

I kept replaying the moment the officers had appeared. The sound of their voices. The look on Abba's face. The joy of my wedding had curdled so quickly into fear.

The night stretched on. Through the window, I watched the stars drift slowly across the sky, indifferent to human suffering. From somewhere in the house came the low murmur of voices, of others who could not sleep.

And outside, on the road beyond our gates, the Temple officers waited. I imagined them there in the darkness, wrapped in their dark cloaks, torches guttering low, patient as predators.

AUTHOR'S NOTE

Thank you for spending time in these pages and walking beside Anna through this part of her life. If her story touched you in any way, through a moment of tenderness, a glimpse of Jesus's nearness, or a reminder of truth, then I am grateful.

Stepping into the first century through story allows us to feel familiar Scripture in a new way. It has been an honor to imagine what it might have been like to live in the days when Jesus walked the earth, the dust on His sandals, the compassion in His gaze, and the presence of God close enough to touch. I hope Anna's journey offered a window into that world and stirred something of His nearness in your own.

Anna and Andrew's journey is far from over. They will walk with Jesus in the seasons ahead through moments of joy, moments of sorrow, and moments that shape their faith. The One they follow will be faithful in every step. Come along with Anna and Andrew as their journey continues in *Anna of Bethsaida*, Book Two of The Arimathea Chronicles.

With grace, *Susanne*

HISTORICAL NOTE

Stories often begin with a question. For me, it was a simple one that stayed in my heart. Why was Joseph of Arimathea allowed to claim the body of Jesus? Who was he, and what kind of story might stand behind that moment of courage? That wondering planted the first seed of this book, but the story that grew was Anna's. Exploring her life offered a more intimate and human way to enter the world surrounding Jesus.

The Gospels form the foundation of this story. The teachings, ministry, and character of Jesus are drawn from Scripture with deep respect. Around that firm center, I wove the details of daily Jewish life in the first century: family rhythms, faith practices, meals, customs, and the quiet joys and sorrows of living under Roman rule. Anna is a fictional character, but her world reflects the kinds of experiences many women of that time might have known.

Scripture identifies Joseph as being from Arimathea, although the exact location of this town has been debated for

HISTORICAL NOTE

centuries. Some scholars connect it to Ramathaim in the hill country of Ephraim. Others place it closer to Jerusalem. For this story, I chose a setting that reflects the likely region and character of a Judean town in that era, close enough to Jerusalem to make Joseph's presence there believable and rooted in the everyday life of the time.

Some elements of this book are inspired by historical and traditional sources outside of Scripture. Early Christian writings such as the *Gospel of Nicodemus,* also known as *The Acts of Pilate,* and later traditions portray Joseph of Arimathea as a devoted follower of Jesus. Some of these writings even suggest a family connection between them. Scripture does not confirm these details, but they have been part of Christian reflection for many centuries. I chose to treat these traditions gently, not as fact, but as a storytelling possibility that helped shape Anna's world.

Where the biblical record leaves gaps, as stories often do, I filled them with imagination. My aim was to stay true to the culture, faith, and humanity of the time. The household details, friendships, personalities, and specific events in Anna's story are fictional, but they were created with reverence for the sacred history surrounding them. I did not set out to rewrite Scripture but to step quietly into the spaces between its lines and consider what life might have felt like for those living during this time.

Thank you for allowing Anna's story into your heart. May the same Jesus who walked the roads of Galilee walk beside you as well, guiding, comforting, and reminding you that the God who wrote her story is lovingly at work in yours.

ABOUT THE AUTHOR

Susanne Blumer is the author of *Anna of Arimathea*, the first book in *The Arimathea Chronicles*. She is also the owner of three magical bookstores: two nestled in the mountains of North Carolina and one in the Lowcountry of South Carolina. She cowrites the Bell Tower Bible Adventures series with her husband Cole and is the author of the Piper Periwinkle series and several other children's books. Susanne is CEO and Founder of Sassafras on Sutton, LLC, a cheerleader for Christian fiction, and adores wandering around her stores, chatting with customers and pretending she's working. She splits her time between the mountains and the coast, has more books than shelves, loves coffee more than she should and is always dreaming of the next story to tell.

Learn more about her stores at sassafraspost.com. If you're ever in Waynesville or Beaufort, stop in and say hey!

You can stay in touch with Susanne at susanneblumer.com.

BONUS CHAPTER

Anna and Andrew's wedding night was stolen by Temple guards and fear. But in Bethsaida, far from Jerusalem's threats, Andrew has a chance to give his bride the night she deserved.

Want to see what happens next?
Get the exclusive bonus chapter "The Wedding Night" delivered straight to your inbox.

GET IT HERE

susanneblumer.com/theweddingnight

ANNA OF BETHSAIDA
Book Two of The Arimathea Chronicles

Coming Spring 2026

Anna thought marrying Andrew meant gaining a home. Instead, she gained the dusty roads of Galilee, the scrutiny of hostile Pharisees, and a front-row seat to miracles that both heal and unsettle.

As a healer traveling with Jesus's ministry, Anna finds her place among the women who follow—women like Tirzah, whose friendship offers unexpected comfort as the journey grows harder. But while crowds press close to touch the Teacher's robe, darkness gathers in Jerusalem's council chambers. Her father Joseph walks an impossible line within the Sanhedrin, and every miracle Jesus performs draws the net tighter.

The cost of discipleship, Anna discovers, isn't counted in miles walked or meals missed. It's measured in the space between what she hoped following Jesus would be and what it actually demands. Between the life she imagined and the one unfolding on these dangerous roads.

From Galilee's shores to Bethany's olive groves to an impossible resurrection that forces the Sanhedrin's hand, Anna must choose whether love means clinging to safety or walking straight into the storm.

"Compelling, heartbreaking, and utterly authentic. Susanne weaves Anna's intimate story through the gospel accounts with masterful precision."

Available wherever books are sold.

Printed in Dunstable, United Kingdom